SPI
EGE
L&G
RAU

pencil lines cross y^e image or middle of colours . . . . . .
^seuerall ^afore named colours was brisk^, ^& where he judg'd y^e breast confine
of them to be, whilst J held y^e paper so y^t y^e ^said image might fall
within a certain compas marked on it. And this J did, partly because my o . . .
eyes are not very critical in distinguishing colours, partly because another . . .
to whom J had not communicated my thoughts about this matter, could hav . . .
nothing but his eyes to determin his fancy in making those marks. This ob . . .
servation we repeated divers times, both in ye same & divers days to see
how ye marks on several papers would agree, & comparing ye observa . . .
tions, though ye just confines of ye colours are hard to be ^distinguished
assigned because they pass into one another by insensible gradation, yet the
^but little, especially towards the ^red end,
differences of ye observations were ~~very inconsiderable~~ & taking meanes be . . .
tween those differences ^that were, the length of ye Jmage (reccond not by ye distance
of ye verges of ye semicircular ends, but by ye distance of ye centers o . . .
those semicircles, or length of ye straight sides, as it ought to be) was d . . .
vided in ^about ye same proportion that a string is, between ye end & ye middle
to sound ye tones in an eight. You will ~~soon~~ understand me best by viewin . . .
ye annexed figure, in wch AB & CD represent ye straight sides about ten in . . .
long, APC &BTD

the semicircular
ends, X & Y the
centers of those
semicircles, XZ

ye length of a musical string double to XY & divided between X & Y so as
to sound ye tones exprest ~~at~~ at ye side, (that is XH ye half, XG & GJ ye third
part, YK ye fift part, YM ye eighth part & GE ye ninth part of XY.) &
intervals between these divisions ~~exprest~~ ye spaces wch ye colours written there too
up, every colour being most briskly specific in ye middle of those spaces.

Now for ye cause of these & such like colours made by refraction,
biggest or strongest rays must penetrate ye refracting superficies more freely
& easily then ye weaker, & so be less turned awry by it, that is, less refrac . . .
wch is as much as to say, the rays wch make red, are least refrangible
those wch make blew & violet ~~be~~ most refrangible, & others otherwise re . . .
frangible according to their colour. Whence if ye rays, ~~as in ye afforesa~~
~~experiment~~, wch come promiscuously from ye sun, be refracted by a Prism
in ye afforesaid experiment, those of several sorts being variously refracted
~~those of several sorts wch fall being variously refracted~~ must ~~fall~~ go to
several places on an opposite paper or wall, & so parted, exhibit every
one their own colours, wch they could not do while blended together. An . . .
because refraction only severs them, & changes not ye bignes or ~~length~~ o . . .
the ray, thence it is that after they are once well severed . . . each o . . .
cannot make any further changes in their colour.

On this ground may all ye Phænomena of ~~colour~~ Refractions be
understood. But to explain ye colours, made by Reflexions, J must f . . .
pose, that, although light be unimaginably swift, yet y^e æthereal vibra . . .

...trary, it may be an hour or two, not more, in moving from ye Sun to us.

...is celerity of ye vibrations therefore supposed, if light be incident on a thin

...in or plate of any transparent body, ye waves overtaking it one after

... excited by its passage through ye first superficies, overtaking

... after another till it arrive at ye second superficies, will cause it to be

...flected or refracted accordingly as ye condensed or expanded

...ye wave overtakes it there, to compress or relax that physical superficies

... thereby augment or diminish its reflecting power. If ye plate be

... such a thickness, that ye condensed part of ye first wave overtake the

...ray at ye second superficies, it must be reflected there; if double that

...ickness y^t ye following rarefied part of ye wave, y^t is, ye space between

...at & ye next wave, overtake it, there it must be transmitted; if triple

...thickness y^t ye condensed part of ye second wave overtake it, there it

...t be reflected, & so where ye plate is 5, 7, or 9 times that thickness

...must be reflected by reason of ye third fourth or fift wave overtaking

...at ye second superficies, but where it is 4, 6, or 8 times that thickness

...y^t ye ray may be overtaken there by the dilated interval of those waves

...shall be transmitted, & so on; the second superficies being made able

... unable to reflect accordingly as it is condensed or expanded. By ye wave

...or instance let AHQ represent ye superficies of a spherically convex glass lens

...on a plain glass AJR, & AJRQH the thin plano-concave plate of Air

...tween them, & BC, DE, FG, HJ &c thicknesses of that plate or distances of

... glasses in ye arithmetical progression of ye numbers 1, 2, 3, 4, &c,

...hereof BC is ye distance at

...ch ye ray is overtaken by y^e

...ost condensed part of ye first

...ve: J say ye rays incident at B, F, K & O

...ght to be reflected at C, G, L & P, & those

...cident at D, H, m, & Q ought to be transmitted

... E, J, N & R; & that, because ye Ray BC ar—

...rs at ye superficies AC when it is condensed by

...first wave that overtakes it, DE, when rare,

...ed by ye interval of ye first & second; FG,

...en condensed by ye second wave; HJ, when

...refied by ye second interval of y^e

...cond & third, & so on for an indeterminate

...mber of successions; & at A, ye center or contact of ye glasses, ye light must

...transmitted because there the æthereal mediums in both glasses are continued

... one uniform medium. Whence if ye glasses in this posture be

...a, there ought to appear at A ye contact of ye glasses, a black

...bout that many concentric circles of light & darkness, ye squares of

...iameters are to sense in arithmetical progression. Yet all y^e

...t exception ought not to be thus reflected or transmitted, for something

...be overtaken at y^e second superficies by y^e vibrations raised by

...ollateral or immediately succeeding ray; wch vibration, being as strong

A Novel

REBECCA STOTT

SPIEGEL & GRAU
New York
2007

BOOK DESIGN BY AMANDA DEWEY

ISBN-13 978-0-7394-9247-5

PRINTED IN THE UNITED STATES OF AMERICA

First published in Great Britain in 2007
by Weidenfeld & Nicolson

AUTHOR'S NOTE

Although *Ghostwalk* is a work of fiction, and all of the characters are drawn from my imagination, the seventeenth-century figures in this book are historical. The details of their lives are based on records, as are the facts about Cambridge in the seventeenth century. For anyone interested in the historical background of the story within the novel, I have provided additional material at the end of the book: an author's note explaining my use of history in more detail, a time line, excerpts from Newton's diaries, and a bibliography.

—Rebecca Stott

For Judith Boddy and a meteorologist in a taxi,
whose name I never asked

All the planets are heavy towards one another.

—ISAAC NEWTON

Things hurtful for the Eyes
Garlick Onions & Leeks . . . Gooing too suddaine after meals.
    Hot wines. Cold ayre . . .
Much blood-letting . . . dust. Ffire. Much weeping.

—ISAAC NEWTON

Prologue

Unrepaired and swollen with rain, the gate in the orchard wall refused to move until Cameron put his full weight against it and pushed, hard. Stepping into the smell of a long-abandoned apple crop, Cameron called towards the house, hoping to catch his mother's attention in the window where she would be sitting working. "Elizabeth?" He waited for her to come to the window and wave, then called out again. This time his voice disturbed a pigeon, which flew from one of the apple trees in a great clatter of wings.

There was so much that needed mending here. The cracks and splits and rustings over bothered him more now that he was getting older. But then there also seemed to be a point when it stopped mattering. His mother had reached it. She was no longer trying to keep all that ageing and disrepair at bay. She'd stopped seeing it. She let the apples rot in the long grass where they fell; she let the Virginia creeper inch over the windows so the house became darker almost by the minute; dust gathered on the books, shells, and animal skulls on her shelves and windowsills; leaves blocked the gutters.

There was no answer from the house. No face at the window. Time had stopped here. Time always seemed to stop around Elizabeth. She wasn't interested in the present; time ran backwards or eddied around her, always finding its way back to the seventeenth century.

Where was she? Where had she gone?

The grass had grown thick and long under the apple trees. The orchard smelled like a cider press; everywhere the gold and russet curves of fallen fruit gleamed through the emerald green of long grass, gloriously lit and shadowed by the late-afternoon sun which had broken through the rain. It was too late to gather them now. The brown of apple bruise had spread too far. Some of the apples had been gnawed, he noticed. Rats again.

Cameron's boot pressed on something hard in the wet grass. A small pink plastic fist gestured at him aggressively. He reached down to pick up the half-clothed doll: his son Toby's lost action man, lying at the base of a wizened tree. He laughed, looking up to follow a twist of wire into the apple boughs. Toby must have suspended this rope last time he had been here, a rope down which this action man had abseiled. The doll was covered in trails now from slugs that had crawled blithely over the plastic muscles in their hunger for fermenting apple flesh. When he pulled the string to see if the voice mechanism still worked, a woman's voice called out: "Action man patrol. This is your commander speaking. Mortar attack. Fall out. Fall out." He tucked the doll into the pocket of his coat where, muffled, it eventually fell silent.

Cameron knocked before he let himself into his mother's house. Its eccentricity still amused him. She called it The Studio, but it reminded him of the witch's gingerbread house in the forest, its wooden-tiled roof sloping precipitously all the way to the ground, cross-hatched by the shadows of the orchard's apple trees. Inside, a sturdy white totem pole held up the entire structure; Elizabeth had commissioned the architect to give her a steep-ceilinged expanse of white studio space to write in and a little bedroom tucked away in a mezzanine floor under the roof, at the top of a steep wooden staircase.

What was wrong with him today? He had a knot in his stomach, an ache cradling a dark sense of anticipation. Elizabeth would say he was out of sorts. What was it to be "in sorts"? He must have dreamed some complicated sad dream the night before, he thought, which had slipped away, leaving the vestiges of itself in his skin and blood.

Where *was* she? Not in the house. The door, opening, swept mail to one side: A bank bill. Oxfam. A postcard from Russia. He called out again, tucking the mail into the ledge on the windowsill: "Elizabeth?" His words echoed back from the wood panelling. The Studio was already darkening as the afternoon slipped away. Perhaps she had gone for a walk: the red wool Jaeger duffle coat his wife, Sarah, had bought Elizabeth two Christmases ago was missing from the pegs by the door.

The house had a different smell. He noticed that first of all. It smelled of lavender furniture polish. He'd not smelled furniture polish here before; dust, yes, and books, and wood smoke, and sometimes the acrid sweetness of lilies—Elizabeth loved lilies and hyacinths—but not furniture polish. He couldn't remember ever seeing Elizabeth cleaning with furniture polish. Her work table was different too. The oak slab on which she worked was usually invisible under piles of papers and books and card files. But now the research papers for her book were—for the first time— all piled neatly into labelled cardboard boxes. The labels read: Newton: Trinity College, 1667–69; Grantham: Apothecary's House; Optics; Plague Years; Glass; European Alchemical Networks: 1665–66.

Along the windowsills the wood had been cleaned and polished and the delicate objects and bric-a-brac rearranged into fresh compositions. Elizabeth had always arranged everything into still lifes: stones cut in spirals on windowsills, strings of pearls draped over oyster shells she had gathered, coral, and, somewhere among the beauty, always the *vanitas*— the bleached skulls of small animals—yes, she collected those too.

How odd. In the kitchen there was no usual pile of unwashed plates, just a single mug upside down on the draining board. And she'd folded the cloth. She never did that.

He left the front door open and strode outside as fine rain began to sweep slantways across the garden. Why was he walking so quickly? he wondered, seeing himself suddenly as if from a distance, watching himself with curiosity from the trees at the other end of the garden as if he were in a film. He could see himself reflected in the glass of the big window: Cameron Brown, fellow of Trinity College, neuroscientist, was looking for his mother. He glanced at himself in profile, the large shambling frame, the long black coat, the Wellington boots, the snagged sweater, un-brushed hair, and unshaved face. Action man head sticking out from his pocket.

A flash of red out of the corner of his eye. Was she playing games? Down by the water's edge.

Now he was running for the river, slipping on rotten apples, pushing through nettles that stung his hands. Then he forgot he was Cameron Brown. Cameron Brown lost his outlines—they dissolved as he waded into the water, seeped away as he reached down for the red woollen shape submerged in the rushes. He heard the howl of Mahler then as he turned the figure over and lifted his mother's small body onto the nettle-veiled riverbank, where he closed her eyes because he couldn't bear to look into the glassiness there, moved the white hair to one side, and blew air into her lungs. She had no shoes on. He rubbed her feet with the wet wool of his coat but could rub no colour into the blue-white flesh. And then, shouting to everyone and no one, he brought his fists down onto her chest twice. But someone had turned the sound off. River water emptied out of her mouth. When he stood blindly, lifting her small body, thinking only that he must get her into the house, he tripped on the long hem of his own coat and fell back into the nettles, his mother's flailing body in a wet red coat falling heavily on his in the mud.

Then there was nothing. He remembered nothing. He could recall only a succession of images and sounds: flashes of light from the police car on the sloping ceiling, river water dripping loudly over the edges of her table and onto the floor and down through the cracks, a body cov-ered with a blanket lifted onto a stretcher, papers to sign, a funeral at which he behaved badly in some way.

And a glass prism returned to him by a mortuary assistant who had pried it out of Elizabeth's clenched fist. "Needs signing for," he had said, before he placed it in Cameron's hand. A wedge of triangular-shaped glass, chipped along one edge.

One

Over the last two years, as I have tried to tease out the truths from the untruths in that series of events that seeped out through Elizabeth's death, like lava moving upwards and outwards through salt water from a tear in the seabed, I have had to *be* you several times, Cameron Brown, in order to claw myself towards some kind of coherence. Sometimes it was—is—easy to imagine the world through your eyes, terribly possible to imagine walking through the garden that afternoon in those moments before you found your mother's body in the river. After all, for a long time, all that time we were lovers, it was difficult to tell where your skin ended and mine began. That was part of the trouble for Lydia Brooke and Cameron Brown. Lack of distance became—imperceptibly—a violent entanglement.

So this is for you, Cameron, and yes, it is also for me, Lydia Brooke, because perhaps, in putting all these pieces together properly, I will be able to step out from your skin and back into mine.

Alongside Elizabeth's body floating in red in the river, there are other places where this story needs to start, places I can see now but wouldn't have seen then, other beginnings which were all connected. Another death, one that took place around midnight on the 5th of January, 1665.

That night, Richard Greswold, a fellow of Trinity College, Cambridge, had opened a door onto a dark, unlit landing above a staircase in Trinity. A draught caught the flame from the lamp in his hand, twisting and elongating the shadows around him. As a thin stream of blood began to trickle from one, then both of his nostrils, he raised the back of his hand and wiped it across his cheek, smearing the blood into streaks, and fell forward, very slowly, into air, through the palest of moon shadows cast through casement windows. He fell heavily, his body twisting and beating against the steps and walls. The lamp fell too and bounced, making a metallic counterpoint to the thuds of flesh on wood. By morning the blood from the wound on Richard Greswold's head had run through and across the uneven cracks of the stone flagging on which he died, making a brown map like the waterways across the Fens to the north, the college porter said, prying a key—the key to the garden—from the dead man's clenched fist. Encrusted blood, as thick as fen mud.

Greswold's death was bound up with Elizabeth's. She came to know that before she died, but we didn't. Two Cambridge deaths, separated by three centuries, but inseparable, shadowing each other. Richard Greswold. Elizabeth Vogelsang.

Elizabeth Vogelsang drowned in September, 2002, the first of three deaths that would become the subject of a police investigation four months later. The police took a ragged testimony from me, which I gave in answer to the questions they asked and which were recorded on tape in a windowless room in the basement of the Parkside Police Station by a Detective Sergeant Cuff on the 16th of January, 2003.

"All the interview rooms are occupied this morning, Dr. Brooke," he said, struggling to find the right key as I followed him down grey corridors. "So we'll have to use the central investigation room. I'm afraid it's not ideal, but it is at least empty this morning. There's a staff training morning—health and safety. We have about an hour. This is not a formal interview, you understand. We'll do that later. Just a chat."

"I don't know whether what I have to tell you will take an hour," I said. My nerves were jangled. I wasn't sleeping. I was still waking in the middle of the night angry with you, and with me, but I had enough self-possession to know that I would have to be careful and alert here at the Parkside Police Station. Very alert. They had arrested Lily Ridler.

"We will have to see you again, Dr. Brooke, without doubt. You will be central to our enquiries."

That's how I came to see another version, their version. Well, not quite *see*, but *glimpse*. The central investigation room at the Parkside Police Station was filled with filing cabinets and four desks with exaggerated curves sweeping in different directions; over to the right, a magnetic whiteboard ran the length of one entire windowless wall. Cuff pulled up a swivel chair for me on the other side of his desk, carefully clearing away papers and notes into a drawer and locking it. A collection of objects and photographs had been attached to the whiteboard with magnets. Curled around those objects were a series of questions, names, lists, and arrows in coloured marker pens in different hands. I couldn't see very much from where I was sitting, so when Cuff went to retrieve a file from another room, I slipped the digital camera out of my briefcase and photographed it. A risky act driven by nothing but a terrible, bereaved curiosity.

A white magnetic board written on in different hands in different colours and a series of photographs—three dead bodies, one woman drowned in a red coat, two men with their faces slashed, a wall of graffiti, several photographs of mutilated cats and horses, the house at Landing Lane, a photograph of Lily Ridler next to some other people I didn't recognise—animal activists, I assume—and a photograph of a pile of shredded paper. When I call up the photo on my laptop and increase the resolution I can pick out details. If you go close enough you can just see that the blue pen lists two of the murder scenes: Staircase E of Trinity College and St. Edward's Passage. And if you go very close, right up into the right-hand corner—it took me a while to spot this—there's a photograph of me next to a photograph of Sarah. It was the photograph of me that you carried in your mobile phone, filed away carefully, so that no one would find it. The one you took on Holkham Beach. They must have gone through all the files in your mobile to find that. Underneath someone had written my name. Lydia Brooke.

Yes, that whiteboard was the sketchy beginning of the police version of what came to be known as the Cambridge murders. Murders that would be discussed in Parliament and produced as evidence to support proposed draconian measures in the Serious Organised Crime and Police Bill, and which were finally instrumental in changing British law. Yes, we were making legal history but, of course, we didn't know that then.

That first conversation did take the best part of an hour because Cuff had so many questions about my relationship with you, what I had been doing in Elizabeth's house, how I had come to know the family, when I had last seen you, what we had talked about, what you had been wearing, and the context for that message I left on your phone. Cuff, who affected a relaxed nonchalance composed, I guessed, to make me drop my guard, summarised my answers and wrote them all out on lined police paper before reading them back to me in a continuous story, which he had somehow made from my fragmented answers. I signed it as a "true account."

A few months later I tried to put together a more coherent description for the lawyer representing Lily Ridler in the court case. She asked me to write down everything I remembered that might have been relevant to the case, from Elizabeth's funeral to the days of the trial. I had no ambivalence then about its truth or about its beginning and ending. That came later. I typed it out in Kit's study looking down over the summer garden, two hours a day, until it seemed about right. Although it read sequentially, I didn't write it sequentially. Memory doesn't work like that. I kept remembering things as I wrote, things I had thought until then were inconsequential, which might have been "relevant," so I went back and tucked them into the story—little details, thoughts, surmisings, speculations.

I've always wondered how the two stories—the ragged one I put together in answer to Cuff's questions and the one I wrote in Kit's study for Patricia Dibb—ended up being so different. It wasn't as if I falsified anything. For the police my story was only part of a much bigger narrative, made up of perhaps twenty witness accounts, so the prosecution knitted together all those reports and circumstantial evidence in chronological order, and bit by bit against and between them, my story got pulled in several directions. When set together with all those others, my story took on a different shape, and it was the composite version, filtered, dragged, and kneaded, that the jury agreed to. It was pretty damning once they'd finished with it, damning enough to convict Lily Ridler of murder and send her to prison for the rest of her life. A tight story, she said to me the last time I saw her. Impenetrable now. A closed case.

The story kept on changing. When the court issued a press statement and the newspapers distilled it back down to the size they wanted, with all the appropriately dramatic, suspenseful moments, it fitted neatly into columns of small type. One journalist even made a time line of events in which the two murders were simply a notch in the straight passing of time through Lily's life, like a single-track train with stations that began with her birth and ended with her arrest. She was charged with three murders and sixteen acts of unlawful animal killing and mutilation, but because they couldn't pin Elizabeth's death on her, she was convicted of only two murders. Once they'd added those killings to the time line and filled in the details about her grandfather and her parents, Lily Ridler had become a psychopath, a monster. Now, nearly two years later, Lily is dead.

So if we thought it was finished, we know it isn't now. The ghosts have not been laid to rest after all, you see, not yours and not hers. If they were to question me again I think I would have to say that I see it differently now—the connections, I mean. Time does that. There were missing parts then, a historical dimension that no one asked any questions about and which, then, I could only half see.

What was missing? The seventeenth century. But how do you say that to a policeman who has just switched on his tape recorder to record the words "Parkside Police Station, 16 January, 2003, interview with Dr. Lydia Brooke"? How do you say, "There's a missing witness account and a missing suspect . . . Sergeant Cuff, the seventeenth century is missing. And you need to talk to a man called Mr. F."

How do you tell him that you think there's a link between a female scholar found drowned in a river in Cambridge and a man who fell down a staircase nearby three hundred years earlier? Not a simple causal relationship but something as delicate as a web, one of those fine white skeins you see around the tips of grass stems in the spring when the dew is heavy.

A crow has just flown off my study roof, launched itself into the air to my left down over the garden, just as the right-hand corner of my map of Cambridge has curled itself noisily away from the wall. The syncopated sounds of the scurrying of crows' feet on roof tiles and the curling of old paper is enough to make one think that there might be something else in the room beside me as I write. Which of you restless people is it? What do you want with my story?

No. If Elizabeth were here she would say that history is less like a skein of silk and more like a palimpsest—time layered upon time so that one buried layer leaks into the one above. Or like a stain in an old stone wall that seeps through the plaster.

What would Cuff have said or done if I had told him that he needed to know about the man who fell down the stairs of Trinity College on the 5th of January 1665, the fall that stained the floor, the stain that leaked through Elizabeth's life and Lily's, that held us all together, in thrall? Cuff would not have known the significance of the date—1665—or at least I don't think he would have done. Perhaps 1666 would have rung some bells: the year the Great Plague abated in England and the Fire of London ravaged the capital in its wake. He might have remembered that from his secondary school history classes.

If I had told Cuff about Greswold and about Isaac Newton's complicated friendship with a Mr. F., he wouldn't have written any of it down. He wouldn't have considered it relevant. A man falling through air and shadows in Trinity College, 1665. A secret friendship between two young men, forged in alchemical and mathematical calculations. How could that have any bearing on a series of murders in Cambridge that took place in 2002 and 2003? If I had suggested that, Cuff would have raised one of his thick black eyebrows and his pen would have paused in midair. Elizabeth Vogelsang would have understood. Cuff wouldn't.

Lily went to prison because the seventeenth century was missing from her court records, from her story. Her time line needed to be longer, much longer, and there were many sidelines and tracks, twistings and turnings and yes, it was a labyrinth, a skein of silk that began to weave itself in 1665, 339 years ago.

I've been thinking about labyrinths this summer. Ariadne giving Theseus the thread so that he could find his way back out of the labyrinth, away from the black void of the flesh-eating Minotaur. Unravellings have to start somewhere. Now that I see, for the first time, how connected everything is, I know that the threads between Isaac Newton and us were all attached, like the ground elder under Kit's soil.

That summer in which I wrote my story and yours for Patricia Dibb, Kit and I declared war on the ground elder that had taken over her flower beds at Sturton Street. As we began to dig, we could see how each of those separate plants, uncurling above ground, was joined to a great network of root systems underground. There was no point in digging up *part* of it; you had to pull up the whole thing, and if you didn't, it would start reaching out again in the wet darkness of the soil, another green leaf curling up a week or so later. Grace, Kit's elderly neighbour, leaning over the chicken wire fence, uttered her warnings about the impossibility of ever killing it off. She had spent fifty years trying, she said. Break those roots just once, she said, and the wound on the root will make scores of new shoots.

From my study in the attic of Kit's house, I looked down on the long stretch of her garden, with its rose beds and gravel path twisting through tall shrubs and Mexican orange blossom, and imagined the ground elder stretching itself luxuriously under the lawn, under the iris bed, unseen in the dark. We had pulled out most of it by the end of June, but a root or tendril here and there would have clung to the root systems of other plants—the iris bulbs, the tubers of the gladioluses—so I knew we would see it again.

As I write, Grace's grandchildren play in raincoats on the trampoline under the apple tree. Before the rose garden and the shrubs and the trampoline and the shed, before any of that, the elder had made its way up through the orchards that stood here for centuries, before Kit's house and before all the others in this terrace were built. Kit has a sepia photograph in her kitchen of the building works for her street, a skeleton row of houses being built on the orchards. Before the orchards, there were marshes here to the south of the city, southeast of Newton's Trinity College, and the ground elder would have rioted then in the wet earth, unrestrained. Before the orchards and marshes, Roman farmers and the gardeners of Roman villas built on this land would have kept it at bay or used it in herb gardens to make soups and broths or to cure their gout. Builders found the remains of a pretty villa under the road only a stone's throw from here—three rooms with painted plaster walls, bright red, yellow, green, grey, and deep blue, some patterned to imitate panels of marble, a tiled roof, mortar floors, glass windows, under-floor heating built on blocks of imported chalk. It was probably the last house on the edge of the settlement, marking the boundary between civilisation and the marshlands.

Every cut in the ground elder root is a failure; every cut will make a redoubling of effort necessary. That's how I came to understand Isaac Newton's fear of sin, I think, and how embroiled Mr. F. became in Newton's name, and how neither of them could stop what they had started, and, finally, how I have come to see the way the consequences of their seventeenth-century acts twisted and turned their way to us, underground and overground, splitting and redoubling. Organic and botanical.

My story, both of my stories, the police tapes in the Parkside station and the typed account I wrote for Patricia Dibb, began with Elizabeth Vogelsang's funeral.

Now, Cameron Brown, I am starting to tell it again so that I can make you a thread for your labyrinth. Yes, I am putting the seventeenth century back into the picture. I hope you can hear me.

Two

O n the day of Elizabeth's funeral I'd been in a hurry, as usual, and
once I reached the motorway I couldn't quite remember if I had
pulled the flat door closed. It was too late to go back. Could I call my
neighbour and get her to check? Gripping the wheel with one hand, I
pulled out my phonebook with the other to see if I still had Greta's number listed there, but then swerved too closely towards the central reserva-
tion. Stop rushing. One thing at a time. Just pay attention. And don't lose
your way. Head directly north with the sea behind you up the M23, over
the massy chalk of the south downs to the open eye of the M25; trace a
line around its rim anticlockwise, crossing under the Thames through
the Dartford Tunnel and then north to the top of the circle, then north
again up the M11 and into the flatlands of East Anglia. Drop into Cambridge from the north, then find the Leper Chapel from the ring road on
the east side.

To compensate for my lack of a mental compass, Kit had taught me to
turn directions into a painting or a drawing, a charcoal line stretching
across white paper. Lack of direction? Now, don't put that down to me being a woman. If being male and female can be reduced to a set of stereo-
types, you know I have more male instincts than female ones. Perhaps it's
the writing. Writers, apparently, often have a diminished sense of direction: too many maps—time maps, road maps, character maps—all laid

one on top of another, like the stories of a building. It gets to be difficult to separate them out.

I shouldn't have been late. It wasn't as if I went to funerals very often. That morning I'd taken ages to get out of the flat, unable to decide whether to wear black or not, so I'd pulled on black clothes and then dark blue ones and pulled them all off again until they had piled up on the bedroom floor. Christmas, Easter, weddings, and funerals. I hated all those sentimental empty rituals made stiff and unyielding by rules and protocols. Elizabeth wouldn't have cared what any of us wore. She refused to go to funerals.

Elizabeth Vogelsang—what kinds of things had she cared about? Misused semi-colons; mistakes in dates; poor logic; "dodgy reasoning"; mixed metaphors; the Leper Chapel on the Newmarket Road. Oh, and smells. Elizabeth always noticed smells. She could smell if you were getting sick. She'd said something to me once two years or so ago when we'd met in the University Library tearooms. That day I watched the shadow of your remembered mouth pass over hers as she talked. Her mouth. Your mouth. Mother and son. "Lydia, are you feeling quite well?" she'd asked, stirring her tea and refusing to meet my eye. "It's just you are giving off a particular kind of smell . . . not an unpleasant smell exactly . . ."

"What kind of smell? Sweat?" I blush easily. No one had ever talked to me like that before. Not even my closest friends. Not even Kit. I'd felt affronted, angry, and fascinated. *You are giving off a particular kind of smell.* Giving off—it made me think of exhalations, steam rising from the backs of saddled horses, dragon's breath on frosted mornings. For one bad moment I wondered if your strange mother could smell you on my skin, but then you'd not been near my skin for three years. Could you have left your smell on my skin after all that time? You were certainly still *under* it then, especially as I was sitting there with that mouth, her mouth, just on the other side of the table.

"Oh, wet newspapers. Newspapers that have been wet for several weeks. Ink, the edge of mould, wet leaves . . . It's just your glands. You're probably coming down with something."

It was only then that Elizabeth had looked up. Thankfully, by then my scorched cheeks had returned to their natural colour. I raised my hand to my glands and found swellings there like invisible bruises. Three days later I had a temperature.

She wasn't finished with me. "It became something of common knowledge in Cambridge, you know. You and my son."

"I know," I said, trying to match her directness with my own. It was perhaps more of a relief than anything to have broached the subject. "Did
someone tell you?"

"No. I saw you with him in here once. You didn't see me. You were
walking together from the South Wing to the North Wing. There was
something about the way you were walking, the way you didn't smile, like
friends do. So I asked some questions. But don't worry. I'm not one to
judge—how could I? Life is complicated. Mine has been . . . complicated."

"That's why I left Cambridge," I said, realising I was lying a little.

"I wondered." She laughed and gathered her papers together. "Well,
that's a relief. I thought if we were going to be working together again, it
might be better to avoid tiptoeing around all of that. We don't need to
talk about it again."

Now, years later, here I was driving from Brighton to Cambridge, from
the sea to a Leper Chapel that looked like a ship on the marshy common
outside Cambridge, for my last appointment with Elizabeth Vogelsang.
And I was late.

The Newmarket Road was traffic-bound enough for me to risk checking my phone and to reach for my bag of makeup. I had covered only one
cheek and part of my nose with foundation before the traffic began to
move again, and in trying to manoeuvre the makeup and the steering
wheel, I spilled a single drop of foundation onto my black skirt, which
wouldn't rub off. I needed makeup that morning—I'd had almost no
sleep the night before so that I could finish the manuscript and e-mail it
to my agent before leaving for Cambridge. Miranda would have opened
my e-mail by now, I knew, saved the attachment, printed it out in her office onto the thick cream-coloured paper she used: *Refraction: A Screenplay*, by Lydia Brooke. Then she would have set it aside. Judgements later.
I decided I wouldn't think about the script today. Only Elizabeth. Wonderful, clever, obsessive Elizabeth.

The Newmarket Road, as it passed out of Cambridge through Barnwell, always made me think of prostitutes: seventeenth-century prostitutes and brothels. Barnwell was where the undergraduates came to pay for sex: a seventeenth-century traveller to Cambridge once wrote that for 18 pence (that's just £8 now), a scholar and his mistress could have a brothel all to themselves, and, he added with a crow of male triumphalism, there hadn't been a maidenhead to be found among the sixteen-year-olds of Barnwell since the time of Henry I. The undergraduates, they said, would take off their gowns and roll them up outside Christ's College at the Barnwell Gate, so as not to be seen leaving the city eastwards, because no under-graduates were allowed there—officially, at least. There weren't many who stuck to the college rules. Newton was probably one of the rare rule keep-ers, at least as far as brothels were concerned. As far as anyone knows.

I found a parking space on Oyster Row, finished my makeup in the car mirror—coral-pink lipstick, dark mascara, cappuccino brown brushed onto pallid cheeks—climbed out, and locked the car. That's when I re-alised that in my half-asleep state I had found my way to exactly the same place where I had parked on the winter afternoon when Elizabeth showed me Stourbridge Fair. It was part of the research for the screenplay I'd been writing then, just after I had come back from France. The sign on the old scrap-metal yard brought that memory back, the memory of the two of us walking this street six years before. I leaned back against the car and closed my eyes hard. I was tired. I was sure to cry.

"If you want to write about the seventeenth century you'll have to know how it smells," Elizabeth had said. I could hear her voice as if she were standing there beside me. "Find me an afternoon and we'll conjure some smells. Then you'll know where to start, I promise." One snowy af-ternoon in February, Elizabeth had driven me up and down the warren of streets off the Newmarket Road called Oyster Row, Mercers Row, Garlic Row, and Swanns Walk. I took scores of pictures through the open car window with the digital camera that I used as a kind of visual notebook—graffiti, overturned bins, scrap-metal yards, bungalows, warehouses, and corrugated iron. Modern streets built on the site of the old Stourbridge Common, where the mayor and aldermen of Cambridge had hosted a fair since the twelfth century. At the foot of Garlic Row, Elizabeth had parked, climbed out of the car, and then, standing in the forecourt of the scrap-metal yard, she'd turned into some kind of historical shaman, her voice raised against the clamour of the industrial machinery behind us. I gave myself up to her. You had to do that with Elizabeth.

"Use your imagination and get your bearings. It's September in—let's say—1664. You are standing at the bottom of Garlic Row, which is the main thoroughfare of the fair, a wide dirt track that runs north in front of you. It's muddy; sticky underfoot. Over that way, northwest, is the River Grant, down which most of the traders have arrived, many from the north, from King's Lynn, weaving their way across the waterways of the Fens. Their boats are moored on the river now. Between us and the river are arable fields. The harvest has just finished, so the fields are cropped close; there's stubble as far as you can see and a few wildflowers. But there's not much room for anything to grow now because already every- thing has been trampled by hundreds of traders and merchants, who have set up their coloured booths in row after row. Over near the river is the Coal Fair and the Tallow Fair and a little mound called Fish Hill. Right in the centre near the mayor's temporary house there's the Oyster Fair, stalls selling thousands of oysters brought down from King's Lynn and kept fresh in barrels of ice and straw.

"Between the Oyster Fair and us is Soper's Row. Over to your right are the bookstalls and beyond them the White Leather Fair and further north the Horse Fair. Now add the others in their stalls. Think of the trades, the guilds who have come here: goldsmiths, toymakers, braziers, turners, milliners, hab- erdashers, hatters, wigmakers, drapers, pewterers, china warehouses, pup- peteers, and prostitutes, and among them all coffee shops, eating houses, brandy shops. There are jugglers, acrobats, and clowns. You are standing among all the tents and booths. What can you smell? Close your eyes."

Manure, brandy, the seawater smells of oyster shells, the perfumes of soaps, tar, tanning, leather, oil from wool fleeces piled around the Leper Chapel. Smells and perfumes mingled into each other as the sun rose. I walked through the thoroughfares, invisible to the ghostly sellers, run- ning my hands over wool, silks, spices, oyster shells; I felt dried hops running through my fingers, the marbling of books on my fingertips; I heard cries, accents from all over England and northern Europe, men and women from Lancashire, Holland, Germany, Yorkshire—chickens, horses, iron, the chains of scales working. Sex, riot, and desire.

"The greatest medieval fair in Europe," Elizabeth said quietly. "Now that you can smell it, can you *see* it? Cambridge is just a palimpsest. All of this is. Just one century laid upon another upon another. Nothing is ever quite lost while there are still a few old buildings standing sentinel. Time bleeds here, seeps, perhaps more than anywhere else in the city. You'll see. *Now* you have to see the chapel."

We walked back onto the busy Newmarket Road up the brow of the hill, where the Leper Chapel stood facing the road in a miniature valley of its own. "In Newton's time it was used for storage; it was semi-derelict," Elizabeth began, pulling a wrought-iron key from her coat pocket and slipping it into the hole in the door. "Just think, it's been here for nearly a thousand years from before the city was anything more than a village with a castle and a fort. In the seventeenth century Samuel Pepys would have stood in it and John Bunyan—he used Stourbridge Fair as the model for his 'Vanity Fair' scene in *Pilgrim's Progress*—which, of course, Thackeray stole for the title of his novel—"

Now I was late for Elizabeth's funeral, walking towards the Leper Chapel, lost somewhere in Stourbridge Fair with the ghost of a dead woman and a whole host of imagined smells I didn't know what to do with, and Pepys and Bunyan and Thackeray. "Your fault I'm late, Elizabeth," I said aloud, stepping to one side to let a woman pass who was pushing a child in a buggy and talking on a mobile phone at the same time. We were both talking to the air, to ghosts.

Time had begun to bleed in the way that it did around Elizabeth. Yes, I had turned my back on Cambridge and you, Cameron Brown, for five years, but the feelings the city dragged from me were always the same—a physical oppression, a sense of mouldy suffocation and bad air, low grey skies on most days suddenly transformed to arcs of blue that made your heart ache. Cambridge made me think of Madame Bovary trying to draw breath in the prim protocols of suburbia and yearning for she knew not what, angry with she knew not what. And yes, like Emma, your eyes were never quite the same each time I saw you—black in shadow, brown in daylight, and close up, like the stem-cell slices you photographed, they had all the richness and variety of hue of medieval stained glass.

Three

It was the smell I noticed first as I pulled the heavy door open and stepped into the dark chapel. Someone had filled the church with blue hyacinths. Though the lights were off, in every corner the Delft blue of the flowers and their emerald leaves gleamed against whitewashed deep-cobbled walls. At the far end of the tiny church, which was not much bigger than a small barn, under the arch and beyond the altar, a projector threw a photograph of Elizabeth aged about thirty onto the far wall. The photographer had called out to her and she had turned towards him, glass of champagne in one hand, cigarette in the other, turned towards the voice and the camera, had smiled and raised her glass, her eyes distant, daydreaming. Just like Vermeer's girl with the pearl earring, I thought, and then I knew I was going to cry.

A CD player, propped upon a pile of red plastic chairs at the back of the church, played Mozart's "Requiem." An old woman standing at the door passed me a programme and a packet of tissues in plastic wrapping, printed with red roses, and gestured towards a seat marked "Reserved" on which someone had placed a small sign with my name written in a child's handwriting and a small smiling daisy in the bottom left corner. I had to cross through the beam of the projector to reach my seat, and as I glimpsed my silhouetted limbs, posture bent apologetically, passing across Elizabeth's much-magnified face, I remembered a shadow theatre my stepmother had made for my birthday once in the old barn—the screen had been stitched together from white sheets with black boot threads.

Faces turned towards me—how could I have arrived late to a funeral? A woman in black pressed a white silk handkerchief to her face; her mascara had already stained her cheeks and the handkerchief. I heard Elizabeth laughing irreverently somewhere.

Once I'd sat down, I saw the thick dust motes in the beam of light passing down the aisle of the church only inches from my right shoulder—illuminated particles of a photographed Elizabeth, travelling kaleidoscopically through centuries of dust. Elizabeth wasn't a palimpsest; she was dust. Dust didn't disappear. Dust was immortal. What dust might a Leper Chapel contain? Fragments of leprous skin, seed spores from the fields, ash from the altar candles.

The music stopped abruptly in mid-aria as a tall man stood up to speak over to my left behind the pulpit. He wasn't a vicar. There didn't seem to be a vicar here at all. The tall man had probably been waiting for me to sit down, I thought. Waiting for the last guest, the bad fairy. It was only when you spoke that I could tell it was you—your voice, as deep and rich as it always had been, now breaking. I could see the shape of you, but not your face. You stooped uncomfortably and kept running your hand through your hair as you spoke so that it stood up, spiked and dishevelled.

"My mother chose this place for her funeral—it was very important to her. She called it a guardian of history. She was a historian. She saw herself as a sentinel between her history, her seventeenth century, and what she called 'the uncountable daily acts of forgetting.' She used that phrase many times in her work: the uncountable daily acts of forgetting. Those of us who speak today will be writing a kind of collective obituary—we are then the guardians of her life history. But which history are we to tell? What would it mean to tell the history of Elizabeth Vogelsang?"

You looked up. Your carefully modulated words began to break up. You had abandoned the script. I knew what that felt like, the leap from solid ground into air, the rhetorical free fall. I did it more and more in my talks and public addresses now that I was older—balancing on the edge of a cliff and jumping into something that was fragmented but at least stood the chance of escaping the already framed, weary, and laboured phrases in which we find ourselves too often. You went on:

"Which of us will ever know, for instance, what it was about seventeenth-century alchemists that obsessed her? Kept her researching and visiting archives for fifteen years? Which of us will ever know now what she was looking for? I knew many things about my mother—I could tell you the things she loved: blue hyacinths, lilies, her cat Pepys, dark chocolate, her orchard, apple pies, good punctuation, Verlaine, Baudelaire, and Camus." You smiled, and someone called out, "Chateau Lafite" from the back of the church when you paused. Laughter. You pointed to a patch of light on the cobbled whitewashed wall, light that stretched out tautly and then was gone. "And she loved sun on stone. But I couldn't tell you what she was looking for. Perhaps I should have asked her. I wish I had." There was a murmur of understanding from the congregation.

"I keep trying to bring her image into focus in my mind, but the pictures slip away. Some of them are stills and some are moving. I am only just beginning to understand the way grief works. When I think of my mother she is usually bent forward concentrating on a book. My mother," you said with deliberation, turning your head back towards your script and picking up its safe and orchestrated rhythms, "liked to read. The last time I saw her she was working her way through a pile of maps and manuscripts. She was trying to work out what stood on the ground under the Wren Library before it was built. Not approximately but *exactly*. She was reading maps and she was reading words, travel accounts and scholars' journals. She was drawing her own maps. My history of Elizabeth Vogelsang is, then, the history of a woman searching for something. I don't think she found it. I think we would know if she had. Two months before she died she was digging down under the foundations of the Wren Library.

"She only read aloud to me once after the days of children's stories and fairy tales. I was sixteen. She read me her favourite poem. We were eating breakfast, and she read 'Fifteen Ways of Looking at a Blackbird.' Or was it thirteen? I could never remember. Her copy had jam stains on it."

Now that my eyes had adjusted to the darkness I could see some of the details of your face through tears that had welled but not yet fallen—

receding curly hair, stubble, fine features, a badly fitting black suit, a black tie—Elizabeth's son, Cameron Brown. The Cameron Brown I knew was a man who played games, conjured spells around people, filled rooms with himself. Now you were struggling and diminished.

"I will offer some fragments of my mother to you as the only act of remembrance I am capable of; others here will do better. I have nothing more coherent than that, only memories and pictures and poems. Perhaps that is what a life amounts to in the end. Yesterday, I started looking for her in her copy of Wallace Stevens and in that poem, 'Thirteen Ways of Looking at a Blackbird' and I found that stanza nine goes like this: 'When the blackbird flew out of sight, / It marked the edge / Of one of many circles.' That's what's happened to Elizabeth. She has flown out of sight, but her absence marks the edge of many circles"—your voice broke again—"which we can't see yet. I looked in the family photo albums to find the edge of one of those circles. So here she is in pictures. Elizabeth Vogelsang. I wish she were here to see them. All I know is that she hadn't finished. She hadn't found whatever it was she was looking for."

Yes, you were right. Elizabeth hadn't finished. But would she ever have done? Does anyone ever finish? Isn't it always unfair—death always a kind of outrage? A life ended too soon with jagged and torn edges, a sentence incomplete.

The wind had picked up and the Leper Chapel was now like a ship at sea, its crew and passengers waiting in the hold in the dark while the captain wept. Outside, through the small, high windows, I could see the straining tops of trees and the occasional sheet of wind-tossed newspaper or plastic bag. A window blew open and started to bang against the stone. No one closed it. It banged again, violently, insistently.

Cameron pressed his remote control, stabbing it in the air in the direction of the projector as if in defiance of the wind. A succession of new pictures followed the black-and-white picture of Elizabeth with the champagne glass and cigarette. Someone gave up waiting for Cameron to speak again and turned up the volume on the music: Strauss's "Four Last Songs" this time.

Family photos in black and white: Elizabeth sitting in a 1950s wedding dress at her wedding reception, shoes off, legs crossed, reading. Behind her, people dancing. Elizabeth holding a fat baby on a tartan rug in the garden, reading, crows circling overhead. Black-and-white family photos passed into colour: Elizabeth standing next to a small boy with black shorts, knee-high socks, and a satchel, book tucked into her apron pocket. Elizabeth and her husband, Franklin, at the beach with a seven-year-old Cameron and friends and their children, in a head scarf and sunglasses, book in hand. Elizabeth in a tree, draped across it like a young leopard, in a black trouser suit, reading a copy of Wallace Stevens with a pale yellow cover—with jam stains. A tall, grown-up Cameron and his parents on holiday in Scotland with friends, Cameron in a heavy black coat and long striped scarf, sitting on the same tartan rug. Mother and son both reading. Glencoe behind them. Then a succession of pictures of Elizabeth with Cameron followed by pictures of Elizabeth with Cameron and Sarah, then a baby, then a second baby. Pictures on beaches—families on beaches— the tartan rug among sand dunes. Elizabeth always on the edge of the picture reading or putting a book to one side so as to smile at a camera.

I was lost in those pictures, lost in Elizabeth's life, when the woman sitting next to me suddenly put her hand on mine, making me jump. I remember her hand more than her face now, looking back. The veins stood out and the nails were rather too long, like talons.

"I have something—a fleck of dust—in my eye," the old woman whispered apologetically. "I wonder if you might help me. I can't seem to get it out. It's starting to hurt." I felt my shoulders drop. Some dust in an eye. Nothing more emotionally demanding. An old woman in a navy blue sweater and slacks. A friend of Elizabeth's.

"Of course. We'd better get you out into the sun."

"I've only got one good eye and now I can't see from that one, I'm afraid. It might be a little difficult to get out."

"Take my arm. We'll be out in a moment." I tried to sound kind and unpatronising, but I realised to my horror that I sounded like a nurse in an old people's home. She didn't seem to mind.

I slipped the old woman's arm into mine and talked her through the short distance between our seats and the great oak door, past rows of dark-clothed men and women in hats and children holding hymn books. We had to cross the projector beam again—to cross through a photograph of Elizabeth with her grandsons and a copy of a book open in her lap, this time inauspiciously called *The Draining of the Fens*. Cameron was now reading more poetry. Heads turned towards us when I tripped loudly over a pile of hymn books. Cameron stopped reading for a moment and looked up, but though he looked straight at me, he couldn't have recognised me in the half-light beyond the projector.

It was when I stumbled that I first noticed the tattoo on the old woman's right forearm, dark against her white skin. An anchor about three inches long, which rose out of the dark blue of her sweater sleeve under some indecipherable letters. She might have been a sailor recently returned from the sea, swarthy and broad-shouldered, with forearms that were remarkably muscular for a woman who must have been around seventy. But if she had the build of a sailor, she was cross-dressing in the way that large old men passing as women sometimes do—the twinset-and-pearls version of womanhood. Her hair looked as if it had been sculpted. It was probably naturally white but had been dyed a pale orange and curled carefully and hardened with hairspray so that the little tongued curls of hair looked like a wood carving. I imagined her weekly trip to the hairdresser, the curlers and the hairspray, the gentle back-combing, the gossipy exchange of stories.

Outside, in the absence of a bench or other seat, I asked the old woman—she was definitely a woman in the daylight—to lean against the church wall, while I eased open her eyelid and dabbed at the black fleck on her iris with a silk handkerchief I'd found in the bottom of my bag. She began to wince and thank me all at the same time. The eyeball was swollen and heavily veined with blood; the pupil contracted and dilated with the light of the sun and my hand flickering in front of it. The other eye didn't move at all. It had a milky absence, a dark blue cave filled with white mist. You could see deep into its hollowed-outness. I felt nauseous. Glad I didn't have to touch that one.

"Well done, well done, it's out now," I heard the old woman saying in a high-pitched, rather aristocratic voice that reminded me of the women's voices in films from the forties. I heard the voice of the woman in *Brief Encounter* and for a moment the air was filled with steam from steam trains and the sound of Rachmaninoff. The old woman was talking on: "I hope you don't think me rude, but you do remind me of someone. You have her hair—heavy and silky. It's remarkable. I'm Dilys Kite. And you?"

"Lydia Brooke."

"And what are you, Lydia Brooke?"

I didn't even think before I answered, "A writer."

A writer. Yes, I was a writer. That was what I was more than anything. Funny. I could think of a whole list of things I *wasn't*—a wife, a mother— a whole list of negatives that, for some reason, I wanted to tell Dilys Kite about. Why was that? What was the half-blind woman drawing from me?

"A poet?" she asked, turning her good eye, still bloodshot, towards me.

"No. A writer of novels and now screenplays. But until quite recently I used to write pretty much anything for money: legal documents, letters, advertising copy, family histories, and memoirs."

"And Elizabeth? How do you know Elizabeth?"

"I've known her on and off for years. She helped me out with my post-doctoral research and then much later when I was writing my first screen-play. I was living in France then. The film company insisted on a historical consultant. And I remembered Elizabeth. I came to stay with her in Cam-bridge a few times, and we wrote to each other. She wrote great letters."

"You did well to find Elizabeth. Find Elizabeth, find the seventeenth century, we always say. She has a gift."

"You talk about her as if she's still here." I put my hand to the back of my neck suddenly. Something—the wind, a twig, a wind-blown leaf—had touched me there.

"Oh, but she *is* still here. I haven't seen her yet, but she's here all right. There are others here too. Don't you feel them?" Now the milky eye turned upwards under the lid and I found myself looking intently at the tangle of blood vessels on either side of Dilys's nose, broken, angry veins as if something had bled invisibly beneath. Safe to look there. Better there than anywhere else. I had started to fall.

"*He's* here. Over there, leaning against that tree. But not Mr. F. He's not here. He knew to stay away. Oh, you mustn't be frightened. And there's Greswold, Cowley, and the boy." When she laughed, I glimpsed a gold tooth at the back of her mouth. "They've come to pay their respects. And they've been waiting for you. There are several people who have been waiting for you."

I could see nothing, nobody, among the trees where she pointed.

"You've taken your time, Lydia," she said, reaching out her hand, that hand with the veins and the too long nails, and running it tenderly down my hair. "So heavy—I thought as much. Like hair running with water . . . like heavy copper-coloured satin. Not a kink in it."

I was six years old again, standing in front of my bed, waiting for the green hand to reach out from under the bed and fix its grip around my bare ankles. I could feel the warm, slightly wet clasp on my ankles but I couldn't move, couldn't step away. Fresh sweat made me suddenly cold in the fen winds. I could feel every inch of my skin under my clothes. It was Dilys who broke the spell.

"We had better get back inside, don't you think? Lydia. Might I call you Lydia? Listen. They're singing 'Rock of Ages.' How beautiful. You go in first. You can slip in while they're singing. I'll be along in a few minutes. Just need to collect myself."

The wind picked up again as I walked away from her, back to the church, so I lost her last words, but I am sure she said something like "I will seek you out."

I looked for the old woman after the service, walked around the perimeter of the chapel twice, pushing through brambles and nettle patches, stinging myself, but she had gone. The mourners disappeared quickly too, escaping the high winds. From the hill I watched you leave, alone; a few minutes later Sarah followed with Leo and Toby, a tall woman neatly dressed with her two pretty sons (they must have been around eleven and fifteen years old then, I guessed), one who looked like you in profile; Sarah spoke kindly to one or two people, touching hands. I watched myself, too, to see what, if anything, I would feel after five years, seeing you, Sarah, the boys. Like pressing on a place where a bruise has been once.

Branches had fallen during the service; leaves and rubbish from the scrap-metal yard and landfill sites lay strewn across the thick grass.

I spoke to no one. I wonder why I took the pictures of the scrap-metal yard and the graffiti that day. Something to do? I didn't want to cry again. I took them as a gift for Anthony, who weaves graffiti tags into his sculpture. Something to do with inscription and stone and rituals for staying time: Anthony's sculptures are carved to look like menhirs, ancient marks on receding landscapes which have lost their meaning to us, just as graffiti tags are a kind of private code, a means of memorialisation as a way of saying: "I have passed here on my journey through time. I leave my mark." For years I'd been photographing tags and graffitied walls in every city I visited and e-mailing the photographs to Anthony's computer from Internet cafés in Calcutta or Berlin.

Dine and Duplo had branded their names here in this scrap-metal yard one dark night or early morning, curling their torchlit foot-high letters respectfully around another tag I'd not seen before: one word, written seven times vertically in green letters against metal: NABED. I'd not seen NABED before. I imagined boys dressed in dark clothes with balaclavas and rucksacks full of different coloured spray cans, perhaps skateboards strapped across their backs. Urban warriors. Graffiti artists. Street bombers, they called themselves, Anthony had said. Anthony had pictures of Duplo's tags from as far away as Peterborough. I imagined Cambridge trains riding through the night carrying Duplo's signature through fields and industrial estates and into sidings. I'd seen Duplo's tags on a warehouse hoarding farther along the Newmarket Road and on the back of an Argos lorry. His name moved—they all moved.

Once I'd finished, I sent Kit a text: "Funeral over. Be with you in half an hour. Still OK to stay over? Tell Maria I have a present for her." Kit would know how to be, how to put words around this terrible sadness, not my own but a borrowed sadness—one of the many circles the blackbird had flown from.

Four

For as long as I can remember I have dreamed a dream about a warehouse. I write "warehouse," but it might easily be a derelict stately home. The point about this building, whatever it is, is that it has scores of rooms full of things. Old furniture and armchairs and lacquered cabinets painted with birds, glass cabinets full of little boxes. Trapdoors and secret corridors and disguised doorways and hidden staircases and no one but me in there. Me, curiosity, and the dust. In my dream, I walk around all the rooms and sometimes I find new ones, open a door I hadn't seen before which leads to a new staircase. I touch objects piled on tables and display cases—glass, fur, metal, jewels, feathers—until I find a long mirror and racks of clothes and jewellery. Standing there, I try each piece on one by one: the chiffon dresses, the Spanish shawls, the fur coats, and I drape paste diamonds over myself, diamonds I've found laid out in the velvet-lined drawers of mahogany cabinets. Each time I dream my way to that place I feel I've come home. Sometimes I feel someone else is there in another room. I hear a noise like a chair being dragged over floorboards or the creak of a door. But I haven't seen anyone there yet. It's always me looking—in drawers, behind trapdoors, down corridors, me looking at myself in the mirror as various people I don't recognise—never me *being* looked at. No, *being watched* is something new.

Maybe that's how I found Kit Anderson. She's run a vintage-clothes

stall at the Cambridge market all the time I've known her, which is sixteen years or so. Back then, when she was a history student at Clare, she
just had the stall on Sundays, but now it's a proper business and she's
made money from it, enough to live on. None of us thought she could.
That's where I first met her, at the market one day just before Christmas.
It was almost dark and there were Christmas lights coming on all around
us, and the crinoline-shaped netted skirts attached to the metal frame of
the stall were blowing in the wind. I was trying on a black velvet jacket in
the dressing room she had constructed from old eiderdowns and in that
half-light I found myself telling her about the carved wooden dressing-up
chest in the conservatory of my father's house which my stepmother had
bought and stuffed full of old clothes donated by friends, the ladies from
the conservative club in Bradford. Down in the dark corners of the chest
were pieces of jewellery, beads, thick leather belts, hats, and scarves. Then
Kit quoted me some lines from an American poet friend of hers who
wrote about still-life paintings and the way they worked to stop time, to
distill memory into a series of intensely arranged objects. Vintage clothes
were like that too, she said. Even when they passed on to new bodies, they
kept their old people about them.

Kit got pregnant before she finished her Ph.D., and though we'd try
to guess sometimes, she never told anyone who the father was. She always
said she'd go back and finish the thesis when Maria got older but she
never did, and in the end she joined that subcommunity of people who
live in Cambridge who've been finishing their Ph.D.s for decades. Like
most of them she still has a room full of books and papers, even something like half a completed thesis, but the whole academic field has
changed now. To finish it she'd have to start again. And the world, she
says, is too crowded with academics working on Restoration theatre. Instead, Kit Anderson runs the clothes stall and does something much
more interesting: she rewrites revenge tragedies—*The Duchess of Malfi,
The Spanish Tragedy, Titus Andronicus*—for an experimental theatre company she's put together called Mainspring.

Kit poured me a gin and tonic when I arrived at her house in Sturton
Street after the funeral. I walked down the side passage between the ter-

raced houses and the rosebushes and through into the garden and there she was sitting in the conservatory kitchen she'd built since I'd moved out, sitting with Maria; Kit was reading the newspaper and Maria was at the sewing machine again. Kit looked up, laughed, and stepped out into the garden to meet me.

"I never thought we'd see you back in Cambridge again, Lydia Brooke. You said you were done with Cambridge."

"I had. But Elizabeth . . ."

"I know, I know. I'm just teasing. It's great to see you. Hey, this is a sodding big bag. You planning on staying for a bit?" I couldn't be sure from her voice whether I heard approval or disapproval.

"If that's OK with you people," I said. "I've got a bit of free time and I thought I might stay for a few days, perhaps even a week, if I won't get in the way."

"That's good news," Kit said. "Maria will make you up a bed in her room, but I'm afraid you'll have to put up with Titus—he's noisy at night." Titus was Maria's guinea pig, a ridiculous creature whose long curled hair made him look as if he'd been crossed with a Barbie doll.

"You OK?" I asked, as Maria left the room.

"Tired, a bit hungover. We had a party here last night, as you can see." She gestured towards the kitchen and a sink full of unwashed glasses. "The last garden party of the summer." She twisted her hair into a knot, pulled a couple of chopsticks from a drawer, and stuck them through the knot of hair. Maria's face had brightened by the time she reentered the room, Titus on her shoulder.

"Good party?" I asked.

"Brilliant. Mum bought those red paper lanterns from the Chinese supermarket on Mill Road, so when it got dark they were all lit up all the way down the garden to the pear tree."

"It was too cold, really," Kit said, "but we just wanted to squeeze one more party out of the autumn, didn't we, rabbit?" Maria blushed. She was thirteen and her mother had begun to embarrass her. So, Kit was still squeezing parties from the summer like blood from a stone. Kit was afraid of the dark; she hated the winter. Dreaded it creeping up on her. Maybe that's why she worked on revenge tragedy—those sudden bloody stabs in the dark, a violent death in an alleyway, meaningless and cruel. She'd been dancing the night before, pushing back the dark.

Maria moved her sewing to one side to clear a space among the sequins and buttons on the conservatory table to make room for the plate of Moroccan lamb Kit pulled out of the microwave. I ate and drank my gin and tonic looking down over the darkening garden, while Maria and Kit talked about funerals they'd been to, exams, mobile phones, the garden, and the party. I wasn't really listening till Anthony's name came up.

"Anthony stayed over," Maria said, eyes wide. "In Mum's bed."

"Maria!" Kit exclaimed with mock outrage. "You make it sound like we're lovers or something."

"Well, you are in a way, aren't you? I know, I know. He's always here and he brings you flowers and presents and sometimes he stays over. You can never be really, really sure that someone's gay, can you? People fall in love."

"If Anthony was going to fall in love with me he'd have done so fifteen years ago."

"Not necessarily," I said. "You're more interesting *and* more beautiful now."

"Bugger off," she said. "That's a hollow compliment if I've ever heard one."

"But she's right," Maria said, scanning her mother's face. "You *are* more beautiful now. Well, a bit."

Kit raised her eyebrows at me. "I can just see it all now. You can just drive back home to your fancy Brighton flat, Lydia Brooke. I'm not having you stay here to shift all the alliances in my house. This daughter of mine is supposed to be on my side. Look at the pair of you ganging up on me. You were always trouble." The pupils of her eyes narrowed. She meant it. She was still angry with me from before. I would have to be careful.

"I've got some pictures for Anthony," I said. "And some flowers for you and a case of pinot noir in the back of the car."

"More graffiti pictures? You were always his main supplier. Does he know you're back? What have you got? Show me."

"Oh, the usual," I said, passing her the camera so she could scroll through the tiny pictures illuminated on the screen. "I picked up some great tags from Amsterdam earlier this year, and there's new tagged walls from the skater park in Brighton. I took some pictures this afternoon too in Cambridge—the scrap-metal yard next to the Leper Chapel. There's a tag I'd not seen before: NABED. Green letters, black shadow. Does he have that one?"

"Christ. Yes. Trust you to find that one on your first afternoon. NABED. It's not really a tag. It's political. An animal-rights group. They target the animal-lab people and leave their tag after an attack, like a signature."

"What does NABED stand for?"

"No one really knows. They're completely silent."

"No Web site? No manifesto?"

Maria left the room—pointedly. Kit watched her go.

"No, just the tags—so far at least." She changed the subject.

That night, as I lay listening to Maria's breathing and the interminable wheel of Titus's cage turning and turning in the dark, I thought of Dilys Kite and all the questions I hadn't asked her and I thought of the black-bird and the edges of circles. *I will seek you out,* the old woman had said.

I found Kit in the kitchen around midnight, making tea. She was wearing my favourite kimono from her collection of 1920s silk dressing gowns, the one with a blue background and gold water lilies, and her thick black hair was still piled on the top of her head. I'd thrown on a black silk robe from the back of the bathroom door. They were everywhere in Kit's house. Even her dusters were made of scraps of old velvet—and she doesn't dust.

"You not sleeping either?" she said. "Titus needs shooting. I swear he's got more energetic as he's got older. But guinea pigs don't live long. By my calculation he's only got four months to go. I could put him out in the shed while you're here—might speed up the process. Chamomile tea?"

"Maria would have a fit if you turned him out for me. No, it's not Titus. I'm just overtired, I think. I've been writing late for a couple of weeks and now that I've stopped I'm dead tired, but I can't seem to switch off. I'm like Titus on that bloody wheel."

We sat in the back sitting room in the dark, where Kit lit some of the candles in the red Chinese lanterns that she'd strung across the fireplace. The two armchairs had lost their springs years ago so you sunk down deep into them, almost to the floor. Kit had slung fleece rugs over them, and in the warmth of wool and the wood fire I suddenly felt I could fall asleep looking at Kit's feet curled under the blue silk of her kimono. She had silver nail varnish on her toes.

"Funny seeing you in that robe," she said. "It's the one Anthony wears when he's here."

"Yes, I thought I could smell him. Where is he? Christ, I've missed you all. Funny how it all seems to stay the same. This house. The smell."

"Just looks that way to you. It isn't the same, though. I've fixed all sorts of things since you were here last . . . the bathroom light switches work, the back door doesn't stick anymore. I bought a DIY book."

"So if this is now Anthony's robe, it's not the first time he's stayed?"

"God, you're as bad as Maria. No, it wasn't the first time, though Maria thinks it was. When Anthony stays I sleep better. He's been very good to me."

"He's always adored you. He's never sold that white marble head you sat for, has he?"

"No, he hasn't. He's had some important commissions lately; he's working on an enormous bronze for a shopping centre in Gateshead. Another menhir. You must see it."

"You're not lovers, then?" I didn't look at her.

"No, we're not lovers—though . . . it's complicated. What about you? How's that dreadful man of yours?"

"Peter?" I said and she brought her heavy eyebrows together into an exaggerated frown. She never called him by name. "He's OK," I said. "I've asked him to move back into his flat, though. I need a bit of a break. Living together isn't working out."

"Bet he hasn't gone yet."

"No. He hasn't."

"Surprise, surprise. You shouldn't have let him move in in the first place."

"It was good to start with."

"What, for two weeks?"

"Yes, about that." I'd brought Peter to one of Kit's parties once and he'd offered to mend her broken gate—he had a tool kit in the back of his car, he said. I should have warned him. She hates people pointing out the broken things in her house and she won't be helped, especially by a man with a toolbox, though in those days she'd never got round to mending all those things herself. I felt oddly defensive. "He's good company. He's a great cook. It's nice to have him there when I get home. We get on."

"Not enough reasons to have him live in your house, though. You don't need a housekeeper or a handyman. Not you."

"I know, I know. I made a mistake. But that's boring. I don't want to talk about Peter or even think about him. You know, I don't think I'm going to go back till he's moved out again. Elizabeth's funeral yesterday changed some things, like a switch had been thrown in my head. It's a cliché, I know, but I suddenly saw it, in black and white: life's too bloody short. I've had enough of all that wadding—you know, the day-to-day stuff, the habits, the routines. I want something else. Want to go back on the road for a bit. Somewhere a bit wilder."

"*Again?* Jesus, Lydia. You should hear yourself."

"So you'd have me settle down, would you? A little house in the suburbs and some children? I can't do that."

"There's other ways of doing it." Kit hesitated, ran her finger over her bottom lip and pulled her gown around her feet. "You stayed put for Cameron. Long enough for him to mess up your head."

"Now, that's complicated. I gave up trying to understand that years ago. But you're right, I did stay put—in a way. Have you seen him?"

"I bump into him at parties from time to time. Anthony sees him when he's in Cambridge."

"He's not around much?"

"Cameron Brown's a big shot now. He travels a lot. Anthony says he's working on some major neuroscience project. Top secret. He's up for some big European science prize. Can't remember which one. He looks older these days. Works very long hours at the lab, apparently. And he has to be very careful who he sees and who he talks to. Security levels have been stepped up in Cambridge because of the NABED group. Cameron's right in the firing line, doing what he does."

None of this surprised me. If you joked about your mother's obsessions, it was because you knew how it was to pursue a question so far that it began to consume you from the inside. You were always your mother's son. When you were at the lab or working late on your papers in your office at Trinity, you'd forget to eat for whole days. There were times for both of us, when I was writing too, when we could only claw ourselves back to sanity in the depths of each other's skin in the dark of the night, desperate and mindless and hungry for something we couldn't name.

You'd wake sometimes in those nights and reach for paper to write something down, some solution that had come to you in the night, some formula or some new question. You'd laugh in the daylight, looking at the words you'd written, nonsensical words scribbled on the back of anything you could find: paperbacks, bills, even once the corner of a lampshade. Though you claimed otherwise, it was never the academic rewards and adulation that drove you, but the head rush of unearthing something no one had put together before, being the first one to see it. Sometimes, ecstatic with some new breakthrough, you'd begin to tell me something, then stop yourself, remembering the silence that had to wrap itself around your work. You thought I didn't notice. Then the man of silences would make up stories. First thing in the morning, before dawn sometimes, spinning stories, ridiculous, brilliant stories. Write that down, you'd say. Do something with that. And I did. Stole your plots and the made-up people you brought me.

Once, eight years ago or so, when we were sitting talking about everything and nothing, nursing hangovers and drinking tequilas in a cabaret bar buried in a flea market in northern Paris, right at the heart of a knot of streets lined with shops selling chandeliers the size of upturned trees, jewelled swords, antique clocks, medical models of men and animals with every sinew labelled, jewels and glass and piles of lace and linen, boiled and ironed to stiff whiteness, I said:

"You're a pretty good person to get annihilated with."

You laughed. "Annihilation," you said. "Yeah. *Killing Time* by Cameron Brown and Lydia Brooke." An aged woman with dyed black hair and eyebrows had begun to sing "La Vie en Rose" very loudly on a platform in the sawdust depths of the bar.

"You know, you could annihilate me, everything, at any moment," you said, darkly, when she had slipped off the stage again. "Just by sending her a letter or ringing her up. It frightens me sometimes to think about it. Armageddon. Your armies and mine—just think what they could do to each other. If we let them."

"I think about that too," I said. "And it frightens me that I do think about it."

"It all hangs by a thread," you said.

"No. Not really. It's a robust thing; it's weathered and adapted down the years. It's all much stronger than you think."

"You're talking about yourself—"

"No, I was talking about you. I was hoping it was true and afraid that it wasn't. I sometimes think I'm stronger than you. I think I am." Yes, I could see your mounted armies and mine lined up to face each other on the hills of Montmartre, before the city spread that far, waiting, paused. A lowering sky behind. The glint and clink of metal. The exhalation of horses in cold air.

"Think you are what?"

"Stronger than you."

"One of the animal-lib people wrote that to me once. Funny the language they use. Passionate. The letter said, 'We know your every weakness. We are stronger than you. We have greater resolve and we will never give up.' That scares me too." You were running your finger around the edges of a stain on the table.

"Perhaps I should give you up," I said. "Release you."

"You can't."

"I could try."

"But I will never give *you* up. Never. And I don't care how that sounds. I need you. I won't let you want to leave me. Not yet." I could see the ring of gold around the dark iris of your eye.

We were both afraid suddenly in the smoke of that Parisian café. Afraid to leave and afraid to stay. We came to be afraid in those months before I disappeared, before I left you, from that day we lined up our armies on the hills of Montmartre. A game of Risk. You with the blue dice and me with the red. So many battalions to lose.

. . .

I had just begun to fall asleep, remembering that bar in Paris, my head against the fleece, when Kit told me about the phone calls. She tried to be casual, even offhand.

"Don't answer the phone while you're here, Lydia. Maria's not allowed to either. I've been getting weird phone calls. So I just use my mobile."

"What kind of phone calls?" Now I was wide awake.

"Look at you," she laughed at me. "Bristling like a cat. Don't get wound up. It's been going on for a bit. They don't bother me anymore. And they don't happen that often either. It's the fur coats."

"You're getting strange phone calls about fur coats? What kind of pervert is that?"

"It's not a pervert. Look . . . I have a rail of vintage fur coats on my stall. This person, the woman who calls, belongs to some animal organisation—not NABED as far as I know, thank God. This woman says I shouldn't sell them. To start with she was reasonable, but then, you know me, I got angry and told her to sod off, and since then she keeps on calling once a week or so."

"Are there threats?"

"Oh yes."

"And you're still selling the coats? You could just stop. It's not like you *have* to."

"Think about it. Would you stop if someone started ringing you like that? I mean really?"

"But you're so exposed there on the market. Anyone could—" I stopped.

"Anyone could what? I've thought about all of that. Yes—they could what? Graffiti my stall, poison me, burn the coats . . . bomb my stall? I'm a little person. They won't do anything to me."

I moved to sit nearer the fire, taking one of Kit's feet into my hand and massaging it. "They might."

"It's not a bloody film, Lydia. This is just some crank. You can't give in to these people. Actually, I'm pretty sympathetic. Anthony's friend belongs to one of these groups, and they've got a point. They say there's an animal holocaust going on and that anyone who is complicit with it, by selling animal products or experimenting on animals, is a collaborator. I kind of see that. They want to bring down the institutions, the meat industry, the clothes manufacturers, the pharmaceuticals—all the institutions that hurt and exploit animals. It makes sense."

"So why don't you stop?"

"You wouldn't."

"No, I wouldn't. But . . . What about Maria?"

"I've talked to her about it. She thinks I'm right. So just don't answer the phone, that's all. They'll stop if I ignore them for long enough. Now go to bed, look at you. You look a hundred and five."

I was cold, suddenly, and sad; I wished I'd known. Wished I'd been up to Cambridge to stay more often. That's how it started . . . slowly, piece by piece. With a bristle. Yes, it did make me bristle. I wanted to protect Kit and Maria and even those bloody fur coats. After all, I had time. I could stay. That's what I said to myself then, but there was something else too. Something about not being finished with the city or it with me. I wasn't going back to my flat till Peter had gone. Not now. I had some wadding to throw off. And you? Well, you might have had something to do with it, too.

Five

I called you early. It ought to be easy, I thought, after five years—what trouble could there be? We were over it. It was finished. I had two books Elizabeth had lent me that I wanted to return. I only had to see you once, after all, to make my point and satisfy my curiosity. Best to get it out of the way, I thought, so it was eight-thirty A.M. when I phoned; Kit and Maria were still sleeping, and there was no chance of being overheard. I didn't want to be thinking about Cameron Brown today: the day was fine and I had promised to take Maria punting on the river. The punts would be packed away for winter from the beginning of October, so there wasn't much time left now that she'd started school again. As soon as I had pressed the buttons on Kit's phone I realised it was Sunday and probably too early to call. But it was too late.

I would never have used your home phone before, but I was lucky; it was you, not Sarah, who answered the phone.

"Cameron Brown. Hello."

I began to speak, but my voice was too high. I started again.

"Sorry. I have a cold. Cameron, it's Lydia."

"Lydia *Brooke*?" Did I detect anything in your voice? Had I forgotten how to read it? Already?

"Yes." Safer to say as little as possible. For the moment.

"That's extraordinary. I have a piece of paper on my desk here on which I've written your name. It says 'Call Lydia,' but I thought it was too early to call. I thought you'd still be sleeping. Last night I called your home in Brighton. Your husband gave me your mobile phone number. But here you are calling me instead. Are you in Cambridge?"

"Yes, I'm in Cambridge. That was Peter you spoke to. He's not my husband. He's a friend. He's staying in my flat."

"Oh, OK, sorry. I'd heard you were married. Are you in Cambridge for long?"

"Yes, well, about a week. Maybe longer. It depends. I came for Elizabeth's funeral and I'm staying with Kit. And . . . you didn't hear I was married. You made that up. You know I don't believe in . . . You know I wouldn't." You had me, and you knew it. I'd lost my composure.

"You're staying in Sturton Street? Shit. I wish you hadn't told me that. Same room?"

"No. I'm sharing with Maria. Kit's turned my old room into a storeroom for her clothes."

Same room? Not your business, Cameron Brown. "My old room"—*our* old room. Yes, you were at Sturton Street for most of the time I rented a room from Kit there. We'd been talking for less than two minutes and already we'd talked our way back to *that room*. Change the subject. Get out of there, away from the crimson sheets, the white muslin curtains and the light that hit the bed around midafternoon through trees that dappled it. Keep to the point.

"I have some books of Elizabeth's I wanted to return. I wonder if I might drop them by the lab sometime in the next few days?"

"Yes, yes, that would be great, but I wonder. Might we meet? I have some things I wanted to ask you. Elizabeth left a letter for me in which she gave me your phone number. Oh, look, it's impossible to explain over the phone. I have some questions I want to ask you about the goddamned seventeenth century."

"You have some questions about the goddamned seventeenth century? You probably need someone else then, not me."

"No, it's definitely you I need to talk to. Let me explain. Let's meet. Are you free later on today? Let me buy you lunch. I have to go into Trinity to pick up some files, so how about the pasta place on Market Square? Twelve-thirty?"

"OK. Sounds interesting."

"Mmmm. Don't know about that. It all seems very complicated to me. But I will explain. Or I'll try to . . . It's so good to hear your voice."

So I abandoned the plans to take Maria punting. Just like old times. You always made me do that. But then I suppose I didn't *have* to abandon friends, films, plans, and trips whenever you texted me that you had an hour or a day free. I was in love—was that justification enough for always putting you first?

I saw you reading a book in the restaurant window looking over the market—the Sunday market full of craft stalls and ugly objects, cartoons of cats and painted glass. A market among the chiselled and inscrutable stone of Cambridge colleges, walls marking their borders from the town. The first word Maria had recognised, Kit told me once, was the word *private*. Kit said she hadn't noticed how often you could see the word around Cambridge on walls and doors till Maria had pointed and repeated it. A city of keys and locked doors and private secret inner courtyards—gardens to which only fellows had the key.

Kit's stall was empty; she didn't work on Sundays. She'd gone to a yard sale; Maria was still asleep. Hidden in the shadows I locked Kit's bike, caught my breath, and ran my fingers through my hair, checking my reflection in the window of the CUP bookshop. Cameron Brown, Doctor of Neuroscience, Fellow of Trinity College, Cambridge. You never looked quite like an academic. Cambridge male academics dress badly, Kit always says; that is axiomatic, that is the dress code: trousers at least an inch too short, patterned sweaters from the eighties, jackets with shorts, socks worn with sandals, and once, Kit swore, she'd seen a split seam on a pair of trousers that had been *stapled* back together. You dressed positively elegantly compared with most of the men I'd seen in the University Library. That man's dishevelment, Kit used to say, is different; it's carefully arranged. Studied even. There's nothing contingent about it.

"So sorry I'm late. Hope you haven't been waiting long." Why did I sound like I was a hundred years old? Or about to interview you? The cuffs of that grey sweater I bought you had begun to unravel. You had shaved. It always made you look younger.

"I knew you'd be late. I had a bet with myself." You knocked the salt and pepper pots over as you stood to shake my hand and tried to put your book away in your briefcase at the same time. I thought I'd be the awkward one. I felt suddenly at my ease as I took off my coat and watched you stand the salt and pepper pots up again, smiling urbanely, looking me up and down, thinking I didn't notice. But then I was doing the same to you. A man with long limbs, I remembered, who doesn't quite know how to carry himself.

"I'm not late," I said. "And you know I'm not a generally late person. You must be mixing me up with someone else."

"No, I don't think I am, as it happens," you said, passing me the menu. "I've ordered us a bottle of wine—the wine's good here. And some olives. Are you hungry? The seafood's good here too. You like crab, don't you? It's fresh in from Lowestoft. Probably scuttling across the seabed up there only yesterday."

"Are you having crab?" I asked. I didn't like crab. Not at all. My step-mother had tricked me into eating a crab sandwich once in a café in Cromer, told me it was tuna. I'd never forgiven her. You once knew I hated crab. Had you forgotten or were you pretending to have forgotten?

"I'm having the eggplant and chickpeas. And bread—a basket of bread. My kind of food."

From where I was sitting I could see the stall where the young man mended wicker chairs, and stalls full of market vegetables and organic meats and the smoke from the stall round the other side where they bar-becued ostrich burgers. I remembered talking to you and Sarah at the market once, before any of us had become entangled. The three of us had been at the same party the night before and there we were, quite by chance, at the water hydrant on the marketplace, sitting on the same wall, eating lunch. It was May, I think. She'd gone rowing at six A.M., she'd said, despite her hangover, and she was going home to sleep. She had magnifi-cent arms. I remember that. Rower's arms.

You poured me a glass of wine and, draining yours, poured yourself another. It was a brown earthy red, a Rioja. We were both doing every-thing we could to avoid looking at each other.

"We could have gone to the vegetarian café across the road," I said. "You're still vegetarian, I assume."

"Yes, I am. But that café's not very good anymore and anyway—you like seafood."

"How do you know I still like seafood?"

"Oh, that won't have changed. It's in your blood."

"I'm genetically programmed to always like seafood?"

"Yes, I wrote the programme. It's the finest I've written. My master-piece." You must have seen my eyes narrow. You could still read me then and put your shields up as fast as ever. "Lydia, shit, it's just a joke, OK? Don't look at me like that." You were winning.

"None of your manipulative jokes, eh?"

"Maybe later? A little one?"

"Have I told you how much I dislike you?"

"Many times." The corners of your mouth had curled into the faintest of smiles. You wanted to fight. I didn't. Today you would win. Perhaps I didn't care anymore.

"I'll have the duck salad. Did you finish your book?" I couldn't tell you that I had bought and read it; that would have given you too much advantage.

"Yes. I finished it—finally. That was a burden. I *had* to finish it once you'd gone. What are *you* working on now? Actually, I know the answer to that question. I asked Anthony. You've just finished a screenplay. Yes?"

"Yes, I've just finished a screenplay. Suddenly I know why I live in Brighton, not Cambridge."

"Why's that?"

"Because you can be private in Brighton—even, on good days, anony-mous."

"Oops, sorry. You're right. In Cambridge everyone knows everyone else's business. Especially if you're famous."

"I'm not famous."

"I think you'll find you are. Famous by Cambridge's standards. Doesn't take much."

"Cameron, stop it now. Enough."

"Stop what, Dr. Brooke?"

"Your games."

"So you're back? You're looking good. Different. Your hair's longer. Something's different. Not sure what. Something about your eyes."

"Yes, I'm back." *But not to you. I haven't come back for you.* "I came for your mother's funeral. I'm so sorry about Elizabeth. You must be . . ."

"It's been five years since I saw you."

"I know." *Five years and three months, actually.* "Shall we order? I'm very hungry. I didn't get much sleep last night."

"Jesus. I know how you get when you're hungry. We better eat quickly or you'll have one of your tantrums. Were you working late or just anxious about seeing me?"

"Neither. It was a noisy guinea pig."

"I was up late last night too. Sick child."

Cameron Brown up at night with a sick child. Toby or Leo? That seemed strangely incongruous and implausible. Then I saw it all again— the house, the wife, the boys who played football and got sick. The smell of couples, sentences routinely finished by the other, clothes hanging in the same wardrobe, schedules for cleaning the toilet or for picking up the kids. Was Sarah still arranging for your bike repairs and taking your clothes to the dry cleaner? You probably never even questioned all of that, took it for granted. Life was disappointing, I thought, when you looked close; full of mediocrity and domesticity. Everyone went down in the end, martyrs to the golden marital dream. Then the compromises and the bandages, the arguments about who cleans the toilet. Cambridge was full of wives who tolerated their academic husbands working late and did everything for them, looking firmly away from their affairs. And full of women like me who didn't want all of that and in return got to be called mistresses and were whispered about in libraries and college corridors. Pretty, suffocating Cambridge. I didn't like to look at it. Didn't want to see inside your house and find a repetition of a thousand Cambridge middle-class households. It bored and frightened me.

I blushed and you noticed. I saw your eyes linger on the base of my neck, which is where my blushes stain most red. What were you thinking then? Only the most obvious interpretation, I thought: confirmation that you were still under my skin.

But you didn't misunderstand me, did you? Not then and not later.

You misunderstood other things but you knew then, you knew why I blushed. I never gave you credit for that.

"And how is Sarah?" I asked when that blush had receded. I made an effort to meet your eyes head-on. I must have looked confrontational. No more misreadings.

"Sarah? She's fine. She's had a book out too, on seventeenth-century trade relations between England and Spain."

"She finished that book? You *both* finished?"

"Yes, it's been, Christ, what's the word? Peaceful. We just got on with our lives. Worked hard, finished certain projects. Lydia, I want to ask you something."

"Yes, you said. About the 'goddamned seventeenth century.' Can't you ask Sarah? She's a seventeenth-century historian."

"Not the right kind, unfortunately. OK. From the beginning . . . It's about Elizabeth's book."

"The history of alchemy book?"

"You know how it meant everything to her, night and day, summer and winter."

"Yes. I don't know much about it, though. She never really talked about it to me."

"She didn't really talk about it to anyone. She'd started out with that history of alchemy project thirty years or so ago, but in the last decade she'd narrowed it down to just Newton's alchemical work. She published a few articles in the nineties, all of them highly scholarly but uncontroversial. She gained a reputation; even something of a following. There were certain important historians who were waiting for her to finish the magnum opus with a degree of anticipation, I think."

I noticed several patches on your neck that you'd missed in shaving. I hated noticing things like that. You leaned forward, suddenly conspiratorial, and whispered:

"Don't look now but there's an old girl two tables away who's trying to hypnotise me." I glanced in the direction you indicated. An old woman dressed in dark blue sat with a group of friends, talking and chain-smoking. She looked away as I turned towards her. An older woman in a tweed jacket passed her a pint of golden-coloured beer, and she lifted her hand to the glass. She drank half in one go without putting down her cigarette. I was impressed. She didn't look like the sort of woman who would drink pints.

"That's Dilys Kite. A friend of your mother's. I met her at the funeral. Strange that she should be here."

"Well, I don't care whether she's a friend of my mother's. I've never met her and I don't remember seeing her at the funeral. She's definitely trying to hypnotise me. I won't look. See her off, won't you?"

"She can't be trying to hypnotise you—at least not from there. She's only got one good eye. The other is false. Don't turn your head right now but take a look at her right forearm. She's got the most magnificent tattoo."

I don't know why but, though I was laughing, I was suddenly afraid Dilys would disappear again. I didn't want to speak to her this time. At least not in your presence. She would have made me say too many things I didn't want to say. You would have been rude. I knew that. I took my camera from my bag. You raised your eyebrow.

"Don't ask," I said. "Just humour me. I need a photograph of her. Shift into this seat so that I can see her over your shoulder. That's right. I'm going to make it look like I'm photographing you but the zoom on this camera is good enough to catch her. She can't see us anyway, but just in case."

"I'm too old for photographs."

"Don't worry. I'll edit you out later. It's her I want."

"Why?"

"It's a long story. You wouldn't get it."

"Oh, OK, it's a writing thing. Your dark art."

The flash of the camera made several people glance in our direction at the same time. I opened up the screen. There was Dilys, now a series of pixels in my digital camera. Fixed. Framed. Imprisoned. Her head rose over your shoulder, the smoke from the cigarette she held in her left hand curling upwards, a snake trail against the polished metal door of an old bread oven set into the fireplace behind her. Your cheek and jaw filled a third of the screen. I zoomed in past you to see how clear the cropped picture of Dilys would be. Her eyes were half closed but she was looking straight at the camera, as if she knew she was being photographed. I took the focus in several times so that her face filled the frame.

But you had poured me some more wine and begun to talk about Elizabeth and her book again, so I turned off the camera and put Dilys away. When I looked across at her table she and her friends had gone.

Since then I have gone back to that picture several times. I never did edit you out, though I meant to. And it was only later that day, when I transferred the picture to my computer screen to crop Dilys's face, that I noticed the bloody weals that ran down your cheek—angry wounds. Funny, I thought. He must have cut himself shaving. Why hadn't I noticed at the time? You hadn't cut yourself shaving, had you? Something unaccountable had started.

Slowly you wove Elizabeth's spell around me all through lunch with your silk threads and hers, like a cocoon. I was now very interested in your goddamned seventeenth century. Elizabeth's seventeenth century. You said suddenly, seriously:

"I'd like you to finish Elizabeth's book. Don't say anything yet, just listen. You can make up your mind later. I've thought about this a lot. Elizabeth would have wanted this—she left your name among her papers on the last day."

"But that doesn't mean anything—"

"Shhh. Just *listen*." You were cross, impatient. You were already talking to me as if we were still lovers. There seemed to be a great deal at stake.

"I want to pay you to finish it," you said. *I want to pay you to finish it.* What a strange phrase; what an unnerving proposition. I thought of courtesans then, you know, in silk kimonos, in those still moments as I took in your words and dwelled upon them there, running my finger around the ring of the half-full wine glass so that the sound seemed to hold out a taut meditation between us which I could not sever, could not take my finger from. Silk kimonos and hushed peignoirs and a poem by Wallace Stevens. I blush to tell you even now what I thought then because—but you know, you knew— to tell you about seeing silk kimonos and courtesans is to tell you of books, and dust, and seduction, to tell you now that it is too late, that even then I was already in your bed, or you were in mine. Again. Yes, that was your story and mine, as it wrote itself, as it wound itself into sheets and stories through Cambridge winter afternoons as the shadows lengthened. How much seduction was in the air; even then, even in that lunch amid the eggplant and chickpeas and the smoke from the Sunday market.

"I propose to pay you a salary for six months. No, no, don't laugh. Don't dismiss it. I am making a business proposition: you have made others like it, I know. I'm asking you to finish my mother's book between now and the spring; that's around six months. It might not even need that long. It's practically finished as far as I can see. Her footnotes look impeccable, as always."

"But I live in Brighton. Elizabeth had notes and papers. I would need libraries and access to her books . . ."

"I've thought about that. It makes sense for you to live in The Studio while you're writing. It's obvious. All the books you could possibly need are there, and it's only a half-hour walk from The Studio to the University Library. Pepys is still there. A neighbour has been feeding him."

"You want me to live in Elizabeth's house? But if there's more research to be done—how . . . ? I'm not a proper historian, Cameron. You know that."

"You won't need to be a historian. She's done all the research. There are a couple of incomplete chapters, but there are files with notes for each of those. The rest just needs redrafting and editing. The manuscript is in her computer; there's a printout on her desk."

"Have you read it?"

"No, I can't bear to. But I have glanced through it, just to see what sort of state it was in."

"And?" I was biting my nails.

"Well, it reads well. The bulk of it covers Newton's life from 1661, when he arrived in Cambridge, to 1667, when he was given his fellowship. Like a mini-biography. It's very detailed."

"Just six years? Why those years in particular?"

"Alchemy. She was using Newton as a way of showing how all those European alchemical networks and secret societies hung together. That's how I always understood it, anyway. She wanted to challenge that myth of Newton as a lone genius, working completely in isolation. It was a passion to her—she hated all those genius myths and eureka moments in the history of science books. She talked about it a lot. She wanted to show how much, like all other scientists in the seventeenth century, Newton depended upon European secret societies, Freemasons and alchemists, groups of men in The Hague and in London and Cambridge and Paris.

That he wasn't in isolation and that the network to which he belonged controlled him in some ways, too."

"Depended on them for what?"

"Oh, for almost everything—for knowledge, secret manuscripts, books, libraries, scientific instruments, patronage, formulas, introductions to other people. Newton was apparently connected up to a group of alchemists working in London and Cambridge. She'd been tracking them down one by one. She had an index-card box full of their names and dates. Some of them were easy to identify apparently, but others just had code names like 'Mr. F.' or initials like 'W.S.' or pseudonyms like 'Philalethes.' She was working on identifying some of the last alchemists in Newton's circle when I last spoke with her, just before she died. I helped her with some of it."

"OK. Sounds interesting. That does happen to be a decade I know relatively well because of *Cobalt*—end of the civil war, the plague, the Fire of London, the establishment of the Royal Society. I'd like to read it, though, before I make up my mind."

"You can't. This is an act of trust. I can't let you read it unless you agree to finish it. You have four days to make up your mind."

"Why?"

"I'm going to Berlin until Friday. A conference."

"Lucky you."

"I won't see anything of Berlin. We're not allowed to leave the hotel."

"Why?" You looked away. Waved for the bill.

"The usual reasons. The lab managers have stepped up security to high alert. There's a new animal-liberation campaign going on in Cambridge that's getting nasty. Three car bombs and acid attacks since the summer. One of the car bombs was mine. I seem to be towards the top of their hit list now that the book is out. That's a measure of professional success, I suppose."

"Christ. They got your car? Not the little green Mini."

"Yes. The fucking Mini. I've had that car since I was a student. We've got a Volvo now. I hate Volvos."

"I know. I'm sorry." *We slept in that Mini, remember, parked in the middle of a field at night, somewhere outside Wisbech.* "Kit's on one of those lists too, it seems," I said.

"Kit's being targeted? Why?"

"The fur coats on her stall."

"Oh yes, that would be reason enough—now. Oh, you know how it is. It's no big deal. I've lived with it for at least fifteen years. Phone calls, letters, e-mails—threats mostly. Since you left, the sponsors agreed to pay for Sarah and me to get proper security for the house at Over so it feels safer. They leave the kids alone, which is something. But it's more dangerous abroad—particularly in Germany, where many of my financial backers are based. The conference will be boycotted."

"Do you have to go?" Was this fear on my part or a sense of foreboding?

"It's my work. Of course I have to go." You smiled. Yes, you knew. It had already started.

"Look. Here's my card and contact details. I've changed labs. You won't be able to just drop by, I'm afraid. No one's allowed in, not now. Even my office at Trinity has a CCTV camera. It doesn't work properly, but the college has insisted on it, even though I'm only there once a week or so."

I looked at the business card you passed me. "Histon BioSciences?" I said. "You always said you'd never go there. Christ, Cameron. Why?" The Histon lab was notorious. There were whole groups dedicated to bringing that laboratory to a stop.

"For a moment there, Lydia Brooke, I might almost have believed that you were concerned for my welfare. But it's the thought of the puppies, isn't it? Contrary to popular belief, we don't torture puppies at Histon." Your eyes had flecks of steel in them now. You were not going to explain anything to me, or defend yourself.

"Here's my mobile number. Would you text me in Berlin with an answer when you're ready? I'm sorry to hurry you, but I have to make arrangements with the executors of Elizabeth's will to release the money to pay your salary, and they're putting pressure on me. If you agree, I'll ring my lawyers and get them to send you a contract to sign. They'll ask for your bank details so that your salary can go straight into your account, on the last day of the month, every month until March. Money. Christ, yes money. Sorry, I forgot. The salary. The details are all in this envelope.

Someone contacted the Writers' Guild to find out the upper end of the current rate for ghostwriting."

"Ghostwriter? Yes, I guess that's what I'll be."

"Sounds good, doesn't it? Beautiful word. Ghostwriter. Ghost-pale. Ghost-light. Ghost-hour. Ghost . . ."

"Ghost-ridden . . . yes, beautiful. And if I say no? What alternative arrangements do you have in place?"

"None. I don't know what I'll do if you say no. Frankly. Throw something? Lose my temper . . . no, not with you." You laughed and I noticed how your lips still creased like the finest parchment. You were used to getting your way—probably took it for granted now.

"And Sarah?"

"What about her?"

"Won't it cause problems?"

"She never knew about us."

"Cameron, she *always* knew about us."

"So you say. You'll just have to believe me; it won't be a problem. You're the obvious person to finish the book. She knows that."

You made your excuses, paid the bill, and left, handing me a sealed envelope containing a key to The Studio and the paperwork at the very last minute so that I couldn't pass it back. That was presumptuous of you. "Go and look over The Studio if you like," you said. "It's empty."

Empty? The Studio was never empty after Elizabeth died. But you didn't know that.

After I left Cambridge, you sent me a text message out of the blue, one of several. "The world is no longer beautiful," it said. It was the tone you had taken that made me want to be cruel in return. Made me want to send vials of poison back to you. It was the artfulness of those occasional texts you sent me, the fact that—after everything—you still had the audacity to assume that the loss and the pain were yours. That you were the suffering one. I didn't answer. It seemed better that way. Just silence.

And I knew that despite your words of love, in that silence and in my absence you would be purifying yourself again, doing whatever it took to persuade yourself that you could now become an honest man, that you could stop betraying Sarah. And, I guessed, that would mean finding my letters, all those letters I had sent you from Italy and Greece and Istanbul and Syria, envelopes filled with the pressed flowers and the bits and pieces of things I had slipped between the thick sheets of paper, that you would print out all my e-mails, gather all my letters and e-mails together and burn them on that bonfire out in your garden. Once you had seen all those words in flames, I knew, there would be a kind of redemption. Yes, I thought, you would do that, burn my words in exchange for your own redemption.

What was it that made me agree? The prospect of living in Elizabeth's house, which I loved, the promise of quiet, no company but a cat, a project to finish. Was it the money or the fact that I had just finished my screenplay and for once had nothing else to do for a few months? Or perhaps the thought of going back to Brighton, which made me feel buried alive—I glimpsed for a second Peter's orderliness, the handles of the saucepans all facing in the same direction in the cupboard, the list of jobs to be done on the fridge door, and it made me shudder. Was it that I already knew I was leaving him? Or was it you? Or the wine we had drunk? You were uncompromising, determined. You wouldn't have taken no for an answer. You had made up your mind that I was to be Elizabeth's ghostwriter, discussed it with your lawyers, drawn up a contract with my name on it. You had prepared your ground, asked all the right questions. I just walked straight on in.

I texted you that night for the first time, pushing out the letters onto an illuminated screen in the dark of Maria's bedroom before I had even talked to Kit.

"Yes. I will. Yes. Lydia B."

Only two minutes later, as if you had been waiting for me, your reply lit up the screen on my phone with a tiny envelope:

"Thank you, Lydia B. Use the key. Make yourself at home. Will call on my return."

Six

I remember that beginning as a series of flights and drops, certainties and fallings away. After rising to your challenge, sealing my fate in those few short letters typed into my phone, I had a couple of very bad days, days in which Kit's questions challenged my motives, in which I found myself doubtful and resolved by turns. I picked up the mobile to text you several times: if a few words typed into a mobile phone had committed me to writing Elizabeth's book, a few words might also undo that knot. But I didn't undo it. You were in Berlin; I in Cambridge. I sent no further message. What could I lose, I wondered, now that my direction was so unscripted? I would have liked to talk to you. I didn't. I walked on in.

I turned myself into Elizabeth's ghostwriter by a series of small and inconsequential acts over the following week that continued to propel me towards The Studio and tied the knot between Elizabeth, you, and me ever tighter: a long phone call to Peter that started with explanations and ended with raised voices, a phone call in which I sought advice and which ended instead in my telling him I was moving into a house in Cambridge; a deliberately formal e-mail sent to my now ex-lover the following day with a list of things I needed to take with me; a drive to Brighton to pick up the boxes of papers, books, and clothes that Peter had packed up, labelled, and colour-coded; new agreements made over my kitchen table about bills and responsibilities and rent to be paid into my account; an ar-

gument with Kit about risk and your manipulations; boxes that stayed un-
packed in the back of my car until the morning I took my clean washing
from Kit's laundry cupboard, packed my last things, picked up the key to
The Studio, stepped into the car, and drove to your mother's house. Just
keep on walking forward, I said.

The Studio was not as I had remembered it. Quiet roads twisted and
turned down by the river, lined with elegant eighteenth-century houses of
all different shapes and sizes: gardens filled at this time of the year with
hollyhocks that had bloomed; the little pub called the Green Dragon
overlooking the river; the parking place by the cobbled wall; the door in
the ivy which I had to open by pushing my shoulder against it hard; beyond the door the bright September light falling through trees that were
already turning gold and russet. It was only when I pulled the heavy door
to behind me, shutting myself away from the sound of the traffic, and
when I smelled the river and the apples rotting in the orchard garden,
that my ambivalence dropped away. I remember the lawn and the bright
flowers and the blue sky blindingly bright above the sharded angles of the
roof and the sound of my feet on the gravel path and the clustered tree-
tops over which rooks circled and cawed in the glassy sky.

When I circled the outside of the house looking in, taking my time,
Elizabeth's cat, Pepys, a ginger tom, twisted his way like a skein of wool
round my ankles, as he and I followed the path round the woodpile at the
back of the house and through the rose arbours and shrubs planted
around the skirts of the orchard. I remember noticing that there were no
curtains at the windows and that many of the wooden shingles on the
roof, which swept all the way down to the ground, needed replacing. Not
my responsibility, I said to the cat. I don't have to mend and paint and re-
pair here. I'm just passing through. I didn't walk down to the riverbank,
down to those reeds, not just yet. No ghosts here, I thought. No ghosts
and a room of my own.

Two days later a woman dressed in black with short blond hair let herself
into The Studio at around midnight and, finding me sitting at Elizabeth's
table in the dark, reading her papers by candlelight, let out a scream. Of
course: in that light and at that hour, she thought she'd seen a ghost.

Since the front door was still open, the wind blew the candle on my table out, and paralysed by the sudden darkness, she dropped everything she was carrying onto the hallway floor. Switching on the light, I helped her pick her things up: library books, a tobacco tin, and a new bottle of glass cleaner called Shine.

"She's run out of glass polish," she said, by way of explanation.

"How come you've got a key to this house?" I asked.

"How come *you* have?"

"I'm going to be living here for a bit. Cameron—Elizabeth's son—has asked me to do some work on her papers. I'm a writer. Lydia Brooke. I was also Elizabeth's friend."

"Will Burroughs." She offered me her hand and I shook it. "Elizabeth was my friend too," she said proprietarily. "She paid me to do her garden and sometimes I cleaned her house. I stayed here sometimes when she was away—fed Pepys. I'm a graduate student at the university. I've just kept on coming since she died. I love this house and I miss her. She let me work in the back room. Some of my papers are still in there."

"Will?" Even in the dark I could see she wasn't a boy.

"Short for Willow."

I lit a match and found the candle. "Willow?" She was tall and thin. Boyish. Yes, she could pass for a boy.

"My parents were hippies. Bastard name. I hate it."

"Oh. No, you don't look like a Willow somehow. Will's much better. Do you want a glass of wine? I have a bottle open."

"I don't drink wine. I'll pour myself some water, though, and then I'll just get on and clean. Don't mind me. I'm very good at cleaning quietly. Used to working around Elizabeth. She always worked late. She was always awake when I came."

It's only recently that I came to think again about what she said to me that night. I have only recently come to wonder why, if Will had been tending the garden and cleaning the house, it was all so unkempt.

That's how I came to be friends with Will Burroughs. There was something about her I liked from the start. Something enigmatic. So I asked her to come and give the house a thorough clean—it had been standing empty for a while and smelled musty—and to do some late-summer work on the garden. It was an excuse, really. I had been working alone for too long, and apart from Kit and Maria I wasn't in the mood to be looking up old Cambridge friends. I was just passing through. Will stayed late one evening and we played chess on an old board I found under the sofa. That's when I told her that if she wanted she could carry on working in the back room. She had a key and could come and go as she liked. So every couple of days she would appear at The Studio—anytime between dawn and midnight—and work for a few hours. She would bring me flowers or a book she thought I should read or vegetables from her garden. We didn't talk much to start with. She would leave her gifts in the kitchen and disappear into the back room to set up her laptop. After a while, we settled into a pattern. Sometimes I would pay her to clean or mow the grass. One Friday morning she arrived with a bag of spinach from her garden and cooked me a spinach cake after midnight, leaving it in the fridge the following morning with a note that said: "Eat cold with bread and mango chutney."

The first time I saw Will I knew I had seen her before. But it wasn't until days later that I realised that she was in the picture in the alcove in The Studio, one of Elizabeth's oil paintings, signed by the artist, Helen Gould, a friend of Elizabeth's. It was my favourite picture in The Studio. There are two people in it, each facing in a different direction: a woman, Elizabeth, I think, though it's difficult to tell from the back alone, and a dwarf in the foreground looking towards us. It's not clear whether the dwarf is a man or a woman, but his or her face is Will's. Each of the two figures is standing under an archway that looks as though it is the gate to a medieval city, and beyond is a sweeping vista towards the mountains. The dwarf walks towards us and into the city, out of the light and into the dark, and the woman walks away towards the sunlit hills. The dwarf looks straight at us, warily, dressed in a red coat with harlequin markings, and he has no shoes on his feet. One hand, large and disfigured, is a kind of question mark; the other clasps a three-sided wedge of glass. He has something to ask, but he hesitates. He is not sure whether he trusts the person he is looking at.

But Will was neither a dwarf nor a young man. Will was Willow, and Willow was many things: a young woman with a pretty name who dressed as a boy and called herself Will. The daughter of hippie parents who had grown up travelling from festival to festival and who eventually packed their surprisingly serious and studious daughter off to an experimental boarding school at the age of ten, where she got herself six A-grade A levels and came to Cambridge, where she was now working on a Ph.D. on passive resistance in the writing of Henry Thoreau. She lived in a small terraced house in Chesterton that her parents had bought her from money her grandfather had left her, took in lodgers, was painfully thin, and had started to work for Elizabeth Vogelsang when she'd answered an advert on the graduate noticeboard in her college. That was Will's story. But Will had other names too, which I didn't know about then.

A few days later I was still unpacking my suitcases, hanging my winter clothes in the alcoved wardrobe, when I heard Will let herself in downstairs. Sitting at the top of the steep open staircase I could look down on the studio space and watch Will carrying logs from the shed and piling them next to the stove.

"It's getting cold," she said.

"I know—perhaps you'll show me how to light the stove."

"I don't know how to," she said. "Elizabeth always did that."

"Perhaps we can work it out together . . . Is there a reason why there are no curtains here? The house would be much warmer with curtains."

"Elizabeth said she liked watching the light move round the house. Said the apple trees were like curtains—nobody can see in through them."

"Are there any curtains we could put up?"

"You could always look through the cupboards in the back room. But then that woman took most of what was in the cupboards."

"That woman?"

"Cameron's wife."

"Will, do you know why she died?" I asked.

"Who?"

"Elizabeth."

Will didn't answer for several minutes. She just kept piling up the logs carefully, turning them around so that the grain was visible, making a pattern.

"Why she died?" she repeated, without turning to look up at me, though she let a log fall from her hand onto the hearth. "What do you mean?"

"I mean: I know she drowned in the river here, but—no one seems to want to talk about it. Did she kill herself? Was there a reason why she might have done that?"

"None that I know of. She was busy. She was finishing her book."

"Didn't the papers say she had a gash on her head?"

"The coroner said it was probably caused by some sort of collision in the water. Floating debris. After the point of death."

"Floating debris can't cause a gash, can it? It would have to be something sharp and fast moving."

"I know. It's horrid. I'm just telling you what the coroner said."

"So what really happened?"

"I don't know." Now she looked up at me—wanted me to see her face, or wanted to read mine. "No one knows. I was away and when I came back there was a police cordon around the house. I didn't go in. The neighbours told me what happened. Then one day when I came, Elizabeth's daughter-in-law, Sarah, was here with their Volvo and she'd boxed up all Elizabeth's things—clothes, linen, jewellery, letters—and took them away, leaving only the furniture, books, and papers. I didn't stay. Couldn't bear to see that happening. I watched her from the trees. She threw a whole heap of Elizabeth's stuff onto the cage for bonfires down by the riverbank."

"I guess that was in preparation for me moving in here."

"Yes, maybe. I don't know what she did with all Elizabeth's clothes. I keep expecting to see one of her coats in a charity-shop window in Burleigh Street, on one of those mannequins with no heads."

"But there's so much of Elizabeth still here. The pictures. Her shells and bones. Her books. Sarah can't have taken that much."

"I think she got spooked before she'd finished. She seems not to have touched very much down here in the big room."

"There was a postmortem, wasn't there?"

"Yes, but they didn't find anything out. What can you say? She'd drowned. She'd been in the water for two days."

"Who found her?"

"He did."

"Cameron?"

"Yes."

"Christ. I didn't know that. It explains . . . So what do you think happened?"

"Why don't you ask him?"

"I can't ask him. That wouldn't be right."

"Look, she just drowned, right? Leave it at that. There was no note and, well, she just wasn't like that." She had turned to sit cross-legged on the floor. She had soot from the fireplace on her cream tracksuit trousers. She wouldn't look at me now.

"Like what?"

"Depressed. Tired of life. I don't know. She wasn't any of the things that make people do that . . . whatever they are. I've thought about it a lot."

It was Ophelia I saw in the water then, not Elizabeth in her red coat. Ophelia lying face upwards among her flowers. An innocent victim in a revenge tragedy. A conduit. She took the blow that others should have taken. It fused and melted her brain cells so she didn't know who or what she was anymore.

"Elizabeth wasn't like that. She had a book to finish. All of her life was in that book."

I changed tack. "What does Cameron think? Have *you* talked to him?"

Will turned away from me, reaching for the dustpan to sweep the bark and soot from the floor and brushing off the soot from her trousers.

"I don't know what he thinks. We haven't met. I saw him come here once on a Sunday afternoon. I was working in the garden."

"You've never met him? But you've been working for Elizabeth for months. You must have run into him once or twice."

"He doesn't come here often, and when he does it's at weekends. I'm only here during the week. Elizabeth, well, she didn't want him to know about me, didn't see the need." Like mother, like son, I thought. Secrets.

"So if Elizabeth didn't take her own life, what happened, do you think? Could she have had a heart attack? Fallen into the water by accident?"

"No. When they did the postmortem they checked for that. Her heart was sound. Yes, she could have fallen in, but then why didn't she climb back out again? The water is deep there, but she could swim."

"Were there . . . could there have been . . . suspicious circumstances?"

"Yes, but not the kind you think. She had no shoes on."

"What do you mean?"

"The answer's in there somewhere, I'm sure." She nodded towards the table and the pile of printed papers—Elizabeth's book. I stood then, rising to the knowledge she was indicating. I walked down the stairs towards her, into her words.

"In the manuscript? The answer's in the manuscript? You've read it? Don't be cryptic, for Christ's sake. If you know something, why didn't you speak to the police?"

"No one wanted to speak to me. And I didn't want to speak to them. I had no proof; they would have laughed at me."

"How well do you know the manuscript?"

"Well . . ." She hesitated, then decided to trust me, if only a little. "Elizabeth employed me as a research assistant, not as a cleaner, for most of this year, until July. I checked references for her. I followed up on things. I was in and out of the University Library anyway working on my thesis; it was easy."

"What happened in July?"

"We fell out."

"Why?"

"Because her friend Dilys Kite turned her head. She was here sometimes for several days at a time, or Elizabeth went out to her house in Prickwillow. I thought she was losing it. They were always in cahoots. She seemed crazy to me—obsessed."

"Elizabeth was always obsessed."

"Yes, but she'd always been rational. She'd stopped being rational. A few months before she died, she'd become obsessed with this 'Mr. F.,' a friend of Newton's, mentioned in one of his manuscripts, and these deaths—"

"Friend?"

"Well, as far as Newton ever had friends. In June she'd asked me to look for this Mr. F., told me to go through all the Fs in the list of seventeenth-century Cambridge graduates, to make a short list of all the people who fitted the right dates. Then she told me to stop. She said she wanted to do it herself. So I never knew his name, and when she found him in that list—and she did—she wouldn't tell me. She told me he was a fellow at King's, a mathematician, about ten years older than Newton and one of the Cambridge alchemists. Then she asked me to give her back all my research notes, everything, every scrap. I told her she was barmy. Well, she fucking was. She even rang an exorcist in July."

"An exorcist? Why? Elizabeth wouldn't have done that. She wouldn't—"

"She did. Of course she didn't believe in all that crap. That's why we fell out. I told her she needed a psychiatrist, not an exorcist. Dilys had turned her bloody head."

"Where did she get an exorcist from?"

"Tommy Logan. He's a friend of Dilys's. Get this—he's also the manager of the Texaco garage on the A10."

"And?"

"I don't know what happened. I wasn't here."

She picked up the pile of papers, holes punched and threaded through with a silver ribbon, and thrust it at me, so that as she jerked it from the table the stone paperweight fell to the floor and lodged on its side in the crack between the floorboards.

"You haven't finished it yet, have you?" she asked me.

"No, I've only dipped into it. I wanted to read some books about alchemy first."

"I didn't think you had. Just read it. Then ask me . . . if you need to."

With that she left. Threw the dustpan into the armchair, scattering soot, dust, and wood bark everywhere, and walked out. A pool of reflected light that had gathered in the shape of a large silvered octagon high on the wall quivered and stilled. I watched it settle back into its diamonded shards and then begin to move slowly across the wall, inch by inch.

She came back later that day, let herself into the house and then just stood there in the big room with her hands thrust deep into her jeans pockets. I was sitting in the old armchair looking out the window, the manuscript open on the floor beside me, Pepys on my lap, half asleep.

"Lydia. Look, I'm sorry," she began. "It all went wrong. I didn't mean to be like that."

"It's fine. You miss her, that's all. It doesn't matter." I smiled at her. "I'm glad you've come back."

"Lydia, I don't think you should be here. I've been trying to say that since you arrived."

"Where?"

"In Cambridge. In The Studio."

"Because . . . ?"

"Because there are things you don't know about."

"I know. There's lots of things I don't know about. That's why I'm here. Look, it's just a job, Will. I'm enjoying it. And I want to finish the book, for Elizabeth's sake."

"Can't you work at your friend's house?"

"At Kit's? But I need all Elizabeth's books and papers."

"You could take them with you." She was very winning. Like a child.

"*Why* shouldn't I be here?"

"I can't say why. There are several reasons."

"No, I can't move now. How come it's OK for you to be here?"

"Oh, I'm safe enough."

"Look, I'm staying put until spring at the latest. I'll probably be gone by March. That's only a few months. Then I'll be off. And you're right. It's time I finished this manuscript and started writing. I wanted to read as many of the biographies as I could before I started Elizabeth's manuscript, so that I could see where she was taking a different line, and I needed to know more about the history of alchemy. But I've mostly finished that now. If you've got good reasons for thinking there's a risk, then tell me; otherwise, let's just go on as we were. I'm not going to give this up because you say there's something strange going on that you won't—or can't—talk about."

"No, you're right," she said. "Forget I said anything. I'll be back the day after tomorrow." She disappeared into the hall.

"Did you mean it?" I called out after her.

"Mean what?"

"That Elizabeth's death has something to do with what she was writing."

There was a pause. She closed the front door and came back into the room.

"I shouldn't have said anything. It was stupid. Look, I've been a bit stressed lately, for reasons of my own. Probably a bit paranoid. You mustn't listen to me."

"But you *do* think so, don't you?"

"You've no idea how it was towards the end—before I went away in July. She was already half mad. She'd discovered these suspicious deaths in Trinity in the 1660s and she thought Newton might have been connected in some way. Read the book and make up your own mind. Maybe she did just . . . *lose* it."

"No, she didn't just lose it," I said. "She's not the type. She was out there in the rain and slipped. Or waded in to reach something in the water and lost her footing. Her coat might have got tangled up on something . . . it doesn't take long to drown."

"Yes, and anyway she's not coming back. So there's no *point* in wondering . . . is there?" She was mocking me, my rational explanations. Sarcasm. *There's no point.*

I didn't say, but I might and probably should have done. I didn't say: Look, I want to know too. I want to know why she died. I want there to be some reason for her death other than a chance slipping of a foot on a wet riverbank in the middle of the night. I didn't say: There's so much that doesn't make sense. What if it wasn't accidental; what if it wasn't suicide? But, no, I wasn't going to get drawn into conspiracy theories or superstition or hauntings. Someone had to keep some perspective. And yes, if you had asked me then, if you had said, "Do you know why my mother died?" I would probably have said that yes, I did think Elizabeth Vogelsang had lost it. That's what it looked like to me. She'd lost it because . . . ? Well, because she was searching for something she couldn't find. And it drove her mad.

I watched Will's hunched figure slump through the garden in the rain, towards the riverbank. She never left by the street gate, always the river path. I didn't think anything of it then.

Seven

I sat at the long oak table the following morning, with the pages of *The Alchemist* laid out in front of me, feeling Elizabeth at my back. A tortoiseshell butterfly beat away at the apex of the triangular roof as shards of watery light passed across the white walls above, twisting infinitely slowly, aggregating and disaggregating like amoebas or hydras under microscopic illumination, coming in and out of focus as the sun brightened or dulled. I'd never seen light circuses like this in any other house. No wonder Elizabeth had never hung curtains here.

I remembered standing on the shore of a Scottish loch once at night, watching the aurora borealis pulse in the northern sky. Behind the mountains, thin stubs of rainbows undulated red and green, like ripples of water. I heard the sky vibrate, crackle, like a whispering way up above the sound of Peter's voice explaining about particles driven into the earth's magnetic field by solar winds charged up and streaming down towards the magnetic poles. Or at least I heard, but Peter and his friend Simon didn't. Now, why is that? If I could hear the aurora, why couldn't they when they were standing only a few feet away? What was it about the sound that was so particular?

I sat for perhaps ten minutes before I lifted the stone paperweight holding down the sheaves of paper—slate grey with a lightning bolt of white quartz through it—in order to try out some of Elizabeth's sentences

on my tongue. The words conjured her. The dark began to gather outside. It was like lifting the latch and walking into an empty house without
an invitation.

Play the word-association game and throw in *alchemy*. Most people,
even clever people, will say *gold* first of all, then follow up with phrases
like *philosopher's stone* or *elixir of life*. Most people have this idea that
alchemists were all medieval wizards trying to find the philosopher's
stone, a mythical powder that would turn base metals to gold, and that
they had some kind of clandestine brotherhood with secret handshakes.
But there were important reasons for the secrecy. Alchemists knew that
the precious knowledge and formulas the ancients had carved out over
hundreds of years, in Babylon, Mesopotamia, China, and Egypt, could
only be passed among people who knew what they were doing, the initiated—people who spoke the secret language. Men like Nicolas Flamel,
Paracelsus, John Dee, Agrippa, and Agricola. And they believed in the
ritual of discovery, thought that every generation coming to these sacred questions had to seek these things out for themselves, as Hermes
Trismegistus insisted. The knowledge was dangerous, and its potency
would be lost if it were not kept hidden and concentrated. It had to be
forever rediscovered.

There are so many different kinds of alchemists and alchemy, across
so many cultures and beliefs, it's almost impossible to say precisely what
alchemy was, or is, in any absolute sense. Alchemists, like our scientists today, were trying to uncover nature's secrets, her patterns and processes,
trying to work out how the five elements—earth, fire, water, space, air—
transmuted into and out of each other under various astrological conditions to make up all forms of matter. They believed that everything, even
those things that *seemed* inert, was actually teeming with spirits and that
therefore everything could be raised or provoked into fuller form. They
believed that all matter was on the move, moving into and out of everything else, waxing into or waning away from fullness so that lead fell short
of gold, just as mortal man fell short of immortality. Under a certain pattern of stars and through fire, any matter (like lead) or spirit (like the human soul) might be "healed" or "killed" or "perfected" or "transmuted"
into a greater state. A blooming would take place. It had a rare beauty,
this secret hybrid art made up of magic, chemistry, philosophy, hermetic

thought, sacred geometry, and cosmology, a beauty in that passion to make things bloom into a fuller being. It made me think of transubstantiation—the wine into blood, the burning bush, Lazarus raised from the dead.

The first words after the title page of *The Alchemist* were not Elizabeth's. She had set an epigraph on the front page, like an inscription carved over the entrance porch. It was a quotation from Richard Westfall's definitive Newton biography *Never at Rest: A Biography of Isaac Newton*, published in 1980; I found the quotation marked up in Elizabeth's copy in a footnote on page 21 of Westfall's book in her library. She'd drawn a pencil ring round it. It may have been only a footnote, but it sat there in the foundations of Westfall's book like a talisman to ward off bad spirits. A disclaimer. A statement of incredulity.

All the Newton scholars knew that the great man practised alchemy— there was no getting round that. Like hundreds before him, Newton believed that the riddles of the universe were to be found in certain secret papers and traditions handed down by the initiated in an unbroken chain from the time of the great hermetic revelations in ancient Alexandria and China. Richard Westfall—his friends called him Sam—honest and meticulous, confessed in that footnote that he was embarrassed and confounded by Newton's alchemy. He had to say this somewhere in his book, get it off his chest, though he'd written all the way through to page 21 before he did so:

> Since I shall devote quite a few pages to Newton's alchemical interests, I feel the need to make a personal declaration . . . I am not myself an alchemist, nor do I believe in its premises. My modes of thought are so removed from those of alchemy that I am constantly uneasy in writing on the subject, feeling that I have not fully penetrated an alien world of thought. Nevertheless, I have undertaken to write a biography of Newton, and my personal preferences cannot make more than a million words he wrote in the study of alchemy disappear. It is not inconceivable to most historians that twentieth-century criteria of rationality may not have prevailed in every age. Whether we like it or not, we have to conclude that

anyone who devoted much of his time for nearly thirty years to alchemical study must have taken it very seriously—especially if he was Newton.

"My personal preferences cannot make more than a million words he wrote in the study of alchemy disappear." In those words Westfall admitted to wishing that he *could* make those million words disappear; if he could he would excise all that hocus-pocus from the collected works of the English hero of the Enlightenment. A million words.

In putting a floodlight on Westfall's scepticism, drawn out of the shadows of his footnotes, Elizabeth was declaring her own position. She would go where angels and sceptical biographers had previously feared to tread; she would look where they had not wanted to look, at Newton the alchemist—not the scientist who dabbled in dark arts but the man who practised them. Elizabeth Vogelsang would not avert her eyes from Newton the magus.

Then without further comment—for her book worked by a kind of bizarre juxtaposition; she'd put things together as an alchemist would and let them do their own work, make their own chemistry—Elizabeth plunged straight into her first chapter, "Glass Works." The phrase evoked Venice and optical instruments and sand and fragility, stained glass, blues and reds and golds. It made me think of rainbow reflections from Victorian chandeliers.

You would have liked the colour and light of her writing, the ease of her sentences. *The Alchemist* would not have grieved you as you feared it would. You looked for Elizabeth in Wallace Stevens and found a glimpse of her there. You might have looked in *The Alchemist* too, where you would have found her among the opulent materiality and detail of her goddamned seventeenth century.

Your mother's book began with the journey of a consignment of glassware from Venice to Cambridge across the Fens, destined for Stourbridge Fair.

Glass Works

One morning in the early spring of 1664, glassmaker Sr. Allesio Alvise Morelli received a letter, delivered by horse to his glasshouse in Murano, a small island off the coast of Venice, a cream-coloured envelope bearing the thick red seal of John Greene, Glass Seller of London. The envelope contained a large order of glassware, some of it destined, Morelli knew, for one of the largest trade fairs in Europe, Stourbridge Fair at Cambridge.[1]

Morelli could no longer take his English clients for granted. The English king, Charles II, on his restoration to the throne only four years before, had granted a royal charter to the Worshipful Company of Glass Sellers, allowing them to put tight controls on the importation of glassware from Italy, Germany, and the Low Countries. Now that the war was over, the king and his dangerous ally, George Villiers, the second Duke of Buckingham, were determined to forge a new glassmaking industry in England to rival that of the rest of the world. Buckingham was building glasshouses at Vauxhall in London. Orders for Venetian glass were already in decline, but, the other Murano glassmakers bragged, Buckingham's English glass would never rival the fluted, twisted, engraved *cristallo* glasses and flutes of Venice because Murano glassmakers had alchemical secrets, skills learned over hundreds of years. The English hadn't the materials, the knowledge, or the climate.[2] At least not yet.

But now the Duke of Buckingham, who virtually controlled the monopoly on English glass production, was *buying* Venetian glassmakers and glassmaking secrets. His agents, they said, were everywhere along the Venetian coast and islands, offering money, making deals to bring Italian glassmakers to London. It wasn't the first time Venetian glassmakers had betrayed their secrets. Fifty years before, the glassmaking priest and alchemist Antonio Neri had been enticed into the Antwerp house of the Portuguese nobleman Emanuel Zimines and persuaded to write out his spagyrical secrets in a book published in Florence in 1612 called *The Art of Glass*. Persuaded? Some say he was tortured. Now the English Royal Society had paid the physician Christopher Merrett to translate Neri's book into English because the English glassmakers needed the ancient alchemical secrets. No Muranese glassmakers, Morelli intoned, should ever have been allowed to leave the island. The Venetian civic

[1]The British Museum archive of letters written by John Greene to Allesio Morelli dated 1667–72 establish that Morelli had been supplying the London glass sellers Greene and Measey for several years. For Morelli's reactions to the shifts in status between English glass and Venetian glass see Vogelsang Papers, pp. 33–37.
[2]See Dan Klein and Ward Lloyd (1984), *The History of Glass*; Eleanor S. Godfrey (1975), *The Development of English Glassmaking, 1560–1640*; W. Patrick McCray (1999), *Glassmaking in Renaissance Venice: The Fragile Craft*; and R. W. Douglas and Susan Frank (1972), *A History of Glassmaking*.

council had been too weak. Just as Daedalus died for trying to carry away the secrets of his labyrinth, so, they said, Neri had paid with his life in an alleyway in Pisa in 1614. He was only thirty-eight. He would practise alchemy no more. The Venetian brotherhood had seen to that.[3]

But despite the ban on the importation of glass to England, Greene, a member of the Worshipful Company of Glass Sellers, was still ordering Venetian glass in large consignments like this. Morelli knew this meant only one thing: Venetian glass was still far superior to the glass Buckingham's men were making and Greene was prepared to take the risk of importation as long as he could get away with it. The glass seller had drawn page after page of designs and sizes, specifying width of bowls, size of stem, even the thickness of the glass. Morelli's eyes glanced briefly down the order—drinking glasses, claret glasses for French wine, sack glasses for Spanish wine, small beakers for brandy, goblets, a new design for a beaker with a flaring lip, forty dozen goblets, 286 dozen beer glasses—5,400 items in all, including a number of specialist items such as mirror plates, strings of beads, and prisms. This order would easily fill one of Morelli's three ships.

Morelli did not like the change in the Englishman's tone in this letter—an edge of threat and a new sense of power that membership of the Worshipful Company of Glass Sellers had given him, as well as his insinuations, his underhanded way of implying that unless the quality improved he would buy his glasses elsewhere. This time Greene wanted Morelli's ship to sail to King's Lynn, not into London, for, he said, he wanted to meet the consignment there and oversee its unpacking onto canal barges that would carry the chests down the fenland waterways and into Cambridge for the fair at the end of August. The glass would be safer travelling on water than on the road, Greene wrote, even if it did increase the length and time of the journey. It would also be cheaper. Morelli thought for a moment. That would mean shipping by July. They had only May and June to complete the order.[4]

During May, when the sun was high and hot in the sky, Morelli's men unloaded hundreds of barrels of quartz pebbles that had been sailed down the River Po to

[3]For Antonio Neri see W. Patrick McCray (1999), *Glassmaking in Renaissance Venice: The Fragile Craft*, pp. 153–55; for the death of Neri see Richard Westfall's Web catalogue of biographical details on European alchemists, http://galileo.rice.edu/lib/catalog.html.
[4]For Morelli and Greene see R. W. Douglas and Susan Frank (1972), *A History of Glassmaking*, p. 14; Ada Polak (1975), *Glass: Its Makers and Its Public*, p. 115; and McCray (1999), *Glassmaking in Renaissance Venice*, p. 148.

the coast from the beds of the River Ticino, and then sailed around the coast to Murano's port. Here they roasted the quartz in furnaces and when the pebbles were cooled, pulverised them, grinding them to a pure white powder called silica, which they stored in sacks at the back of the glasshouse. Now the master glass-makers mixed up the batch, stirring into the white powder secret amounts of soda imported from Syria and Egypt, which would lower the melting temperature of the silica. The soda, which the Syrians made from seaweed ash, or *allume catino*, Morelli knew, was much superior to the soda the glassmakers used in the Low Countries or in England. Another secret. It was good but was never pure enough, Morelli complained, insisting that his men refine it even further by distilling it. Glass made from this mixture alone would be a pale blue-green, unless the colour was bled out of it. Only manganese would do this, expensive manganese brought from Piedmont and stored in the locked buildings in the yard. Without manganese there could be no colourlessness or transparency.[5]

Quartz powder, seaweed ash, manganese—the fire would transform it all, release its components, separate out and then reunite them. More fires. More heat inside and outside the glasshouse. But the men did not complain. With-

[5]See Antonio Neri's *L'Arte Vetraria (The Art of Glass;* 1612, translated 1662).

out the fire there would be no mystery, no glass, no distillation. God's hands worked in the brick dome; for the glassmakers the furnace of fire was church, the work their act of worship. As the sun began to slip down into the horizon, the men ladled the powder into the earthenware crucibles and passed them through the work openings in the domed brickwork furnace. Here, invisible to the glassmakers, on brick shelves above a fire of wood and coal burning at 1,500 degrees centigrade, the powder in the earthenware bowls turned slowly to thick, transparent glass-honey as the moon made its way across the sky.[6]

From the glassmakers' chair under the arch near the door, Morelli watched the patterns of the men's moving bodies radiating out from the central dome of the furnace. The men worked together in their teams of two or three, the master glassmaker and his assistants, each team working around one of the six work openings in the hot brick furnace. One would blow the molten glass up into the air into a perfect sphere, like a freshly cast planet on the end of a blowing iron, or would let it drop and turn as he blew, so that it formed the perfect curve of a goblet. Then the seated master glassmaker would take the wooden handle of the still twisting blowing iron from the glassblower and, placing the twisting iron against the wooden supports of the chair, would prod and nip the glass into drops and curves and tease out a base like a flower from a perfect drop of molten glass, as round and fine and flat as the finest oyster shell.

Inside the glasshouse, for three hundred years, under the mastery of Morelli's father and grandfather, the men's bodies worked with the perfect regularity of stars moving in the heavens. Twisting, spinning, and twisting, blowing and twisting, the men dripped sweat, working as close as possible to the furnace so that the fire would keep the glass molten and malleable. Flames from the furnace cast all the irons and the moving bodies into flickering, flattened shadows, radiating outwards from the dome, around which the angles made by the blowing irons shifted and changed perpetually in the thin grey smoke. Between the blackened bodies of the fathers and grandfathers, their sons, some of them no older than Pedro, Morelli's own grandson, officiated like sweat-smeared altar boys, stoking the fire, carrying coal, wood, and freshly cleaned tools to the men and ferrying trays of the finished glasses away from them, packing the glasses into thick wooden chests filled with dried seaweed.

[6]See R. J. Charleston (1957), "Glass," in *History of Technology,* vol. 3, edited by C. Singer, E. J. Holmyard, A. R. Hall, and T. Williams, pp. 206–44.

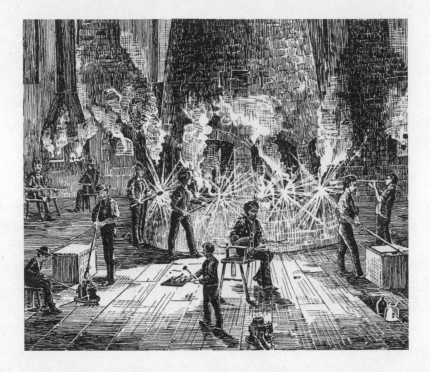

From the curves and arches and circling labour of his furnace, Morelli's glassware travelled its routes across the seas to the damask-draped tables of the aristocracy in England, France, the Low Countries, Spain, even the New World. In Antwerp and Utrecht, they said, painters were putting Murano-made roemers into their paintings of feasts and banquets, glasses with twisted stems or flutes, alongside oysters or lemons. It was a paradox, Morelli thought, that though his glassmakers had taken such care to bleed out all the colour from the glass—to make it perfectly transparent *cristallo,* they said— the painters in Antwerp needed scores of expensive oil pigments to capture in their pictures the colours made by the light reflecting off or passing through the miracle of the Murano-forged transparency. The fire haunted his glass, then; it had just been recomposed and reordered in this alchemical art.

The English Duke of Buckingham must only stand here in this glasshouse, Morelli thought, to see why Venetian glass would always be superior to English glass. Even the glass prisms, destined for chandeliers and for the contemplation of light by those concerned with natural magic, must be flawless, Morelli insisted, consigning all of the smaller glass objects, the glass beads,

the vials, and the prisms, to the hands of the new apprentice, Castelli's son, Antonio. Seven prisms, two dozen vials, and fifteen strings of coloured white beads in white filigree. The last items in the order. There were six-inch-long triangular moulds for prisms in the storeroom. There must be no air bubbles, no colour streaks, no chips; they must be perfect triangular-sided tubes of glass to take the light and throw it into scattered rainbows. Let Murano prisms tell the English about light.

By the time the glass sellers arrived by carriage at King's Lynn in mid-August, the *Scardinelli* had sailed, returning to Italy and leaving its precious glassware freight stored safely in the warehouses at the Norfolk quayside. Greene's agents, riding ahead, had negotiated the customs due and hired local men to move the cases onto the barges which would carry them south to the fair in Cambridge, a journey of several days. If you can't buy glass from the glassmaker at the furnace door, if you must import it, always carry it by water, he told Measey, who complained about the time this was taking them both and about how much quicker it would have been to travel by road to meet the barge at Cambridge. The bargemaster, Samuel Inchbald, warned them that the journey would most likely be slower than usual because the Dutchman Vermuyden and his men had finished draining the Fens and this had made the water levels unpredictable.[7] Some of the waterways had dried up; others were flooded. Those Dutchmen were a marvel though, he said, turning previously miry and waterlogged land to rich meadows and corn land. He told the gentlemen glass sellers how, from the riverbank, they would see plantations of fruit trees and willows and vegetables, the greatest plenty imaginable: flax, hemp, oats, wheat, cole-seed, and woad. Even the weeds that grew on the banks of the waterways, he said, were as high as a man on his horse.

Nonetheless, for all its marvels and sights, the journey to Cambridge took five days through big skies edged with tall reeds and scattered with ducks and geese flying in formation. A wilderness; an emptiness, the land like a seabed exposed to the sky and here and there ploughed to black soil. Down the fen waterways every kind of boat and barge seemed to be moving, peopled by merchants and watermen speaking languages Greene and Measey could not understand. Barges laid with leather or corn or coal or fleece or silk or stacked with hundreds of barrels of oysters from France. The whole of Europe's traders seemed to be travelling down the waterways like arteries into the fair, under the arc of sky which played like a symphony, a drama Greene and Measey watched hour by hour. One late afternoon they lay under their midge nets of silk watching a storm break overhead, blackened clouds in shades of black, purple, and slate grey moving like explosions of smoke in the distance and streaks of rain like water poured on dried paint, under which a triple rainbow arched, its stripes of colour seeping into each other. Worth the time, Greene murmured to himself, for the safety of the glass and for the orchestrations of the sky.

Below the deck of the barge where Greene and Measey lay admiring the riches of the fen land and the drama of the fen skies, while the fen midges found their way under the silk gauzes of the English glass sellers, in the cases of glassware, under the stems of twisted *cristallo* and bowls of ruby, seven prisms packed tightly in a box, in a thick wadding of dried seaweed, waited for light.

[7]For the history of the Fens drainage see H. C. Darby (1956), *The Draining of the Fens* (Cambridge: Cambridge University Press). Sir William Dugdale travelled across the Fens on several occasions between 1650 and 1665 and wrote several firsthand accounts, including "Things Observable in our Itinerarie begun from London 19 May 1657" and *The History of Imbanking and Draining of divers Fens and Marshes both in Foreign Parts and in the Kingdom, and of the Improvements thereby* (1662). See also the account of Elias Ashmole, an alchemist and collector, "Observations in my Fen Journey, begun 19 May 1657" from Elias Ashmole (1717), *Memoirs of the Life of Elias Ashmole* (London).

At Cambridge, Greene and Measey found rooms in an inn in Chesterton, taking the ferry at dawn across to their stall on the common, where servants and dogs slept, guarding the glassware. The fair, depleted by the arrival of plague in the city, still rang at night with the sound of drunken laughter, lewd dancing, and lovemaking. That morning, three days before the fair opened—without, in that plague year, all the usual pomp, ceremony, and parades—Greene and Measey supervised the unpacking of the chests from Venice, watching their servants carefully lift the glassware onto the tables arranged under the cloth awning where the booth faced onto Cheapside.

Somewhere down at the bottom of one of the chests, a servant found the box of glass prisms on which apprentice Antonio Castelli had scrawled his name, in a chest in which all the ruby-coloured roemers had smashed, scattering shards of red glass into the seaweed. John Gresham, apprentice glass seller, severed a small vein in his wrist reaching for that box, which he could see deep in the packing materials. This was how John Greene, hearing the cry of alarm and stepping towards his apprentice, came to have blood on his fresh white linen shirt the morning that a young undergraduate bought the only prism that Greene and Measey sold that plague summer. Newton would have bought a second—he said he thought he would have need for a second prism—if the glass seller had been able to give the young man a special rate for two, but with blood on his shirt and a case of broken ruby glasses to take into account, John Greene was not feeling generous that day.

So that was how in 1665 a Venetian glass prism came into the hands of a young Isaac Newton, natural philosopher, who had wandered that morning among the glass sellers of Cheapside asking for information about glassmaking and lens grinding. While the Murano port and wine glasses found their way from Venice across the sea and onto the gilded dining tables of the colleges, where they would catch light refracted from candles and from the white feathers of roast swans and the opalescent whites of oysters, that prism was to find its way into the darkened and shuttered chambers of a young undergraduate anxious to test a theory of light recently argued by a Frenchman called René Descartes.

Eight

Something had started. Together we were making a new prism, a new way to see our world, but I had no idea why or what it was for. It was early days yet—our glassmakers had not yet even set out to collect the pebbles from the River Ticino. The river water was still playing over those pebbles. Somewhere in Syria someone was burning seaweed and raking over the ash.

A week later, I was reading the manuscript on the bench outside the big window at dusk, watching the long shadows stretch across the garden, when I heard a car draw up on the other side of the cobbled wall and the sound of the gate being unlocked and pushed open. Someone had come into Elizabeth's garden. It wasn't Will—she was away somewhere. For some reason I felt myself to be the trespasser, caught in an orchard that wasn't my own. Someone was pushing the door back into place in all the ivy. I sat absolutely still, counting the seconds I had calculated it would take for whoever it was to reach me down the path and round the corner of the house—thirty seconds, twenty seconds, ten. It was you. I hadn't thought of that—that you might have a key and come and go through the walled garden at your pleasure.

"Lydia?" You looked as surprised to see me there as I was to see you. When you reached me in that pool of light beneath the window, the woods had darkened, filled up with unseen scuttling things between us and the river. You crouched down beside me, your boots wet with grass and mud. It must have been the faintest smell of chemicals on your skin that conjured that picture of the grey interiors of animal experimentation labs at Histon, which I had never seen but often imagined: sanitised, men and women in white coats, the eyes of unspecified creatures looking out disoriented and bored through the mesh sides of cages. Pictures I had seen more often on posters in the Underground or on pamphlets slipped under my door. I tried to put you there in that picture in a white coat and failed. A glimpse of you moving in white light opened like a peephole and then closed.

"You look startled," you said.

"You frightened me. I couldn't think who you could be."

"Sorry. I should have called you first." Our shadows were cast forward onto the grass by the light from inside the house, reaching out for the beginnings of the orchard.

"Lydia, you won't believe this, but I forgot you were here."

"Forgot I was here? What's that?" You were carrying a green canister.

"Petrol. I know, weird isn't it? Since Elizabeth died I've had these memory lapses. I find myself halfway through a sentence or halfway through doing something and then I get lost. Stand there, wondering who or where I am. It's . . ."

"Disconcerting? Yes, I know how that feels."

You sat down next to me. "You get that too?"

"No, not exactly. It's a bit different. Don't laugh . . . I sleepwalk sometimes. It's a similar kind of sensation. In the dream you're really focused on doing something or saying something important, even urgent, you know, like saving the world or your grandmother, or catching a train, and then suddenly you just wake up and you don't know where you are or what you were doing. All that sleep adrenaline and energy suddenly drops away, as if someone has just cut your strings. And you stand there, unstringed, feeling a fool."

"How long have you been sleepwalking, Dr. Brooke?"

"Well, Mr. Brown, you know, I'm just not sure. It started about the time I went to France, I think. It comes and goes."

"Have you saved the world often?"

"Yes, I have saved the world precisely fourteen and a half times."

"The half?"

"Not an entirely successful attempt. Saved half the world population. The other half drowned."

"Not bad."

"Yes, and I have also won several medals for my sleepwalking— marathon, long distance, and sprint. Broke the world record for the sleepwalking pentathlon: that's a combination of sleepwalking, jumping, crossing the road, and typing."

"Typing?"

"Yes, sorry, that's a new one. Kit found me typing at my laptop last summer, eyes open but sound asleep."

"Christ. What did you write?"

"Oh, nothing comprehensible. A whole load of jumbled letters. Shame. It would have been great if it had been some kind of automatic writing. A message from the other side. Kit was most disappointed in me. You know what she's like."

"You were in Cambridge last summer?"

"Just passing through." *Passing through. Passing by. Passed away—Elizabeth. I should be more careful with my words.*

"Have you 'passed through' often since you left Cambridge?"

I left you, Cameron. I left you, not just Cambridge. But you can't say the words, can you? Go on, say it: "Since you left me. Since you left me. Since you left me." You see, I did it, didn't I? Didn't we always assume that it would be you doing the leaving? Strange how differently things worked out from the way we thought they'd be.

"I've been back four times," I said carefully, trimming my untruth, making a note to remember the number if asked again later. "Mostly to see Kit, but also to see Elizabeth." *Actually, Cameron, I lie. It's more like eight or ten times. I stayed with your mother at The Studio a couple of times three or so years ago; I stayed with Kit several times; once with Anthony out at Barton. But I carefully avoided all the places where I might run into you. I couldn't have borne that—glimpsing you across a street or in the market or in the tearoom of the library. I thought I saw you everywhere. I expected to see you, but you never appeared.*

"So you've started writing messages in your sleep? But I'd guess you still don't believe in another side?" you said. *You're thinking too. Right on the edge. Don't speak. Keep it at bay a little longer.*

"I'd like to think I have an open mind. Of course, *you've* seen ghosts, haven't you? You have a stake in 'the other side.' Didn't we used to quarrel about the afterlife? Amazing. I've never quarrelled about the afterlife with anyone before or since. Most people aren't interested. Most people don't even think about it. But it mattered a lot to you."

"Yes. I've seen things I can't account for . . . Don't know that I would call them ghosts, though. More like presences. A smell, a sensation of something. The smell of tobacco in the big house when I was a child."

"Since you were a boy?" The boy growing up in the big house near the river with the crazy mother. Seeing ghosts.

"Yes. As long as I can remember."

"But you don't see them now that you've grown up?"

"Are you saying I've grown up, Dr. Brooke? Now, you know, I would never have thought *you* of all people would say that. But then . . ."

"I believe you do your best to maintain appearances," I said, smiling, letting you draw me nearer that edge.

"Quite. Oh yes," you said. "There is always the maintenance of appearances."

The sound of a sword being resheathed. There was to be a cessation of combat now in the silence that marked the end of something that would have to start again, had already started again.

"Cameron, do you know what you were doing when you came here? Before you woke up, I mean, and remembered that you had forgotten that I was here?"

"Yes, I do remember. I had a bonfire to light."

"Oh yes, the petrol."

"When Elizabeth died, Sarah came here and sorted through all her things. We kept most of the precious things in the house, but I told Sarah to pile up all the rubbish Elizabeth had stored in the cupboards down at the riverbank, in the big chicken-wire cage where Elizabeth used to burn things. I was supposed to burn it all weeks ago, but I've been putting it off."

"So you've come to make a bonfire on a riverbank? At nine o'clock on a Monday night? Why tonight?"

"Yeah. I know. It's mad, isn't it? I was driving back from the airport and I remembered. In fact, it was as if she had suddenly appeared in my car. I stopped on the hard shoulder and remembered her and all the pile of her things. So here I am. I suddenly saw it all—all that stuff of hers was still there under the sky. There was a kind of nakedness about it."

I heard the rustling of silks in that silence. You put your hands on the edge of the bench and gripped hard, as if to stop yourself from jumping down there into the void.

"Aren't you expected home?" I asked.

"Sarah's away with the boys. She wanted to take them away for a bit after what happened."

"What happened?"

"Don't you know? It was in the local papers. While I was away in Berlin someone broke into the garden at Over. Killed Leo's guinea pigs."

"Shit. That's awful. How?"

"Slit their throats. Tied their feet together with wire and slit their throats. Cut diagonal slashes across each of their bodies. A kind of ritual slaughter." You bit your lip.

"Who would have done that?" I said.

"The animal-liberation people who target my lab. They've changed their methods and renamed themselves. They had a policy of nonviolence, but it all shifted for some reason this spring. On the night of the spring solstice—they make a big thing about the earth's seasons—they declared war via an e-mail network I was part of and made this statement about abandoning nonviolence in the war against the animal holocaust. That's what they call it. To them, I'm one of many Hitlers. It was only a matter of time before they would get the kids' pets. I should have been more vigilant. There's been a spate of animal murders in the city since the spring—all in the same way. Haven't you seen the papers?"

"I'm sorry. That's outrageous. Can't the police catch them? I mean, if they are targeting labs and so on, wouldn't they be able to track them through surveillance cameras? CCTV?"

"Oh, there's plenty of pictures, but they all look the same: men or women dressed in black with black hoods. Not much to go on."

"Balaclavas?"

"No, black hoods with slits for the eyes. Scary when you see endless footage of these black figures moving around the perimeters of your house in the dark, fast-forwarded. We have thousands of pounds' worth of surveillance equipment installed at Over, which the police come and sort through every few weeks. There's a squad attached to Scotland Yard, and they've created a special unit now in Cambridge. But so far there's not much to distinguish between all the black shapes. The ones who do the attacks are almost all the same build—similar height and weight. Must be chosen for that. They won't even know each other's names. It's all coordinated via e-mail and text messages—all codes, apparently. So after Sarah saw the footage of the three figures opening up the guinea pig hutch and all the rest of the dreadful charade, she decided to take the kids away. They've all had enough."

Hadn't we all had enough one way or another? Trouble was, no one could find the way out. There were no exit signs. Maybe Sarah had found one finally, after all these years. I envied her. Maybe she'd get away first. There would be a kind of justice in that.

"The bonfire. Would you like some help?"

"I'd love some help." You headed off through the trees to the river. No hesitation. I was surprised at how tall you were suddenly, now that you had disappeared into the flattened shapes of the woods, the light catching your face. Chiaroscuro. I could only see the shape of you receding.

"Won't we need some things?" I called out after you. "Like newspapers and matches? Maybe a flashlight?" By the time I'd fetched all those things from the house and stuffed them into the pockets of my long coat, wound a scarf round my neck, pulled some gloves from a drawer, you had climbed onto the pile, rearranging all its strange objects with a pitchfork, dousing petrol over it all. Behind the chicken wire, barely contained by it, wanting to spill out and over, there were bottles, old boots, boxes of papers, cardboard, old clothes. Moonlit, and with the pitchfork in your hand, you looked like a figure from a medieval painting. You had sweat on your brow, cuts on your hands.

"Some of that won't burn," I said.

"Whatever doesn't burn I'll take up to the dump."

"Why don't we just take out everything that won't burn?"

"It all has to burn."

"Some of it *won't* burn," I said again. "You'll poison yourself with the fumes from some of this stuff."

"Since when do you know anything about bonfires? You're a city girl. How would you know?"

"Antoine was rebuilding Terre Rouge when I moved out there," I said. "We burned everything. There was no dump for twenty miles."

"Antoine—the Frenchman?"

"Algerian."

"Oh," you said, "I don't like to think about that."

I would have answered your questions if you'd asked them. Yes, I was happy most of the time during those first three years, out there in the Pyrenees, in exile, happy enough to write *Cobalt*. There were fig trees and olive trees and when I wasn't writing I made a garden. There was always something wonderfully temporary about it, as if we were holed up during some war. We had no money and the roof needed fixing and the well kept running dry. No, I have no regrets. Why did I leave? Because a film company offered to buy the rights to *Cobalt* and I came back to England, to Brighton. Why Brighton? Don't know. Always wanted to live there. Antoine and I never talked about what would happen then, and he got bored with the silence. He went back on the road with the Dutch wife of the local village mayor. He sold the house and land. No, I didn't have any regrets. Why? Because I'd found success, because I found Elizabeth again and the seventeenth century. Because while I was in France I stopped thinking of you—sometimes. It was possible, you see, for a while.

There you go. You could have asked. But you didn't ask, and I didn't tell you. Not then, at least.

"How's the writing going?" Your turn to veer away from the edge. You climbed back over the chicken wire and I passed you the box of matches, but you did nothing with them. We stood there in the dark in the thick smell of petrol.

"Writing? Give me a chance. I've only been in The Studio for a short while. Your mother's seventeenth-century-history collection is amazing. She's got every book on the history of alchemy. And I'm still reading *The Alchemist*."

"You're still reading it?"

"Yes. It's fascinating. You'd like it. I'm about three-quarters of the way through a first reading, though even this far into the book, I'm not sure what she was trying to claim."

"What do you mean, 'claim'?"

"Well, you were right. The book argues aggressively that Newton didn't work in isolation, that he wasn't the lone genius of the Newton myth. Elizabeth shows how dependent he was on a whole host of European alchemists to bring him things—books, instruments, manuscripts, codes, and formulas—and to do things for him—act as his patrons and secure him positions in the Trinity College hierarchies. And of course she's also saying that you can't separate out alchemy from science in the mid-seventeenth century, that it's a false distinction and that all scientists were alchemists to some degree and that they all depended on the networks. You couldn't work in isolation or be independent."

"Same is true now, of course."

"How so?"

"In neuroscience. You can't do the science without the sponsors."

"Why not?"

"Well, on an obvious level, because you need sponsorship to pay for the labs and the equipment. That means constant fund-raising. The sponsors have their own agendas too, of course, because there's so much money at stake, and so they try to control the questions you ask. And at the same time all scientists are dependent on knowledge and information from so many other scientists across the world, and you have to be connected up to get it. And for that you pay a price. There's politics everywhere—in what gets published, in how it's published. It's impossible to keep out of all of that. Completely impossible." You paused, catching yourself, and changed the subject. "What kind of book is *The Alchemist*?"

"It starts out as a partial biography of Newton and alchemy, but then about halfway through it seems to turn into a kind of historical investigation—except that the end is missing. I have a hunch about what she is getting at or moving me towards, but it's all by implication . . . so far at least . . . Newton's involvement with a 'Mr. F.' seems to have been important."

"Is he in the index-card box?"

"Who?"

"Mr. F."

"I haven't looked. Of course. The index-card box. I'd forgotten. You told me about that, didn't you? The index-card box full of alchemists. Names and dates. God, that will save me some time. I'll see if I can find it."

"The Newton scholars will hate all that alchemy—"

"Does that matter?"

"Of course not. It's great."

"The book's really confident in some places and hazy and vague in others. As if she's undone some of it, and in other places she goes round the houses, embedding us in detail. As if she's taken some of the explanations out. She just puts A next to B and doesn't show what's in between. It might be a plus or a minus or an equals sign."

"Sounds like Elizabeth."

"It's complicated. I'll read the whole thing, then read the last incomplete chapters again alongside the notes she left. Then I may be ready to write."

"When will that be, do you think?"

"Are you going to harass me like this for the next few months? And are you going to light that fire or are we just going to stand and look at all this rubbish?"

"No, I'm not going to harass you. I know you'll finish it. OK, let's light it, shall we?" We didn't. We were both a little lost, I think.

"If I'm right, *The Alchemist* is going to be a very controversial book," I said.

"How?"

"Elizabeth has accusations to make that will seriously undermine Newton's reputation. You know how dangerous that would be. He's practically a national saint. To be honest, I'm worried about the consequences of publishing this book."

"You don't have to worry about anything. Your name won't be on the cover. You'll be safe from all the publicity. The publishers will love it—all that scandal will sell copies. Why don't *you* light it? Just set light to that piece of newspaper sticking out there."

I did. The fire began to curl its way across the paper.

"OK. OK. I know," I said. "I like the fact that my name won't be on the cover. I'll pull out the stopper and lob the hand grenade, then watch what happens from a distance. Watch all the Newton scholars scurrying around, trying to challenge Elizabeth's evidence. Throwing up their hands in horror. There may even be headlines."

"Hand grenades don't have 'stoppers.' "

"Whatever—trigger, plug, cork . . . This book is going to make waves, I'm sure of it."

"They have pins."

"What have?"

"Hand grenades. Look at the blue in that fire. Elizabeth loved bonfires. She used to light them on Sunday evenings all through the autumn. I'd build them for her when I was here and then she and I would drink a bottle of wine while the smoke poured out over the river. It always made me think of you."

"Don't," I said.

"What?"

"Just don't."

"OK. It *never* made me think of you . . . Then she'd compost the ashes and pile the compost around the apple trees and under the roses every spring. Did she manage to decode those lines from the Newton notebook? I always hoped she'd manage that. It was an obsession."

"What code? I haven't come across a code in her papers yet."

"Newton used a code in some of his notebooks. A biographer managed to decode most of it in the sixties, but there were four clusters of letters in one of the most important early notebooks that no one's been able to crack. Elizabeth was convinced it was a powerful alchemical mantra that had been handed down to him. She asked me to help her decode it a few months ago. I'm good at codes, but I couldn't crack that one. She and I spent hours writing out the letters in different combinations. She was convinced that Newton was using it as a kind of ancient purification spell, to protect the rest of his work. She'd found some of the combinations of letters in other alchemical books."

"I'll keep a look out for it in her notes," I said. "Look. I've got a couple of bottles of champagne in the fridge which Kit gave me when I moved in. Shall I bring a bottle out here, or would that be inappropriate? Bad taste?"

"Only if it's definitely champagne and not cava. I won't drink cava."

When I brought out the bottle and the glasses from the house I could already see the glow from the burning newspapers illuminating the river-

bank, casting orange shapes upon the bark of the birch trees and along
the towpath, smoke from the damp leaves brimming through the woods.
I saw your shape silhouetted against the fire, very still. Beyond you, over
the other side of the river in the darkness, there was the empty open land
of Stourbridge Common, invisible now, as if there were nothing there,
just a great black void; and there we were standing on the edge of it, looking into it. You between me and the dark. I thought, My talisman to keep
all *that* at bay. Stourbridge marshland where pigs had scavenged and
where Newton had bought his glass prism. The merchants and townspeople and prostitutes would row across somewhere near here, at Ferry Lane
and Water Lane early in the morning as the chapel bells began to ring,
from the quiet of Chesterton to the roar and lights of the fair. To market
to market to buy a fat pig. Home again, home again, jiggity jig.

It was as if somewhere in the earth exactly under the patch of riverbank where we had built this fire, someone had slid aside a valve and,
through that narrow hole, all the earth's gases were escaping. A fire so
blue and orange and dense that you could have touched it, which began
there in that tangle of bonfire apple wood and the discarded stuff of a
woman's life. Around this blue light, the darkness fell away into shades of
grey and brown.

"Passing through," I said. "It's like something's passing through. A
kind of exhalation."

"You're beginning to sound like Elizabeth."

"Oh yes, I'm with the alchemists. It's amazing how it changes the way
you see things. Putrefaction is the key. Rotting reduces everything to chaos
so then it can be remade. Apples rotted into fire and blue light. Fantastic.
Aggregating and disaggregating. Out of the rot comes the power." You
poured me a glass.

"Like champagne," you said. "Grapes to liquid gold and air and then
assimilated into human flesh. That's you and me and the transmutation
of grape matter."

"Are you making fun of me, Mr. Brown?" You kept your distance. We
both kept our distance.

"Oh no, far from it. Perhaps we're both sleepwalking. Maybe this fire
will only figure as the flicker of a déjà vu next time we find ourselves

standing among friends by the edge of a bonfire. And we will struggle to remember what we think we are remembering—"

"Oh, I'll always remember this."

"Yes. Elizabeth had something to do with this."

"Elizabeth? No. She wouldn't have wanted us working together like this."

"She never knew about us."

"She did, I'm afraid. She spoke to me about you just a month before I left for France."

"She never told me. Never let on in all the time after you left. Though, when I think about it, she was very attentive that first winter. As if she knew I was suffering. But she never said anything."

"No, I asked her not to."

"I'm suddenly very tired, Lydia. I wonder if you might let me sleep in the little back bedroom. There's still a bed in there, isn't there?"

"It's your house." I was cold, suddenly formal. I hadn't meant to be.

"I'm sorry, I shouldn't have come at all. It's not you. It's Elizabeth. It's the first time I've been back since that Sunday."

"I don't think I've got any spare bedding."

"There's a brand-new duvet in the cupboard under the stairs. I bought it for you in case it got cold in the winter. Actually, Sarah did—I can't claim that. She's the thoughtful one. It's probably still wrapped." You pointed up to a pattern of stars I half recognised. "Have you seen the Big Dipper tonight?" you said. "It's like a cup running over."

The constellation *was* a cup running over. We stood there for that moment at midnight looking up at the sky through the white ash particles blown up by the now quiescent bonfire. Cambridge: pretty, suffocating Cambridge.

So you stayed. I found that still packaged duvet in the cupboard under the stairs; you brought in your bag from the car and, for a second, I glimpsed the small presents you had brought back from Berlin for Sarah and the boys: soaps, postcards, chocolate, and books, all thrown in. I wondered if I minded—yes, another place where a bruise had marked me once.

You asked me if I was safe sleeping up on the mezzanine floor and I

asked you why you asked. You said the stairs were too steep and dangerous for sleepwalkers and I said I had never fallen on stairs while sleepwalking yet. Then, while you slept downstairs, with the moon casting its
light directly on your bed through curtainless windows, sometime in the
early hours I dreamed of an old man falling through moon shadows
down the wooden stairs of a Cambridge college I half recognised. I
dreamed of his blood filling up the ridges in the stones beneath his head.
Blood running from his nose.

Since then I've often wondered if it was your presence that made me
dream. I awoke in the night drenched in sweat, remembering the dream
fall. I thought about Dilys Kite and the prism made from river stones and
the fire made from apples. Something was being stoked up somewhere in
that house. We were part of it, but only part. It was the aggregation that
was important. You, me, Elizabeth, and Will in that little house in the orchard—in the glassmaker's furnace. Someone should have seen that coming and not lit a match.

And I should not have walked down those stairs hungry for your body
in the middle of that dream-filled night. And you should not have been
awake and waiting for me.

When I woke at dawn there was blood on your pillow and dried blood
smeared across your sleeping face, as if you had been struck. Had I struck
you? Had I made you bleed? What had happened in one night to make
you bleed?

"How strange," you said, waking to my gaze, glancing at the sheets. "A
nosebleed. I dreamed I'd fallen down a staircase."

"Must have been that conversation about sleepwalking we had last
night," I said, too baffled to tell you I had dreamed that dream only hours
before you. "Can a dream make you bleed, do you think? Or is it just a coincidence?"

"I've never had a nosebleed at night before," you said. "I must be getting old. And I'm covered in bruises—here down my arms and these on
my thigh—what did you *do* to me last night?"

"Perhaps you're a princess," I said.

"Princess?"

"The princess and the pea. The pea that bruised the girl's skin through a hundred mattresses."

"What is it that you do to me, Lydia Brooke? Look at me. Bruises and blood—that's because you've taken my skin off again, turned me inside out. You've always done that."

"I don't mean to."

"But you do. Or one of you does. One of you stalks me, follows me so that I'm never alone. All the time you've been away—every day, every bloody day, you've appeared at some time or other. From somewhere."

"That's not true," I said, pulling my gown around me, turning my back on you, looking out into the garden. "That's just not fair." I pressed my cheek up against the glass, cold and cornered. "I had to get away or one of us would have gone mad. You wouldn't let me go. It hurt to go, nearly broke me, but I went, because I had to. I did leave you alone. That's just not fair. You wouldn't let up."

"You took liberties with me; you still do. You climbed inside my head; slipped your hand through that broken pane of glass and lifted the latch and then climbed on in, made yourself at home, found out where every-thing was, how the electrics worked, the places where I'd hidden the spare keys, worked out the combination lock for the safe. And then you scattered your things around—all your memories, your passions, the way you see things. You can't take all those things out of my head just by leav-ing the country, for Christ's sake. You left them all behind. Here, in my bloody head, so that every time I see a sunset or a sunrise, I see it through your eyes and imagine what you'd say. Every time I hear Chopin, or eat oranges, or read Elizabeth Bishop. You think it's been easy being in love with you all these years? With all that stuff still in here?"

"So don't read Elizabeth Bishop," I said, "or eat oranges or go outside early in the morning or in the evening."

"It doesn't work."

"No," I said. "I know. It doesn't work." *Every sea, every botanical garden, every library, every note of Mozart's "Requiem"* . . .

"What happens now?" You were standing behind me, naked in the morning, one hand on my back, the other writing my name in the fog I had made on the window. I turned to look at you, serious and a little afraid. I could smell the wood smoke still clinging to your warm skin from the bonfire. "What happens now?" you asked again, passing your hand under my gown.

"You're asking *me*?" I said. "Look. Just because you stayed last night doesn't mean it's all started again. We can walk away."

"I don't want to walk away. And you can only walk away if you promise to take all of you with you and leave not the faintest shadow behind, here in my head. You have to promise to take away all the shadows of you that drift across my skin, everywhere, all the time. And you can't promise that, so you can't go. And so you will have to kiss me again, just to make sure I'm still here, and I will have to kiss you again to make sure you are still there, that neither of us are just phantoms in each other's dreams."

"No, I won't kiss you," I said, and kissed you. "No, and a hundred times, no."

"I have a present for you," you said, turning away to pick up a bag you'd thrown in the corner of the room. "We were allowed a half day in the city, escorted. The others all went sightseeing, but there's a dusty sec- ondhand bookshop I like down in a little warren of streets called the Ack- erstrasse—you'd love it. And I found you this. I've always wanted to buy you a copy. Pater wrote it for you, you know, a hundred years before you were born."

It was a tiny red calf-leather copy of Pater's *The Renaissance,* and you'd written in it, on the flyleaf, as if nothing had changed, "For Lydia," and then Pater's words: "and for this continual vanishing away, that strange, perpetual weaving and unweaving of ourselves."

Later that morning, after you left for the lab, after I had watched your blood turn to brown smoke and disappear altogether from the pillowcase soaking in the cold water of the sink, I went in search of Mr. F. in the index-card box of alchemists. The pale brown plastic box was easy to find, stacked under dusty loose papers in the box Elizabeth had labelled "Eu- ropean Alchemical Networks." The box contained records of decades of research, the fruit of trips Elizabeth had taken to archives in numerous European cities, such as Amsterdam, Prague, Milan, Cologne, Genoa, Antwerp, and Copenhagen, where piece by piece she had put together the cross-referenced lives of hundreds of alchemists with names like Olan

Borrichus, Oswald Crollius, and Johann Joachim Beecher, lives recorded in detailed, spidery notes. The box contained one index card for each alchemist she had tracked down; each card listed his or her occupations, education, religion, dates, patrons, and the societies to which they belonged. The life stories of those I pulled out randomly were remarkably similar. These alchemists were travellers, itinerants—they rarely stayed in one city for more than four or five years. They worked in courts, as doctors, as tutors for the sons of noblemen, or they taught in universities. Sometimes the cards listed imprisonment or exile or unaccountable disappearances. They were always on the move, these migrants, travelling across Europe to and between each other, carrying secrets.

There were three names under *F* on the index list: Ezekiel Foxcroft, Robert Fludd, and John Freind. Will had said Mr. F. was a fellow at King's College. Fludd was an Oxford man who had died in 1637; Freind wouldn't be born until 1675. The card for Ezekiel Foxcroft was missing. Another dead end.

I didn't tell you that when I went to unpeg the pillowcase from the clothesline where it had dried in the sun and wind of a brisk October day, under the apple trees, the bloodstain was as brown and deep as it had been that morning. Why didn't I tell you that? How could I have done? I threw the pillowcase on the smouldering fire, where the flames turned it into something else, where I didn't have to think about it.

Nine

How many times can you explain away unaccountable events as coincidences? When does the perpetual blowing away of the same piece of paper in a windless garden, the fourth crashing of a computer that results in the loss of only one file when it is restored, a piece of linen with a bloodstain that disappears and returns—how many of all these repeated events can be given rational explanations? A series of coincidences becomes a pattern. The natural bleeds into the supernatural somewhere in that spectrum.

The laws of probability were severely strained in The Studio, after I moved into its high-pitched silences. I struggled to explain things away from the first day. Sometimes I laughed at myself for the things I imagined. At first, I gave you my stories, told you about the strange lights and the coincidences, offered them up as entertainments, but by late October their frequency and implausibility had become alarming. I stopped telling you either for fear you would think me mad or foolish or because I was protecting you from what I was beginning to see.

I would like to say that the dreams began the night I first read Elizabeth's opening chapter, but they had already started within days of moving into The Studio. It wasn't a time line, one event nudging another, like a series of carefully stacked dominoes, falling and falling, each toppling the next small block in a sequence. I can't say what it was—a heterogeneous mixture, like white light, which through the prism of The Studio began to divide into different colours, reflected upon a wall, shimmering, playing, opening out, and closing down. And, like Newton, I didn't see it all at once. It has taken me two years to see how the patterns fell then, years of dawning.

In the first weeks in which I worked in The Studio I felt it as a slight menace on the edge of my vision and hearing, and almost always at dawn or twilight—something, a muffled cry of something in pain, heard far off, a figure barely glimpsed in the garden, a pool of light that moved in strange ways across a wall. It was nothing. A sense of presence but never of occupancy. Fleeting moments, easily forgotten, even more easily dismissed as a figment of imagination, a writer's mind at work, conjuring. A sense of something forgotten, or of someone missing.

I said that to you once and you laughed. Writing can be a haunting, I said, and you said that was a cliché. I protested. There are few things you can say about writing, I ventured, that are not clichéd. When you laughed again, I persisted. There *is* something haunting about it, I said, perhaps because of that heightened sensibility, because you spend so much time listening for the words. You make a character from nothing, a few words, fragments of people you know or have seen from afar, and once they are up and walking they don't just come and go at your will; they begin to be demanding, appearing at awkward times, doing things you wouldn't have dreamed they could; they come upon you suddenly when you are asleep or making love. And I'm not talking about the sudden apparition of ideas for plots or new episodes—that happens too—I am talking about people who exist only in your head but who appear in your living room when you have temporarily forgotten they existed, when you have closed your study door on them. It's a kind of possession. You begin to feel you are being watched.

The people in *The Alchemist* were different. They'd been alive; they'd had flesh and sinews and blood; they'd had family and friends, rooms and libraries in which they worked. Almost all of Elizabeth's people were Cambridge people; they had wound their way through the colleges, gardens, and labyrinths of this city four hundred years ago. They had talked, argued, exchanged money, drunk together in taverns, and most were long forgotten. They had all been entwined in ways that I could only guess at, entwinings that Elizabeth had sought to map, hooked up to alchemical networks that stretched across the labyrinths of Europe. There were secrets, codes, friendships that Elizabeth could only guess at; many more that she had uncovered and recorded in her box file. But they were Elizabeth's people, not mine. They couldn't haunt me because I hadn't called them up.

Will knew what I meant. I asked her about her people once. She was working—reading and taking notes from Emerson's essays on the sofa near the stove one afternoon while I worked at the long table.

"Do you think about him much?" I said.

"What? Who?"

"Thoreau."

"What made you ask me that—just then, I mean?" She grinned, blushing faintly.

"I don't know."

"I was just thinking about Thoreau when you spoke."

"What were you thinking?"

"I was wondering what he would think about Iraq. What he would do about the war, if you must know. I know, I know. Crazy, eh?"

"But you're reading Emerson."

"Yes, but I can't read Emerson without hearing him talking with Thoreau. They're always at it. Bickering. Trying to outdo each other in my head. Thinking round things, disagreeing. Sometimes I ask them questions. Does that happen to you?"

"No," I said. "Never. I think you should see a doctor about that."

"You're joking?"

"Yes, of course I'm joking. Sometimes I hear all my people talking at once. It's so noisy I can't think. And then there's all the real people too, the ones who aren't dead, talking away. My stepmother, my dad, Kit. So many questions to ask them. So many opinions to think about."

"Yes. Shit. That's right. My grandmother's always in my head somewhere when I'm thinking about politics. Having her say. Like she won't be left out. Yes, there's always Thoreau, me, Emerson, and my grandmother trying to sort out the world, in some car park or other."

"Car park?"

"Yes, weird that, isn't it? The places you have conversations in your head. With Emerson and Thoreau you'd think it'd be a forest or a river valley or a field full of flowers. But for me it's always a car park. Now, are you going to let me work or are you going to come for a walk, if you're ready for a break?"

We talked more and more easily now, especially on those occasional mornings when the library was closed and she would come and work alongside me at The Studio. Lunch would stretch out sometimes for hours and I often walked with her in the afternoons. But, as if I knew without knowing, I never talked to you about her or to her about you. For some reason I thought Elizabeth wouldn't have wanted that.

You were back in my landscape now, in my car park, arguing with me, taking me on. You'd never left it. There was no point in promises or resolutions or rules. We'd done all of that once. For the moment the sense of relief was astonishing enough. And, as before, you brought me objects, to stand in for the missing words. Sarah was away, so you stayed at The Studio night after night, summoned me back at the end of the day from alchemy and plague and smoke and brimstone, and from that still irresolvable question: *What did Elizabeth Vogelsang know?*

"I forgot," you said one morning. "I've been carrying this around for weeks. Forgot to give it to you."

You threw a small block of glass towards me. It landed on the crumpled white of bedclothes I had gathered around my skin, cold in the morning air. A block of old glass. Triangular. A prism. I ran my hand over its cool edges, feeling chips here and there. I held it up to the light. Not a single bubble in the glass. Beautiful.

"Meant to give it to you a while ago," you said. "It was Elizabeth's. She left it behind. It's a prism."

"Is it old?" I said. "Seventeenth century? Where did she get it from?" But you had already disappeared down the stairs, late again.

"She stole it," you called from the doorway. I sat on the top stair, so that I could watch you leave, and held the prism up to the morning light.

"Don't be ridiculous," I said. "What a stupid idea."

"Whatever you say," you called back. "But a prism of exactly that size and description was stolen from the Whipple Museum about a year ago. It was one of Newton's." Then the front door slammed. Your feet on the gravel outside, walking down the path, the gate opening and closing. Silence.

Ten

Newton's prism, forged in Morelli's glasshouse on a tiny island off the coast of Venice and shipped across oceans and through the fen waterways to reach Stourbridge Fair, where Newton bought it from London glass sellers in exchange for a few coins, was now in my hands, back in The Studio. Here, in her own alchemical laboratory, in the furnace of her head, Elizabeth had turned manuscripts and notes and facts into a continuous history, laced not with mercury or antimony but with dangerous accusation.

Now, with the prism on the desk in front of me, I began to read the third chapter of the manuscript of *The Alchemist* again—the chapter on Newton's optics, which Elizabeth had called "The Disaggregation of White," and which describes how Newton learned to use this prism to split light while bubonic plague took its grip on the city around him, turning lithe bodies into corpses. Perhaps I thought that with the prism as talisman standing between me and her words, I might see something new; I might see why Elizabeth had needed to possess it badly enough to steal it from a museum.

Elizabeth began chapter 3 with a comet, describing the young Newton's extraordinary experiments on light in his rooms in Trinity in the mid-1660s, the plague years. "The Disaggregation of White" intricately entwined plague with light.

When twenty-one-year-old Isaac Newton watched a comet pass slowly across
the Cambridge sky in December 1664, leaving a blazing red trail in its wake,
he might have seen it as a sign of his own good fortune, for 1664 had been a
good year. Six months earlier he had been granted a Trinity scholarship, which
had given him a small income of his own, 26 shillings per annum. Now he no
longer had to work his passage through the college as a subsizar,[1] fetching
food, cleaning boots, or emptying chamber pots, and he had more time on his
hands, time for reading, calculations, and experiments. The comet fascinated
him; he stayed up night after night walking in his garden, watching the comet's
trail, and taking notes about how its light moved. He lost so much sleep that
he only later understood that he had become disordered in his mind.

The movement of light had been a question of renewed importance to Newton since he had begun reading the work of the controversial French philosopher René Descartes.[2] He started a new section of a notebook, calling it
"Quaestiones Quaedam Philosophiae"—Some Philosophical Questions—for,
mostly, questions driven by Descartes's ideas. Descartes's explanations of the
workings of the universe both compelled and troubled Newton. For Descartes
everything could be explained in material and mechanical terms. He claimed,
for instance, that light was a pressure transmitted instantaneously through
space from a cosmic vortex. This pressure on matter caused the movement of
certain particles, which Descartes called light "globules." As they reached the
retina they produced the sensation of whiteness, but if they began to rotate
they created a sensation of colour. In other words, white came first, travelling
in lines, and could be converted into colour with the addition of spin.

English philosophers had been preoccupied with light too, of late. Robert
Boyle had published a book called *Experiments and Considerations Touching
Colours: The Beginning of an Experimental History of Colours* in 1664, full of
stories and scores of experiments, problems, and conjectures about how
colour was made.[3] Robert Hooke had published his extraordinary new book

[1]A subsizar was the lowest status of scholar. Subsizars worked their way through their studies in the employment of a fellow. Though Newton's family was not poor, it is interesting that his mother was not prepared
to pay for him to have a higher status.
[2]For Newton's reading in Descartes see J. Lohne (1968), "Experimentum Crucis," *Notes and Records of the
Royal Society* 23, pp. 169–99; Westfall, *Never at Rest*, pp. 345–47; M. Mamiani (1976), *Isaac Newton Filosofo della
Natura: Le Lezioni Giovanni di Ottica e la Genesis del Metodo Newtiano*, pp. 81–94.
[3]Key works on optics in the seventeenth century are A. I. Sabra, *Theories of Light from Descartes to Newton* (London, 2nd ed., 1981), and Allen E. Shapiro, "Kinematic Optics: A Study of the Wave Theory of Light in the
Seventeenth Century," *Archive for the History of Exact Sciences* 11 (1973), pp. 134–266.

about optics and microscopes, *Micrographia,* in 1665; in it he described his extensive experiments with beams of light reflected on different surfaces, such as soap bubbles and transparent films of mica. He had come to believe that colours were impressions made on the retina by different strengths of pulsing light.[4] Newton was sure that light was not a pulse and that colours were not a result of mixed and heterogeneous impressions. He was sure that *immaterial* things, memory, imagination, and will, for instance, also played a part in the miracle of vision.

Through a series of detailed and repeated experiments, Newton determined to demonstrate that both Descartes and Hooke were wrong.[5] Sometime in the early spring of 1665, when the sun provided him with strong enough rays in his Trinity rooms, Newton turned his own eye into an experimental apparatus.

In that clear early morning, autumn leaves blowing across the garden outside The Studio, I read Elizabeth's meticulous descriptions of Newton's optical experiments. She stressed how his own physical pain seemed insignificant to him in relation to the scale and compulsion of his questions. Setting out first to test Descartes's claim that colours were caused by the pressure of light on the eyeball, he bought a blunt, large-eyed wooden needle called a bodkin and, in the quiet of his rooms in Trinity, slipped it into his eye socket between the eyeball and the bone. The idea made me shudder. Pressure did make a difference to vision, apparently. When he pressed hard he saw dark and coloured circles, but though the colours faded when he released the pressure, they did not disappear immediately. They left ghosts of themselves—Newton called them phantasms—on his vision.

Elizabeth had pasted into her manuscript a photocopy of the diagram Newton drew to describe his experiments with his eye. In one of his notebooks he had drawn his own eyeball, exposed and swollen to fill the precious paper, and mapped it out with letters to reference points on its inner

---

[4]Robert Hooke (1665), *Micrographia,* p. 54.
[5]For the most extensively and densely researched account of Newton's experiments with prisms see Simon Schaffer (1989), "Glassworks: Newton's Prisms and the Uses of Experiment," in S. Schaffer and S. Shapin (1989), *The Uses of Experiment: Studies in the Natural Sciences.* See also Rob Iliffe (1995), " 'That Puzleing Problem': Isaac Newton and the Political Physiology of Self," *Medical History* 39, pp. 433–58.

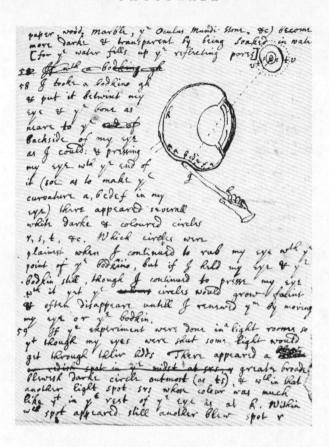

surface. He had sketched the path of light from a tiny sun, as well as a
hand, severed from a body, grasping a bodkin the size of a rapier, pushing,
prodding, and pressing on the eyeball without compassion. The rest of
Newton's body was missing from this picture, represented on the sheet of
paper only by out-of-scale body parts, a hand at war with an eyeball.

The picture made me want to touch my own eye. Sitting there reading
these descriptions at Elizabeth's desk, I also found myself curious—was
the miracle of colour to be reduced then to pressure on the eyeball, pressure made by some vague cosmos out there? My momentary experiment
with the smooth end of a fountain pen produced only a lingering and un-
comfortable pain and dark shapes that seemed to dance over the page. I
couldn't imagine repeating that act, protective of the filmy fragility of my
eye, imagining piercings and burstings, blood and pain.

The bodkin in his eye socket was only a start. Next Elizabeth described how, curious about these stains of colour, Newton tried out and recorded other experiments. When he stared at the spring sun reflected in a mirror for as long as he could bear, he discovered that all the light-coloured objects in his rooms turned red and all the dark-coloured objects blue. The coloured phantasms, as before, pulsed and twisted until they slowly decayed and vanished. Then he found that, as before, in a darkened room he could *still* see a blue spot fading to white, circled by rings of red, yellow, green, blue, and purple long after he had stopped staring at the sun. When he opened his eyes the pale objects in the room had turned red again and the dark objects blue, as if by closing his eyes he had re-created the effect of the sun. Even more extraordinarily, he described in his notebook how he learned to conjure the phantasms by will. Just by *imagining* the sun stains in complete darkness, lying on his bed at midnight, he could bring them back as bright and clear as when he had first seen them.

Eventually Newton's eyes were so damaged by staring at the sun, his retina so singed by these optical ghosts, that he was forced to lie down for three days in a darkened room; it took three long days for his sight to return.

I could, with all these details Elizabeth had described, imagine Newton lying there under a thin blanket in the dark of his rooms, perhaps more frustrated at having to stop working than conscious of his own pain. Among the scattered papers covered with the jottings and drawings of his optical and mathematical experiments, thinking through the new set of problems the experiments had produced: what were the coloured spectres and what made them linger and return at will?

And while Newton lay there, in the spring months of 1665, the plague was creeping towards Cambridge from London. In paragraphs like these, Elizabeth described the plague as a scuttling thing, carried by rats, insidious and malevolent:

The Great Plague of 1665–66 did not appear suddenly—it had been ripening and spreading its tendrils across Europe for years. The particular strain that killed so many in the summers of 1665 and 1666, however, was carried by rats coming ashore in London from ships at several landing points along the Thames between Stepney and St. Paul's Covent Garden in April and May. From there the plague would follow the rats along the trade routes, radiating through and out from London.

Across Cambridge, while Newton lay in the dark waiting for his sight to return, rats, warmed by the spring sun, stirred in their burrows behind wainscots, under floorboards, and in thatches, and gathered their young about them. As temperatures rose, fleas stirred and bred in the warmth of rat down, blankets, and skin. As rats died by the thousands, some in only a matter of hours, the fleas sought out human blood, passing the bacillus into the human bloodstream. Within three to six days of an unfelt fatal fleabite, perhaps scratched for a moment, victims began to shiver and vomit, became quickly intolerant of light, and, seeking darkness, closed shutters, took to their beds, with aching bones in their backs, aches in their heads and limbs, swelling sores under their armpits. Joiners and carpenters boarded up houses; painters daubed red crosses on doors; the rich ordered their carriages and left for the country. Across England clergymen continued to predict apocalypse—God was visiting his wrath on a country of sinners, they said. Babylon is falling.[6]

A drawing of four consecutive panels, reproduced in *The Alchemist*, showed the progress of the plague from London to outlying cities and towns. In the first, panicked Londoners were drawn "flying" London for the towns and villages, climbing onto any half-watertight boat or barge. Then processions of people, miles long, were shown "flying by land," ribboning their way out of the city by foot, sure now that death was behind them, not knowing that it was in their very clothes and skin. In the third box, death struck—here the processions were for the dead, searchers ahead, ringing their bells and heading for the plague pits. In the last panel there were more horizontal bodies than vertical ones—too few people to bury the dead.

According to Elizabeth's sources, Cambridge actually fared rather well during the plague years, because, by careful planning, those "flying" Lon-

---

[6]For the history of Cambridge in the plague years see C. H. Cooper, *Annals of Cambridge*, 5 vols. (Cambridge, 1842–1908), vol. 3; C. P. Murrell (1951), "The Plague in Cambridge, 1665–1666," *Cambridge Review*, pp. 375–406; Raymond Williamson (1957), "The Plague in Cambridge," *Medical History* 1:1, pp. 51–64.

don multitudes were largely kept out of the city. Elizabeth told of how John Herring, the mayor of Cambridge that year, called the aldermen to council to plan strategies as if the plague were an invading army already making its way north. Ahead of the enemy, the aldermen employed labourers to build temporary pesthouses on the outskirts of the city, on Midsummer Common and Coldhams Common.

As the plague approached, the men of the watch and ward, a kind of territorial army, boarded up all minor entrances to the city, purified the few people who were allowed to enter in smoke-filled waiting places, and poisoned all the city cats and dogs. At night searchers carried the sick and dead to the pesthouses, where the sick were put into isolation and tended. If any man, woman, or child survived at a pesthouse for a full lunar cycle—and some did—they were allowed to return to the city at two A.M., on the condition that they fumigate their lodging with lime-slaked smoke with the shutters closed for a full two hours before dawn. A Lazarus returned from the dead.

I could see from the reproduction of the old map pasted into *The Alchemist* that seventeenth-century Cambridge had had its own kind of moat, where the King's Ditch had once been dug to keep out the Vikings, a ditch from one point of the River Cam to another making a protective circle of water. I traced with my finger on the map the irregular arch of the King's Ditch round to where it joined the natural watercourse of the river and down to that strange oval of ground just next to Trinity, where the river passed around Garret Hostel Greene and where they would build the Wren Library in the 1670s.

Turning the map so that the oval lay to the left of the city, so that north was at the top, the map of Cambridge, ringed by water, suddenly seemed to me a reversed image of Newton's drawing of his own eyeball, with the oval of Garret Hostel Greene as the pupil. I put the two pictures next to each other— Newton's eye looking to the right and the eye of Cambridge looking to the left. Another coincidence. One image echoing the other. In the spring of 1665, while Cambridge aldermen were working hard to keep out all infections from the fragile city, protecting and closing down all its borders and entrances, Newton, in his rooms at Trinity, was sticking sharp objects into his own eye socket, opening it up in order to understand the laws of light.

I turned the prism, Newton's prism, over in my hand and watched its imprisoned colours glint at me, pools of blue and the occasional flash of red. It seemed to have a knowledge behind its hard surfaces, pools into which I might never reach, secrets it would never tell; it was as silent as Elizabeth herself.

But Elizabeth *wasn't* silent—I had her words; I could reach into these pages and find her, as she pursued Newton through Cambridge streets in search of better tools to understand light. Why, she asked, did Newton stay in a plague-stricken city after all the other undergraduates and fellows had been sent away for their own safety in July 1665? The answer was the prism.

In August 1665, Newton would have seen the wagons and the searchers making their way around the streets, their bells tolling, carrying the sick and the dead on carts past Trinity and down Jesus Lane to the pesthouses out on the common. He would have watched the strange effects of light through billowing smoke as the wind blew through the city's empty streets, a wind blown across the Fens from the Urals. Cambridge would have been surreal that summer: embattled, boarded-up windows and gateways, tolling bells and silences, smells of brimstone and pitch.

For a man sleepless, half starved, and with his eyes burned and exhausted from experiment, a man whose imagination was fired by thoughts of apocalypse and prophesy, the city must have seemed like a vision from Revelations. At a time when for many others the four horsemen of the apocalypse were virtually at the gates of the city, it was as if the plague simply did not exist for the young philosopher. He saw it, perhaps even felt his own fragility in it, but fragility was no more of any consequence than the pain in his eyes caused by the optical experiments.

Newton stayed because he was not finished; his questions were still unanswered. He would not leave his laboratory rooms, where his optical notes and mathematical papers were laid out with minute calculations and summations of infinitesimal arcs of curves and algebraic symbols, not for the four horsemen, not for anything. Believing in spirits as he did and in the miracles of alchemy, and watching his own extraordinary success, he must have felt that something divine was passing through him, perhaps even that it had conferred an immortality on him that would protect him from the plague. But he had also reached the limits of what he could do with his own eye. Now he needed a prism to answer new questions he had framed about the composition of colour. The prism would come to him if he waited—some of the finest glass sellers in Europe would converge on Stourbridge Fair in late August.

Near the end of that first summer of plague in Cambridge, Isaac Newton bought a prism at Stourbridge Fair. One of his relatives recorded that memory many years later:

In August 1665 Sr I, who was then not 24 bought at Sturbridge Fair a prism to try some experiments upon Descartes book of colours and when he came home he made a hole in his shutter & darkened the room & put his prism between that & the wall found instead of a circle the light made ⟨⎯⎯⎯⎯⟩ with strait sides & circular ends &c. wch convinced him immediately that Descartes was wrong & he then found out his own Hypothesis of colours though he could not demonstrate it for want of another prism for wch he staid till next Sturbridge Fair & then proved that he had before found out.[7]

Puzzlingly, Newton remembered buying a prism at Stourbridge Fair in the year that the records show the fair was cancelled because of the plague.[8] But, given that the cancellation was not announced until August, it is likely that many of the traders who came by water, setting off from their homes in Eu-

[7]Keynes Ms. 130.10, ff. 2v–3 Newton Project. Newton also remembered buying a prism early in 1666, as he wrote to Henry Oldenberg: "In the beginning of the Year 1666 (at which time I applied my self to the grinding of Optick glasses of other figures than *Spherical*), I procured me a Triangular glass-Prism, to try therewith the celebrated *Phaenomena of Colours.*" Newton to Henry Oldenberg, 6 February, 1672; ed. H. W. Turnbull 1959–61, 3 vols Cambridge University Press *Correspondence 1,* 95–96.
[8]Westfall argues that Newton was in Woolsthorpe for the entire period from early August 1665 to 20 March 1666. There is no conclusive proof, however, that Newton did not return to Cambridge for brief periods of time that winter. On Newton's hypochondria and remedies for sickness see Rob Iliffe, "Isaac Newton: Lucatello Professor of Mathematics" in Shapin and Lawrence (1998), *Science Incarnate,* pp. 121–55. London: University of Chicago Press.

rope long before they could possibly have heard about the outbreak of the plague, would have continued sailing the fen waterways to the north, reaching Stourbridge Common without coming anywhere near the city, or its watch and ward. The aldermen might then have taken the view that so long as the traders stayed out of the city, the fair posed only a moderate health risk to the citizens of Cambridge, given that most of the students and fellows had already left the city in July. So Newton stayed to buy the prism and wander through the curiously empty and depleted fair, and when the sun's lowered elevation in late August or September brought those first optical experiments of 1665 to a close, he returned to his hometown Woolsthorpe, where sometime in that autumn or the following autumn, in his mother's orchard, he determined the basis for the law of gravitation.

On his return to Cambridge the following spring, Newton began a new series of light experiments in April 1666 with an additional prism in his rooms in Trinity.[9] This time he turned his largest room into a giant eyeball, with a hole in the shutter of his window acting as the retina. Through the hole in the shutter he directed and turned and reangled the rays from the sun which fell on the shutters of his room for about two hours a day around noon. Newton would be ready, waiting for the sun to travel round, busying himself in preparation or writing up his notes from the previous day, laying out paper and pens, ready to record the details of his complex and varied experiments, for the sun would not oblige him for long. He had been waiting all winter for this.

Other natural philosophers before Newton had used prisms to experiment with light and colour, including Descartes,[10] but no one yet had made the projected spectrum large enough or let the rainbow-freighted ray travel far enough. Newton let the beam of coloured light travel twenty-two feet from the hole in the shutters at his window to the wall at the other end of his room; there, where the beam met the wall, it made a rainbow-coloured shape three times as long as it was wide. He coined the word *spectrum,* or ghost, to describe the lozenge shape that glowed on his wall, narrow in the middle with curved edges. The shape of his ghost was conclusive—the seven

[9]For the location of Newton's rooms in Trinity see Lord Adrian, "Newton's Rooms in Trinity," *Notes and Records of the Royal Society* 18 (1963), pp. 17–24.
[10]Simon Schaffer has discovered several other natural philosophers who worked with prisms; see H. Peacham (1606), *The Gentleman's Exercise*; John Bate (1654), *The Mysteryes of Nature and Art*; G. Della Porta (1658), *Natural Magick*; and T. White (1654), *An Apology for Rushworth's Dialogues*.

coloured rays from the shutter hole were travelling at different speeds, for otherwise they would have made a circle. *This* was how colour was made: rays of light travelling at different speeds.

Gradually, through a series of experiments with several prisms, Newton came to prove that colours are simple; white light is the mixture. Colours make white; colours come first; white is a hybrid. This claim was a simple one, but it also turned current knowledge upside down. Until 1666 white had been associated with simplicity and purity. Now Newton argued—and indeed had proved—that individual colours were *first* principles, pure and simple. White was made of colour. Jan Vermeer had come to know this too by a different route, also using camera obscuras and prisms at around the same time as Newton's experiments in Cambridge. So had the Dutch painters de Heem and Osias Beert, who studied the whites of oyster flesh in their table pieces. White, the Dutch painters knew, was laden with other colours, a heady and complex mixture—never pure. In Cambridge, Newton had proved it.

But with the smoke and smell of burning brimstone and superstition seeping through shutters everywhere in the city, at a time when God's wrath seemed visible on every street and punishment ubiquitous, few might have been interested in a young man's claims that he had worked out how white was made. For the moment the young man was silent. He checked his notes. He honed his observations and kept his own counsel.

It was when I finished that last page of Elizabeth's chapter that I glimpsed the rubbed-out pencil annotations on her script for the first time, in the right margin, next to the section on Revelations and the four horsemen of the apocalypse. Handwritten and erased, surviving only as tiny imprints, those marks might have escaped my notice if the bright morning light, falling on the paper at a certain angle, had not brought them into visibility for a second. Elizabeth Vogelsang had written in the margins of this section two questions:

Did he think he was invincible? Had someone made him think he was invincible?

And then, sometime later, she had rubbed both questions out.

Newton, Elizabeth believed, had come to think himself invincible. In 1665 and 1666 he believed his body to be beyond the reach of plague or death. And she believed that someone had been responsible for that Faustian audacity.

Eleven

I met Kit a week or so later down at the café in Chesterton; afterwards she walked with me down Landing Lane and Ferry Path, the towpath into town. She was heading for her stall, I for the library. We had, for once, time to spend. It was one of those fine October days—the sun on the river, bushes and trees along the riverbank, a spectrum of greens. From time to time runners jogged past us. Reflected colours ran from the brightly painted barges into the water. Greens—so many greens all around us: the silver-green of the underside of the willow trees, the emerald of the grass along the bank, the mottled grey-brown-greens of the scrubland of the common on the other side. Virginia Woolf had once described the river-banks as being on fire on either side of the Cam, but there was no such fire here now. Or at least not yet. There was red—rowan berries, rose hips, pyracanthas—but the red sat against the astonishing palette of autumn green like the sparks of a newly lit fire, like drops of crimson blood in the hedgerows. It was yet to pull itself to a blaze or a haemorrhage. And those famous willow trees she had described as weeping in perpetual lamenta-tion, their hair about their shoulders, had been pollarded since she walked here, so there was no elegant weeping for them anymore, only the flurry of silver-green leaves, shorn demented heads against the sky. The river still reflected everything that passed over it, as it had done for Woolf, who would drown herself in another river in 1941: sky, bridges, red berries, and from time to time the colours melted, forked and quaking, as rowers oared their way through the reflections, only to form again as if their surfaces had never been broken.

"Crimson," Kit said, waking me from a muddled reverie on colour and light. "That's what everyone wants right now. Shades of burgundy and claret. I've just dyed a whole load of cotton shirts—they've all come out slightly different shades, depending on the porousness of the original material. Perfect. Won't look like a job lot. Bet I sell all of them by the end of the week."

"What? Sorry . . . Missed that." I was watching the ripples in the water fanning out from one of the rowing boats.

"Shirts, you know, the stall. Your mind's wandering again. You asked why my hands are so red. I've been dyeing clothes and I forgot to wear gloves. Berry colours are in again, so I've been dying shirts red—for the stall."

"Sorry, yes. Lemon juice might do it. He did that too."

"Who did?"

"Newton . . . dyed things."

"Isaac Newton dyed things?"

"Yep. He had a book full of recipes for colours that he started about the time he came to Cambridge. He was an experimenter. Always trying things out, you know: poisoning birds, putting mirrors on the top of church steeples to test how long the light took to move from mirror to mirror, dropping things from towers, sticking things in his eyes, boiling things, mixing things, writing down the results."

"OK. How did he make red?" Was she laughing at me?

"Can't quite remember. Yes, I can." Blurred words came into focus. "Sheep's blood drained into a bladder, hung out to dry in the sun to make a powder, then mixed with alum water when needed. There was another one in which you boil brasill, whatever that is, and then he writes that if you would have it a 'sad red,' mingle it with potash water; if a light red, temper it with white lead. Christ, I've only read the transcription of that notebook once and I remember it all. What do you think a 'sad red' is?"

"What's Elizabeth's book like? You've finished it?"

"Brilliant—full of the most wonderful detail about Cambridge. I'm completely lost in it."

"I can tell."

"Sorry. I've been sleeping badly. It's as if Elizabeth is there—in the seventeenth century. Not reconstructing it but actually *there*."

"Sounds like that's where you are too. So what's the problem?"

"Problem?"

"You've had a frown on your forehead since you moved to The Studio. You'll have to be careful—the wind'll change and that face will stick." Another boat cut its way through the water, a small blond coxswain driving the rhythms of the oars with a voice too big for her small frame.

Kit was wearing a long purple coat over grey linen trousers and a T-shirt. With her stained hands and the jewellery around her neck, her hair piled on top of her head, she made people turn their heads. She knew she did that. She walked tall and the coat, made of some thick cotton which she had probably dyed, billowed around her in the wind. I imagined her being swept up like a character in a García Márquez novel, in her own billowing clothes, swept off like an angel or Madonna in some kind of purpled apotheosis. Seventeenth-century Cambridge would have been filled with such billowings, I thought, when the winds were high and all the undergraduates wore their gowns—billowings of purple and black in winds that blew into that labyrinth of streets straight from the Ural mountains in Russia.

Today, it blew through my hair, tugged at my skirt, stung my eyes. In France the wind was aromatic, full of the smell of soil and ripe crops. Here it just smelled of mould. That was the marshland.

"When does coincidence stretch to improbability, do you think?" I asked her. "I mean, at what point do you say to yourself that something completely beyond the bounds of probability is happening to you?"

"That's a hard one. Explain."

"There's a whole series of things . . . none of them sounds very significant in itself. OK, there was this piece of paper."

"A piece of paper?" I'd forgotten how sceptical Kit had become. It was reassuring. She'd have an explanation, if anyone did.

"Just listen, won't you? I spotted the corner of a piece of paper in the garden under a lavender bush. I must have dropped it when I'd been working out there the day before because it was from one of Elizabeth's notebooks—I recognised her handwriting, or what was left of it. There were snails crawling all over it."

"Snails?"

"Yes, snails. Just ordinary mindless garden snails . . . They'd eaten sections of the paper and the rain had washed out the ink, but I could still just read what was there. I traced out the words with my pen—they were still visible, and I worked out that it was Elizabeth's transcription of a notebook Newton kept when he was around twenty and had just arrived in Cambridge. It's an important notebook because Newton wrote it in code and it wasn't decoded until 1963 by Newton's biographer, Richard Westfall. Elizabeth had transcribed a section from the decoded notebook."

We stopped now under a rowan tree, its berries scarlet against the dark green leaves. The wind was blowing the river water in arced shapes, like bows stretched from one bank to the other. Kit was out of breath.

"Sorry, I'm not following. What's weird about any of this?"

I passed her the piece of paper, folded into four. It looked more like a paper doily after the snails had finished with it. She began to unfold it.

"Just don't let go of it," I said. "It's blown away four times now. OK, I said it didn't amount to much in itself. It's what's *in* the notebooks that's interesting. Westfall spent months decoding that early notebook in the 1960s. He must have thought he'd find something of scientific importance, judging by the amount of time he spent on it, that he'd uncover—I don't know—mathematical notes or reflections on optics perhaps. You know what he found? Not mathematics or formulas, but *sins*—two lists of Newton's sins. The first set of forty-eight was headed 'Before Whitsunday 1662,' and a further nine were listed as 'After Whitsunday 1662,' arranged as if they were an account book. Imagine the intimacy of that—seeing that list for the first time since Newton actually recorded them secretly, guiltily, three hundred years earlier."

"What kind of sins? Fornication, buggery, bestiality? Consorting with a witch?" Kit unfolded the piece of paper as if it were a page from a pornographic magazine.

"No, nothing so dramatic. Mostly little things. Stealing cherries, sticking pins into people's backs in church, getting irritable, making things on Sundays."

"Newton stole cherries? Was the gravity apple stolen? That would make a good story . . ."

"Be serious. It's awful."

It wasn't until I checked Elizabeth's page against Westfall's typed transcription that I felt how awful it was—the young man writing out his sins
in code. It moved me. There was something bald and relentless about it, a
man's conscience flayed like a rabbit, all glistening sinews and blood. I
imagined him wrestling with his conscience, trying to live according to
his understanding of the Bible, failing, punishing himself, and starting
again, over and over. He had no sense of humour; I could feel how tired
he was with his constant relapses, struggling with a God who was watching
him all the time.

"Poor bloke," I said. " 'Idle discourse on Thy day and at other times;
Not turning nearer to Thee for my affections; Not living according to my
belief; Not loving Thee for Thy self; Not loving Thee for Thy goodness to
us; Not desiring Thy ordinances . . .' "

"You've *memorised* them?" Kit checked the accuracy of my recitation
against what she could read on the paper.

"No, but that's the point. I can practically recite them and I've only
read them once. It's the same with the recipes for colour. You know what
my memory's like—I can't even remember my nine-times table. Don't
you think that's weird?"

"So? Your memory's improved since your undergraduate days. That's
no big deal. Nothing to get alarmed about. Why did Newton have to
count them like this, number them, make a list like an account book?"

"Because they stopped him from being pure. They were the obstacle.
And every now and again, on feast days, on Whitsuntide, they would all
be cancelled out. He'd be given a clean slate. At those points he would be
pure and powerful and his magic would be at its strongest."

"What magic?"

"His alchemy. He was starting to practise alchemy."

"How do you know all that?"

"I don't *know* anything. But when you ask me questions like that I can
just answer them without thinking."

Kit lit a cigarette and passed me back the piece of paper. I went on.

"Kit, do you remember Cameron taking us to that Methodist chapel in
Wales when he and I drove out to visit you at that holiday cottage you and

Maria took for the summer? There was a service on and we sat at the back?"

"Christ, yes—the sermon about sin." She exhaled cigarette smoke into the autumn air. "The sweaty minister."

"He started out by asking us all to think about the very last sin we'd committed; then, he said, think of all the sins committed by all the people in your house since breakfast, and . . ."

Kit fell into the rhythms of the minister's sermon—she remembered it more clearly than I did: " 'Think of all the people in your street,' " she chanted in a mock Welsh accent, " 'think of all the people in your city, in your country, in the world. Now multiply that by three hundred and sixty-five—all the days in a year. Now think of all the years since Christ died—two thousand long, long years . . .' The pile of sins just got bigger and bigger . . . I couldn't keep up with the math. Three hundred and sixty-five times two thousand. What's that?"

A passing runner in shorts and a T-shirt, catching a fragment of a Welsh sermon where he had never heard one before—on a riverbank no less—turned for an explanation, jogged a few steps backwards, then gave up listening and was gone.

"I know," I said. "Those rhythms. Suddenly, after building up and building up, numbers getting bigger and bigger so your head swam, he *stopped*. Must have stopped for about half a minute before he said just three words: 'Then Jesus came.' Cameron laughed out loud at that. Outrageous. I thought we were going to be asked to leave. Then the minister said it again. 'Then Jesus came and took away all the sins of the world.' He told us to imagine the scale of all of that sin and then to imagine it all gone. Just like that. It was a brilliant sermon. I've never forgotten it because it made me think about sin differently—like a kind of infestation, sins multiplying, breeding, like germs."

"Or rats . . . And what about Newton?"

"Newton was an alchemist, but he thought he wasn't pure enough. The first thing you had to be as an alchemist was pure. He knew he wasn't. He could be pure for a few hours; then some bad thought would creep into his head and spoil everything, take his strength and his magic away. Every morning he'd wake with a new set of resolutions and self-punishments, and by breakfast it would have all started again, the spiteful thoughts, the desire for vengeance, like an infestation."

"That's why he was angry?"

There were swans now, six of them, swimming upstream, battling against the wind and the current. Three small children were playing with a silver kitten outside the Fort St. George pub, trailing a piece of string along the ground for it to chase. Great tubs of geraniums and late nasturtiums exploded with colour. Passing under Victoria Bridge we sat on a bench next to the lock to watch children throwing lumps of bread to the uninterested, overfed swans. The day had brightened and the colours of the painted barges opposite glowed surreally in the sun. A pretty couple, both with thickly dreadlocked hair, roped their bicycles onto the flat asphalted roof of a barge called *The Unmissable* and disappeared below, behind rainbow-striped curtains.

Yes, he was angry, I thought. Newton's anger had penetrated my dreams now—it happens sometimes with writing, when it matters, when there's something at stake. Yes, I was dreaming the dreams of the boy who was angry with his sister, his mother, and his stepfather, who dreamed about killing them all when he went back to Woolsthorpe, who hated himself—and it all went round and round and he couldn't stop it, and it was getting in the way of his work, his experiments. Too much noise in his head. He couldn't get out of that. There was no way out.

I said to Kit, "He was desperate. When he was at school in Grantham, when he was *twelve*, for Christ's sake, he wrote in a notebook: 'I will make an end. I cannot but weep. I know not what to do.' "

Kit was persistent despite my absences, wanderings. "So he started writing his sins down in a notebook to cheer himself up?"

"Yes, and to try to keep track of them. And he started doing alchemical experiments. Making potions with chemicals. He boarded with an apothecary in Grantham when he was at school, so in those days he had access to lots of chemicals."

"Apothecaries are often the poisoners in Renaissance drama. Romeo and Juliet—the poison that goes wrong."

"He collected recipes for mixing colours: purple, crimson, green, russet, charcoal black, colours for painting nakedness and colours for painting corpses."

"A colour for painting corpses? Did he paint them? How do you mix a colour for painting dead bodies?"

"The colour for corpses? Do you really want to know?"

"Yes. Go on. Tell me." She put out her cigarette and watched me closely, as though she was looking to find the hidden trick in this strange new memory of mine, as if I was some tin-pot street magician. "Go on," she said. "Surprise me. Let's see how good your memory really is."

I did surprise her; I surprised both of us. That recipe was in a drawer in my head somewhere. All I had to do was read it through: " 'A colour for dead corpses: Change white lead with water of yellow berries and wash the picture all over and change it with blue Indie and shadow it in single hatches, and in the leanest places then take soot, yellow berries, and white lead, and with it shadow the darkest places.' "

Shadow the darkest places. If my beginning was Elizabeth's funeral, and yours was finding her body in red in the river, Elizabeth's entanglement started much earlier—I'd guess around the time she found that notebook full of sins. Yes, that was Elizabeth's beginning—in the dark corpse-washed corners of a seventeenth-century notebook written by a boy who turned his sins into coded accounts and who wanted to paint dead bodies. I walked that way much later. As Elizabeth's ghostwriter I had to walk the road she walked, trace its meanderings and speculations back to their origins, start where she started. She'd been working on alchemy and had found Newton's sins while looking for something else. A moment's curiosity had set her thinking about how far he would go to find the answers to the questions that stopped him from sleeping. How violent could he be? Would he kill? Could he? What happened to him to give him so much power—real or imagined—in 1665 and 1666?

Kit was sceptical. "So what's the series of coincidences that's spooking you? Apart from the fact that you can remember Newton's sins and his recipes for red and for corpses?"

I passed her back the piece of hole-riddled paper. "Look again at Elizabeth's transcriptions—she's marked out some of the sins. You can just see the remains of red highlighter pen on sins thirteen, fourteen, fifteen, and then if you turn it over, she's also marked out number forty." Kit read them out: " 'Thirteen: Threatning my father and mother Smith to burne them and the house over them. Fourteen: Wishing death and hoping it to some. Fifteen: Striking many. Forty: Using unlawful means to bring us out of distresses.' Why those ones in particular?"

"That's what I've got to work out," I said. "They're all about Newton's violent feelings. I think it's a clue to what the last chapters are supposed to say. The key one is 'Using unlawful means to bring us out of distresses.' Elizabeth has underlined it twice as well as highlighted it."

"Unlawful means? What did he mean by that?"

"You tell me. You're the one who knows about crime in the Renaissance and Restoration. What would 'unlawful means' be a euphemism for?"

"Could be anything. Murder. Conspiracy. Almost certainly violence of some kind. So you've got to fill in the last two chapters."

"Yes, using her annotated notes and the rest of the book as the only source materials. Extrapolate the rest."

"And what have you done so far?"

"Well, read it through several times. Started to read the notebooks."

"Sounds to me like Elizabeth was turning him into a character from a revenge tragedy. You know: the boy wound up like a spring by parents who neglect him or favour other siblings over him, the boy who buries himself in secrecy and makes plans for revenge. Smoulders and smoulders. In the end the whole world has to be punished, burned, and tortured. Like Edmund in *King Lear*—the ambitious, vengeful bastard son. Too easy. Almost a cliché."

"In her book, Elizabeth makes claims that have no sources. I simply don't know where she got them from."

"What sort of claims?"

"In the footnotes she often references what she has called the Vogelsang Papers—Vogelsang—she gave the archive her own surname."

"Which means what?"

"That it's a collection of primary sources that she discovered and that only she had access to. Eyewitness accounts, I guess, and historical documents that almost certainly won't have been copied or microfilmed. I've looked everywhere in The Studio, but there's nothing. Without the Vogelsang Papers these claims just won't stand up."

"Do they need to?"

"Well, I'm safe from being sued because as a ghostwriter, I am technically invisible. And Elizabeth can't be sued, because she's dead. The author is dead either way, beyond challenge. Absent from the court. But that doesn't solve the problem. If I am going to get the publishers to take this book as it stands, I have to provide some kind of proof of the allegations I think she's making. She knew these things to be true, but *how* did she know? Without the Vogelsang Papers there's nothing absolute. That's the problem—she's missing, the evidence is missing, the last chapters are missing, and I'm invisible."

Kit laughed. "There are some advantages to being invisible. If you're right—that there are certain things that she just knew—maybe you just have to take those things for granted, even though she's not proved them to you—yet. Maybe she found another way to know—beyond looking in archives. Maybe she got to the end of the archives and still wanted to know so badly that she went places where academics don't usually go."

"Such as?"

"Oh, I don't know. Where would you go if you really wanted to find out something about the past and yet you got to the end of what was known?"

"I have absolutely no idea. I'm just standing there at the edge looking out and I can't see anything. I'm becoming less and less certain that I know anything at all. I mean, there is so much I just can't explain—everyday things, not just Elizabeth's book."

"Like what?"

"Pieces of Elizabeth's notes, important keys to the last chapters, keep disappearing and reappearing as if someone wants them to disappear. Files have gone missing. There are coincidences. There are weird light effects all over the house that I can't find sources for."

"What kind of lights?"

"Light that looks like water—as if it's been reflected off a bowl of water. Rainbows that appear in little stubs and stretch out till they disappear, really slowly. I've tried photographing them, but my camera doesn't seem to be good enough to catch them."

"The river?"

"It's too far away."

"Mirrors?"

"No, I've checked."

I didn't tell her how one morning I had collected every piece of glass in The Studio, lifted down the decanters and the glasses from every shelf,

unhooked all the mirrors and pictures still hanging on the walls, even removed the light bulbs from their sockets and put them in dark places—in
cupboards or under Elizabeth's bed. Then I had sat and waited, clutching
my camera. The light came just the same, spreading around the wall,
pooling, slanting, stretching out, even with nothing there to catch and
throw it. Light thrown, hurled, pitched. Light caught. Illumination. But
the brighter the house became, the more I was thrown into darkness. I
couldn't see anything. And the camera showed nothing, caught nothing.

"Don't you think that maybe you just need to get out more?" I'd lost
Kit. She stood up from the bench to walk again, so we followed the path
along the river's edge, towards the boardwalk that meanders round past
the punts moored at Quayside. She was impatient. I could hear it in her
voice. She would come with me so far and would go no further into these
speculations. She was laughing at me. "Look, Lydia. I'm going to a party
next week. Want to come? We might find someone to share your bed.
Then I bet you won't be watching light move across walls."

"And there's another thing . . ." I was getting desperate now. *Don't
leave me alone with this, Kit. Don't look at me like that.*

"What?"

"The one bit of the list of sins that nobody has been able to decode is
a line that Newton wrote at the top of the list, on the flyleaf, like a heading. Every Newton scholar who knows anything about codes has had a go
but has failed to decode it. Cameron told me that Elizabeth had been trying to decode it for months. She even asked *him* to try."

"And?" She was checking her watch. Thought I didn't see.

"Well, it's another coincidence. Look." I passed her my notebook with
the transcription of the undeciphered heading:

Nabed Efyhik, Wfnzo Cpmkfe.

"What am I supposed to be seeing?" she asked. "It's gobbledygook."
Behind her a street juggler had started to throw coloured balls into the
air. But it was too windy, and he kept dropping them.

"Same bloody word," I said. *Was she being deliberately slow?* "Nabed. Newton used it as a code word in his notebooks in 1662. A code so obscure
that no one in four hundred years has been able to break it. Because it's

so obscure, it may have been some code he had been passed by someone else—a pledge, a spell, or a mantra passed to him along the alchemical networks, something so powerful it would work as a kind of protection there on the flyleaf of his notebook where he kept the list of his sins."

"So . . . and?"

"Well, now, three hundred and forty years later, the same word turns up in the same town as a secret code word used by an animal-liberation group. OK, so it's just a coincidence. I can see that. But what kind of coincidence is that? Just random—like monkeys on typewriters?"

"Yes, just that," she said. "You are making as much sense as a monkey with a typewriter."

I was about to tell her about the bloodstain that disappeared and reappeared, but I stopped and changed the subject. Why didn't I tell her? Because then I would have had to explain that the blood was yours. To do that I would have had to explain how your blood came to be on the pillowcase I had washed. Yes, Kit, Cameron stayed the night at The Studio. Yes, I did go to his bed. No, nothing is happening between us. It's finished. History.

No, I wouldn't have said all of that. I could hear how hollow it all would have sounded. There were so many things that I had started to *not say*. Lydia Brooke, previously the soul of indiscretion, had become rather quiet about many things. That was part of the trouble.

Kit and I had followed the boardwalk round the edge of the river on to Quayside, where on that late afternoon in October a few last punt touters in white shirts and straw hats tried, with a tired charm, to persuade too-cold tourists to take river tours. One of them, with a blond ponytail and a goatee, approached us and then, recognising Kit, smiled and changed his mind. She'd had run-ins with him before, she explained triumphantly. Now she had plans to cast him in her next play. "He'd make a great Bosola," she said, "if I can flatter him enough to agree. He has the right kind of swagger. Looks like an eighteenth-century pirate."

As Kit prepared to leave me to walk down Magdalene Street to the market, where she would relieve her assistant and check on the sales of her crimson cotton shirts, she said, "You have too active an imagination. And you're working too hard. Come and stay at Sturton Street for a few nights. Have a break."

"What? So that I can exchange my strange lights for the sound of Titus's wheel?" I said. "I think not. And, hey, thanks for all the sympathy."

"Let me know if you want me to find you an exorcist," she called deliberately loudly from the corner of Nadia's Bakery. "I'll look in the Yellow Pages." She grinned and disappeared into the crowd. I watched her patch of purpled clothes move up the street.

But I knew where to find an exorcist—Will had told me. In the Texaco garage on the A10.

Twelve

I was heading for the library and would need to turn left onto the bridge but, determined to catch the last of the afternoon sun, I took a table outside one of the cafés on Quayside and ordered a coffee. This was, after all, part of what I was supposed to be doing—taking in Cambridge, finding the seventeenth century. This was research.

The mottled green of the scrubland along the wild riverbank from Chesterton had given way to lush green grass, hedges, flower borders where Magdalene College began the great sweep of colleges lining the river as it curved its way down to Queens' College, past Silver Street, and on to Peterhouse. From here the river belonged to the colleges. For hundreds of years men and women labourers employed by the colleges had kept this water's edge spruce, mended its bridges, trimmed its hedges, tended its flower beds, painted its windowsills, polished its glass. Beyond this point on the river Cambridge became a kind of miniature Venice, its river water lapping up against the ancient stone of college walls, here mottled and reddened brick, there white stone. Stained, lichened, softened by water light. Here the river became a great north-south tunnel, a gothic castle from the river, flanked by locked iron gates, steps leading nowhere, labyrinths, trapdoors, landing stages where barges had unloaded their freight: crates of fine wines, flour, oats, candles, fine meats carried into the damp darkness of college cellars.

Great Bridge, carrying the great north road into Cambridge and on to London in a diagonal stroke from northwest to southeast, had been the single most important entry point to the city, where all northern traffic moving by water or by road made its way south. Now Bridge Street was lined with bag and hat shops, little boutiques selling jewellery.

I had Elizabeth at my side again, the Elizabeth who'd conjured Stourbridge Fair from February winds for me, Elizabeth the shaman of the seventeenth century. "Find Elizabeth, find the seventeenth century, we always say," said Dilys Kite. What could Dilys have wanted with the seventeenth century? Or it with her? *Find Elizabeth, find the seventeenth century.* "Find it for me," I said, under my breath. "Find me the seventeenth century."

Somewhere close by council workers were emptying glass-recycling containers into a refuse lorry. I heard the pouring torrent of breaking and splintering and crushed glass bottles stop and start, echo and subside. I wondered whether glass bottles sounded different, in their breaking, once they had been sorted by colour.

I watched the men and women come and go across the bridge, negotiating their way past the punt touters with their placards, stopping to lean over the edge of the bridge to look at the river traffic or take pictures. But instead of finding the seventeenth century, I began to wonder where you were at that moment, whether you might be walking this way, how you would meet my eye. Yes, it was when I was thinking about you that I first saw him. Not out of the corner of my eye or on the edges of my vision but there on the bridge, directly in front of me. How far away? About fifty feet. What did he look like? He had white hair and a red gown.

I saw the white hair first. A thin young man, about the same age as the punt touters, but looking old before his time, his hair worn to his shoulders, so that it blew slightly in the wind as he leaned against the metal of the bridge, flanked on either side by Japanese tourists taking photographs. He wore no hat and his university gown was scarlet, not the usual black. It was the shock of recognition that made me gasp. He met my eyes. Mutual recognition, a raised eyebrow, the slightest upturning of the edges of his mouth. Or did I imagine that? What was I doing hallucinating Newton on a bridge in Cambridge?

He was as definite as a picture in a frame, yet around him everything fell away. There was a smudge around him. As if what I was seeing was something *underneath* the surface of my reality, as if someone had rubbed away the surface of my Cambridge, its boutiques, cars, bicycles, and hat shops, so that now, for this moment, there were shades instead—even smears—of men and women from his world walking behind him through the optical smudge he occupied, or had made. Perhaps he had done the rubbing through from his side. How, then, was it that I could see him, see through into that?

As we stood there confronting each other—he on the Great Bridge, me on Quayside—there was a falling away such as even Elizabeth could not have conjured. Yet nothing much changed. Neither of the Japanese tourists on either side of him seemed to show any surprise at his presence. I can hear again, as I write, the intense hush into which the sounds of the afternoon fell away. Quayside lost for a moment its clamour. I might even have said that for a moment it lost its colour; they faded into a kind of black and white. That would happen again, later, much more sharply, that draining out of colour, but then you wouldn't know that. I didn't tell you.

How long did it last? You ask that now? You, who understand about the contractions and spasms of time, about that world and this. It lasted longer than I could breathe my way through it. He seemed to fix me from the bridge with a question, a scrutiny through the fading light. He had both hands on the ledge, and as he turned away from me, his hand grazed along the length of it. I can still see, as if I am seeing it now, the passing of his long fingers along the stone. He turned away; that was all I knew, and was gone.

Thirteen

If it was the smudge on the bridge that made me find Dilys Kite's telephone number, it was Pepys's death that made me pick up the phone and call her. When I got home that afternoon, the cat's body was lying on the doorstep. From a distance, even before I saw that his legs had been tied with wires, I knew something was wrong. Even asleep or sunning himself on the front step, he didn't lie like that.

The blood was still wet, darkening as it dried from crimson to brown. It had fanned out from the first incision with coagulating skirted folds of red velvet. His eyes were open, head thrust forward. What did he see and hear in his final moments? How many hooded figures in black had gathered round him? They had bound his feet with wire, sending a message to Cameron Brown, to you, through me, Elizabeth's ghostwriter, marking out their territory. Using Pepys as a surface to write on, to save the others, to change the world. I didn't understand till later how much more complicated that message was. I couldn't have understood then, though you would have. You would have known what that dead cat meant. Things might have turned out differently if I had told you, if you had received the warning, meant for you, that Pepys carried.

But I couldn't tell you. It was a postponement of telling, not a conscious evasion. All I knew then was that you couldn't see Pepys's body mutilated like that. Not so soon after Elizabeth's death. There had been too many deaths at The Studio. I buried him in the garden near the river-bank where the soil was already turned over, so you wouldn't notice. I could keep all of this from you, I thought. Stand between you and it. I tried to unbind Pepys's feet before I slipped him into the ground—it seemed right—but when his front paws twitched for a second as I un-twisted the wire, as the blood rushed back into his feet, I thought he might be still alive and I dropped him from my lap back onto the step. I had blood on my clothes and hands. There were ants already working around his wounds. I couldn't do any more for him. It was beyond me. So Pepys went into the ground with his back legs still tied. I don't like to think about that.

Burying Pepys there in that peaty ground beside the river made me think of the bodies they pulled from the bogs of Ireland, humans slaugh-tered to appease the gods: young women with their hands bound, buried alive, or drowned in bogs, their skulls smashed in. I imagined someone digging there at the riverbank some hundred years from now, raising Pepys's bones on his spade and finding the wire binding his back legs to-gether, contacting the archaeology unit at the university.

If you were the archaeologist driving out to Chesterton to see the cat bones laid out for you in the rain on the riverbank, you'd be thinking of witchcraft, wouldn't you? A cat with cut marks on its bones, feet bound, and buried beside a river just outside the city's boundaries. You'd be ex-cited. Date? Oh, seventeenth century at the latest—part of the witch trials of the seventeenth century, you'd say. A cat, a witch's familiar, tortured and buried. You might have started to imagine a project, research assis-tants, a dig. If the cat was buried as part of a witchcraft trial, you'd say to yourself, you would need to look for the remains of an old woman's body too, close by, and that would take time. Once you'd found her bones and determined whether she'd been burned or drowned, you'd almost cer-tainly be able to tell when she was executed with carbon dating. You'd be expecting to find the burned remains of a house too, and perhaps the shadow of an herb garden.

But on your arrival at the riverbank the wire would be an instant disap-pointment. Naturally, in your excitement you wouldn't have thought to ask the caller how the cat's feet were bound. Garden wire. Dated in the lab to the early twenty-first century. No witch's cat. No witch. No burned house or shadow of a garden. No article in the future equivalent of *New Scientist* or television interviews. So what do you do with your nameless cat? He has to be placed, an explanation found, if only for curiosity's sake. A search in the online local history database tells you that in the first years of the twenty-first century there was a spate of animal killings in and around Cambridge that were part of a new and more violent animal-liberation campaign that would get uglier yet. And once you had found those articles and found the descriptions of the type of killings—the seven slashlike cuts, the bound legs—that would be your answer. You would have looked no further. This would be evidence enough to provide the explanation, fill out the quota of footnotes for a short scholarly article that would swell your number of publications for that year.

And would anyone have blamed you for not asking any more questions? For returning in a moment of speculation to your first instinct, that there was something decidedly seventeenth-century about this dead cat, buried by a river with its feet bound. What was that, exactly? Revenge, blood rites, and scapegoats. The children of the Duchess of Malfi strangled. Macduff's children murdered. The fierce violence of the act of vengeance, its appalling motivelessness; the villain, who, even with the blood of murdered children still warm on his hands, cannot say *why* he acts. Ferdinand in the *Duchess of Malfi* knows that his villainy is beyond explanation as well as redemption, that he is as unfathomable as quicksand (or a fen): "He that can compass me, and know my drifts, / May say he hath put a girdle 'bout the world, / And sounded all her quick-sands."

Did *you* think you knew me? Had you fathomed me, Mr. Brown? You haven't yet. Though you watch my every move. I've not told you everything yet.

They asked me in the court why I hadn't reported the cat's death. There was a lot of criticism about that in the papers. Knowing about the cat's mutilation might, they said, have given the police a chance to stop the NABED campaign before it had escalated to murder. But how was I to know that, then? I told the prosecutor that I picked up the phone to call the police but at that point I realised that they would almost certainly need a statement from you. And I didn't want you to know. I didn't report the death because I was protecting you, I told them.

"Why did you need to protect Mr. Brown, Dr. Brooke?"

"Because he was still grieving for his mother. Pepys was his mother's cat."

"And that was a strong enough reason to decide not to report a crime?"

"Yes, sir. It was. I didn't want Cameron to see his mother's cat cut about like that. And, frankly, I didn't know whether killing a cat *was* a crime."

"Did anyone else know about the cat?"

Though Will had never known about Pepys's death, I said: "Will knew about the cat. She was with me when I found him. We had been walking all day, up to Fen Ditton." There was a good deal of noise from the gallery at that point, where the journalists were sitting. Will picked at the skin around her fingernails.

"And how did she react?"

"She was upset. She told me to phone the police. She was angry when I didn't."

Will stopped picking her fingers and sat very still. She looked confused. The prosecutor repeated my statement in that way that prosecutors do, with clear implications, slowly, stressing certain words, glancing at the jury to check that they understood the import of my words, repeated, headlined.

"She told you to phone the police?"

"Yes, and she was right. I should have called the police. But what would I have said? We hadn't seen anyone in the garden or in the house. There were no footprints. Someone had got into the garden, found the cat, and killed it. It was terrible. An act of brutality. But we couldn't add anything to what the police already knew."

There was now a lot of noise in the courtroom. I heard a woman say something about irresponsibility. Yes, I know now how stupid it was not to have reported the cat's death. The police might have been able to trace the wire around his legs or find some fingerprints on the gate. But at the time Pepys was just a dead cat. None of us knew how it was all going to spiral. That there were to be human lives at stake as well as animal ones.

"How did she seem—emotionally?"

"She seemed agitated and upset."

"Was she fond of the cat?"

"Yes, I think she was. We all were. Pepys was a very affectionate cat."

Distortions. A few words here and there. A few words to pull a story in new directions. It doesn't take significant untruths to do that, just a few words like drops of arsenic into wine. Why did I do it? I had no plan. But I had an instinct to do what I could to slow the process down. I couldn't do much. But I could be a stone in the stream. I would be like one of Edgar Allan Poe's narrators, I thought. I would be seductive and mendacious in the courtroom.

You learned about lying on the river when you were working as a punt chauffeur. To lie on, to lie under, to lie close, to lie in wait for.

That was around the time when we first met. You had a postdoctoral fellowship; I had just started working on my Ph.D. I knew who you were, of course; you had something of a reputation. Not for womanising, but for general misrule. Then there were the stories people told about how brilliant you were. People always wanted to talk about your brilliance as if it explained your misrule. Someone who knew you, a geneticist, I think, had used phrases like *cutting edge* and *paradigm shifts* and, yes, everyone used the word *clever* about you. Elizabeth said that once: "Oh yes," she said, "my clever son." It had a sting in it, that word *clever*.

In your postdoctoral days you had short hair, which made you look aggressive. Funny that. Most undergraduates had long hair. We were at a pub called the Fort St. George. It was a Friday night in October and I was with Kit. We'd bought our drinks and were looking for a table. There weren't any; the pub was dark, candlelit, like a series of smoky caves by the river. Kit saw Sarah sitting with you and Anthony in a corner by the fire—the best seats—and she walked over and introduced us. Anthony found some stools.

When I told you I was doing a history Ph.D. you laughed and said you were a historian too. "Ask me about any aspect of Cambridge history," you said. "I am a punt chauffeur, the very best kind of historian. I know every-thing there is to know about that stretch of the river and the colleges along it. Just that—nothing more."

"I guess," I said, "that makes you a liminal historian with a fluvial spe-cialism." Kit glared a warning at me, but I was thinking of you standing on the end of the long sliver of a boat, pole in hand, slipping it deftly into the depths of the water, pushing against it, muscles flexed, propelling the boat forward.

"I like that," you said, and repeated the phrase. "A liminal historian. Limen. Threshold. A historian of thresholds. Go ahead, Lydia Brooke, ask me any question. A pound for every question I can't answer." You laid out five pound coins on the table. Anthony went to get another round of drinks. There were oars from famous boats lining the walls like primitive weapons. Crossed.

"OK," I said. "When was Trinity founded?"

"My college. Far too easy: 1546. Founded by Henry the Eighth."

"How are we to know if that's right?" Kit asked.

"It just is. You'll have to believe me."

"Hah," said Kit. "Trust Cameron Brown? That will be easy."

You ignored her taunts, downed your pint, and pulled off your sweater, brushing the sleeve across the candle flame. It didn't catch. Sarah caught her breath. Her eyes were on me. What was she looking for? What was she looking at? Me caught in the beam of your charm. I dared not catch her eye. What did she see that I hadn't even begun to guess? I reached for your cigarette box.

"May I roll one?" I leaned forward to smell the acrid fragrance of the tobacco. A gesture to give me something to do, I thought, to give me a reason to get out of your gaze, but that was not how you wanted it. You were slightly drunk.

"Please do. I love watching women roll cigarettes. Especially if they have long fingers like yours." Even in this low light I knew my rising colour would be visible to Sarah. I pulled out a cigarette paper from the packet.

Kit rounded on you. "I've heard you lot down there on the punts, making up stories. The dates are almost always wrong."

"My dates are never wrong," you said. "I take a great deal of pride in the accuracy of my dates. I just embroider some of my stories, that's all. Improve on history. The tourists want to be entertained, so we entertain them."

"Does anyone ever challenge you?" I asked, putting the rolled cigarette to my lips. You leaned forward and lit it with the candle from the table. One of my hairs caught the candle flame and hissed.

"Not so far. Academics wouldn't dream of hiring a punt chauffeur, so we're usually safe from challenge. Plausibility is the key."

Sarah was scornful and irritated. "Plausibility? That's ridiculous. Most of your stories aren't at all plausible. You just romanticise everything. That's what the tourists buy into. They'll never challenge anything you say so long as it's beautiful or fascinating." She turned to me. "He made up a story about Trinity Great Court being haunted by the smell of oysters. Told the tourists that Great Court was haunted by the ghost of a fifteen-year-old oyster seller who'd been Byron's lover and whom he'd taken swimming in the well there. Now how plausible is that?"

"She caught a cold and died, leaving the smell of oysters perpetually in the dusk of Trinity Great Court," Cameron interrupted self-mockingly. "But it's *almost* true. Byron did smuggle girls into his rooms at Trinity. As often as he could. He was an iconoclast. God. Imagine how suffocated Byron must have been here. So the *spirit* of my story is true."

Anthony passed me another pint of bitter from the tray he carried from the bar, and a pickled egg in a paper cake case.

"Ever had one of these before?" he asked, grinning. "Speciality of the house. Egg, vinegar, and beer. Perfect combination. As is Cameron's story. The smell of oysters is an objective correlative for sexual repression. It's perfect."

"Objective correlative?"

"An object that stands for something complicated—an emotion, a knowledge, an instinct. The ghost oyster seller is the return of the repressed, haunting the court with the smell of oysters. What's repressed in cerebral Cambridge is sex, except that it's everywhere, because it's repressed. In the stacks of the library, in public toilets, alleyways. Drive it out and it'll find its own corners. I saw a group of Chinese tourists in Great Court the other evening at dusk sniffing the air. Trying to smell oysters. Brilliant. They'd been on Cameron's boat, I'd swear."

You were on a roll. "The point is that my oyster-seller ghost works as a historical *metaphor.* My oyster-seller ghost is a metaphor. For a tourist, she's much more eloquent than any dry-as-dust history book that tells them about what it was like to be a student in the early nineteenth century and all its manifestations of sexual repression. There's a plaque over in that far corner there, a page from a guidebook for undergraduates published in 1807. It reads: 'Suspect danger from . . . those women . . . who haunt the lanes, and ends, and corners of the town, who are Hebes at night, and Hecates in the morning.' Isn't that great? Hebes at night and Hecates in the morning. Beauty and the beast. That's my kind of night. Sounds more like an advert than a warning to me. What are you, Lydia Brooke? A Hebe or a Hecate?" I'd had enough of the games now.

"She's a Hecate every time," said Kit, preparing for a fight. Kit would say that. She had her theories about people. No room for Hebes in her world. All her people, men and women, she would say, were Hecates in one way or another, even if they travelled in disguise, even if they didn't know they belonged to the Hecate tribe.

"No, I'm not," I said. "Hecate was a witch. I'm not a witch." I sounded like a child being taunted in the playground.

"You work on witchcraft, though, don't you?" Was Sarah enjoying my discomfort? You had fallen silent. Your hand was on my thigh. I couldn't move it without being seen. Why did that make me feel guilty?

"Not exactly. I'm writing my dissertation on the classification of spirit manifestations in the seventeenth century. That doesn't make me a witch."

"And how would you classify a ghost who smells of oysters?" Anthony asked. "You have to admit, it's a stroke of genius."

"I'll drink to that," you said. "The point is that oysters have no smell. But that doesn't seem to matter."

That was 1988; sixteen years ago. You and Sarah were already married, though you didn't tell most people. Six years later you had a Trinity fellowship, a string of accolades and awards, your own lab, and two children, and you were finding your way to my bed most afternoons. Yes, dates were always important for you because, once we were lovers, storytelling became your great art, the way you kept the machinery of two lives moving.

If you weren't already a genius in rewriting the daily acts of the present, you became one. The great skill in lying is not lying, you'd say. Just leaving things out. Keeping everything as close to the actual truth as possible. Nothing overblown.

"The train's just pulled in at Cambridge Station," you'd say, phoning Sarah from my bed. "But the taxi queue's pretty long. It might take me another forty minutes to get home." You'd make up the names of conferences so that we could travel across Europe. You told her that cars broke down. Trains broke down. The lab went through yet another crisis. Friends got sick. Did Anthony ever know that you'd used him as an alibi for almost two years? There was no bravado in the fabrications, nor were they an act of display. They were just necessary.

You learned to lie on the river. You lied in my bed and from my bed.

Fourteen

After I'd heard the phone ring three times I realised I wasn't even sure what I was going to ask Dilys Kite. I told myself it was idle and harmless curiosity, but I knew this was an act of desperation—I could see that desperation in my face in the hall mirror, in the way I was clutching the phone. Someone had to be able to tell me what was going on and how it—the lights, the man on the bridge, the cat's death—all fitted together. Someone who wouldn't laugh. And Dilys had been there with Elizabeth in those last months from July, when Will left, until September, when Elizabeth died. She must know something, I thought, be able to explain something.

Nonetheless, I had more doubts than certainties about what I was doing even then, even with the phone in my hand. I could always put the phone down right now, I thought; I could always pretend I had the wrong number. I needed to hear that strange high voice again, the precise syllables. I had, in fact, almost put the phone back onto the receiver when I heard her voice calling my name, sharply but from a distance, as if I had fainted and she was waking me, slapping my face hard, waving smelling salts under my nostrils. Lydia. Lydia? She came into focus. Her voice became louder. I put the phone back to my ear.

"Yes?" I said. How strange. It was me who was supposed to be calling her, and in control of the questions. Now everything was inverted.

"Lydia Brooke. We expected you much earlier than this," she said. I saw I had soil under my fingernails from digging the little grave down near the roses. The mirror framed a face with pale skin and darkened, hollowed-out eyes. Lydia was looking thin.

"I'm sorry. It's late to be calling," I began.

"Will you take tea?"

"I'm sorry, I don't understand."

"On Wednesday, when you visit. You've forgotten?"

"Forgotten what?"

"You *have* forgotten."

"I'm sorry, I don't understand." I had begun to think I might hang up after all. This was like a Pinter conversation—jigsaw shards that didn't seem to fit together, with so much more underneath. I remembered the tattoo on her right arm, the chiselled hair. Who was this woman to be talking to me like this? What was I doing ringing her? I repeated myself: "I don't understand. Have we made some kind of appointment? This is Lydia Brooke—we met at Elizabeth Vogelsang's funeral a few weeks ago. I am doing some work for . . . I am doing some work on Elizabeth's book . . ."

Did she perhaps think I was somebody else?

She continued. Still in control but more emollient now. "Yes, hello, Lydia Brooke. We know you are working on Elizabeth's book. That's why you are calling."

"I don't understand. How could you know that?"

"If you have forgotten, of course you won't understand. You want to come to see us. And we would very much like to see you. Wednesday would be best for us. Wednesday afternoon at around four o'clock. Would that suit you?"

In the mirror, the woman who looked like Lydia Brooke put her hand to the back of her neck. The surface of the mirror was so old that its glass was both flecked and watery. I watched how its rippled surfaces distorted her face as Dilys talked. Haunted, willful, maddening, the light was playing tricks again. As I watched, the surface of the mirror began to undulate, shoaling, burnished, as if it were a pool into which I sought my reflection at the very moment that someone behind me had dropped a stone into the silvered water. Someone was behind her, or between her and the mirror, his face overlaid on hers, mouth open, asking a question that she can't hear. The man in the red gown, with the white hair. The man with the question on his lips. He was there in the ripples of the mirror, at the centre of a series of waved circles rippling outwards from a glass centre, her face and hair and eyes over his, washing outwards to the chipped oval frame. Then it was gone, her face all back in place, still, sharp, outlined.

I blinked, but my eyes would not clear. They hurt. It was as if I was now looking through water.

"How did I get here?" I asked Dilys.

"Precisely."

"Pardon?"

"That is precisely what we will help you find out," she said, briskly. "How you got here. Do you know where to find us?"

Elizabeth's address book was lying open in front of me on the hall table. I had marked the place with the snail-bitten doilied sheet from her notebook.

"Prickwillow, River View, Padnel Bank?"

"Yes, that's right. Prickwillow is up past Ely—you'll need to take the A10 north and then take the ring road underneath Ely and out to the east, taking the signs to Soham and then to a village called Queen Adelaide. Take the road to Prickwillow, then turn left into Padnel Bank just before you reach the bridge over the river. We're about halfway down the row of bungalows." I wrote down the details. Couldn't trust my eyes or my memory now. *Padnel Bank. Prickwillow.*

We? Us? I wondered who Dilys Kite might share a house with. Husband, sister, a family? Perhaps they all lived in the village—one great spilling family, the butcher, the baker, the candlestick maker—and the half-blind clairvoyant. The Happy Family Kites: Mister Kite, Mistress Kite, Miss Kite, and Master Kite, flight-sight makers. But perhaps Dilys, with her tattoo and twinsets, was very undistinguished in Prickwillow, just one of the local characters. Perhaps she organised coffee mornings and church fetes, arranged the church flowers, minded the grandchildren, played darts in the pub on Wednesday evenings. No, not darts. A half-blind person with psychic powers couldn't play darts, surely? But perhaps she baked cakes. Apple and blackberry pies. Or sewed lavender dolls for the local crafts market.

In Newton's time a half-blind woman who had visions would be branded a witch, hounded, taunted by day, visited by night along the back wooded paths. She would have lived on the outskirts or beyond the village boundaries, in the woods, where she could be called upon by villagers seeking exorcisms, spells, and potions. Love potions for already lovesick girls. Chants to quiet the spirits of dead children who had settled on their mothers' hearts. Spells for the harvest, for the spirits of the corn or the sky or the waters. Incantations. Predictions. *Tell me when the rain will fall. When will my mother die? Why has my crop failed? Give me a potion to appease the spirits. Give me a poison for the man who has taken my daughter's maidenhood. Make me a rainstorm.*

"I'm frightened," I said, speaking a thought I didn't know I had.

"Of course you are," she said in a motherly tone. "You would be very foolish not to be frightened now. If you don't mind me saying so."

"Can you explain? Will you be able to explain?" I had been drawing on the piece of paper near the phone—scrolled shapes, triangles, boxes, joined by cross-hatched shapes around the few words I had written. But there among all the scrolls was the word NABED. Capitalised. The word I had seen on the green metal hoarding near the Leper Chapel on the day of Elizabeth's funeral. The first word of the coded sequence that Newton had written on the flyleaf of his notebook:

Nabed Efyhik, Wfnzo Cpmkfe.

"Do you know what NABED means?" I asked Dilys just as she was bringing the phone call to a close.

"If you want to ask questions you will have to bring something of the person you want to speak to."

"Something? What kind of something?"

"Something that belonged to them. Something that carries them."

"With her smell on it? Like a walking stick or a piece of clothing?"

"No, smell doesn't matter; it's spirit that matters. Whatever object you choose must have her spirit on it. But there's no point in bringing anything of Elizabeth's. You won't be able to talk to her yet. We've tried. It's too early."

"Elizabeth?"

"You can't speak to Elizabeth yet."

"Him then?" Him? Who did I mean? The man in red on the bridge in the smudge.

"You're ready to talk to *him*? We wouldn't advise that yet. Not at all. Too early. You will have to talk to the boy first."

"The boy?"

"Yes, there's about two weeks now, only two weeks left."

"What boy?"

I heard Dilys speaking to someone—or some people—in the same room. I heard her say, "She's asking 'What boy?' She's forgotten." There was a murmur of disappointment and frustration. The voices sounded like a Bible group or an old people's home. How many of them were there, I wondered, and all waiting for me to call?

"If it's the boy you want to speak to, we have something of his. You won't need to bring anything."

"Wednesday at four o'clock then?"

"Yes, Wednesday at four. We look forward to seeing you, Lydia. Very much." I might have been booking a bed-and-breakfast, I thought.

As I pulled up to the kerb outside Dilys's house, I reached over to turn off my phone. Your text came through as I touched it, and a memory of you flicked across some nerve in my brain, a nerve you would have a name for. Another text. Now there were several every day. Oh yes, something understood. A pitch of intimacy ratcheting up. I remembered how you did that. Back then, all those years ago, when you began to seek me out for the first time, it was cigarette papers, then postcards, then letters. You left flowers and other objects on my doorstep: a piece of amber with a cockroach sealed inside, a Roman brooch, a book of poems by Neruda. I resisted at first. You were married. You had children. I turned away and refused to reply. So you stopped. And in the silence that rang round my head when I looked for objects on my doorstep and found none, you broke me down, made me ache for you. One week after the silence began, I drove out to your house and placed a single oyster shell on your doorstep. Later that night, I heard your car draw up outside Sturton Street. Kit let you in, though it was past midnight.

Now that we were lovers again and now that you could send texts and picture messages, your powers of seduction were at their strongest. Not that you would for a moment admit that you were engaged in an act of renewed seduction with, or for, me. No, not that. There was a curiosity driving both of us—the bodkin pressing on the eyeball—a compulsive desire to know what would happen—*this* time. I'd said, hadn't I, that despite a night in your bed, we could walk away? It meant nothing. But with a text here and there, stolen moments, e-mails, it took no time at all for us to be back in the spell we had always made in and around each other.

I opened up the little envelope on my phone, into the in-box, where your name, Cameron, sat listed with fourteen other Cameron messages, a sequence broken only by texts from Kit and Maria. You had written to me only minutes before: "I couldn't find you in the library. Everything all right? Back in the lab now. CB."

"Working up in the stacks," I texted back. "Sorry to have missed you. LB." Well, I couldn't have written: "In Prickwillow visiting a half-blind psychic," could I?

I never lied to you, exactly. They were sins of omission. I was airbrushing constantly by that October, brushing out people from my stories, brushing out lights, mirrors that turned to water, dead cats, coincidences, missing words, and now a fenland clairvoyant. It was very important that you didn't see. I could protect you from it. And I would because I could.

Fifteen

To find Prickwillow and Dilys Kite I drove out across the Fens. The road beyond the great north roundabout gave way eventually to the flat blackened land of the Fens, where once there were meres and reedbeds, alders, curlews, and sedge warblers. The road seemed to curl its way along a ridge newly and only slightly risen from a seabed, only recently exposed to the sky. Above it the sky was a great arch of clouds, shades of blue and crisp white that afternoon, shading to grey and pale purple bruise over towards Ely, where diagonal streaks of light and dark marked out the edges of a rainstorm behind the flattened outline of the cathedral.

The guidebook to East Anglia describes this landscape north of Ely as "the black Fens, where celery and onions grow in endless weedless rows down hedgeless billiard-table fields." It's more beautiful than that, though, and darker too, particularly in winter, when nothing breaks the black soil for miles, except for the straight edges of roads, drains, and hedgerows, and the rusted corrugated iron of sheds and bunkers. Black as black. No, not really like a billiard table—more like the flattened shapes of a Mondrian painting, in black, greens, browns, and greys. Here and there reeds fringe the waterways and feather the wind that blows in from the Urals.

The poet Tennyson came out to the Fens when he was a student at

Cambridge in the 1830s, already sick with love for poetry and for his friend Arthur Hallam. He used this thin light and flattened, river-riven landscape and lowering sky in several of his poems, but it's the Lady of Shalott I see when I'm watching the willows trail their leaves on the edge of rivers. The lady who left the tower by the river, where she'd been imprisoned by a spell, because she'd fallen in love with a beautiful knight who had ridden past her window. She sailed down the river to Camelot, knowing that she would die now that she'd broken the spell. And as she passes down the river, consumed by her desire, "willows whiten, aspens quiver, little breezes dusk and shiver." The Lady of Shalott, entangled in her web, *falls*; she is always falling, or fallen. Tennyson found her in this black, wet land.

Prickwillow's not old; even the pumping station, which is now a museum, only dates from 1922. The land the village stands on, where the River Lark meets the River Ouse, would have risen from the marshy waters in the late seventeenth century, when they drained the Fens and brought the land up out of the marsh. Before that this village, the land where Mrs. Kite's bungalow stands and the pub, the pump-engine museum, and the church, were all waterlogged peat, covered with sedge, dangerous black land, full of exhalations of gas bubbling up from long-rotted ancient bog oaks, their long-limbed shadows turning invisibly beneath apparently solid surfaces. Apart from the church and the stone houses clustered along the bend in the river, Prickwillow looks temporary, half rotted and rotting: rusting corrugated iron sheds, abandoned gardens, the metal shells of cars and boats scattered about like fossils emerging from mud. There's a stagnancy about it like a still-life painting, objects caught suspended in the act of passing. Even the river is apparently still, like glass.

After the draining of the Fens, willows found a place here along the riverbanks, making perfect mirror images of themselves in the water. Then thatchers brought their boats upriver to cut skewers of flexible willow wood here to hold down the thatch on their roofs. They called them prickets. Willow pricket. Prickwillow.

There's no burial ground in Prickwillow—the water table is too high even now and the ground too saturated. The dead must be interred instead at Ely. Death would somehow be suspended here too, like time.

Dilys Kite's house looked like a bed-and-breakfast—a bungalow in what appeared to be a housing estate to the side of the village. Two brightly painted gnomes stood squatly in the garden, one fishing, the other with trousers round his ankles. Curved borders hosted late snapdragons and nasturtiums, curling around a well-manicured lawn, in the centre of which someone had placed a mock Tudor well. Now why, I wondered, would a medium live in a bungalow and not, as one might have thought, in a cottage with thick walls and low beams? Perhaps it would be too noisy. If you are picking up traffic all the time from the other side, an old cottage would be deafening. Much better to live in a fifties bungalow among the picket fences and gnomes of village life. Empty walls. And a well with no hole down into the peat below.

Dilys Kite—psychic, medium, clairvoyant—didn't advertise, of course. People just found her when they needed her, she often said. Found their way to Prickwillow from America, New Zealand, London, Cambridge. Wind chimes hanging from the porch, in this wind, were hectic and out of key. I had a cold sore on my bottom lip, just pushing its way through to the surface. My eyes were hot and seemed to be getting hotter. I had to blink now to see sharply—fen light, I thought.

I had imagined, or tried to imagine, a husband for Dilys Kite, but there was no husband. She came to the door alone, her glass eye turned slightly askew, slippers on her feet. Yes, this particular memory runs like a dream. I can't see too well. She can't see at all but she also sees everything. When she has made the tea in her little kitchen and I have taken a seat in her dark sitting room and talked a little about her roses and the autumn weather, she asks me to turn off my phone, explaining, as if she were telling me about stain remover, that mobile phones disturb the spirit world.

"Shall we go through?" she asks. She takes my tea from me, puts it on a tray, opens a little door into a conservatory overlooking her garden, and carries the tray through there, into the light. I follow. There's an element of showmanship in all of this, the rustle of expectation. She motions for me to take a seat on one side of the room and she takes another—her seat, I knew that. It has that air about it.

"I've come because . . ." Someone had to start somewhere.

"I know why you are here, dear," she began, closing her eyes and settling back into her chair. "You've come because you've seen what Elizabeth left unfinished in that house. You must try to finish it, close it down, but you won't be able to do that on your own. You don't know enough."

"And you do?"

"Elizabeth came here often, especially towards the end. She had a theory, and she was looking for evidence to prove it."

"By contacting the dead?" I failed to erase the sneer in my voice. "Elizabeth wasn't like that. She was a serious scholar."

"No, she wasn't 'like that,' as you put it," Dilys said, without taking offence, "but she came to believe, when there was no other way. She wanted to know certain things for which there were no records. It was a kind of obsession for her."

"About Newt—?"

She put her finger to her lips quickly. "No, my dear. You mustn't say his name here. We've made that mistake only once before." She motioned to a burn mark on the wall, high up above my head. I didn't ask.

I thought of you and wondered what a neuroscientist would say about parapsychology. Would you see clairvoyance as a version of schizophrenia? How would you diagnose what people called Dilys Kite's "gift"; what drugs would you give her? There's a chemical in the brain that produces hallucinations and visions, I think you showed me an article once in *New Scientist* about that—some stupid headline about how all those medieval mystics just had more than their fair share of this chemical. No angels—no, in the end it's all a matter of chemicals surging through the frontal lobes.

"There's a boy," Dilys said. "One of those who died. Elizabeth should have left it all alone. She would never admit that. She just did what she had to do, I suppose. The boy has been here often. He's here with us now."

She pointed behind me. I ignored it. I wasn't going to be spooked by any of this hocus-pocus. I'd come here to find out what Dilys Kite knew about her friend, not to contact the dead. I wouldn't lose it, as Elizabeth had done. I knew where reason ended and irrationality began, even if Elizabeth had forgotten how to find that edge.

"What did she find?"

"You've not finished reading her book?"

"Yes, I've finished reading it, but it doesn't say. The last two chapters are missing."

Dilys sighed with a degree of of exasperation. "But she *did* finish it. That's the point. She rang me that last weekend to tell me she had finished it. There were no missing chapters."

"Well, it's not finished now," I said. "The last two existing chapters are only in note form. I've checked all her computer files. There's one computer file with the entire text in it labelled *The Alchemist,* and there's a printout. They are both exactly the same—the book dwindles into notes."

"Well, well. Perhaps that's best after all. What kind of notes?"

There were posters of Native Americans on the brick-wall end of Dilys's rather draughty conservatory. Roses, drifts of red and pink and orange beyond, another well-manicured garden. Wicker easy chairs. A coffee table. Green mock-marble vinyl on the floor. This was just a suburban conservatory in October.

"The last two chapters of *The Alchemist,*" I said, trying not to let my eyes wander around the walls. "Some of the text is polished, probably even finished. She describes Newton's appointment to the fellowship at Trinity in 1667. Most of that material, right down to his buying clothes for the celebrations and being given a key to all the rooms and to the bowling green and the tennis courts—all of that is there; it's wonderful. But then there are pages in between that are just in note form. Names, places, dates. Some sections in the hard copy are scratched out. The electronic version is full of gaps and little notes to herself."

"As if the file had reverted to an earlier draft?"

"Yes, how do you know?"

"My dear, Elizabeth talked to me a good deal about that manuscript. We did many things for Elizabeth and with that manuscript. Nothing made any difference. What computer are you using? Hers?"

"No, mine. I brought a laptop."

"Good. Don't use hers. Best not." She poured more tea into tiny ornate cups from a small metal teapot and passed me a ginger biscuit on a china dish.

"Why? Viruses?" I asked. Would Dilys Kite know about computer viruses?

"Oh no. She never had any viruses in that computer. She was very careful about that. Just accidents. Electricity shortages. Files that disappeared. Words that came up on the screen on their own when she would be working on a chapter."

"What words?"

"NABED was one. That came up many times. Upside down. Back to front."

"NABED? The name of the animal-liberation group?"

"Yes, but that, I believe, is entirely coincidental. I've been trying to work out what it stands for. Probably something like National Army Against Biochemical Experimentation and Death or Destruction. Interesting, don't you think?"

"Could someone have been hacking into her computer? Some kind of propaganda campaign by the group? It could have been a simple malfunction. Or even a virus."

"She wasn't connected to the Internet there."

"She could have picked up a virus in all sorts of ways."

"Yes, I expect she probably could. I'm sure there's a rational explanation. Is that what you think it was . . . or, should I say, is? Your computer is doing the same things, isn't it? Your laptop?" She stopped and looked at me rather intensely. "Are you remembering yet? Are you beginning to remember?"

This was no kind of remembering I knew. It started in the form of a déjà vu, or at least it had all of the sensation of a déjà vu—the vividness of colour and taste, the confusion, the absolute certainty that I had been there before, sitting and drinking tea, eating a ginger biscuit, looking out into that garden. But I know that the memory as it came to me in Dilys Kite's conservatory that afternoon, thick and embossed and finely textured, was not my own. I had to put down the teacup—porcelain, delicate, with its lilies of the valley—because my hand was no longer my own. Déjà vu is a sensation in the head, a kind of rush of perception. The rest of that memory, such as it was, came up from my loins and spread outwards, filling my chest, and stayed, steadied, in the base of my throat, so that I couldn't swallow. I closed my eyes. It filled me up—from my loins to my fingers and toes, down all the arteries and sinews and down all the optic and fibrous nerves. It filled me to the brim. I had a sensation of bursting in my chest, like a plum that is about to split its skin. I sat still so that I wouldn't split. I tried to breathe slowly.

When you don't believe in the paranormal, as I didn't and might even say still don't, such sensations, even if understood in material terms—as something, say, brought on by a mind-altering drug or as distortions of perception caused by powerful suggestion—are very unsettling. Part of you just absents yourself, looks on with curiosity, while whatever "it" is just walks on in.

"What do you see?" Dilys sighed. Somewhere out there in the conservatory, she had put down her teacup and switched on a tape recorder. Though she was silhouetted against the garden window, her features indistinct, I could see that she was watching me. But I also knew she could see nothing. I wondered whether she had put something in my tea. Perhaps that was how she made her money—by stimulating hallucinations. I was quite powerless to refuse her now. Everything here in this conservatory was falling away.

"Give it up," she said somewhere to my left. "Give it up."

I closed my eyes. I remembered that she had done nothing to hypnotise me. I tried to remember that she was half blind, and a friend of Elizabeth's. I could see her tattoo and the pearls around her neck now in the darkness behind my closed eyes, but I could also see flowers unfolding, shapes and shadows passing across the darkness, coming closer. Somewhere there I thought I saw oysters, whites and fringed black edges against the darkness.

"A river," I said. "At least I think it is a river. I can see ripples on the surface of the water. There's a mist along the edge of the water. There are two swans over on the other side where the grass is longer. And a moorhen. It is cold. Dark. I can hear an owl in the trees on the other side of the river."

Not my words. My voice, yes, but not my words. What was I doing here in this conservatory bungalow in Prickwillow with a madwoman, sliding into the crazy place she lived in? Seeing things on a dawn riverbank.

"What is your name?" Dilys's voice was very still and slow, as if she was talking to a child.

"Lydia Brooke. My name is Lydia Brooke."

"No, what is your name?"

"Richard." I didn't even have to hunt for that. I was Richard, answering Dilys's questions.

"Richard?"

"Richard Herring, son of Alderman Herring, the draper."

"Where are you, Richard? Can you tell us what you see?"

"I can't see very much. My eyes hurt. It is dark."

"Where are you?"

"Near the river."

"Near the river?"

"By the river. Between Garret Hostel Bridge and the tennis court. I can't see. I feel sick. I want to go home."

"Where have you been?"

"At the Red Hart in Petticury. Playing dice with the man from London."

"What time of year is it?"

"The eleventh day of November, 1668."

"Have you seen anyone else tonight?" Dilys's voice was gentle and knowing. I had the feeling that she and I had talked like this before. It was a kind of ritual. My part to conceal; hers to open up. A game of cards.

"Master Newton was there in the Red Hart with his friend. He nodded to me, standing tall, his white hair up above the crowd, and then when I looked again he'd gone. I was using Captain Story's money to play dice."

"Did you win?"

"No, I lost the money to Master Newton's friend. And I lost Master Newton's money too."

"Did he have a name—the friend?"

"I'm not supposed to know his name. He changes it. He gave me money."

"For what?"

"I can't tell you that. I am not supposed to tell anyone about that."

Dilys spoke to me as if she knew me, had known me for a long time.

"Did you help Master Newton, Richard? Did you buy things for him? For his potions? Help him in his rooms? With the furnace?"

"Yes. They're not potions. He's a magician. He said I had a gift and he told me secrets. He promised me more secrets."

"Did he give you money to keep you quiet?"

"Yes."

These were leading questions; they would never stand up in a court of law. Court of law? How did that thought drift across my mind? Once I thought of Richard Herring in the dock, being cross-questioned by Dilys Kite in a black gown, once I saw the carved wood, the gallery of men and women watching, I lost the column of blue light. I lost the river tinged with pink and the two men. I lost the dice, the cards, the smell of the smoky tavern, the dawn light. As if someone had turned off the phone, or the light.

How long did we sit there, Dilys and I? I watched the shadows lengthen across her garden, a blackening shadow theatre across the vibrant emerald of her lawn. I watched the honeysuckle tendrils blow in the wind, the soft rain, the late flies, a crow. I was nowhere and somewhere. Lost between a river and the Fens, between the seventeenth century and the twenty-first, between scepticism and belief.

Sixteen

He's gone again," Dilys said somewhere on the other side of the room, but she was not speaking to me. She was with them again, whoever *they* were, her Bible group, the voices in her head.

"She's let him go," she said. "No, no, she *had* to. He won't stay. He never does."

"What was that?" I said. My throat wasn't tight anymore. I wanted to get out of my chair, but I was still cold and my limbs were not yet my own. I clenched my fists, rubbed my hands. Mrs. Kite passed me a glass of water and draped a tartan rug around my shoulders.

"It takes some people hard," she said. "It's not an easy thing—being the road they walk down. You won't want to be doing that too often. It's always the same with the boy. He can't seem to speak for himself. He borrows people."

"Who . . . ?" I could hardly speak.

"That was the boy, Richard Herring, one of the people Elizabeth found. He was the fourth in the series. How did it go? Richard Greswold, James Valentine, Abraham Cowley, and Richard Herring. There's a fifth man, apparently, but we were never quite sure how he fitted in. Funny, you know, I'm not sure that Elizabeth ever knew his name, or if she did, she never told me. She always referred to him simply as the fifth man.

Herring was number four, yes: Greswold—one, Valentine—two, Cowley—three, Herring—four, and then the fifth man."

With Dilys's rounded vowels and clipped consonants, the list sounded like an incantation. I could have sworn that someone sighed somewhere near my right ear as she took out two pieces of paper from a file in front of her, photocopies from a book.

"Elizabeth called it serendipity," she said. "I wouldn't have called it that."

"*What* did she call serendipity?"

"Wait. It's important to get this all in the right order. When did it start? When she was writing the Stourbridge Fair chapter—it must have been last fall, November, perhaps. Elizabeth was in the library going over the eyewitness accounts of Stourbridge Fair in the seventeenth century. Defoe and Pepys, I think, and some others. She was very conscientious about her sources. She had her own facsimile edition of a diary written by a Cambridge alderman in the 1660s that she used as a kind of reference book which was especially good on the fair. She'd taken the diary into the library to photocopy some passages so she could mark them up."

"The diary of an alderman. As in town councillor?"

"Precisely. Alderman Newton. Strange coincidence in the names, eh? Alderman Newton was *Samuel* Newton, no relation as far as I know. Elizabeth put the page she was copying on the photocopier and then pressed the button, but two sheets came out of the machine. Neither of them was the page she had photocopied. She nearly threw them away, but something caught her eye. Each of the two pages, from widely separate parts of the book, parts of the book she'd overlooked, contained a short extract in which Alderman Newton described the death of a Trinity scholar—the death of a Mr. Greswold on the fifth of January, 1665, and of a Mr. Valentine on the ninth of November, 1666. It was the similarity between the two deaths that held Elizabeth's attention to begin with: they had both fallen down staircases in Trinity during the night, apparently drunk."

This account sounded familiar, but I couldn't think why. Something else I had forgotten or was trying to forget. A staircase.

"Not that unlikely really, I suppose," I said. "What with dark staircases and academics drinking too much."

"Yes, that's what I said. But she said there was something in the way Alderman Newton described the deaths that showed that he thought they were suspicious. She knew the diary well enough to know the diarist pretty well. He kept repeating the phrases 'as was thought' or 'as was supposed,' as if he didn't believe the explanation the college had put forward. It didn't mean very much to her—just a coincidence—so she put the two sheets in a file with her other notes. Then she photocopied the section on Stourbridge Fair she wanted—it worked the second time—and she went back and finished writing the Stourbridge Fair section of the book."

"I've read that chapter. It's very good."

"It should be—she read every surviving description of the fair. But she didn't just rewrite the sources. She reconstructed it in her head. She had a gift."

"So what happened about Greswold and Valentine?"

"When she went to look for the two pages in her file a few weeks later, the pages had disappeared. So she started again—on a whim. First, she went back to the bookshelf in her study, but the book was gone. So she went to the University Library, but their copy was listed as missing. So she went to the City Library, found the book in the local history section, though it had been shelved in the wrong place, and spent the best part of an hour searching for them. She'd forgotten their names, of course. When she found them, she photocopied the two passages again. She said it seemed as if she wasn't meant to find them again. And then, of course, she was determined that she would find them."

"And where do you come in?"

"I bumped into her in the library tearooms a month or so later. She told me the whole story. She wasn't usually so—how shall I put it?—unguarded, indiscreet. She was an excellent researcher, but she'd drawn a blank on these two and it was getting to her. There was almost nothing to be found in the Cambridge archives about Greswold and Valentine. Venn had entries for them, of course, but nothing else. Absolutely nothing except the Alderman Newton account and Venn."

"What's Venn?"

"Venn's *Alumni Cantabrigienses*. A list of all the students who have graduated from Cambridge. Goes way back. It gives a short entry for each graduate: date of birth, schools attended, date of graduation, fellowship, father, and family, if known, and date of death, if known—you know the sort of thing. If she hadn't looked so desperate I wouldn't have suggested it . . ."

"What?"

"That she try a less conventional way. I asked her out to Prickwillow, suggested that she try my way. She laughed. She wasn't a believer, you see, though we'd been friends since our university days and she was never rude about what I did. She'd read history, I'd studied English—medieval specialism. Over the years, we'd only ever talked about our research— archives, libraries, and search engines. She was particularly good at checking footnotes. She always checked mine. We avoided talking about what I did. So it was all a bit of a surprise when she said she would."

"What do you write?"

"I'm a biographer. Several articles and short books now. I'm slow. It takes me such a long time to read, with only one good eye. The articles are mostly for the *Spiritualist Inquirer.* Julian of Norwich. Women mystics. That's my forte. So I said to Elizabeth, Come with an open mind. I always have an open mind, she said. She didn't. Very few people do really, though most think they do. Especially academics. It was hard for her to come here."

"What did she come out here *for*?"

"More information. A lead. I suggested that we contact Greswold and Valentine directly to see if they could tell us anything. Give Elizabeth something more to go on. She'd been through all the death records, the annals of the city, all the town records and college records."

"Nothing?"

"No, nothing. Greswold and Valentine died during the plague years, of course, so it's not surprising that the death records are a little patchy and incomplete. She said she had nothing to lose. It seems she had a lot to lose. Poor Elizabeth. She was an unusual woman. A bit aloof some-times, a bit prickly too. But really. All of that shouldn't have happened. It shouldn't. It's a damn shame."

Dilys picked up a bundle of papers, photocopies and other materials, from her table. She pulled out a single sheet, following up on details. "Yes. Greswold," she said. "Fellow of Trinity. Number one in Elizabeth's series. Sometimes called Gresould, with a *u*, sometimes Gressald, with a double *s* and an *a*. He died in January 1665 aged only about twenty-eight years old. James Valentine, fellow of Trinity and professor of Greek. He died on the ninth of November 1666, aged about forty. He's number two in her series."

"Series of what?"

"Suspicious deaths. Five men—Trinity men—died suspiciously within a span of about five years. It starts with Greswold's death in 1665; then Valentine in 1666; then Cowley in 1667; then Herring in 1668 . . ."

"How do Herring and Cowley fit in? How did she find them?"

"Well, we tried to contact Greswold and Valentine and the other two turned up instead."

"The other two?"

"Numbers three and four—except we didn't know they were in the series at all, so we didn't know they were numbers three and four. The poet and the boy. Cowley and Herring."

"What do you mean, just turned up?" I pictured them, poet and boy, pitching up in Prickwillow by coach from London or Cambridge. Ringing Dilys's doorbell, waiting under the wind chimes among the gnomes.

"Here. On the board—the letterboard." She lifted up the lace-and-brocade tablecloth to reveal the corner of a pretty, antique table beneath. The top was a highly polished rosewood and walnut, I'd guess, inlaid with the letters of the alphabet.

"My mother's," Dilys said, smoothing the tablecloth back into place. "Made in Wales around the middle of the nineteenth century. Lovely, eh? A nice bit of inlay. They turned up here, on the letterboard. We were calling up Greswold and Valentine, but it was Cowley and Herring who answered—the glass kept spelling out their names on the board. Over and over. Serendipity. Elizabeth set a lot of store by serendipity. Finding something when you are looking for something else. I wouldn't call it serendipity, of course. Much too chaotic a notion. Too dependent on chance. There are guiding hands at work in the world. You have to have an open mind and you have to empty yourself out and let them show you where to look. Do you have an open mind, Lydia?"

"I don't know," I said. "I really don't know."

"Well, that's a good start," she said, turning her blind eye on me. I hated the way she did that. She must have known what she was doing.

"Cowley and Herring—numbers three and four," I said. "If Greswold and Valentine were the men who fell down the stairs at Trinity, and Herring was the boy in the river, who was Cowley?"

"Abraham Cowley, poet and fellow of Trinity College, one of the founders of the Royal Society in the early 1660s—but Elizabeth always called it—"

"The Invisible College?"

"Precisely. As it was originally called informally. Elizabeth guessed that the Cowley on the board might be Cowley the poet, so she looked him up. Cowley also died in suspicious circumstances in 1667. Aged forty-nine."

"In Cambridge?"

"No, in Chertsey, Surrey. He seems to have been lying low for some reason. He was found asleep in a field near his house—apparently drunk. Died a week or so later on the twenty-eighth of July, 1667. When Elizabeth checked the biography, it seemed he'd had a bad fall two years earlier—in May 1665. He almost died from that fall. If it had killed him in May 1665, he would have been number two in the series."

"So that's how he came to be on Elizabeth's list. A Trinity man who died in suspicious circumstances, though not in Trinity."

"Yes, it seemed Cowley and Herring wanted Elizabeth to know they were part of the sequence too. Or someone did. The apparent drunkenness, the closeness of the dates, the link with Trinity, the fact that Cowley had had a fall that nearly finished him off two years earlier . . . The files," she said, apologetically. "I forgot. I was to give them to you when you came. As a kind of contingency plan."

She put the four bundles of papers back into a pale green file, marked in Elizabeth's handwriting with my name.

"A contingency plan?"

"You are the contingency plan, dear, Elizabeth's contingency plan."

"I am? She *knew* I would come here?"

"Oh yes. Once the seventeenth century had found you, that is. Once *they* had found you. We had expected it to be a little earlier than this. But you are a braver woman than we thought. Living in The Studio for—what is it now?—weeks. Not an easy thing to do."

"What do you mean by brave?"

"You've not seen anything odd?"

"Well, I wouldn't say that. Lots of things have gone missing and there are strange lights that pulse round the house and a number of . . . coincidences."

"Coincidences? You're still calling them coincidences after all this time? If Cameron Brown had any idea what goes on in that house he would never have suggested that you . . . It's most irresponsible."

"How would you explain them, Mrs. Kite?"

"It's all part of what Elizabeth left unfinished. There were people she raised. Things she stirred up. Stories that have to be finished."

"And as her contingency plan, what am I to do? Will finishing the book *un-stir* everything?"

"That, my dear, is a very interesting question. We are beginning to wonder whether finishing the book is a good idea at all. It seems to have got worse since you've been in The Studio. But we do have to do something to stop the repetitions."

"OK. You've lost me now. What repetitions?"

"Elizabeth had a theory and a set of questions about Newton's fellowship and the company he kept and the alchemists he worked with. The deaths seem to fill in some gaps. She had a theory about how those four—or possibly five—men all died . . ."

"Something that involved Newton and the Invisible College?"

"Yes, in a way. You could put it that way. You see, it didn't happen all at once. The facts—or what she came to see as facts, though they can never be proven by methods that rationalists would accept—seemed to find her, rather than she them. Once she had put together those two sheets of paper, the one that described Greswold's death and the other Valentine's, and once she had seen the similarities between them, there was no undoing anything. She said it was a kind of alchemical reaction that seemed to have its own momentum outside her. She had started it and it seemed to need her to work, but it was making . . . *taking* its own way, using her . . ."

"Richard Herring—the boy—was the fourth in the series? How did he die? Did he drown? Was he a Trinity fellow too?"

"No, he wasn't. He was the son of an alderman called John Herring, a draper, who was very important on the city council and had been mayor of the city until the year before his son's death. His son, Richard, got tied up with things alchemical, Elizabeth thought. He drowned at dawn in the river in 1668. Yes, at dawn. It's all in the file. He was the fourth in the series but not the last. But then it's not really possible to talk about beginnings and endings as far as the dead are concerned."

"So Elizabeth came here and you 'called up' Greswold and Valentine? Then Cowley and Herring turned up on the letterboard. What did they tell you?"

"Nothing coherent. That was the trouble. It was all a jumble. We kept a record of everything the spirits told us through the glass on the letterboard. There were references to the Bible, to what we assumed were alchemical texts, initials, and what we assumed were code words, as well as the words *Herring* and *Cowley*. It was all just fragments. We failed to make any sense of it. Elizabeth eventually gave up and went back to the archives to see if the names were significant. She found Cowley pretty quickly."

"How did she find Richard Herring?" I asked. Dilys passed me a sheet of photocopied paper. "It was under her nose. She looked up Herring in Alderman Newton's diary and found this," she said. The photocopy was headed, in Elizabeth's hand, "Richard Herring—fourth in the series" and showed an extract from the diary. Alderman Newton had described the events of the night of Richard Herring's death—the game of dice in the Red Hart, the riverbank walk—events that I had just glimpsed or dreamed in that strange trance:

11th November, 1668. *Wednesday:* Richard Herring the sonne of Alderman Herring draper, did drowne himself as it is thought, betweene 6 and 7 in the morning before it was light between Garrett Hostle Bridge and Trinity Coll Tenniscourt, he had bin at play at dice the night before being Tewsday night at John Dods at the Red Hart in Petticury and lost (as was thought) there with a London gamester, and cheater above 100 which as was thought was the onely reason he offered violence to himselfe, the money was said to be tax money received by him for Captain Story. He was buryed in the South Churchyard of Great St Maryes the same night.

"But," I said, suddenly chilled. "I've never read this."

"Precisely."

"So how . . . ?"

"Oh, it all depends on what you believe. Sceptics would say you have an active imagination or that you have yielded to my powers of suggestion—though I am not quite sure how I might have suggested those particular details. *We* would say that earlier this afternoon you received a spirit who passed through you. You were not hypnotised. Richard Herring is very insistent on using other people to speak for him and to remember for him. He has been very insistent since Elizabeth first came here." She lowered her voice and leaned forward. "He is, frankly, a nuisance."

"How so?"

"He gets in the way of the other spirits. My work is terribly important to the people who come here. I have to speak with those who have passed through to the other side: fathers, sisters, dead children. People rely on me. There are messages to be conveyed backwards and forwards. People get upset very easily and there's so much room for misunderstanding, so one needs the lines to be very clear and one needs to be very tactful. It is all rather delicate. I'm afraid that since Elizabeth first received him, Richard Herring has been more than a nuisance."

"What does he want?"

"He won't say. But he's got much worse since Elizabeth died."

"Don't most ghosts come back for resolution or justice? If they are still around, isn't that because they have unfinished business?"

"That's all a little clichéd, if you don't mind me saying so," said Dilys, mild disappointment in her voice. "And all rather *Catholic*. People who think of spirits as the unquiet dead, well, that's all based on very old-fashioned notions of a place called limbo. We don't like to call them ghosts. Smacks too much of white sheets and chains. Marley's ghost. Spirits is a better way of thinking about them. Spirits make contact for all sorts of reasons."

"But revenge might be one of them?"

"Oh yes. Revenge is an important motive for many of them. I wish it weren't so. But there you have it. You have to work with what you've got."

I scanned the report of Herring's death again. The details were all so vivid: the Red Hart in Petticury, the dice, the tax money, the boy drowned at dawn. "Might Herring have been drugged and then drowned?" I asked. "Is it possible that the card game was a smoke screen, an attempt to make it look like suicide? If Herring was murdered for whatever reason, wouldn't he have a motive for revenge? Wouldn't that be reason enough for him to come back?"

"Yes, but if we are being detectives, then surely we're looking at either Newton or his friend as possible suspects, if only because they are the people Herring saw at the Red Hart just before his death."

"But, Mrs. Kite, we can't be detectives with evidence like this, based on communion with the dead. Nor can ghosts be suspects. Not in twenty-first-century law in any case . . . You talked about repetitions. What repetitions?"

"Elizabeth rang me on the sixth of January to tell me that the dates of the deaths of Greswold, Valentine, Cowley, and Herring had begun to coincide with another series. She was very agitated. Felt responsible, she said."

"Coincided with what?"

"Elizabeth had noticed two deaths last year very close to each other in Chesterton: on the ninth and eleventh of November. Two street drinkers found dead, one at the bottom of a car-park staircase, the other drowned in the Cam, a suspected suicide. She'd noticed the coincidence of the dates but hadn't thought any more about it. Then on the fifth of January this year there was another death by falling in Cambridge—a young man who fell down a staircase in a local hostel."

"Christ. The dates coincide. OK. And what did she make of it?"

"She said she thought it was a warning of some kind—a warning to her to stop investigating. I think someone violent was trying to contact her from the other side, drawing attention to the dates. But she kept on going just the same, all through the spring and into the early summer. We tried calling them up again, and Elizabeth kept on taking down all the combinations of words and fragments of things that came up on the board. Then she told me one day in the library that she'd been in contact with a Mr. F. She wouldn't name him—said it was too dangerous, but she said he knew things about the Trinity deaths. Then on the twenty-eighth of July there was another death—another young man from the same hostel found dead in one of the stretches of grass near Trinity; a heroin overdose, they said. The police started an investigation, and in a few weeks they'd shut the hostel down."

"The twenty-eighth of July—the date of Cowley's death?"

"Exactly. Elizabeth was frantic. She was convinced there was a connection between her research and the deaths, that it was her fault in some way. The police weren't investigating—they didn't see anything suspicious. There was a big fuss in the papers about drug cultures and street drinkers, and people were campaigning to have the hostels shut down. When Elizabeth rang me after the July death, she said she'd decided to burn all her papers. I told her to wait. I wish I hadn't. She wouldn't say anything else. She said she didn't want to put me in danger. I was worried, so I went to see her. She wasn't in. Then I went away in August to a convention in Scotland. At the beginning of September she left a message on my answer phone saying she'd finished the book. But by the time I got back, it was too late. She died on the seventh of September. Cameron found her three days later."

Something over to my left. A shadow in a doorway. The outline of a man, his face illuminated from the left. The light touches only the white of his shoulder-length hair, the sheen of his forehead, the side of his lip, which curls faintly with a tincture of malevolence; dark shadows fall across all the rest. He passes in red through the open space between the two sides of the door frame and then is gone.

"Well, my dear. You are up to your neck in this now. Nothing you can do about it. One thing at a time. There will be a suspicious death in Cambridge in the early hours of Wednesday morning, the ninth of November, the date of Valentine's death, then again two days later, on the eleventh of November, the date of Herring's death. I will stake my reputation upon it. Unless we can do something before then. There's been a death on each of the dates since Elizabeth started investigating."

"How do we stop it?"

"I have absolutely no idea."

"And the fifth man? The fifth in the series."

"He's gone missing from the files."

"Who was he?"

"We never knew. Elizabeth found him somewhere in some archive or other. She only told me that he was a fellow at Trinity, sent down in 1666, one of the two plague years. But she never told me his name."

"Sent down?"

"Insanity, Elizabeth said. She'd found a reference in some Trinity archive or other, but it's disappeared. I've been through everything. It happens. Elizabeth considered him to be the fifth in the series, but I'm not sure why. There's no way of finding out now—not without a name anyway."

Bring something that belongs to him, Dilys Kite had said. The prism. Newton's prism. Why would Elizabeth, conservative, law-abiding, reclusive Elizabeth, have stolen a glass prism, least of all from a museum, unless something very important depended upon it? She and Dilys had already spoken to Newton, then, drawing him in with his own prism, despite the fact that Dilys said it was too dangerous.

Seventeen

One night snow began to fall. Will and I were sitting in the window seat in The Studio watching the snow powder the trees and rose-bushes in the garden when she began to tell me a story about being stuck with her grandfather on a broken-down train in a snowstorm between Norwich and Littleport when she was fifteen. Her grandfather, she said, who ran a butcher's shop in Norwich, was taking her home to her parents. She didn't want to go. Sometime in that void of whitened and blizzarded time he told her a story about blood and snow. Back in the forties, he said, after the war, he'd given up his job at the Smithfield meat market for a job at a small abattoir in Norfolk, right out in the middle of the fields, near Littleport. He wanted to find a place to settle down and start a family, now that he'd met Elsie, Will's grandmother.

They built abattoirs in the fields then, he said, so that the local farmers could plough the blood straight back into the soil. Will winced when she described what she imagined as a glistening mixture of black soil and red-brown blood, but, she said, her grandfather insisted that the blood was good for the crops. Potent. And what else were they supposed to do with it? he said. You couldn't just flush it into the drains.

Eventually, once he'd found his feet in the new job, Elsie took the train from London to see him, turning up at the Littleport Station in a snowstorm with her dog, a white terrier. Frank took her for eel and chips in the village pub and then they set out across the fields to walk in the snow. It was, he said, one of those perfect winter days—imagine, he said, white fields under a lowering and white sky, broken only by the spires of a few churches on the horizon and the cross-hatching of hedgerows, dusted white. He took Elsie diagonally across the field towards the setting sun. He had a question to ask her.

Elsie kissed him in the middle of the field. It was when he opened his eyes after that kiss, he told the fifteen-year-old Will, that he saw the blood on Elsie's boots, but it was too late to stop his question or her expectation of it. It had to be asked. In front of them the landscape was so beautiful that it hurt to look at it, he said. Behind them, like a chain connecting them to the gate through which they had passed and where she had kissed him, two sets of red footprints in the snow punctured the whiteness. The farmer had sprayed blood onto already frozen fields the day before and, unable to plough the blood into the frozen soil, had taken himself home. Then the snow had fallen in the night to cover the blood. Their small steps that afternoon had been enough to melt the thin snow and bring the blood to the surface.

"I've never been able to get that picture out of my head," Will said. "The fields were bleeding. Can you imagine that? My grandmother and grandfather were standing out there alone in all that blood and he was about to ask her to marry him. And then my grandmother laughed," Will said. "She just laughed at the line of blood in the snow, laughed at her dog now stained red and barking, at his boots and her boots, thick with coagulated blood. And then she said, 'Yes, I'll marry you.' He hadn't even asked her, he said. My grandmother was like that—she always seemed to know what you were thinking before you'd even thought it yourself.

"Think of the number of animal lives," she said, "that it must have taken to produce enough blood to cover a field, not just once but again and again, enough for radishes and spinach and beets to grow fat on. There's slaughter everywhere," Will said, "deep in the soil, infecting the whole food chain. My grandmother and grandfather could live with that—they had to. He went straight from all the slaughter of Smithfield to the war and back to Smithfield and then to the abattoir near Littleport. She was a nurse. You just washed it away, Elsie said, when Will asked her about the blood. You used bleach and chemicals and strong soaps and the best twin tubs and you just washed all that blood out of his white and striped cotton aprons and her blue uniforms. Blood comes out. You just don't think about it.

"I never went there," Will said. "To the abattoir. Though I dreamed about it a lot when I was a kid. Still do. Maybe it would have been better to see it for myself. They've knocked it down now. Does it ever go away, though, do you think? All that blood? My grandfather came back from the war and spent the rest of his life killing animals and selling meat. How many animals did my grandfather slaughter in his lifetime, would you guess? Ten thousand? Twenty thousand? Could you ever wash all that blood away?

"That's what it's like up there on the Black Fen," Will went on. "Since the Romans and the Dutchmen came, people have spent all that time draining that land so that they can use it, plough their fields and lay their railways, but the water is only ever a few inches or feet below the surface, like the blood welling up around the abattoir. My grandfather has a picture of the floods at Littleport in 1939 just as the war was about to break. There's a train brought to a standstill and a man standing on the track surrounded by water. To me it looks like blood," she said. "An ocean of blood. A tide." She pulled her feet into the window seat, rested her head on the window frame, and closed her eyes.

And that same marsh lies down there, I thought, watching Will's face in repose, down there under the weight of Cambridge stone and quadrangle and manicured lawns. Waiting. Inscrutable. Like Conrad's jungle. Biding its time before it rises to take its revenge upon its oppressor. Lying close. The city of reason may have declared all that lies beyond rational knowledge to be obsolete, but it hasn't gone away; it's just slipped into the unconscious, down there into the water table. Lying low. The gardeners have to keep the marsh at bay by perpetually trimming the hedges and peeling back the ivy from the stone. T. S. Eliot knew about the malevolence of water too:

> . . . the brown god is almost forgotten
> By the dwellers in cities—ever, however, implacable,
> Keeping his seasons and rages, destroyer, reminder
> Of what men choose to forget. Unhonoured, unpropitiated
> By worshippers of the machine, but waiting, watching and waiting.

Will had fallen asleep in the window seat; from the armchair I saw her closely cropped head fall forward slightly and her lips part as her breathing deepened. The story had unsettled me, but so had the way she told it. I was beginning to understand something.

As I sat watching Will sleep, wondering about her, I knew I was being watched. I turned to look through the window and saw a man with white hair standing near the apple tree closest to the window, looking in, lit only by the light that fell from behind me. He appeared so much closer than before that as I met his gaze, his nearness made me catch my breath and turn cold. There was a terrible intimacy in his appearing there in The Studio garden; it was an alarmingly forward stride for him, I felt. He was the same—the white hair, the curl of the lip—and seen only, this time, as I had seen him before, from the waist up, the window blocking the rest of the view. And, also as last time, it was as if he had rubbed through from somewhere else because, though the snow fell heavy and slow in the garden and across everything, it did not fall across his thin figure or the space in which he stood. And behind him people seemed to be moving in sepia inside a kind of oval frame with smudged edges, crossing and recrossing. I couldn't see whole figures, just the edge of a gown or part of a face—smoke too, grey smoke softening the edges of the moving figures. Among the trees, in the slanting snow.

He stood there looking in at me only for a few seconds—long enough to convince me that he also saw and recognised me. It was the strangest sensation, as if I had been looking at him for years and had known him always. Though he fixed me with his gaze, I watched as his eyes wandered, picking out various objects in the room behind me: the manuscript on the table, the shelves and boxes of papers. I was suddenly quite sure that it was not for me he had come. He was looking at Elizabeth's manuscript.

I gasped, suddenly angry and territorial, rising from my chair towards him, kneeling on the window seat, pressing my face and hand to the pane of glass which clouded up instantly; I wished I could pull a curtain across the glass to shut him out. Will woke, startled by the noise and movement I had made and, seeing me staring out into the garden, turned slowly to look at whatever it was behind her that had frightened me. All we could now see of the orchard was empty with a great emptiness. Will turned back to look at me. My face and expression had shocked her.

"Fuck. You look awful. What's happened?" Her hand tightened on mine as she followed the line of my gaze. "What is it?"

"I thought I saw something in the garden," I said. "Spooked myself. It's just the snow—plays tricks with your eyes."

"Jesus, you frightened me," she said, looking at her watch. "It's so late. How could I have fallen asleep like that?" She paused, dragging her fingers across her face to wake herself up. "You OK now?"

I nodded.

"Look," she said. "I'm going to have to go away for a while. I came to say good-bye."

"You'll be back?"

"Oh yes, I hope so. Depends on what happens over the next few weeks."

"How long?"

"Could be a week or a month. Probably not any longer. And I've arranged for someone to keep an eye out for you."

"An eye on *me*? Why?"

"Because you're caught up in something complicated and it might be dangerous. I can't explain because I'm not allowed to and because I can't just give you bits—I'd have to explain it all."

"To do with Elizabeth's manuscript?"

"No, absolutely nothing to do with all of that. Something very un–seventeenth century. Now go to bed and don't think about it. I'll be back as soon as I can."

Don't think about it? How was I supposed to do that? I had only just begun to think . . . as if for the first time.

Eighteen

I imagined you turning over the words you texted me as you wrote them, trying them on your tongue, writing them, erasing, and beginning again. Texts passed backwards and forwards between us, weaving through days and nights. Word associations, fragments, lines of poems. In that delicate exchange of words did you feel, as I did, the grinding of the stone, the disaggregation of stone to powder, the beginning of the process practised, rarefied, and perfected over hundreds of years in those hot Italian courtyards? I could feel the touch of white powder that day, smell the soda and the silica as I climbed into your bed that night and all those long nights that followed.

The day after I saw the man in the garden, I placed myself behind the thickly book-lined and high-windowed walls of a great library, beyond his gaze. Your words reached me there, travelling invisibly through the Cambridge air from your laboratory to my library. Was that text an act of impetuosity or of calculation? My days were already bookended by your enigmatic messages, which would arrive in the morning as, I imagined, you made your way to the lab and in the evening as you took yourself to bed. The text that reached me in the library that day read: "Your presence is immanent today—you seem to be hanging in the air I walk through."

Hanging in your air. I thought of you typing out those words on your mobile phone in the shadowless halogen-lit white air of your lab. Different worlds, one infinitely measured, a world of tests and reports, the other, mine, seeping and borderless, a place of inferences, guesses, half-truths, and shadows. I thought of the phrases you used in your lab, those you had used to explain your work to me: terms like *cognitive dysfunction, burst firing of brain cells, dampening of emotional responses, potentiation.* Potentiation: to increase potency by using two or more drugs in combination. Potency. Potentiation. The vowels rise and fall. Yet in the hard white edges of your lab you could write that I seemed to be hanging in the air you walked through.

I did not reply, could not reply to those words. Phrases came and went, reordered themselves. I wrote several and then erased them. I couldn't think. I wanted to take your words in. How was I hanging? Like a spider on a single thread of its own making or like a woman hanged for a crime or like a torture victim or a slab of curing meat or, or, like mist rising from a river . . . ? Hanging. Hanging on. Hanging in. Hanging fire. Hanging up.

I wondered how far you would go with this most dangerous of risks, where the limits would be. I could feel limits here, gratefully cocooned in the University Library: beginnings and endings, chronologies, dates and facts and reference books, like consonants holding the vowels in place. But, like Elizabeth, you always had to push on through the limits, didn't you, find what the library didn't hold, knowledge that had never been framed in a paragraph or footnote. What else might you do if you were desperate enough? How far would we go—Elizabeth, Cameron, Isaac, and Lydia—to know, to really know, to bring the invisible into visibility? Faustus travelled to every corner of the globe in his hunger for knowledge. Alone with his Mephistopheles, tempted and desperate, he came to trade with spirits; he was prepared to trade his own soul for knowledge forbidden to the living.

I packed up my books and papers and drove home along Queen's Road, which they call the Backs, because it follows the river northwards on the outside of the city, curling up and around the colleges. On the other side of the river, through the trees to my right, the colleges were already flattening in the twilight against the sky. Trinity lay over there behind the trees with its secrets perfectly sealed away.

"All you have to do is turn your phone off," I said out loud to myself, over the sound of the radio. I turned the phone off, and at the next set of traffic lights I turned it on again. I could not sever the connection, not now. I was lost in a labyrinth and the phone, your voice, might be the only thread between me and the world outside. I might need it. Yes, I had come to need you—again. "Yes, everything is immanent now, translucent," I wrote, framing another untruth. *Send.*

And what did you believe? What were you hunting?

"What are you working on now?" I'd asked while we were driving back from the restaurant on the coast on the night of my birthday—the 25th of October. You had to look at me then, decide whether my question was motivated by interest or politeness. You would not answer me until your gaze had determined the degree of integrity in my question.

"Morazapine," you said, just one word. And I thought of marzipan being rolled out on marble slabs, silken-wrapped packages of frankincense and myrrh carried in leather cases on the steaming sides of camels travelling through deserts under starlit skies. "Morazapine. It's an antipsychotic drug," you said, "that ameliorates severe cognitive dysfunction."

"What does that mean?" I asked, impatiently. "Translate."

"You don't need me to translate, Lydia. OK. OK. It keeps people on the right side of sanity. The tests have been incredibly successful, but we don't know *how* it works. We have an idea though."

"If it works, isn't that enough?"

You quoted Wittgenstein at me: " 'What we cannot talk about must be consigned to silence,' " you said. "It's never enough to know that it works; we have to be able to say *how* it works, must raise that dripping thing from silence and name it, drag it into words. And with Morazapine, it's . . . difficult . . . virtually impossible."

"And what's *your* theory? What words have you gathered to explain it?"

"My theory? *Our* theory; I work on a team. You *really* want to know?" You drew breath before you began, tripping out the words from your reports: "We think that Morazapine works by burst-firing a part of the brain called the locus coeruleus and that, in turn, creates noradrenergic projections to the prefrontal cortex and hippocampus . . . You asked," you said, when I raised my eyebrows. "You did ask."

So strange to me, that language of yours, that language of disembodied brains, so that when you talked I pictured brains of different sizes, stripped of their species, faces, skulls, and sinews, lined up and attached to pumps of differing chemicals.

"How do you go about proving something like that?" I asked. Outside, the moon silhouetted the trees along the sides of the road. There were rabbits in the hedgerows.

"Thousands of small tests and experiments," you said. "Some with people but mostly with rats. We use pumps planted inside the rats' bodies to release the Morazapine in different doses, and then we test their reactions by using behavioural neuroscience to set up scores of different working-memory tasks using mazes. Then we use computerised confocal microscopes to watch what's happening inside slices of their brain-stem cells as the different levels of chemical take effect."

What would my brain-stem slice have looked like in Mrs. Kite's conservatory—hypnotised? I wondered. Would Richard Herring's presence have been visible? What colour would it have been?

I saw you there in the brilliant white of your lab surrounded by brains of rats and humans pumped with chemicals. You asking carefully phrased questions in those lab meetings with your precious team. You waking and walking in the night with more questions, infinite gradations of the first. *Aggregate, disaggregate, transmutate.* How far could a neuroscientist see? Rats and human brains reduced to brain-stem-coloured patterns on a screen— was a slice of rat-brain colouration very different from that of a human when you were tracing the burst-firing patterns of your chemical? You would look at these, I knew, for hours at a time, investigating minute differences between one pattern and another, extrapolating, interpreting.

"Surely," I said, "your microscope can't see everything that's happening in the brain? Surely there's more in heaven and earth than in your image analysis. How do you explain what happened to us, for instance, in those first months after we became lovers? Science can't explain that."

"Oh that? The way we started doing the same things, unconsciously? The way we used to wake at exactly the same second every morning, miles apart, as if one of us was waking the other—even if there was a hundred miles between us? That weird synchronicity. The radar?"

"Yes, and the way we used to see the same things with our eyes closed when we were making love, as if we'd become the same pair of eyes. How does a neuroscientist explain that?" As I was speaking, a white owl, disturbed by the car wheels, abandoned its carrion in the hedgerow and flew across the road in front of our car in a great unfurling blur of white against the night. You put your foot on the brake.

"Jesus. Did you see its eyes? Look. You forget. As a neuroscientist I'm up against the edge of what's known all the time. Every new thing we map or understand brings a whole new set of unknowns with it. Science is really unsettling. Take quantum mechanics. The theory was so weird that Schrödinger, one of the founders, famously said, 'I don't like it and I'm sorry I had anything to do with it.' In the quantum world particles can be in two places at once, they disappear for no reason, and even act differently depending on whether we're watching them or not."

"Like ghosts."

"Yes, and that weird connectedness we've always had is just a replay of one of the big mysteries in quantum mechanics. They—Schrödinger and Einstein and now Reznik, Ghosh, Vedral—they use the same word for it that you use: *entanglement.*"

"Entanglement? You're serious? *Entanglement* is a word used in quantum mechanics?"

"You've not heard of it? Schrödinger called it the defining trait of quantum theory. Einstein called it *spukhafte Fernwirkungen*—spooky action at a distance. For him it *was* spooky. *Spukhafte.* Isn't that a great word?"

"And what does it mean?"

"Well, what they discovered is easy enough to explain; explaining how it works is almost impossible." As you concentrated, searching for translations and metaphors, the car slowed down to around fifty miles per hour on that narrow empty road heading west across the Fens. At midnight, I was now more awake than I had been all day. You began. "They discovered that when two subatomic particles—that's photons, electrons, or qubits—collide or interact and then move apart, they retain a kind of connection even if they're at opposite ends of the universe. They have become entangled."

"What kind of connection?"

"It's incredible. If one of them changes the direction of its spin, the other will do so too—*simultaneously,* even if they're light-years apart, at opposite ends of the universe."

"How does that explain what happened to us?"

"It doesn't. At least not directly. But if quantum entanglement controls chemical processes, it must also have some effect on biological processes. When we talk about the chemistry between two people, aren't we really talking about a kind of quantum entanglement?"

"Two light particles mirroring each other's movements at opposite sides of the universe. Yes, that's beautiful. A kind of shadowing."

"And the weirdest thing of all is that some theoretical physicists are beginning to speculate that entanglement might happen between moments in time too."

"How?"

"If moments in time become entangled in the same way that photons become entangled, then there might be strange connections between the past and the present, moments in time acting in the same way, like the particles; one moment turns one way, the other follows—shadowing. And that's mind-blowing. See, I'm a rationalist who believes in a supernatural world, because I live in it. Science doesn't reduce things, or explain mysteries away; it just discovers stranger and stranger things. And that rationalist once made love to a writer who absolutely didn't believe in the supernatural, and they became—entangled. Now, how did that work?"

"It didn't work," I said. "Don't you remember?"

"You remember what you like," you said. "Your story about us will always be different from mine."

And Newton's way? Like Elizabeth three hundred years later, Newton failed to separate the natural from the supernatural, the material world from the spiritual. Failed? No, he refused. He actually saw no separation. Those exact moments of judgement—when to stop a process of distillation, the reading of "signs," the delicate blending of alchemical proportions, the separating out of light—he believed that all of these moments depended on the purity of the philosopher's spirit, for the philosopher was like a glass through which the spirits passed. One couldn't separate the experiment from the experimenter. Just as a glass that was flecked or bubbled or stained would always distort results, so would the spirit of the experimenter if it was stained or flecked. The philosopher must be a pure medium, as transparent as the glass of Murano. Yes, for Newton the material and the spiritual worlds were a continuum. Without purity and knowledge of what was invisible to others, an alchemist would be a mere chemist, a potion maker.

Elizabeth, also a wanderer in the spirit world, saw her meagre reflection in the works of the irascible, hungry philosopher she pursued. And through her visits to Dilys Kite, Newton's way became Elizabeth Vogelsang's way—she came to believe that there was no distinction or binary between the knowable and the unknowable, just a spectrum, different ways of knowing, which, in the world in which she moved, constituted a range of legitimate and illegitimate knowledges. Newton the alchemist would not have laughed at the techniques of Mrs. Kite, reaching out to the spirit world for facts not recorded in this world. He would not have marvelled at the way in which spirits moved among the ornaments and lace of her conservatory. That was the point, wasn't it? The unseen moved among the seen. Elizabeth understood Newton's fascination with alchemy. Unlike Sam Westfall, she did not seek to make it disappear. She was an alchemist too. Like Newton, she had conversed with spirits so as to reach for a knowing that was beyond words. " 'Tis strange," says Banquo to Macbeth, that "to win us to our harm,/The instruments of darkness tell us truths,/Win us with honest trifles, to betray us/In deepest consequence."

Nineteen

I poured myself a glass of wine and spread out all the pieces of Elizabeth's evidence from the file that Dilys Kite had given me on the table in The Studio. Outside, a low autumn sun picked out single skeins of spiders' webs floating across the garden, like the faintest tetherings upon the house, set loose, as if the house itself could be lifted by this perfect luminosity. Light pulsed around the spaces above me, moving like water. I had long since given up searching for the source of the water that seemed to be reflected across every wall, just as I had given up looking for the source of the sound of water dripping far off and echoing as if in ancient tombs. There was no water for light to reflect in The Studio. No sink left full and projected by sunlight onto a ceiling. Nothing. I had learned to live with the radiant poolings in The Studio, come to take them for granted. It had its fascinations—light that made fire, or water, or ovoid shapes that twisted and pulled themselves into crystalline jewelled angles, stretching, sharding, undulating, and yawning wide across those great white spaces.

Was there a rational explanation to be scratched out of all these mirages, apparitions, lost files, and coincidences? If so, it would be found somewhere in *The Alchemist* or in the file Dilys had given me, or in the lost Vogelsang Papers. I looked at the mass of typewriting and newspaper print in Dilys's file. Here it all was; somewhere here on this table. Elizabeth had formed the hypothesis that sat at the heart of her book *with these materials.*

What had Elizabeth Vogelsang come to think? The papers in the file showed that she had formed several hypotheses in the last year of her research—nothing spelled out, just *implied* by the way she had grouped her source materials.

The first hypothesis was easy. She believed that a sequence of four, perhaps five deaths that took place in seventeenth-century Cambridge, mostly in or near Trinity College in the 1660s, *were connected and were suspicious*. In this bundle of papers Elizabeth had included the photocopied accounts of two of the deaths from Alderman Newton's diary, those of Greswold and Valentine, the two Trinity fellows who fell down Trinity staircases apparently drunk. The third death—Abraham Cowley, another Trinity fellow—took place in London and was also characterised by apparent intoxication; the fourth, also described by Alderman Newton—Richard Herring, by drowning—I had already read. Alderman Newton's reports of the deaths of Greswold and Valentine did indeed show that he regarded them as suspicious, or at least to my mind:

January 5th 1665: *Thursday*. This morning being a great frost Mr Greswold Master of Arts and Fellow of Trinity Coll in Cambr. fell downe the stayres wch are next the chappell north by the Kings gate, and with the fall was killed, being found dead there lyeing, (about 5 in the morning by the bed makers) and was cold and stiff, he had the key of the garden dore in his hand and lay with his head downwards at the feet of the stayres and his heels upwards upon the stayres, with his neck (as was supposed) choked with his high coller, some bloud had come out of his nose, being seene on his band. Humfry Prychard the coll porter lett him into the coll about 2 of the clock that morning and was supposed to have bin drinking somewhere, and having bin as was supposed through the garden at the house of easement at hys retourne goeing up the said stayres to his chamber fell downe and was killed as aforesaid. *(p. 8)*

Alderman Newton recorded James Valentine's death nearly two years later:

November 2nd 1666: On Fryday night about 11 of the clock Mr James Valentine goeing out of his chamber downe the Stayres into Trinity Colledge

Court, gott such a fall that for a good space he lay as dead and bruised and cutt his head and blead much, and its feared much that he will not recover it. Mr Valentine dyed of this hurt on Wednesday/Thursday morning being the 9th November 1666. *(p. 16)*

Elizabeth's second hypothesis was that there was a connection between these suspicious deaths in the 1660s, Newton, and a group of alchemists working in Cambridge, including a man referred to only as Mr. F., whom she had found reference to in Newton's notebooks. This was scandalous—Newton implicated in murder—but certainly within the realm of the rationally possible. She hadn't *proved* Newton's involvement: the bundle of papers here—her attempt to gather proof—contained only scraps and snippets that documented Newton's violent temperament. On one sheet of paper, Elizabeth—speculating—had copied out numbers 13 to 15 and number 40 from Newton's list of sins, recorded back in 1662:

13. *Threatning my father and mother Smith to burne them and the house over them*
14. *Wishing death and hoping it to some*
15. *Striking many*
40. *Using unlawful means to bring us out of distresses*

This bundle also included descriptions of mysterious fires that had taken place in Trinity in or around Newton's rooms between 1662 and 1677—Elizabeth clearly saw a connection between Newton's threat to burn his mother and stepfather and their house and these subsequent fires. The first was a description of a fire in Trinity Chapel on Advent Sunday on the 30th of November 1662, in which the altar was completely burned away; the second an account of a fire in Trinity Old Library between Michaelmas and Christmas in 1665; and the third a report by a student of St. Johns called Abraham de la Prynne of a fire in Newton's rooms sometime in 1677:

In a winter morning, leaving [his manuscript of his book on optics]
amongst his other papers on his study table, whilst he went to chapel, the
candle which he had unfortunately left burning there too cachd hold by
some means or other of some other papers, and there fired the aforesaid

*book, and utterly consumed it and several other valuable writings, and
that which is more wonderful did no further mischief. But when Mr
Newton came from chapel and had seen what was done, every one thought
he would have run mad, he was so troubled thereat that he was not himself
for a month after.*

A further sheet of paper described Newton's famous breakdown in the
summer of 1692, when he became paranoid and consumed with violent
feelings and during which he may have set fire to his lodgings. On this
sheet, Elizabeth had copied out two short extracts from letters Newton
had written at that time—to indicate his state of mind, I assumed. In September, 1692, Newton sent a letter to Samuel Pepys in London in which
he wrote:

*I am extremely troubled by the embroilment I am in and have neither ate
nor slept well this twelve month, nor have my former consistency of mind.*

Three days later he wrote to John Locke:

*Being of the opinion that you endeavoured to embroil me wth woemen &
by other means I was so much affected with it as that when one told me you
were sickly & would not live I answered 'twere better if you were dead. I
desire you to forgive me.*

So Newton had violent fantasies and suffered from attacks of madness
and paranoia. Not enough to implicate him in murder, surely?

The third of Elizabeth's hypotheses was *not* rationally plausible, or not
in any way that I could formulate. In the last months before she died, Elizabeth came to believe that a series of deaths that had taken place in Cambridge since she'd started investigating were connected in some way with
the seventeenth-century murders. This bundle in the file was made up of
a series of press cuttings from the *Cambridge Evening News,* short records
about four deaths that had taken place on one of her four dates: January
5th (Greswold), July 28th (Cowley), November 9th (Valentine), and November 11th (Herring). This hypothesis seemed to be significant only in
that it revealed the extent of Mrs. Kite's influence and the paranoid and

delusional state of Elizabeth's mind just before her death. What had she thought? That these deaths were somehow being replayed for her, either to warn her off or to lead her in a particular direction in her investigation?

The final hypothesis was also a mere speculation. On a photocopy of Alderman Newton's account of Richard Herring's drowning Elizabeth had circled the date and had written underneath: "Almost two years to the day since James Valentine died on 9 November 1666."

What was the connection between the deaths by falling of two Trinity fellows, Greswold and Valentine, and the death by drowning of the son of the draper and former mayor almost exactly two years later? The boy Richard Herring had drowned in the river only a few hundred feet from the spot where Greswold and Valentine had fallen to their deaths. The answer was there in Elizabeth's notes. She had written a single word underneath the account of Richard Herring's death, accompanied by a question mark: "Blackmail?" Of course, I thought, beginning to see the thought that had formed in Elizabeth's mind. Elizabeth had come to believe that Herring had been involved in the Trinity deaths. As the son of a draper, he had perhaps been employed in the college in some way, as a porter or cook or a delivery boy. Offered enough money by a third party, might the servant boy have acted as a poisoner? At some point Elizabeth had attached the question "Blackmail?" to Richard Herring's name. Herring had enough power in 1668, two years after Valentine's death—to attempt blackmail of an unknown "third party," an act of such consequence as to make his death inevitable.

A final scrap of paper, torn from one of Elizabeth's notebooks, I assumed, began with a name and a question mark:

Mr. F.? Newton refers to Mr. F. in his notebooks as a man who supplied him with alchemical manuscripts. Who was he?

This page must have been a record of the beginnings of Elizabeth's speculations about the mysterious Mr. F. She had spent the last few weeks of her life searching for him; she must have found out more than this. He might have been the man in Newton's company in the Red Hart in Petticury, the night the boy Richard Herring died—but that was speculation too. Elizabeth had also told Dilys that she'd seen Mr. F. in the weeks before her death. She had actually seen him. If she had discovered his identity, she had left no record. Elizabeth's pursuit of this question had been interrupted by her death.

Twenty

At midnight on the 2nd of November I let the file drop to the floor over the edge of the bed and fell into a series of confused dreams in which I and a number of people, all of us dressed in black, burned down your house with you in it. You had to see me do it. I could make out your silhouetted frame behind the flickering window, pressed up against it, you inside, me outside. I woke suddenly, covered in sweat and swollen with rage, the smell of burning still in my nostrils and the word *embroilment* on my lips.

Embroilment. Newton had written about embroilment and madness in letters to John Locke and Samuel Pepys, just as he lost his edges. "You endeavoured to embroil me," he wrote.

The woman in the mirror is also embroiled. She knows that. She has known that for some time.

Transitive verb, *embroiled, embroiling, embroils.* 1. to involve in argument, contention, or hostile actions 2. to throw into confusion or disorder, entangle— from Old French *embrouiller,* to throw into confusion.

How to describe one of those dreams that soon becomes so familiar that I struggle to remember how one was distinguished from the next? Only by degrees of force, like volume of sound.

It did not surprise me, then, that when I woke in the middle of the night from that dream and walked to the window, I saw you on the river-bank. I didn't recognise you at first, but I was not afraid of the outside; out there the world seemed benign and uninhabited. It was your frame that I recognised, your silhouetted bulk against the faintly illuminated water, looking across the river to the scrubland on the other side, Stour-bridge Fair, where a few cows cast long shadows. Did you feel my eyes on your back?

Eyes on the back of the neck. I've read about that. No, *you* told me about it. "Given how much research has been done on the brain and how it works," you said, "it's amazing how little work has been done on the mind. People don't even know *where* it is." Your theory was that the mind was a kind of force field. It was "out there," all around us, not inside our heads, like the brain. Our minds reach out to touch what we are looking at, you said. So that's why people can feel someone's gaze on the back of their neck as a touch. It's such common knowledge in the world of sur-veillance that security guards and intelligence officers are trained not to look directly at a subject's back when they are in pursuit. One of your se-curity men had told you that, you said. One of the men employed at enor-mous cost to watch over you, in that house.

That night, Cameron Brown, I began to feel a new kind of power. I touched the back of your neck with my eyes from your mother's bedroom window, through the rain, and made you turn towards me. I watched you turn briefly towards the house, glance up at the upper windows, follow the line of the roof there. But you couldn't see me up in Elizabeth's bed-room in the dark, so you turned back towards the river.

I determined not to be stirred by your presence or by the passing through of those who, like you, would embroil me. *You are the road they walk down,* Mrs. Kite had said. I climbed back into bed and pulled the sheets up over my head. I turned off the phone, then turned it back on again. You might text me, after all. When I went back to the window you were still standing there, your back to me, but the rain was heavier now and your body was hunched and stiff against the cold. You did not move.

I pulled on a raincoat over my nightgown. In the kitchen, where I checked that Pepys's bowls were still standing by the back door so that you would not notice his absence, I poured a glass of whisky into a heavy tumbler and walked through the rain to you. We said nothing, but instead we stood together watching the rain making intersecting circles on the moonlit water. I passed you the tumbler of whisky, which you took from me and drank.

"Come in from the rain," I said.

"I'm glad you've come back," you said, looking away, across the river, hiding your face. "You don't know how it was. Don't go away again."

"There are no happy endings for us," I said. "Just a scattered present. It's always been like that. It's enough, more than enough. But let's not think about futures or make promises."

The moon made a path to Stourbridge Fair across the water.

"There were prostitutes, puppets, and acrobats," I said, "across there during the fair. There are plague victims buried across there too, down there, under the scrub. Bones girt about with buttons and oyster shells and all the detritus of the fair."

"Are they still down there?" you asked. "Does the earth ever give them up?"

"Who? What?"

"A friend of mine has been attacked. He's in the hospital."

"A friend of yours?"

"Emmanuel Scorsa. He works with me at the lab. A young Italian neuroscientist with a fellowship—from Milan. Someone or some people attacked him in Cambridge this evening, in St. Edward's Passage. I've just come from Addenbrooke's. He's in a coma lying on a life-support machine. I hardly recognised him."

We stood on the grass in the rain. You wouldn't come in. It was cold. I was wet. My hair had begun to stick to my face. My feet were bare. I had nettle stings.

"Shit," I said. "That's terrible. Attacked with what? And why?"

"Why? Because he works on animals. Rats. Because he experiments with the brains of rats. Enough reason to stab someone in the dark in an alleyway in the back, don't you think? Rats, for Christ's sake. Just fucking *rats*."

"Have they caught anyone?"

"No. He was found slumped in a doorway by a couple passing by. They thought he was a drunk at first, until they saw the blood and the cuts to his face; then they called the police. The doctors have operated, but he's 'critical,' they say. He has a punctured lung and a cracked skull. They think he might have been attacked somewhere else and then dumped in St. Edward's Passage. The police found his card with my name on it— that's why they called me."

St. Edward's Passage. Too awful to imagine lying there bleeding slowly to death. Listening for the sound of footsteps. Drifting in and out of consciousness. Had he been tortured somewhere to have been beaten up like that? Also too awful to imagine; but Emmanuel Scorsa would have information that the animal activists—if it was animal activists who attacked him—wanted. I couldn't protect you from this. Animal killings were one thing—guinea pigs and cats slaughtered and mutilated—but this accelerated everything. Pepys was now part of a sequence that tied The Studio and me dangerously into your world. So for a moment then I thought how clever I had been to keep Pepys's death from you and from the police, because he was an invisible link in the chain between the guinea pig deaths and Emmanuel Scorsa. You didn't know about Pepys—you never would. If you'd known about Pepys then you would have seen that I was in the firing line now. You being at The Studio at all that night put us both in danger.

"When I got to his bed in the hospital he was all wired up to drips and monitors. He has wadding and bandages on his face where they'd stitched up the cuts."

"Cuts?"

"Yes, of course, cuts. Seven cuts to his face."

"Like the animals?"

"Yes, just like the sodding animals. A policewoman was sitting next to his bed reading a book; she asked me for identification and took down my name. She wouldn't leave me alone with him. They want to see me in the morning. They'll want to interview all of us from the lab in the morning."

"You'll go back to the hospital tomorrow?"

"Yes, his parents should get here by tomorrow. They were leaving for the Milan airport an hour ago. I had to make the call. If he makes it to the morning they're going to do some tests. He has stains around his lips too, which they think may mean he'd been drugged or poisoned. He's in

such a bad way. Bastards. Bloody bastards. Such a brilliant beautiful boy."
You kicked a tree. You threw your glass into the water. It floated for a moment, then sank.

"And Sarah?"

"She took the boys and went back to her sister's this afternoon."

"They'll be all right there."

"She says that's it. She liked Emmanuel. We all did. He took the kids tenpin bowling. He used to babysit for us. He made her laugh."

"She's said that's it before. She'll come back."

"If I were her, that *would* be bloody it. I wouldn't come back. I don't think she will. Not that it matters in the scale of things. None of it bloody matters. Maybe that will be it for me too."

Sometime before dawn in the early hours of the morning, when you talked in your sleep, I put my arms around you, tracing the contours of your naked back and hips with a single fingertip. Sometime in that same night I walked—sleeping—from that bed and your body to the front door. How do I know? The way I always know—because I'm awakened by the cold on the threshold, the open door in my hand, looking out into the night. For a moment in that flickering between sleep and wake, on the threshold between that world and this, I remembered, as I always did, what it was I was supposed to be doing. But in that same second, as always, it was gone, like sand through a sieve. I reach for it, but it's gone. I tried to wake you—I called to you from the bottom of the stairs—but you didn't hear me. I spoke to you as I climbed back in beside you and slipped my cold hands between your thighs, but you were too deeply asleep to hear my voice or feel the touch of my fingers or the silk of my gown. You stirred and said something I couldn't make out. I lay still for a few minutes, watching you, wondering how my defences had been so ineffectual against you in the end, after all my resistance. Would I always come back? Then I gave up trying to work it out, and slept with the word *embroilment* on my lips.

I was washing my face the following morning when I saw the letters and numbers written on the steamed-up bathroom mirror, almost certainly traced by my fingertip on the mirror's surface the night before, while I was sleepwalking. EZ35/6. I didn't recognise them as letters and numbers at first, because the characters curled around each other and mirrored each other, the E and the 3 looking towards each other separated by the Z, and the 5 and the 6 looking towards the right with the slash separating them. They could have meant anything: letters from the license plate of a car; a code from a security lock; a password for a file on Elizabeth's computer; or something from the dream that had pitched me into walking.

You were in the shower, your voice raised above the sound of the running water, talking about someone in the lab. I took a bath towel and rubbed it across the surface of the mirror. I couldn't let you see those letters.

"Did you walk in your sleep last night?" you said suddenly, turning off the shower and climbing out through the curve of the glass door and pressing your wet body up against my back, your arms around my waist.

"I don't think so," I said. "What makes you ask?"

"A dim memory of your body disappearing for a while. This robe of yours is going to have to come off again, I'm afraid." Green silk slipped to the floor, its folds curved and undulating like snakeskin.

"That's strange," I said, appalled at how motiveless my lying had become. There was no need to protect you from knowing that I'd been sleepwalking, after all. I took the toothbrush from my mouth. "How long was I gone, do you think?"

"Oh, best part of an hour, I'd guess. I assumed you'd gone downstairs to read or answer some e-mails." As you massaged my shoulders and neck, ran the tip of your tongue up the back of my neck, I saw my face and yours framed for a moment and then disappearing into the mirror as it steamed up again. The letters I had erased from the surface of the mirror reappeared where your face had been. EZ35/6. My hands were grasping the side of the sink, taking the weight of you against my naked back: your hands were over mine. I was trapped. I couldn't erase the letters this time.

"What's that you've written there?" you said, lifting your head for a moment to make out the letters sharpening in the steam, and then biting the skin just beneath my ear.

"Something in one of Elizabeth's notebooks. One of the codes I have to work out," I said without hesitation. "I was afraid I'd forget a minute ago. Couldn't find a pen." So quick. So quick. So easy to falsify, even like this, even when so aroused that my head was spinning.

"There's a Bible next to the thesaurus on the desk downstairs," you said. "I'd guess it means Ezekiel, chapter thirty-five, verse six."

"Christ, how do you know that?"

"This towel of mine is going to have to come off now, you know. No choice. Might I just put my hand there for a moment? How do I know about Ezekiel? Boarding-school education. You had to know how to find your way around a Bible. Just as I've learned over the long years since how to find my way round this body . . ." You placed the palms of my hands up against the wet tiles of the bathroom wall and, running your hands down the curve of my back and buttocks, traced the letters—EZ—on the base of my spine with your fingernails.

Lydia Brooke and Cameron Brown have lost their edges again. Bodies seen from above a bed. Impossible to tell where one begins and the other ends. Impossible to see the other bodies there, caught up with them, between them, shadows of their own.

Lying to you. Lying with you. Lying for you. Can I remember the difference?

Elizabeth's Bible, on her desk in the big room, fell open at Ezekiel, chapter thirty-five, because there was a card marking the page. An index card with the name Ezekiel Foxcroft written in capitals along the top. This was the card missing from Elizabeth's index file of alchemists. Elizabeth had worked out who Mr. F. was, then, before she died. She'd found him and recorded his details here on this index card. Then, for some reason, she'd moved the index card and hidden it in the pages of her Bible. Perhaps she'd thought it would be safer here, that whoever wanted it might not be able to reach it here. Whoever had left the message on the mirror, using my fingertips in the night, had meant me to find this, hoped I would be smart enough to work it out. I wasn't, but you were. The card read:

Ezekiel Foxcroft *(1629–1674), mathematician, protégé of Henry More. Schooled at Eton, then King's College, Cambridge. B.A. 1652–53; M.A. 1656; fellow 1652–74. Fellow of King's College. Nephew of Cambridge Platonist and philosopher Benjamin Whichcote (1609–1683), provost of King's. Son of Elizabeth Foxcroft née Whichcote (1600–1679), a theosophist, alchemist, and the companion of alchemist-philosopher Anne Finch, Viscountess Conway, with whom she lived at Ragley Hall. Elizabeth Foxcroft cotranslated work of the German mystic Jakob Boehme with Henry More at Ragley Hall. Ezekiel Foxcroft translated the seminal alchemical manuscript* Chymical Wedding *by Christian Rosenkreutz in the 1660s, the third manifesto of the Rosicrucian movement. Moved between Cambridge, Ragley Hall, and London throughout the 1660s. Died in London in a brawl in 1674.*

So Mr. F. was Ezekiel Foxcroft, fellow at King's, a mathematician, ten years or so older than Newton, son of an alchemist mother, named Ezekiel after the great prophet celebrated by alchemists, translator of *Chymical Wedding*, nephew of the founder of the Cambridge Platonists, Benjamin Whichcote, protégé of the most powerful Henry More. Ezekiel was an alchemist, all right; he'd practically been born one. It was in his blood. Elizabeth had underlined the words from the Bible she had meant me to read in Ezekiel, chapter thirty-five, verse six: "I will prepare thee unto blood, and blood shall pursue thee." Elizabeth had sent me that message about him, perhaps even for him: "Ezekiel—blood shall pursue thee."

Twenty-one

It's only when you've pieced together a story in several different ways that you realise where the holes are, discover the knowledge that is still missing, the questions you still need to ask. It's not like a jigsaw, which can only fit together one way, each piece carved out of the side of another so that it will nudge back, skin to skin, bone to bone. A jigsaw exists in two dimensions. But there were so many of these fragments, layerings of narratives with jagged edges, your story, mine, now, then, seventeenth century, twenty-first century, and all the spirits that seemed to pass—or bleed—between. There were horizontal patternings, vertical and diagonal patternings, and those were just the ones you could see. If each part of this narrative of Elizabeth's was a playing card, they had to be reshuffled. So many sequences were possible. But when there are so many players in the frame, so many potential motivations in play, almost any consequence becomes possible.

You had another piece of that jigsaw that I didn't even know was missing. "Have you seen the light here?" you said, lying in my bed one bright morning at the beginning of November. "I've never really noticed it before. It's as if the house is awash."

Have I seen the light? Seen it? I live in it. I didn't answer. I didn't need to. You were about to give me something. Something that would fit.

"Funny that," you said, turning over the prism in your hand, the prism that I carried with me around the house now, slipped under my pillow at night.

"Funny what?"

"People in glass houses . . ."

"What glass house?"

Fragments of your thoughts did that sometimes—surfaced as if they had become detached from the rest of whatever it was you were thinking about. Suddenly you'd say something like "Most people look different in the morning" or "It was probably cowardice," and I'd say, *"Which* people?" or *"What* was?" and you'd come back into focus. But you never did tell me which people or what was probably cowardice.

"Elizabeth built The Studio on the site of an old boathouse," you said. "I used to play down here in it with my friends when I was a kid. It was just a shed really, full of old wood."

Your eyes, close to mine, were of every colour, like Madame Bovary's. A base brown but flecked with gold and blue. I often wondered how many people you were and how many possible combinations there were with all the people I am. Enough newness in that for several lifetimes, I guessed. That's what potentiation means. All those combinations make a kind of potency. But potent for what?

"No boat?"

"Yes, there was a boat, an old rowing boat. My mother—ridiculous woman—renamed it. It was called *Primrose,* I think. She painted that out and renamed it *Harmonium*—after the Wallace Stevens book of poems. She painted green letters down the side. We used it for a few summers when I was back from school, but no one took care of it, and the wood started to rot. It never got mended."

Your body arched as you turned onto your side, facing away from me. I watched the sinews stretch taut across your back. You sighed and arched your back again. Arching against my touch.

I remembered Mrs. Kite insisting on the impossibility of serendipity or coincidence. There are guiding hands at work in the world, she'd said. You just have to give yourself up to them. And you, Cameron Brown, will you give yourself up, into my hands?

When you turned back towards me all the colour and light had gone from your eyes. I could see myself, my white face against the pillow, reflected there in the great darkness of your eyes. You said: "Last time I came here, back in July, you know, the last time before she died, we had lunch. She'd banked up the fire; it was incredibly hot. We piled the dishes from the lunch in the kitchen sink, and opened another bottle of wine—Crozes-Hermitage. I can see her sitting in a pool of sunlight downstairs, in jeans and sweater, on the sofa with the broken springs, feet folded beneath her, her white hair twisted into a knot at the back of her head, with a book of maps out on her lap and a magnifying glass. I sat in the armchair and she just carried on working like she'd always done."

"As if you weren't there . . ."

"Yes, as if I wasn't there. I picked up a book of Flaubert short stories, but I couldn't read. My eyes kept slipping off the page. So I sat and watched her working, the light catching the tendrils of white hair on the nape of her neck, her breathing slow as she sipped the wine, absentmindedly, from her glass. I had to say *something*. 'What are you doing?' I asked. And you know what, when she turned round to look at me and smiled, I felt guilty. And though it was so damned hot in that room, I was suddenly really cold—as if someone had walked over my grave. But it was hers, wasn't it?"

"Her what?"

"It was *her* grave that was making me cold—her grave and all that cold water she died in. I felt it then—that Sunday afternoon. Her death."

"Did she answer your question?"

"About what she was doing? Yes, she said she was trying to work out what was on the land before they built the Wren Library, in the 1670s. She said the seventeenth-century map records of Cambridge were very difficult to read because they weren't drawn to scale, but she thought they'd had to fill in the King's Ditch and dig up an old tennis court. And then she told me there were rats in her garden again and that Pepys had caught three or four of the young ones. And I said, 'That's good.' Just that. 'That's good.' "

The great oval in the river that you can see from Elizabeth's map. Garret Hostel Greene. The pupil in the eye on the map—that's what was there before the Wren Library.

"What was *here* before, besides the boathouse? On *this* land?"

"Under The Studio? Oh, you should have asked Elizabeth that. She was never able to live anywhere without tracing its history, the lay of its land. She had a gift for it. She was tenacious, like those women you see in the local history section of public libraries. But she wasn't looking for ancestors or mapping out family trees. She was never interested in that. Just land and what had been on it. We lived in the big house, of course, where the Morrisons live now. Grange End. They planted the beech hedge so you can't see it from the orchard anymore, but there isn't much to see. It was an ugly house, really. There's been a house on this land for centuries, right back to the sixteenth century. I liked to think of that when I was a boy, sitting in the apple tree. It was an apothecary's house once. My parents took down an old wall in the late seventies to build an extension, and the following summer the field next to it was full of poppies—my father said that the seeds had somehow lain dormant in the wall. You could still see the lines of the herb garden from up in the big tree."

"Poppies? Why poppies?"

"An apothecary would have grown poppies for the opium. Along with an herb garden. Christ, I don't know. You tell me."

"Why did she sell the house—Grange End? Money?" I imagined the beautiful Elizabeth in the big house like that woman in E. M. Forster's *Howards End*. Walking around a sunlit garden, her skirts trailing the long grass.

"My father died. The house was too big for her, and she'd never really liked it. She just wanted a place to store her books and papers and to write in, so she sold off the house and most of the land and had The Studio built by an architect friend of hers, where the boathouse was in the orchard. Just enough. It was quieter here, she said."

"And did she ever find out what came before the boathouse?"

"Oh, yes. Even before she had the plans drawn up. She had to be sure it was good land. The boathouse was only built in the early nineteenth century. You'd never guess what was here before—even Elizabeth hadn't expected that."

"Boatyards for boatbuilding?" I guessed as you pulled on your clothes, gathering yourself for the day, for the lab, finding your papers, books, wallet, watch among the pile of objects you had discarded on the floor the previous night.

I used to think that it was unfair that you were always leaving me. I used to complain that I never got to have a turn at being the one to walk away. But there were all those times when I engineered it so that I could. Slammed the door, left town, left the country. Yes, I guess that's true. It was pretty even, really—the leaving. We always thought *we* were in control, didn't we?

"A ferry?" I pulled the bedclothes around my skin. Of course: you had come here to fill in some of the missing bits for me. You were drawing in some of the lines on the dot-to-dot, but you had no idea what you were doing. The air was thick with threads and skeins. I couldn't quite see it yet. But I could sense that it was there somewhere. You passed me the prism.

"Glass, Lydia. Sometimes you are very slow. *That* was what was here before. A glasshouse."

"A house made of glass?" I pictured a single-story building made entirely of glass so that it was skinless, so that you could watch everything going on inside. It was your house I saw—the one at Over—*turned into* glass. The one that had CCTV cameras trained on it permanently now. In my picture I was outside looking in. People with second sight like Dilys can tell—apparently—even when they're being watched through CCTV. The touch of the eyes reaches them even through all that technology, the glass, metal, and wiring. Like the bruises on the sleeping princess.

"No, a house where they *made* glass, stupid. Look, I'm going to have to go. Should have left twenty minutes ago. I've been late for almost all the lab meetings in the last two weeks. All your fault."

"Bollocks," I said. "You just won't go. Not my fault. Am I keeping you? Are you restrained in any way? What kind of glasshouse?" There was a health club in Cambridge called the Glass House, I remembered. Very expensive. I think you had a membership once.

You sat down on the edge of the bed again, resigned to being late. "OK. An *ordinary* kind of glasshouse—if glasshouses can be ordinary, which I guess they can. I'm not sure about the dates, but I think it was built in the seventeenth century. Part of all that revival of English glassmaking in the 1660s and '70s. Sarah knows about all that stuff. You want me to ask her? Is it important?"

"No, I don't think it's that important," I said. "I'm just curious, that's all."

"Only curious? There's never been *only* curious with you. Well, I only know bits and pieces. Elizabeth insisted on having the oak worktable built right in the middle of the big room because it's where the glasshouse furnace would have been. She was very exact about that. The architect didn't like it at all. Said it spoiled the line of the room."

For once I didn't feel that dropping away when the front door slammed and when, almost exactly two minutes later, I heard the sound of your engine start up. Too full for emptiness, I was framing a question while the sound of your car diminished to nothing: if the walls of a sixteenth-century apothecary's house can leave poppy seeds behind, can a seventeenth-century glasshouse leave the light of its furnace in its wake? And if a boathouse is built on the same land, bringing together all that fire and water, is that potentiation? Alchemy? Particles of fire and water moving and mirroring through and into each other? No, of course not. Seeds can survive for years in cracks in walls if the conditions are right, if it's dry enough, but light, even light freighted with water, doesn't hang about. Light is always long gone. It doesn't have a history, a past or a future. Like people, it just disappears into nothing. Yet some light—like sunset light—*lingers*. You'd say that, wouldn't you? Or a poet might say that. But that lingering is of seconds—surely no light can linger for *centuries*.

Coincidence? No such thing. It was no coincidence that you brought me the prism that Elizabeth had tracked across the sea from Murano into the hands of Isaac Newton or that she had built her house on the site of a seventeenth-century glasshouse. It was no coincidence that she drowned with that prism in her hand.

Everything was turning into new forms on the land around The Studio, or so it seemed to me then. Blooming. It had always been so. Benign. Malign. Who could say? When we were both unaccountably awake at dawn a few days before, you took me out into the garden to show me the fairy ring you'd seen under the beech trees, and instead of the fairy ring we found the fly agaric mushroom in the grey cold, colours washed from trees, soil, leaves, a sepia morning, in which the mushroom's red cap bled like a pool of blood in the undergrowth, flecked with white.

"Jesus," you said. Just that. "Jesus."

A pool of red poison in the grey of the morning.

"If I tell you not to touch it, you'll touch it," you said.

"You think I'm that predictable?" I feigned offence. I'd often tasted the mushrooms you'd not been able to identify, and because you were always so careful about the poisonous ones, yes, it was always an act of defiance. Taste was a way of telling what it was. The books said that certain mushrooms tasted of apricot or cucumber or ashes. You had to taste them sometimes to know.

"Eat it," you said. "Go on, eat it. I could tell you that you'd hallucinate, vomit, and feel your head explode, but it wouldn't be true. You'd need scores of dried ones to do that, but you just can't be sure how strong they are. Several people have died from eating agarics. Go on, you know you want to—eat it. Then I'll drive you to Addenbrooke's to get your stomach pumped."

"What do we do with it?"

"Leave it there . . . there'll be several others in a day or so."

Which of us was Red Riding Hood and which of us the wolf? It had become difficult to differentiate roles now that the tables had turned.

"You've gone back into his bed?" Kit asked, across the reading room desk. The old man to my right leaned a little more closely in our direction, ears pricked. The boy with the ring through his lower lip who was writing on Marvell was listening too.

"After everything you said? Just like that? What is it with you? I told you to be careful years ago. And you've been reckless ever since. That man is bad news."

"It wasn't supposed to be like this," I said.

"Yes, I remember it wasn't supposed to be like this at all. You had other plans then, didn't you?"

"This is unfinished business, I think," I said.

Yes. I had really thought I could finish you off. Exorcise. Dispossess you. Lay my ghost. But there doesn't seem to be a finishing in sight anymore. Kit wanted an explanation that day, a defence even, but I didn't have much of one to give her. I tried: "It was a kind of dare to myself: the haunted house I had to just step back inside."

"Yes, I know you and I know the next bit," she said. "Once you were inside, the door slammed shut and the candle went out. You always did have to prove that you were brave."

I found no records of Elizabeth's glasshouse except on one of those wayside markers on the riverbank near the house, which included a scrap of a

seventeenth-century map on which appeared the word *glasshouse* where Elizabeth's house now stood, and a tiny picture of a simple single-story building
with a flight of steps leading down to a landing stage on the riverbank. I never
found the original map. So there was no proof, unless you are prepared to
count as evidence the light that sharded around The Studio, light that was,
by the beginning of November, full of shadows, passing across the light like
shoals of fish. You never saw them. I never saw them directly; they were always
just to the side, just beyond my vision—something would move across the
light on the wall, a figure, a hand, a shoulder, a sudden break in the beam
that wasn't a beam.

The riverbank in Chesterton was a likely enough place for a glasshouse, I
thought—woodland to keep the furnace going, far enough outside the town
for the furnace fire not to cause any trouble with local farmers, and a town
that would provide a rich market for the glassware (almost certainly mirrors,
beer glasses, beer bottles—not the fancy twisted glass and *cristallo* whose production the Venetian glassmakers monopolised). Elizabeth had put together enough notes on seventeenth-century glassmaking for a book on the
subject. She'd only needed enough information to write her opening chapter, but she was thorough. She read everything. Her bibliography for that
chapter alone ran to seven books and fifteen articles.

Glass, alchemy, and politics. You couldn't separate them out in the 1660s.
Once I'd started to see through Elizabeth's eyes, I could discern all these networks and corruptions and conspiracies. There are other historians who have
seen that too, understood that there was something peculiar about the 1660s
and the restoration of the monarchy. It was a time of reckoning, especially so
because of the comets and the plague. Many of the royalists expected to be re-
warded for their loyalty to the king in the civil war, and many were. The Duke
of Buckingham, for instance—the glass monopolist, the king's friend, and an
alchemist—was caught up in all sorts of deals and scams stretching across Europe. And when the patrons were caught up in deals and conspiracies, their
protégés got caught up too. Sometimes, when I was meandering around in
Elizabeth's notes, it seemed as if everything passed through Trinity in one way
or another, at some point or another. Buckingham was at Trinity College in
the 1640s and he became the poet Abraham Cowley's patron around that
time. He was a powerful Trinity benefactor. These glassmakers and alchemists
and Trinity fellows seemed to be all in cahoots in one way or another.

Twenty-two

I went back to the chapter in *The Alchemist* in which Elizabeth described Newton's initiation into alchemy. I had resolved to track down Mr. F., find some trace of him, somewhere in this book. Elizabeth had called this chapter "The Green Lion," a reference to the alchemical code for mercury, or quicksilver.

The arguments in the later chapters of her manuscript were increasingly dependent upon evidence from the elusive Vogelsang Papers, frequently referred to in the footnotes, but I had still not been able to track down this archive of materials among the papers at The Studio. This time, following Elizabeth through the thickets of her prose, I resolved to keep my eyes on the undergrowth, look for marks in the ground where the soil might have been disturbed. The chapter began:

The Green Lion

There are many complex and contradictory myths about Isaac Newton. There are those who would have his life expunged from all associations with the occult in the quest to establish him as the hero of the Enlightenment, the first scientist to separate natural philosophy from superstition. Then there are also those who have co-opted Newton as the great sorcerer and magician, in possession of secret arts. Whatever the accuracy or otherwise of these accounts, it is the *older* Newton who is described as the member of these quasi-Masonic groups, not the boy.

The problem of how and when Newton became an alchemist has vexed Newton scholars. Both questions are difficult to answer because alchemical practice and alchemical networks have always been shrouded in secrecy and because so little documentation and correspondence has survived. Most scholars argue that Newton began making alchemical experiments between 1667 and 1669 in Cambridge, although some would set the date a little earlier, at the point at which he began to put together the beginnings of an alchemical library, soon after he arrived in Cambridge, almost certainly purchased from the specialist booksellers who put up their stalls along Cheapside at Stourbridge Fair.

Certain facts, however, suggest that Newton's initiation into alchemy began *before* he arrived in Cambridge. There is an alternative history—a story about a "sober, silent thinking lad" being initiated into secret arts by a group of older men, a story in which a series of European alchemical networks run through an apothecary's shop in Grantham, where Newton was schooled. After all, as Richard Westfall points out, "an alchemist was not made; he was chosen."[1]

Alchemists rarely worked alone. Alchemical experimentation was sometimes a solitary activity—the man working alone at a furnace late at night—but acquiring the secret knowledge necessary to begin depended upon being connected to a network that stretched across Europe and had numerous geographical centres, many of them in towns built on Rosicrucian or Knights Templar sites at crossing points on the great Roman roads. Grantham, where Newton was schooled, was one such place. It was one of two or three major stopping points on the Great North Road (now the route of the A1); Grantham's largest inn, the Angel, had been built on the site of a former Knights Templar hostel and grounds. Alchemical practice almost always required patronage.

At the age of twelve, Newton was sent to the King's School at Grantham at his uncle William Ayscough's instigation. Because the school was seven miles away from his home at Woolsthorpe, his uncle and mother arranged for him to board with a friend of the family's, Katherine Clark, the wife of William Clark, the apothecary in Grantham, who had premises next to the George Inn,

[1]Westfall, *Never at Rest*, p. 23.

on the High Street. Newton lodged here for the best part of seven years, growing up alongside the other children living in the house: the children of Katherine Clark's first marriage, the boys Arthur and Edward Storer and a sister whose first name has been lost. There were also young apprentices working alongside Clark, according to an early draft of William Stukeley's memoirs.

William Clark, the apothecary, had a younger brother called Joseph Clark, who was the physician in Grantham when Newton was a lodger there and was a daily visitor to the apothecary's house. Joseph had also attended the King's School at Grantham and then studied at Christ's College, Cambridge, where he had been tutored by Henry More, the man who would become an important mentor to Newton at Cambridge. Joseph kept a small library of books in the garret of his brother's house, just next to the room where Newton lodged, and it was undoubtedly books from this small collection that inspired Newton's first experiments. Stukeley, Newton's first biographer, described Isaac's activities in Grantham as a young man:

> insted of playing among the other boys, when from school, he always busyd
> himself in making knick knacks, & models of wood in many kinds: for which
> purpose he had got little saws, hatchets, hammers & a whole shop of tools,
> which he would use with great dexterity.[2]

Stukeley collected tales of Newton's machines and contraptions: a model of a windmill to which the boy added a treadmill run by a mouse, doll's furniture for Clark's stepdaughter, a four-wheeled cart run by a crank, a lantern of "crimpled paper" to light his way to school on dark mornings and which also doubled as a burning kite at night, and a range of different clocks powered by water moving between different contraptions. Who provided Newton with his "shop of tools"? It was almost certainly not his mother.

These inventions, which were made by Newton over these years and were reputed to have spilled out of the attic and into the downstairs rooms and hallway of the apothecary's house, were inspired by a book he read at the time, borrowed from the attic library and from which he copied many chemical experiments, recipes for mixing colours, and instructions for building

[2] Keynes Ms. 136 (part 3): William Stukeley's memoir of Newton, sent to Richard Mead in four installments (26 June to 22 July 1727), each with a covering letter to Mead. Newton Project.

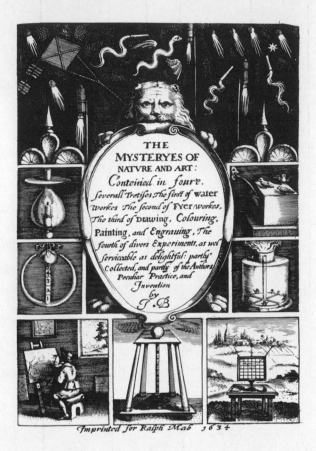

THE
MYSTERYES OF
NATVRE AND ART :
Conteined in foure.
severall Tretises, The first of water
workes The second of Fyer workes,
The third of Drawing, Colouring.
Painting, and Engrauing, The
fourth of divers Experiments, as wel
serviceable as delightful: partly
Collected, and partly of the Authors
Peculiar Practice, and
Invention
by
J. B

Imprinted for Ralph Mab 1634

models: John Bate's *The Mysteries of Nature and Art,* a "book of secrets" first published in 1634.

Thus began Newton's obsession with time and light. He kept an almanac and taught himself how to chart the equinoxes and solstices by the different periods of the sun. He made a series of complex sundials in the apothecary's house, driving pegs into the walls of the hallway, his own room, all rooms with sufficient light to cast sharp enough shadows, and then he tied strings with running balls on them to the pegs so that he could measure the shadows and mark the hours and the half hours. They were so accurate that Grantham neighbours came to consult "Isaac's dials."[3]

Katherine Clark's brother, Humphrey Babington, a Trinity fellow and a future patron and benefactor of Newton at Cambridge, came and went through

[3]See Westfall, *Never at Rest,* p. 62; Stukeley, p. 43; Keynes Ms. 130.2, p. 24.

this household, visiting his sister's children and tripping over the strange con-
trivances the boy lodger had made; so, by apparent coincidence, did Newton's
second supposed Cambridge patron, Henry More, the leading member of a
group of philosophers who would become known as the Cambridge Platonists.[4] Most scholars argue that Newton came to know More in Cambridge in
the 1670s.[5] But it is more than likely that Newton met More *before* he arrived
in Cambridge—in Grantham—for when More visited Grantham, his hometown,
he lodged in William Clark's house.[6] More had also attended the King's School
and, as a fellow at Christ's College, Cambridge, he had tutored Joseph Clark.
Did his friendship with his ex-pupil, now a Grantham physician, merit his staying in William Clark's house, or were there other reasons for lodging with the
apothecary rather than at the perfectly respectable inn next door?

Humphrey Babington, Henry More, and the Clark brothers are all linked to
the Grantham apothecary's house and to Cambridge. Might there have been a
kind of knot in the network here, a small group of alchemists working out of
Grantham with the chemicals provided by Clark, perhaps even using a secret
laboratory at the apothecary's house?

Newton left Clark's house at the age of seventeen and returned to Woolsthorpe with the expectation that he would now run his mother's estate there.
But despite his expensive schooling, Hannah Smith found that while her son's
handwriting and reading were excellent, he was absentminded, inept in prac-
tical matters, and lacking in business sense. He infuriated everyone around
him. Every time he returned to Grantham on his mother's business he would
disappear into the attic library in Clark's house for hours at a time and fail to
remember what he had been sent for.

John Stokes, Newton's Grantham schoolmaster, probably at the instigation of Humphrey Babington and the Clark brothers, wrote to Newton's
mother to ask that her son be allowed to return to school to prepare for uni-

---

[4]More was not a practising alchemist until quite late in his life, but he was driven from the 1650s on by
philosophical questions and beliefs that are inseparable from those of alchemical and kabbalistic writings;
this is especially so in his passionate quest to demonstrate the intellectual inadequacy of any purely materi-
alist account of either nature or man.

[5]Newton referred to More's book *The Immortality of the Soul* in his notebook, under the heading "Of At-
tomes," describing it as the book in which the existence of indiscernible small particles is "proved beyond
all controversie": Cambridge University Library Add. Ms 3996, fol. 89r.

[6]See More to Anne Conway, 8 May 1654 and 18 April 1655 in Marjorie Hope Nicolson, ed., *Conway Letters:
The Correspondence of Anne, Viscountess Conway, Henry More and Their Friends* (New Haven, 1930). See also Vogelsang Papers, pp. 34–41.

versity entrance. When Newton's uncle William Ayscough also intervened, Hannah Smith reluctantly agreed. Newton returned to Grantham, where he lodged with John Stokes and was given private tuition in order to prepare him for entry to Cambridge. Humphrey Babington, fellow of Trinity, knowing that Newton's mother would not provide much towards her son's education, suggested that the boy might enter the university as a subsizar in his own employment. Trinity was to be his future.

Among them, these men—John Stokes, the schoolmaster; William Clark, the apothecary, and his doctor-brother; and the apothecary's friends, Humphrey Babington and Henry More—had almost certainly already introduced the clever solitary boy to the beginnings of alchemical practice and alchemical philosophy before he came to Cambridge, either through direct tuition or in conversation, or by giving him access to a specialist library or hidden laboratory.[7] Certainly the maturity of the knowledge Newton displayed later in his chemical dictionary, written in 1667–68, serves as evidence that he had had substantial laboratory experience before he came to Cambridge. After all, "an alchemist was not made; he was chosen."

Henry More was well connected in alchemical circles and would have been a powerful patron. When he was not in Cambridge he spent most of his time at the country estate of his friend and patron Anne Finch, the Viscountess Conway, at Ragley Hall in Warwickshire, where he had a suite of rooms and where he hosted meetings of European alchemists and natural philosophers. He also had access to vast specialist libraries—his own, those at Ragley Hall, and those at Cambridge—though it is doubtful that he undertook any alchemical experiments of his own until the 1670s.

My instinct had not failed me. This reference to Ragley Hall was the first sign of disturbed earth in this chapter, a glimpse of something buried, perhaps a name or even a paragraph removed. Ezekiel Foxcroft had been here in these lines once, I was sure of it. According to the card I had found in Elizabeth's Bible, Ezekiel's mother, Elizabeth Foxcroft, was the mysterious alchemist companion of Anne Finch, Viscountess Conway, close friend of Henry More and owner of Ragley Hall. Elizabeth Foxcroft lived at Ragley Hall and worked with More. Ezekiel Foxcroft was a linch-

[7]See Vogelsang Papers, p. 55.

pin between these people, a Cambridge alchemist living both at Ragley Hall and at King's College Cambridge, perhaps also visiting Grantham regularly as the protégé of Henry More's. He was practically More's adopted son. But why did Elizabeth not mention Ezekiel here? Why was this linchpin missing?

"The Green Lion" chapter continued with a description of Newton's first months at Cambridge, months marked by secrecy. Elizabeth described how, for instance, the young undergraduate bought a lock for his desk and in his rooms at Trinity continued to practise the secret code he had been taught at Grantham. He also observed the complex purification rituals essential to the practise of alchemy, recording his sins meticulously in code, rarely socialising, drinking and eating almost nothing, and keeping mostly to his rooms and his books.

Newton's Cambridge connections saw to it, she argued, that he was given rooms in Trinity which were of particular value to an alchemist. His first-floor rooms butted against Trinity Chapel, but through an external door he also had access to a physic garden and a laboratory, a shedlike building constructed up against the external walls to the chapel. The significance of this, she suggested, was that Newton's garden, filled with herbs and medicinal plants, would have been shared with other botanists and alchemists, a further point of connection with a larger, largely secretive community. The drawing of Trinity completed by mapmaker David Loggan in 1690 shows a garden and a laboratory exactly at the place where Newton is said to have had his rooms, between the Great Gate and the chapel.

The physic garden was important. If it was a private garden, in Newton's care but shared with others, it would have been locked. Anyone using that garden regularly would have had a key. Trinity was full of keys. Keys to the tennis courts, the bowling green, keys to rooms, hidden keys to gardens, secret keys to locked desks, ciphers to codes.

By the time Newton arrived in Cambridge, Elizabeth claimed, purification had become an obsession for him. Whereas modern biographers might have seen Newton's behaviour, particularly his records of his sins, as evidence of some psychological disorder, Elizabeth read it as essential to his alchemical practise. For her, the fact that Newton had listed his sins in 1662 made perfect sense. It indicated that he had begun the next stage

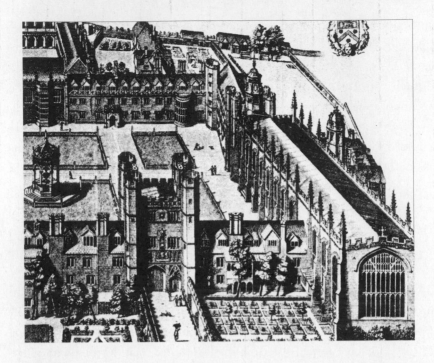

of his apprenticeship. He had also begun to read every alchemical book and manuscript he could find.

Throughout these later chapters of *The Alchemist* Elizabeth deftly, assuredly connected Newton to a group of semivisible Cambridge men who had links across Britain and Europe, collapsing the lone-genius-in-isolation myth piece by piece, summoning other figures—mostly hooded and shadowy—onto the historical stage. Some had names, some didn't, but one had a special significance: Ezekiel Foxcroft, who brought him alchemical manuscripts from London and Ragley Hall.

These manuscripts were important. Like Henry More and the Cambridge Platonists, Newton believed that certain ancient philosophers were in possession of all knowledge. This lost knowledge (what was called the *prisca sapientia)* could be dug out of codes and symbols embedded in a number of ancient, secret kabbalistic texts. From his first days at Cambridge, Newton, searching for these truths, pored over virtually the entire literature of the older alchemy in a way that no one had studied and assimilated it before. In this he had guidance. He wrote over 166,000 words on alchemical matters before 1675, one-sixth of his total writings on alchemy.[8] He was taking notes on books which included, for instance, Michael Sendivogius's *New Chemical Light* (1608), Jean D'Espagnet's *The Secrets of Hermetic Philosophy* (1638, translated 1650), Michael Maier's *Symbola Aurea* (1617), George Ripley's *Opera* (1649), and Basil Valentine's *Triumphal Chariot of Antimony* (1604).

Trinity was Newton's kingdom, and in 1664, after he had embarked on this course of powerful reading, he came dangerously close to exile from it. His mother still wanted him back at Woolsthorpe to run the farm; she couldn't see the point of all this time spent with books. By 1664 Newton had moved into rooms with John Wickins, a fellow student, and the two men would have discussed their future in the college. Newton knew that to escape a Woolsthorpe fate, he would have to be elected a fellow at Trinity—this would give him an income, rooms, food, and libraries, *for life.* To be eligible for a fellowship at Trinity he would first have to win a Trinity scholarship, for only Trinity scholars could compete for the fellowships. But this would not be easy. The system of promotion to scholarships and fellowships at Trinity, as in other colleges, depended upon corrupt systems of patronage. Students from Westminster School in London automatically received at least a third of the Trinity scholarships, and as the scholarship elections took place only every three to four years, Newton had only one chance to compete—in the spring of 1664. If he did not succeed, he would have had to return to Woolsthorpe and give up alchemy and his ripening experiments on light, gravity, and motion, and in mathematics and physics, and become either a farmer or a country clergyman like Humphrey Babington.

In April 1664, Newton's tutor at Trinity, Benjamin Pulleyn, sent him to Isaac Barrow, who held the prestigious Lucasian Chair of Mathematics, to be examined for the scholarship. Newton recalls in his memoirs that Barrow chose to test him on Euclid, which he had not read.[9] Instead Newton had been reading René Descartes's *Geometry,* but he failed to tell the professor this, or to ask to be questioned on the more difficult book. In any case, Barrow would not have believed that any undergraduate could have read Descartes without first reading Euclid. The professor, the story goes, formed "but an indifferent opinion" of the awkwardly reticent undergraduate.

[8]Westfall, *Never at Rest*, pp. 290–91.
[9]Keynes Ms. 130.10, f.2v.

How, then, was it possible that on 28 April, 1664, Newton was elected to a scholarship? Was this election, given Newton's poor performance in the viva voce examination, due to the intervention of a patron? Richard Westfall suggests that Babington intervened, of course, which is the most likely scenario given that Babington was now one of the eight senior fellows in Trinity who ran the college in conjunction with Isaac Barrow, the master. But in persuading Barrow, Babington almost certainly acted with others. Newton was not isolated. As a trained alchemist, he was one of the elect.

Newton had entered the world of British alchemy at an unusually rich and productive time. In London a further group of alchemists had gathered around the late Prussian educationalist, intelligencer, and philosopher Samuel Hartlib, who had died in 1662 and whose money financed many of the translations of ancient manuscripts. This group included the greatest of England's alchemists, Eirenaeus Philalethes (otherwise known as George Starkey), Sir Kenelm Digby, Thomas Vaughan, and Robert Boyle.

There were more alchemical books published or translated and reissued between 1650 and 1680 than at any time before or since. Such publications and translations were opening up alchemical secrets that had been buried or hidden for centuries. Across Europe networks of alchemists shaped and reshaped, forming new centres around powerful patrons. Alchemists travelled, carrying manuscripts and memorised secrets across national boundaries, searching out other alchemists.

But this was also, curiously, a decade in which a very high number of prominent alchemists and intelligencers who promoted the dissemination of alchemical secrets *died*: Samuel Hartlib in 1662, at the age of sixty-two, just after his son-in-law and fellow alchemist, Frederick Clodius, died mysteriously in his thirties in 1661; Sir Kenelm Digby in 1665 at the age of sixty-two; George Starkey (Eirenaeus Philalethes) in 1665, at the age of thirty-seven; Thomas Vaughan (Eugenius Philalethes) in 1666, at the age of forty-four; Nicolas Le Fevre in 1669, at the age of fifty-four. By the end of the 1660s, plague and accident and old age had left many of the major British alchemists dead.

Elizabeth's "The Green Lion" chapter was muddled and labyrinthine in a way that her earlier chapters had not been. I sensed that direct claims had been made and then taken out, leaving behind only questions and inference. The implications worked by juxtaposition: Newton badly wanted to stay in Cambridge. The alternative was almost certain obscurity. He was awarded the scholarship in 1664, but the fellowship still seemed beyond reach. And then the fellows started to die. By 1667, when the elections for the fellowships came up, his chances of election had been significantly increased, but the odds were still against him. There was no avoiding the next question: how far had Newton been prepared to go to secure his future? As far as murder?

Now that I had followed Elizabeth into the beginnings of Newton's alchemy, the whole root system seemed to rear up out of the soil, like the elder or the mandrake. Somewhere, conjuring dark figures and soil and gardens and poisons from Elizabeth's words, I heard the sounds of a body falling heavily down a staircase in Trinity and remembered a man who died with a key to a college garden in his hand. Richard Greswold.

Twenty-three

Over the next few weeks, the radio reports became more and more alarming. A graph printed on the front page of the *Times* showed that the number of animal experiments was the highest it had been since the 1970s, which was when whoever it was began to count them. The official term, it seemed, for animal experiments was "acts of intervention," used to describe all forms, from injections to blood taking to vivisection. The animal activists, outraged, changed their tactics, began to increase their "acts of intervention" in response. Clouds darkened over Cambridge.

There was something ancient and pagan about the animal-liberation campaigns. One morning, rising from a deep sleep in which I'd dreamed that my eyes were on fire, I heard a radio report about the desecration of a grave in a village north of Cambridge called Thorney. It sounded more like a story from the Middle Ages or from the early nineteenth century. A grave dug up in the night and a body stolen—snatched. (I always thought that was an odd word to use about the theft of a corpse—snatching a purse, yes, or even a small child, but snatching a heavy, decomposing body?) The body of an old woman called Ruth Webster, buried there only a week earlier, had been dug out of black fen soil and smuggled away in the back of a truck. The police had nothing to go on: the tyre tracks had been mostly washed away by rain; there were no footprints. The early-morning reporters had resorted to interviews with local residents, who all claimed they knew who had done it. The family of the dead woman, they said, ran a rat farm. They bred brown and white rats for laboratory use, rats you could order by the hundreds from a catalogue, the journalist reported urbanely, with no hint of judgement in his voice, though it was easy to tell that he thought it a repellent practice. Rats that had been pre-bred with cancer cells to save scientists time in the lab.

The radio journalists interviewed Tom Deakin, the owner of the local pub. Thorney was, he said, a small village. Everyone knew everyone else. The Websters, who ran the rat farm, had been effectively isolated from the rest of the village by the campaigners for the last fifteen years. Years ago, they had come down to the pub on a Friday night, but when the phone calls and threats began, he'd just had to ban the whole family. Well, not exactly ban them, just ask them to stay away. Difficult to know what else he could have done. Other neighbours described how they drove a four-wheel drive and kept German shepherds; how the children were never seen out alone and were all homeschooled. Why didn't they just give up? the journalist asked. Would you? I guess you just keep on going, the neighbour replied. They wouldn't be bullied. They had enough trouble just staying afloat, having to compete with the big lab-rat-breeding companies.

The presenter, to be balanced, also interviewed a spokesman for the right-to-animal-experimentation group, who worked himself up at the outrage exacted on this community, living in a state of terror. Acts of terrorism, he called them. He even implied that the local police were complicit with the animal campaigners. "They've never acted, never found anything," he said, "not a single clue to lead them to the terrorists. These people have to be stopped," he insisted. "Enough is enough."

I turned off the radio when I heard your key in the door. How long did we think we could keep it out? How much more could we keep from each other?

"Are you careful?" I said.

"About what?"

"Not to be followed when you come here?"

"Yes," you said. "I know what to do. I take care."

At The Studio you were not escaping from the campaign of intimidation; it simply did not exist. We didn't talk about it. It was a kind of agree-ment. At least we didn't talk about it until Emmanuel Scorsa was attacked. Then there was a cloud in the air between us for days, much more than your preoccupation with the young Italian in the hospital. Something was lying heavily on you. You wanted to tell me something, let go of some-thing. I waited, knowing it was just a matter of time.

"There was a girl," you said finally, as we left the Fort St. George pub one night and you walked me back across the bridge to your car. It was al-most midnight; the night was cold and the stars sharp. No cloud cover. There were satellites moving alongside the stars, in their orbits. Cameras trained on us from up there, I thought, cameras trained on everything.

"What girl?"

"After you left for France, I met a girl."

"What kind of girl?"

"She was a student at King's. A postgrad."

"Not a girl then, a woman."

"OK, if you like. I met a *woman*." You smiled. "It was just a flirtation at first." The gold around the centre of your iris had all but disappeared.

"Ha," I said. "I know about your flirtations. Did you sleep with her?"

"Yes."

"Poor woman. How long did it take you to make her fall in love with you? Did you tell her you'd leave Sarah?"

"She did the running. I tried not to, Lydia. I couldn't. Not after you left. Everything was empty. Colourless. Thin."

"How long did you hold out after I left before you let yourself be 'con-soled'?"

"Fuck it. Stop it. Lydia. Stop being sarcastic. This is important. I know. I know what you think of me. Just cut it out for a minute and listen."

"Keep your voice down," I said. A dustbin lid crashed somewhere. A cat scavenging. We had reached your car, parked on Pretoria Road. You sat on a wall. I could have gone. Could have just walked away. But I was curious. I hesitated, and then I sat down beside you.

"I was trying to be 'good,'" you said, your voice almost a whisper. "I decided after we stopped seeing each other that, well, I would just throw myself into my work. No more affairs. I hadn't the heart for them. Life had become more serious. I met her in the library. She was twenty-three—so yes, OK, a woman—but there was something fragile about her. Rather boyish. I liked her company. She made me laugh and she sent me poetry. I felt responsible. I knew I'd encouraged it even though I'd promised myself I wouldn't. It was more than a flirtation, but it didn't last very long. A summer. Two summers ago. April through to September 2000."

"Between the two solstices," I said. "How very romantic. Sorry, sorry. I will stop being sarcastic. I'm listening. Why do I need to know this?"

"Well, it turns out she was an infiltrator. She's a member of NABED. One of the most senior in Cambridge. They're very secretive, so she wouldn't have known more than a handful of the others. Perhaps none. They have cells. She was a cell. She was just the particular cell they chose to get at me."

"Blackmail?"

"Yes, but that's only half of it."

"Sarah. Did she get to know?"

"Yes. Sarah got to know. There were pictures, sent to her at work. She picked them up from her pigeonhole at Caius, opened them in front of the porters, pulling them out of a brown envelope while there were students walking by. No note. Nothing. Just the word NABED printed across the back of the pictures. The police had to check for prints. That was humiliating. Whoever took the pictures made sure you couldn't see Lily's face. So she couldn't be identified. Very clever. No prints on the envelope either."

"They must have taken a lot of pictures to be able to choose ones in which you couldn't see her face." His limbs; her limbs. All tangled up. No faces, just limbs. Sweat around his brow. Pictures taken from a concealed camera in her room.

"Yes, they must." You were embarrassed. Perhaps even ashamed.

"But you must have been able to give them an address? You knew where she lived."

"Yes, she had a flat, the ground-floor flat in a house on Mawson Road. The police went there. It was empty, nothing but a pile of blank paper on the floor. There had been a Lily Ridler living there, but she'd not left a forwarding address, the landlord said. She'd paid her rent by cash every month, so there was no way of tracing her through her bank details. There was no Lily Ridler on the college register. No one fitting her description among the postgrads at King's—so the police gave up. It was just a case of revenge, they said. Driven by jealousy. Such things happened all the time. They refused to see any connection with any animal-rights group, and NABED meant nothing to anyone then. It's their new name—the name they called themselves when they started the direct-strike action."

"Christ," I said. "Poor Sarah." I was grateful it wasn't me. What would I have done if I'd been sent pictures of you in bed with Lily Ridler? Pictures? Once I'd seen them I wouldn't have been able to get them out of my head.

"Why are you telling me? Why the confession?"

"Because she's still around."

"Lily Ridler?"

"Yes, or whatever her name was. Imagine making love for a whole summer to someone who hates and despises you. Someone who wants to harm you. She *must* have wanted to kill me, every time she took me into her bed. It would have been like sleeping with a monster—Hitler even."

"Sleeping with you, Mr. Brown, is, I imagine, a very long way from sleeping with Hitler. And Sarah? What happened with Sarah?"

"We went back to marriage counselling. I was sorry. Very sorry. It was easier this time. She could see I was sorry for what had happened. I lost a lot of weight. Had to go on medication."

"She took you back again?"

"Yes, she did."

She didn't know how to do anything else. Other women were always your instruments of torture. You confessed flamboyantly now and again, holding your breath. Would she leave this time? Would this be *it*? But it never was. Was this a love story? I wondered. Was this your love story? Cruel and dark.

"Cameron, why do I need to know this? I don't see the point."

"Because she's a friend of yours."

"I don't know anyone called Lily Ridler."

"But you know someone called Will Burroughs."

"Yes and . . . ?"

"Same person." You had turned to look straight at me now, to study my reaction.

"Don't be ridiculous," I said, standing up. "You want me to believe that

Will is the woman who seduced you . . . Will Burroughs? A member of NABED? How ridiculous. Someone's made a mistake."

"Where is she?"

"I've no idea. She went away a couple of weeks ago. I haven't seen or heard from her since. How do you know that I know her?"

"Did she say where she was going?"

"No. She didn't." My voice betrayed my sense of violation. *How do you know that I know Will?*

"Look. There's no point in blaming me for this. I've only just found out too. I thought Lily had long gone. The police came to see me this morning—they think she's got something to do with the attack on Scorsa. I'm not supposed to tell you. I'm telling you because—well, because you're my lover and because that puts you in danger. How do you think I bloody feel? Finding out that Lily—Will—has been in and out of my mother's house without my knowledge for over a year, that she's been making friends with you. She's clever. She's capable of anything."

"This is more than ridiculous. It's just not possible that Will Burroughs and Lily Ridler are the same person. I've never heard anything less likely. Will is a Ph.D. student at King's, working on Thoreau."

"Lydia. Stop. In the end it doesn't matter what you think. Has she got a key? Does she know about you and me?"

"Yes, Will has a key. No, she doesn't know about you and me. Or at least I've never told her."

"That's something. And there's no immediate danger to you, though I'll send a locksmith round to change the locks tomorrow. I had a phone call from the police. She was seen up in Leeds and Bradford earlier today. It's only a matter of hours before they bring her in. I've kept you out of it as best I can. Pulled some strings."

"My interest's in the dangerous edge of things," I said. " 'The honest thief, the tender murderer, the superstitious atheist.' "

"Robert Browning," you said, as if to prove my point. " 'Bishop Blougram's Apology.' Let me drive you back to The Studio. It's so cold."

"I'd rather walk," I said and walked away, without kissing you good night.

"You can't blame me, for Christ's sake," you called after me. "If she's dangerous, that's not my fault."

Infiltrator. You'd called her an infiltrator. Permeating. Pores. Under your skin. Behind enemy lines. Where were the enemy lines? I could think of nothing coherent then in the cold night air. Just that word—*infiltrator*—and Will Burroughs's new name, Lily Ridler, following me as I walked fast, wanting to get home, trying to erase those pictures from my head: you in that room, you with her . . . lips, skin. Her in that room with me. Ridler, riddled, riddling. Riddled with . . . I thought of plague. But we were all infiltrators now, weren't we, I thought, especially where we loved, seeping into each other's lives, insinuating, stealing secrets to empower us, to give us a little strength, though we loved, though, yes, we would also love—beyond everything. We may have boarded up all the gates to the city but the plague was inside the walls now; there was nothing but smoke and silence and the tolling of bells.

I got lost in the University Library today. *Got* lost? Must it always be a passive act? Let me rephrase myself. I lost myself up on the fifth floor of the South Wing looking for a reprint of an alchemical work by Agrippa von Nettesheim called *Three Books of Occult Philosophy*. It's a strange part of the building. It seems to have an atmosphere all of its own. Rows of books stretch from one long, windowless wall to a wall full of windows looking across Cambridge towards King's and Trinity. But somewhere in the middle, the rows begin to twist back on themselves, so that in order to reach some of the catalogue numbers you have to take several turns into darkness. And in the middle there's no light, except from the electric switch on a timer, which you have to turn on before you go in there. Inevitably, I forgot which way I had come; then the light clicked off. For a moment I knew someone was behind me, watching me.

I made a note to ask you about hallucinating presences. There must be some physiological explanation, I thought, some reason for this sensation I live with now of being perpetually watched. Cameron will know, I thought. But then I remembered that I can't ask you. *Because you're the one doing the watching.*

Twenty-four

Fifth of November. Remember. Remember.

One last look. One last kiss—remember this, she tells herself. Hand cradling his jaw, she takes another. Only five days, she tells herself. Five days beyond texts and mobile phones, disconnected, five days in this house alone—but never alone. A plane, different time zones, an American conference. In the early-afternoon light, she memorises Cameron's head in profile through the glass of a car door. Then listens to the hum of an engine, the crunch of car wheels on gravel; the sound diminishing to silence—its vanishing point. A crow's cry fills the absence.

"I've printed out the e-mails," you'd said. "Do you know how many there are now? Thousands. Ten years of e-mails. I've put them on two different disks, left them in the drawer in the bedroom. I felt superstitious somehow. You know—transatlantic flights. I just wanted to be sure they were safe, in case anything happened. Look after them."

"They're safe," I'd said. "And thank you. Nothing's going to happen to you."

I didn't ask you about Will or whether she had been arrested. I watched the news. Waiting. You had sent round locksmiths to change the locks; you had given me a new key. Several things had come to make a kind of sense. Will had never turned up at The Studio when you were there. She might have done. She never did. She must have been watching too.

The police failed to find the disks when they searched The Studio. The disks are somewhere at the bottom of the river near the house. I like to think of all those thousands of words down there at the bottom of the river, seeping into the water. I have so many fragments still in my memory, but I lose as many every day. Soon they will all have dissolved. What will be left then? "I wish to lie with you without interruption for ever and ever," you wrote. "Love is blindness, wrap the dark around me . . . With your Latin and my psychic powers we could do some dark artistry . . . You must not haunt me all night long . . . when I think about endings and abandonment I don't feel that if you turned away from me it would be a casting away . . . I am abandoning the future for the present . . . I feel sometimes like I have returned to something that I might never have been to before . . . I do so love you."

All those words lying down there, in the water.

You told me there were no other copies and, you know, I think I believe you. The police found no other copy on your computer. So many Achilles' heels you had, or at least you had by the fall of 2002, flaws in the fabric, dropped stitches. You had grown careless. It was just a question of choosing one starting point and pulling out those first loose threads.

I followed you in my head that afternoon when you left for the airport, trailing you on the road, listening to the news with you on Radio 4. You will be thinking about the war, I thought, the election, thinking about the route, turning on the headlights when the sun sets finally, squinting your eyes against the glare of cars coming through the night towards you. Cambridge to Gatwick. Two hours—your flight was at seven, you'd said, so you'd have to be there by five-thirty at the latest. You'd allowed yourself plenty of time. Didn't like to rush these things. Should you go? I asked. You had no choice, you said. Emmanuel was stable; he had his people about him. The police had asked all the questions they needed to ask for now. It would be time to think. *Time to think.* You used that phrase for over a decade as a weapon against me, a rapier for my heart. *I need time to think.* You had a way of saying it as if you were capable of making a decision that we both knew you would never make.

I looked in the fridge—only cheese and eggs and some bottles of beer. Don't forget to eat, you'd said in those last moments of the morning. You're getting too thin. You slid your hand under my shirt, caressing the skin around my ribs, running your fingers over the muscles of my stomach. I pushed upwards, reaching for your neck, pressing my ribs against your hand; my lips sought out the soft skin at the base of your neck.

Once you rowed for Trinity on the cold river every morning at dawn; now you row in the gym on a machine with your head turned towards a TV screen, watching daytime television with the sound turned off.

I made soup to eat later, when the missing of you stopped being a pain in my loins and belly—a soup made with the mushrooms you had left. Their brown gills closed, they were dry and rubbery to the touch; severed from damp wood, moss, and wet grass. Some had roots still where you had torn them from the soil, clinging to leaf mould. Pores and gills and caps. I peeled and sliced and cleaned. Inside one of the heads, maggots ate away at fanned gills.

Lack of appetite was punctured by ravishment. I ate the soup, which burned my tongue. I put my head down on the desk among all my papers, and, half asleep, imagined myself there with you in Florida, in that conference audience as it would assemble the following day, watching you on a stage with a microphone fixed to the top of a carved podium, a screen behind you on which you had shown your PowerPoint presentation. Statistics and graphs became a series of brain images, which became a single image of a cross-section of brain stem. The *experimentum crucis*. Rat or human? Your triumph—no, sorry, not *your* triumph, of course—the lab's triumph. Emmanuel Scorsa's triumph too; he should have been at the U.S. conference with you, but couldn't be because his brain was wired up to machines in the intensive care unit of Addenbrooke's Hospital.

This conference was important, I knew, because it was the first time you would unveil the evidence of your hypothesis. If this went well you would be able to apply for more funding, employ more researchers for the lab. You had the first tentative visual evidence that morazapine does indeed burst-fire the locus coeruleus—all set out there in the stained circle of colour projected onto the wall: the brain-slice image, taken in your lab (human or rat?), stored in your computer, and carried to Florida in a jet across the sea.

In my dream I watched you there in that room, using a long stick in semidarkness to point out patterns in the stains, places where the colours bled into each other, red into blue into green. You could read it. I couldn't. It never made any sense to me. All I could ever see was the shape of the top of a skull covered with blotches of colour, mostly red. *The evidence.* They always looked to me like pictures of stained glass, not brain tissue, stained glass windows in fourteenth-century churches in Venice. They made me think of crumbling walls and painted statues of virgins, of bleeding saints and tiled floors. Stigmata. But they were brain-tissue slices processed by a computer, not stained glass at all.

In my dream the conference audience was hushed, listening intently. They took notes. You stopped talking, eventually, with a final flourish of your stick towards the enormous panel of stained glass, projected like a rose window on the screen behind you. When you stopped there was a moment's silence, then applause. Louder than usual. You took a sip of water. Sat down. There was the slightest of smiles curling at the corner of your mouth, that mouth I reached for in the night. Then the chairwoman asked you if you would take questions. You nodded consent and shortly afterwards a young woman with Will's face stands up. She says: "Mr. Brown, might I ask you, would you be so kind as to give us your views on the ethics of using animals in research?" There is a murmur of mild outrage. How did an animal activist breach the security? You look tired. You say: "You will find my views on the ethics of animal research set out in an interview I conducted recently with the editor of *Nature* magazine. It is, I believe, published in the latest edition. I suggest you read that interview."

"With respect, Mr. Brown," she continues, "your views on animal research, which I have not had the pleasure to read, have, I believe, an important bearing on this conference. Many people here would very much like to know your views. Might you, do you feel, be able to offer them to us in a summarised form?"

A university security officer in a black uniform, no doubt completely unaware of the complex philosophical and moral issues now beginning to play themselves out in this hotel room, moves discreetly around the back of the conference room towards the standing woman. Under orders.

"This is not the place for such questions," the chairwoman intervenes.

"May I remind you that this is a conference assembled to discuss developments in neuroscience, not animal rights."

"Madam Chairperson," Will continues, "it is impossible to consider one set of questions without the other—"

The security guard has reached her. Now he takes her arm. She leaves the room without a struggle, saying only as she retreats, "I repeat, it is impossible to consider one set of questions without the other."

I woke from that dream ten minutes later with a stiff neck, asleep over my books and Elizabeth's papers. I was not sleeping well; I often fell asleep at my desk. I calculated, watching the time and pretending that I was working. Five o'clock. You'd be at the airport, changing your money from pounds to dollars, checking that you had packed both your phone and plug adaptors. Three pins; two pins. You buy a newspaper and check your luggage. You have manuscripts to read for the journey, you said. When I asked you about the length of the flight you told me it was two manuscripts and an article long. It had to be. You couldn't give that conference paper on Friday without having read them. Keeping up with your subject. Sailing close to the wind. You always did that. We both did.

You sent me a text from the airport at around five-thirty: "Only five days. I can still feel you." Smaller and smaller. The last few words. A man disappears to vanishing point. A woman returns to her desk for the fourth time that afternoon. Yes, she can still feel you. She drinks Earl Grey tea and she texts you: "I love you," she writes. Three words. Then adds four more: "however raw things get."

I liked to feel you watching me. When I worked in your mother's garden in those frosty mornings in late October when I couldn't sleep, I liked to feel your eyes on me from the window, you watching from the warmth of my bed, just woken to the sound of blades cutting. I didn't look up, but my every movement acknowledged you: clipping the garden to shape; tying tendrils to fences and stone; pruning roses; gathering the last few apples from the tops of the trees and carrying them into the kitchen. And sometimes, before I stepped out into the still dark garden, I liked to stand and watch you sleeping, holding the scythe in my hand.

You hung the prism at the base of the stairs. It will catch the light, you said, and make rainbows. It never did make rainbows, but the shadows darkened and sharpened in the pools of light that day you hung it. No rainbows, just the sharpening of shadows crossing light. Something passing through.

"You should get out more," Kit said every time she rang or when I stopped at the market to watch her moving among swathes of velvet, satin, cashmere, and linen. What did she think? That I stayed in all day, looking at Elizabeth's papers? Did she think I never left the house? She forgot that I walked to the University Library most days, swam at the Abbey pool twice a week, crossing the bridge over onto the common and continuing straight over to Newmarket Road, where the ferry once crossed. She didn't know that you came to The Studio most evenings. I couldn't tell her that. You should know better, she'd say. Out of the frying pan, into the fire. You've had your fingers burned often enough. So instead she just told me to get out more: "Staying in with just a bunch of papers and books for company is enough to make anyone demented. You can't stay in the seventeenth century all the time."

So eventually I said yes to the party on Guy Fawkes Night, on the day you left for the airport. The host was the mother of one of Maria's friends, Kit had said, not someone she knew well. Should be interesting, she said. This daughter of a famous poet, I forget which, had a party every year, Kit said, timed to take place just before the bonfire celebrations began on Midsummer Common. A Cambridge party—I yawned, imagining rooms full of the great and the good, and thinking that exhausted as I was, I couldn't even begin to make conversation, least of all about writing or art or poetry. But I needed distracting, I thought, with you being away and the worry of it. The *Cambridge Evening News* had reported three more attacks on animals in Cambridge in just the last few days: a horse and two more cats—all animals owned by employees of the targeted labs. The police were following up leads on Scorsa's attack; they had arrested a man seen in the area but had released him without charge. A drunk. He knew nothing. They wouldn't confirm that they were looking for members of NABED; they had no evidence to go on, except the pattern of seven wounds on Emmanuel's face, which matched the seven cuts on the mutilated animals. But, they said, they did not consider that fact significant at this stage. No point in me telling them that seven was one of the most powerful numbers in alchemy, that there were seven sacred forms of matter, seven veils of initiation; no point in telling them that in Revelations there had been seven plagues, seven angels, seven churches, seven seals, and seven vials.

Kit had stopped selling fur coats weeks ago. Even she could see the writing on the wall. Yes, now the writing was even etched into broken glass. All the butcher's shops had their windows smashed on a single night—Samuels on Mill Road, Wallers on Victoria Bridge, Pranklins on Arbury Road. The pet shops followed. You could see the emergency glass-replacement vans out everywhere. Bricks apparently, carried in a small rucksack and then thrown at the window with some force. Elsewhere they'd used some kind of battering ram. Pranklins had reinforced glass, so they'd driven a car into his shop window. They'd even had time to daub red letters across the broken glass—*murder,* it said. And the letters NABED etched on the brick.

Police helicopters were out every night. I could hear the persistent sound of their wings, like giant gnats or like that terrifying sense of violence coming through the skies in *Apocalypse Now.* From Elizabeth's window I could see their great beams of light angled across the night sky, illuminating something somewhere out there.

Kit knew she couldn't hold out anymore. She bundled up four fake furs, three astrakhan-fur coats, and some fox stoles in a black garbage bag one afternoon and drove to the back of Oxfam, pulling up in the car park next to the cinema. But the woman who opened the door at the back of the store a crack wouldn't take them. Too dangerous, she said. We've had orders from the head office. In the end, Kit had driven to the recycling center and, without asking, had put the coats, still in their bag, into the back of the lorry that collected clothes castoffs. Hundreds of pounds' worth of vintage fur. Recycled.

There was no point in a cocktail dress, I thought, eating a second bowl of now cold mushroom soup. Kit would wear a vintage silk dress and pull on a pair of wellies. Kit did that. She always looked magnificent. I was far too tired to wear anything but jeans, a jacket, and wellies. I remembered how cold the mud could be down on the common and how long you had to stand there looking up at the sky watching the fireworks. Jeans were not quite right for a party, but since I was a writer, no one would mind. I twisted my hair up onto my head the way Kit did hers, fastening it with a single clasp. With a little lipstick, it would do.

I was just about ready to write those final chapters, just summoning up the courage. I knew what Elizabeth wanted from me, knew how it had to be written now that I'd found some of the traces she'd left. Tomorrow, I thought. Tomorrow I would start. It would take me at least a month to write up the new material from her notes, which would leave me almost four months to edit the rest of the manuscript and check all the footnotes and sources. I had a chapter title—one title, but not yet two. This chapter title would fit the colour palette Elizabeth had created for the book: the existing chapters were titled "Glass Works," "The Black Death," "The Dis-aggregation of White," "The Green Lion," "The Refrangibility of Blue." My title would be "The Crimson Room," the last in the sequence. Then I would be finished with her and it and . . . you. Free to go. Not long. I could hear the door closing and the silence on the other side of it.

So that's how we ended up at the door of that party in Chesterton at six-thirty a Friday evening. Maria, Kit, and me in our wellies being handed cocktails mixed at a makeshift bar in the conservatory of a beauti-ful house—polished oak floorboards, arum lilies, landscape paintings. Groups of teenagers drifted across the hall, disappearing into a front sit-ting room to play on a PlayStation; Maria joined them, carrying in cans of beer and plates of tiny round crispbreads piled with cream cheese and prawns.

I had not dressed right, I could see, but I didn't care much. I was work-ing on being invisible. I talked and moved around, conducted by the hostess here and there. "Lydia, you must meet . . . John, Andrew, Julian." All men. Kit's doing—a quiet word to the hostess, no doubt. *You should get out more.* So the daughter of the famous poet brought me to an architect whose wife had just left him, a scientist who was working on the tempera-ture of black holes, a surveyor for the Ministry of Defence who played bass in a band. Did they sense my lack of interest in the wandering of my eyes, or my boredom in the shifting of my feet? "The trouble with the schools in Cambridge . . ." "The interesting thing about contemporary architecture . . ." "Do you know anything about drum and bass?" The poet, thank God, never materialised.

But you did.

No, you didn't see me. I left before you could. Cameron Brown was not at a conference in the States, nor were his wife and children in the country with her sister. No, I didn't see your face—except in the mirror. But it was you. You were in the hall—just arrived. Susanna, the hostess, was holding the coats you had just taken off—a fawn-coloured coat and a black one. That black one. The one that smells of you around the collar. The one you had put around me just that morning when I climbed out of the bath and asked you to find me a towel. "Put this on," you said. "Then I can take the smell of your body with me."

Sooner or later, Mr. Brown, one has to take sides if one is to remain human.

From the conservatory I watched you and Sarah talking to Susanna, a tall man in an ill-fitting black suit and a woman. A man and wife. I knew them both, even from the back. I couldn't hear what she was saying, or you. Sarah was wearing that lovely emerald green dress you bought her in London for her fortieth birthday and the pearl necklace. Your hand on her lower back. Your hand. I watched it. At the base of her back—you touched her there, tenderly, your fingers just stroking the bare skin, up and down. It was all in that gesture—what I could never see because I turned away always, because I couldn't bear to look at what was there in front of me. Your fingertips on the base of her back told me why you were still there in Over with Sarah—tenderness, mutual dependency, yes, and love. Your hand on her back. Touching her there, skin on skin.

"Gatwick?" the hostess is saying, her hand on your arm in sympathy. "You're flying to America tonight, for a conference? How very tedious. You poor, poor man. You'll miss the fireworks."

"We can't stay long," you say.

"Darling," I can see the side of her face for a moment, as she turns to you, "we've got easily an hour before we have to go. It only takes two hours to Gatwick. That's plenty of time."

I climb the stairs behind me to fetch my coat from the pile in the master bedroom; then I make my way carefully back down. But you've both gone, drawn into one of the inner rooms. I catch no one's eyes. There'll be an explanation, I say to myself. A reason. The lies have always been a kind of protection, a way of making it possible for all three of us to live with this. One of me was reasonable: "So he didn't leave this afternoon. He's on a later flight. Sarah is driving him to the airport and she will kiss him good-bye there. He only lied about the time of the flight; he just let you assume that he was going straight to the airport; that the last person he said good-bye to was you at The Studio under the dripping trees." Not such a crime.

"Why did you come back, Lydia?" Kit had asked once. "You said you were finished with Cambridge."

"Cambridge hasn't finished with me. I have some business to settle."

"Cameron?"

"No, not Cameron. Christ, no. That was all over years ago." I laughed, as if the thought was ridiculous. "Why must all matters of importance always be assumed to be matters of the heart?" I lied, of course, but well enough for Kit to believe me.

I was sitting on the stairs, pulling on my boots hurriedly, when I saw him, through the carved posts of the elegant staircase. At the party, in the beautiful house. The man in red, glimpsed only for a moment through an open doorway, in a mirror in the hallway. No, he was not a figment of alarmed and violent emotion. It *was* him. White hair, thin and unbrushed, fringing the edge of a long white face, the sneer round the corners of the mouth, brows furrowed as if in concentration or as if he couldn't quite see sharply. Just for a second, he passed across the mirrored surface, on the wall behind where you had been. Just turned and looked straight at me there, for a second. Framed, like a portrait. His mouth opened slightly as if he had something to say.

Maria's voice calls after me from the gate of the house I am fleeing, the house of the daughter of the famous poet.

"Lyddie, where are you going? What's up? You OK?"

My smile is as brittle as glass. "Yeah, I'm OK. Just tell your mum I'll call later. Not feeling great, that's all. I need to go home."

Home? The Studio was the last place I wanted to go. I was going to the river. Don't ask me why.

"Do you want me to come with you? You don't look very well."

"Hey you, don't fuss," I said. "You're just like your mother. Tell her I'll call later. Enjoy the fireworks."

Out into the street, the crowds are all heading in one direction—the river, the common, and the fireworks. Small children clasp sparklers, wide-eyed, unaccustomed to the night. Cambridge in November. The colours stream horizontally as if someone has taken a comb through wet paint.

Twenty-five

L ydia. Is that you? Christ. What's happened? Can you move? Wiggle your toes."

It's Will Burroughs. She's in black. Everything else is black and blue. I concentrate very hard, try to remember where my feet are. I move my toes. *Doesn't she have another name?*

"OK, try to sit up—slowly." I can feel a hand behind my head.

Will winds her scarf around my face. It smells of garlic and patchouli oil. She takes off her jacket and puts it around my shoulders. She rubs my legs with her long fingers. I am sitting upright against a brick wall, among rubbish bins, the acrid smell of blood, rotting food and urine in my nostrils. There's a box of empty champagne bottles a few feet away. Will rings for a taxi on her mobile phone. "Hello, Panther? Can I have a taxi for Garret Hostel Lane?"

I see a black panther coming down Garret Hostel Lane, prowling in the shadows by the rubbish bins, swaying slightly, ready to jump. Its coat glistens.

"Trinity Street?" she says. *I remember Trinity Street.* "Christ. You can't get any closer? OK. Outside Hobbs then, ten minutes." There's silence for a moment. I hear Will drawing in her breath somewhere close by. Gathering herself for something. "Shit," she says. "Shit." *Isn't she supposed to be in*

Leeds? Will Burroughs is Lily Ridler . . . is violent, is violet, is vile, is—in his bed with her face missing . . . photographs with no face . . .

"Don't say anything," she tells me. "I'll get you home. Can you stand? We've got to get up to Trinity Street. The taxi driver won't come down here. It's too narrow, he says."

"I don't want to go home," I say. I would cry if I could, but my face isn't mine to cry with. *Don't take me back there. There's too much light. Too many shadows.*

Cameron. Where are you? Why won't you answer? I'm hurting. I think this is your fault.

Will's talking slowly as if I am sick but I'm not sick, am I? I can't see her properly. I can't see anything properly. My head feels as if it's in a vise and someone's still tightening it.

I stand very slowly, with Will behind me, or is it Lily, her arms under mine, my eyes closed. I can see stars, brittle white stabs in my eyes. I am sick, down the wall.

Where are you?

I see the podium, the woman asking you the question, the slice of brain stem behind you like stained glass. With the taste of vomit in my mouth and more rising, I say to myself: "Might I ask, Mr. Brown, could you tell us your views on . . ."

Mr. Brydon, the prosecutor, was very insistent. "Could you tell the court once again, Dr. Brooke, the reasons why you didn't call the police the night you were attacked? Your nose was broken and your jaw partially fractured. You had three broken ribs. Someone had attacked you with a blunt instrument. You were bleeding."

"I was frightened and confused. I think I had also been poisoned. Will offered to take me home. I wasn't thinking straight."

"But, Dr. Brooke. Was it not possible that Will—Ms. Ridler—might have called the police?"

"I told her not to."

"You told her not to? You had been badly beaten. You told her *not* to?"

"Yes."

"Why was that, Dr. Brooke?"

"Because I didn't want anyone to know. I was trying to finish a book. I thought that if the police knew and there was an investigation I wouldn't be able to finish it. That there would be a lot of fuss."

"You didn't phone the police because you had a book to finish? It must have been a very important book. Perhaps you might be able to tell us what it was about?"

You bastard. You knew what it was about. You just wanted to sneer.

"It was a book about alchemy. Isaac Newton. Yes, well, it's more complicated than that, but essentially yes, that's how it was. I had to finish the book."

"So you didn't phone the police that night, when it was conceivable that you had been attacked by the same people who had left Mr. Scorsa for dead, because you had a book about Isaac Newton to finish?"

"Yes, I guess that is about right."

"No further questions."

How could I have said how it really was? That by then I had become absolutely sure that everything—even lives now—depended upon me finishing Elizabeth's book. What would the lawyer for the prosecution have said if I had told him that NABED was also part of a coded preface to the young Isaac Newton's notebook of sins, possibly an alchemical mantra or even a formula of some kind? That there was the seventeenth century and three dead fellows of Trinity College lying in doorways and a drowned boy to consider, as well as the rat farms and the labs and the balaclavas and the slashed bodies in twenty-first-century Cambridge alleyways. Who, Mr. Brydon, was the fifth man in Elizabeth's sequence? And, most importantly, how much had Ezekiel Foxcroft known?

The phone rang at midnight. It wasn't you, it was Kit. Will and I were watching TV—a game show—or at least she was watching; I had closed my eyes. It will be a distraction till you sleep, she said. She switched it off when the phone rang. The arnica bottle was out on the table. She had made me take four of the tiny blue pills cradled in the palm of her hand—for the internal bruising, she'd said. She'd dressed my wounds, soaked my bruises in witch hazel, and given me painkillers.

"Lyddie. You OK?" Kit asked. "Your voice sounds weird."

"Just a cold starting, that's all." *Christ, you should see my face, Kit. I have bruises across it. I think my nose is broken.*

"You missed the fireworks. And guess who was at the party?"

I know, I know. I saw him. He was with her. He was supposed to be on a plane to America.

"Who?" I asked casually.

"Cameron Brown. He asked after you, but he didn't stay long. He was flying somewhere, he said."

America. He was flying to America. She was driving him. The boys were there too, on the PlayStation with Maria in the front room. They must have all gone to the airport together, en famille. *He'll be on the flight now. She'll be driving home, the boys playing computer games in the back seat.*

"How did she look?" My voice betrayed me.

"Sarah? She looked like a woman who'd won, Lyddie. After a long fight. She looked tired."

"She did win. She won years ago."

Yes, but what kind of victory is that?

"Did you see him at the party? Is that why you left?"

"No, I just wasn't feeling well. I'm getting a cold. I ended up talking to this dreadful man about black holes, and he was going on and on and my head started to spin. I just wanted to get home."

"So how come you've not been answering the phone?"

"I took a sleeping pill, that's all. I can't keep my eyes open, Kit. Let me go back to sleep, eh?"

"I'll call you tomorrow," she said, her voice slightly hesitant, as though she knew there was something not quite right.

"Yes, please call me tomorrow. Late."

Will passed me another large glass of whisky—Laphroaig. Twenty minutes later I fell asleep in Will's arms on the sofa in front of the late news, despite the ache across my face from the ice pack. The following morning I couldn't open my eyes at all. I was still on the sofa. Will had laid a blanket over me and a pillow under my head. She had also hung blankets across the windows.

· · ·

"Can you identify Exhibit D, Dr. Brooke?" I hated Brydon's aloofness, that special sneer of contempt he reserved especially for me in the court-room. He passed me a plastic bag containing two keys on a key fob.

"Yes," I said. "It's a set of keys to The Studio."

"Your set?"

"No. These are Will's keys. Her key fob was purple like this."

"How long did she have keys to The Studio?"

"I'm not sure. From when she started working for Elizabeth, which was, I think, in 2001, until Cameron changed the locks in November 2002."

"Cameron Brown changed the locks?"

"He sent a locksmith to change the locks. Yes."

"Did he tell you why?"

"No sir, he didn't. He was always preoccupied with safety. He had to be." Now that I understood that only a fragment of what I knew could be produced in the courtroom, that the fact that a series of seventeenth-century murders which had become entangled with a campaign of violence in the present could not be admitted as an explanation for any of the questions the prosecution would ask, it didn't seem to matter what I omitted or kept to myself. I might as well omit evidence that would damn Lily if I could. I couldn't stop what was happening, but I could do my best to slow the accretion of evidence that would end in her sentence.

"Can you tell the court why these keys were found on the riverbed by police divers?"

"I have no idea. Perhaps she threw them away when she realised they no longer worked."

"Will Burroughs—Lily Ridler—was in possession of keys to The Studio at the time that Elizabeth was found drowned?" Brydon repeated.

"Yes, she was. But she had nothing to do with Elizabeth's death."

Brydon suddenly turned on his heel and drew very close. He sensed a mistake about to happen. He had taken me off guard. I had shown par-tiality.

"Do you know that to be a fact, Dr. Brooke? Do you know that beyond all doubt?"

"No sir, I don't."

Ask me about Mr. F., Mr. Brydon. Then we might get somewhere. Ask me about the book Elizabeth was writing or about how she knew she was going to die. Ask me, Mr. Brydon, about the goddamned seventeenth century. The keys mean nothing. They lead nowhere. Elizabeth died when she fell down a flight of stairs that no longer exists leading from a riverside glasshouse that was demolished nearly three hundred years ago to a landing stage that has left not even a shadow behind it. She died with a prism of seventeenth-century glass in her hand and a gash on her head. She knew she was going to die; she knew the man in red wouldn't let her finish assembling that record of seventeenth-century deaths.

Then again, Mr. Brydon, it would also be true to say that Elizabeth died because the Syndicate chose to make her death a warning to Cameron Brown—the most powerful message of all. But then you don't know about the Syndicate, do you?

Yes, both these explanations of Elizabeth Vogelsang's death are true. So why don't we start there, with the most difficult question of all: not about Lily or her keys—that is a distraction—but about how both explanations of her death might be true simultaneously. It's called entanglement, Mr. Brydon; the word describes the snares of love as well as a mystery in quantum physics. It's not just particles of light or energy that can become entangled; it's time too. Yes, moments of time can become entangled. The seventeenth century and the present have become entangled; they have become connected across time and space.

Twenty-six

What ever happened to Lydia Brooke? Did anyone know? She can't tell you because she doesn't know. The people who attacked her didn't come forward. Never have.

"Where were you going, Dr. Brooke, on the night of the fifth of November 2002?" The courtroom was hushed. Mr. Brydon wore a green wool suit. His white shirt was slightly grubby around the cuffs.

"To Trinity College. I had some research to complete."

"For your book? At seven-fifteen in the evening?"

"Yes, I needed to go to Trinity College."

"Despite the fact that you knew that Cambridge was not then a safe place? You knew about the attack on Mr. Scorsa three nights before?"

"Yes, I knew about Mr. Scorsa. But the city was full of people because of the fireworks. It seemed safe. I guess I didn't think I would be attacked. I didn't think there would be any reason why they would . . . I didn't think."

I had a key to Cameron's rooms in Trinity, Mr. Brydon. I was going there. I wanted to look in the drawers in his desk. I wanted to look in his computer. I wanted to know everything. Everything he had kept from me. I wanted to know all his secrets.

"Can you tell us in your own words what you *do* remember of your walk that night?"

"I am afraid, sir, that I don't remember anything very clearly after I turned into Trinity Lane and before I heard Will's voice. There was nothing unusual until then. The doctors have told me that the memory failure is due to the blow to the head. I'm sorry. I wish I could remember."

In my own words, Mr. Brydon? Oh yes, I will tell you in my own words what happened to me, to Lydia Brooke—what she remembers at least, or what she thinks she remembers. She remembers more than she will tell the prosecution at Lily's trial. Why does she not tell? Not to protect Lily or herself, but because what she remembers will make no sense to anyone there, or at least to anyone but the woman who looks like a boy who sits in the dock and the woman with the tattoo who sits in the gallery. They have already heard it, several times. They have gone through the story piece by piece with her. But otherwise, it is a story that can't be told. It's a simple matter of plausibility.

Did you know, Mr. Brydon, that the way you and I use the word *plausibility*—you know, to mean reasonable, fairly argued, believable— that that meaning only came about in the seventeenth century? No, I don't expect you did. Did you know that Jonathan Swift, the satirist, once described an excuse as having "more plausibility than truth"? More plausibility than truth. Yes, that's something. Your story, the one you are stitching together right now about Lily Ridler and the murders, has more plausibility than truth, I am afraid. But you would never understand that.

Lydia Brooke walked into the dark, wet Cambridge night that lay behind the fireworks and the party in the house of the daughter of the famous poet, behind the bright lights, the candles, and the mulled wine. She walked with her back to Midsummer Common, where thousands of people in jeans and Wellington boots stood watching the fireworks make patterns across the sky just as hundreds of Cambridge townspeople and students had watched the comets in December 1664 and April 1665, gazing skyward while standing on the very land where in the following summer and the one after it, hundreds of them would be buried as plague victims.

Lydia Brooke walked down Jesus Lane from east to west, imagining the few men, women, and children who also walked this way in the plague years, this way, not the other, *back into* the city, towards life, not death. They walked at dead of midsummer night, released from the pesthouses, back from the dead—frail, tired, wide-eyed, incredulous. The resurrected returning to houses where they must burn fires with unslaked lime until dawn, when they would open their shutters to the day, purged and still alive, to the wonder of their neighbours.

Where the streets were then pockmarked and cratered, and elsewhere sticky with mud or heaped with human and animal refuse, excrement, oyster shells, discarded meat bones and rotted vegetables, as well as ash and burnt wood, now they were paved and littered with burger packs and Coke cans. Where then the shop fronts were boarded up, their owners fled to the country, now glassed shop fronts illuminated the newest leather bags or shoes or winter coats on mannequins, which looked to Lydia that night as if they were theatrical dolls, menacing and grotesque, watching her, smiles too wide, too eager, their lipsticked cupid mouths too perfect.

She was not herself. Something was wrong. Her head ached, her skin crawled and sweated, glands throbbed beneath her arms and in her neck. She was nauseous, her stomach turned to liquid. She was afraid that she would have to throw up somewhere in a back alley, or stumble and fall, cornered like a wounded, hunted animal. Sickness had muddled her head and intensified her vision. She could see pinpricks of light across the night, flashing on and off in time with the pulse she could feel in the base of her neck and in her temples, even across her stomach. Sometimes everything seemed to contract as if it was running down a hole in her head, running to a still point. From time to time, fascinated, she would stop to watch the pulsing stars on the black night, and then time would slip away like a sand glass, to the sound of the fireworks somewhere behind her, which lit up the buildings in red and green in time with the pulse in her head. How long did she stand there, staring at the wall?

He must have been there all that time as she stood at the corner of Trinity Lane opposite Hobbs, but it was only when she turned to follow the arrow someone had painted on the corner wall over the words TO THE RIVER that she first heard the footsteps. Why did she turn there? Simply because the sign said TO THE RIVER and that seemed reason enough, an instruction even. She was very thirsty and she thought there might be water there in a river.

So she didn't enter Trinity through the great gateway under the carved unicorn and the lion into the courtyard beyond, for that would have meant talking to the night porter, explaining who she was. Instead she turned right off an empty Trinity Street lined with glittering shop fronts, into the dark of Trinity Lane. At the corner, she slipped under the CCTV camera lashed to the wall watching the shops, and into the lane that for centuries has snaked between the walls of Trinity to the right and Gonville and Caius to the left. She'd enter Trinity from the back, near the river.

That's when she first heard the footsteps, in step with her own. Turning to see who was behind her, she glimpsed, only for a moment, a shape, a human form, silhouetted against the lights from the shops on Trinity Street. But here there was not enough light to see by. The streetlights weren't on that night. She has no doubts about that part of what she remembers. It wasn't that the streetlights for some unaccountable reason had not been turned on, nor that there had been a power cut, but that *there were no streetlights at all.* They had disappeared. And there were footsteps.

Don't let him see you. Don't let him know you are afraid. Keep walking. Don't speed your pace. Don't look back. Remember Lot's wife: transformed into a pillar of salt. Yes, she is thirsty. Perhaps she is already a pillar of salt. Candles flicker in college windows. The man in the doorway is a pool of red in the night.

Wellington boots chafed against the back of her calf muscles, boots that felt as heavy as lead that night, and loud against the cobblestones. But how could they have been loud? Rubber soles make no noise against stone.

"What was it you saw that night, Dr. Brooke? In your own words."

"I'm not sure what they were." *The earth has bubbles, as the water hath, / And these were of them.*

" 'They'? You saw more than one figure?"

"Yes, sir, I saw more than one figure, but I am sure it was only one person I saw."

"Would you say the figure you saw—the one that followed you—was male or female?"

"I couldn't say. I never saw it clearly enough."

Actually, Lydia Brooke saw much more than she could say. Something broke for her that night. When she turned and could no longer see the figure at the top of Trinity Lane, she went to find it. When she thought, *He's gone,* something happened: a bolt shot somewhere, a tide turned.

Tears shall drown the wind. Did the alchemist think he was invincible? Was he? Did he think he was some kind of god, now that he had split light into colours, discovered the laws of motion and of gravity, scratched out the outlines of the calculus? Did he think he had divine protection? Do you? Is that it? Are you immortal already, Isaac Newton, or do you just think you are? Did you make a pact?

Tell me. I'll keep your secret.

And the man in red does what she does, turns, feeling her tide turn against him. He heads for the river down Garret Hostel Lane. How far will Lydia Brooke go? Her pulse, sickeningly fast, drums in her ears and eyes and in her temples. A cat, in the shadows, rummaging among piles of rotten food and rubbish, hisses, seeing what she sees: the figure in the red gown, the man with the white hair, the man who shouldn't be there.

She wants to know, to see. He wants to stop the seeing. She must know. She must not know. *"I am in blood / Stepp'd in so far, that, should I wade no more, / Returning were as tedious as to go o'er . . ."* Tell me.

Lydia shadows the figure in red, moving swiftly now, his gown made of crimson wool, drapery forming and re-forming heavily in the wind, like the folds of the statues they would make of him everywhere, in churches and chapels and outside libraries. She penetrates the dusk of distances and the gloom of shadows, watches him through the shifting effects of perspective brought on by sickness. Was she bringing him out, or he her? A game of hide-and-seek, inside outside, stalker and stalked. *He's behind you.* But then he has gone again, into an interstice in the stone, an opening she cannot see, leaving only a trembling of red upon the wind, the only colour in that Cambridge night now except for the fireworks still breaking over her head like red and green chrysanthemums and corals, over the crenelated and towered edges of college roofs.

But he has not gone. She can feel him bristling somewhere close by, a hunted thing, or a hunting thing, filling out every corner of Garret Hostel Lane. She knows she has to draw him out. He has to run again so that she can follow. She hears steps ringing on stone. She can see him on the other side of the river now, a red figure bleeding into the rain-circled river, a figure reflected in water walking upside down, his leather boots echoing on stone. Over Garret Hostel Bridge into—what?

She has crossed the river. She is standing now where she had stood only three days before, looking across the Backs to Queen's Road, Trinity College behind her, Garret Hostel Bridge behind her. But now where there should have been a paved road in front of her leading from Trinity across a scrublike stretch of meadow, once marsh, to meet Queen's Road, the Backs, a road receding through linden trees to a vanishing point in the night, now there was no road, no linden trees, no vanishing point. Instead she stood on a perfect oval of grass, an island in the river; she was looking from Garret Hostel Greene across water into marsh and darkness. Except that Garret Hostel Greene had been dug up some 330 years ago to make way for the Wren Library.

Lydia knew the patch of oval ground in the middle of the river from the photocopy of George Braun's map of sixteenth-century Cambridge pasted into the pages of *The Alchemist,* and from the second copy, which Elizabeth had taped to the wall of the bathroom in The Studio, above the jar of toothbrushes. George Braun had drawn the oval of Garret Hostel Greene as an enormous pupil in that map of the city, which itself looked in some lights like a cross-section of an eye, one of those seventeenth-century anatomical drawings. On the map there were swine and strange dragonlike creatures, perhaps even a kind of unicorn over on the land beyond the river on the outskirts of the city of stone, glass, and reason.

How could she feel the spongy marshy ground of the green under her feet unless she was already mad?

Something falls into the water. Or lifts out from it. He, the figure in red, is now standing behind her on the bridge, apparently waiting for her. She closes her eyes for a long minute. When she opens them the night seems lighter, but stained with red, the water, the bridge. A phantasm. Newton's sun-stain.

It takes her several moments to work out how the view from the river, from this bridge over which she now follows him, differs from what she knows should be there, because the stain sits there between her and the world, tearing her retina. How can you look at an absence so immense and not see it? *No library.* A hole where it should be and in its place, where that great library designed by Sir Christopher Wren should be, its gracious arches reflected in the river, only a tennis court and a cluster of half-timbered single-story buildings.

She follows him into Trinity through courtyards and corridors thick with wood smoke, where shutters are closed, where cracks of candlelight through shuttered windows spill out and radiate. He stops and waits on the stone flagging; she follows him to the bottom of a wooden staircase, then climbs after the flash of red, through the smell of camphor, slaked lime, and balsam. Odours of the apothecary's shop. He is there, at the top of the staircase, waiting, holding his ground. She turns, still looking up, and stumbling to protect herself from something falling towards her, a glint of glass; she falls in an unlit corridor to the bottom of a flight of stairs in a building which has been demolished to make a great library some 330 years ago.

That was something of the reason why Lydia Brooke kept certain things to herself in the courtroom. There had been moon shadows and red stains on the night of the 5th of November that she could not have begun to describe. Her silence was, she knew, at least technically, a kind of perjury. She had sworn that she would tell the truth, the whole truth, and nothing but the truth, but she had long understood that there were whole truths and half-truths and truths that simply could not be put into words and would not be heard even if they were.

Twenty-seven

It took me some time to open my eyes. Perhaps I didn't want to. Some-where in my head, somewhere in a mass of swollen flesh, my eyes were hot. The painkillers had worn off. I could hear someone else moving around in the room—that was Will, I guessed; she had promised to stay for a few days. Once upon a time. What was Will doing here? Was I now a kind of hostage? Would Lily Ridler use me to reel you in? Kit would come; Kit would know where to look for me.

I struggled to piece together the fragments of the night before as if it were as simple as waking hungover after a long party. I was lying on the sofa in the big room, covered with musty patchwork quilts that Will had dragged out from some cupboard somewhere. I opened my eyes a crack. I could still see; that was something. Will was between me and the win-dow, her body flattened by the thin morning light. She was pulling off her nightgown over her head, unaware of my presence. A Rembrandt painting—a Saskia. Your Saskia. Arms stretched high over her head, dis-robing, long limbs, white skin, blue-white in this light. Will Burroughs. Lily Ridler. Your lover in my house. No, your lover in Elizabeth's house. No, Elizabeth's friend in Elizabeth's house. Will Burroughs.

I understood something of Lily's spell on you as I watched her limbs moving against the morning, the enigma you had fallen for and been so enmeshed in. The Lily Ridler who, you said, took you into her bed in that room in Mawson Road. The eyes that were always somehow absent. She'd changed since I had seen her last. She seemed bigger, or maybe that was because, black and blue as I was, I felt smaller. Or perhaps it was because there were two facts now that I couldn't reconcile: she had been your lover and I knew I was in her debt.

The air in the big room was thick with the smell of wood smoke, the sleep smells of two women and dried blood. My clothes were still piled on the floor near the desk—a pair of jeans, a T-shirt, a scarf, and a cream cord jacket. That jacket would have to be dry cleaned, I thought. What do you say to a dry cleaner about caked blood? An accident. What kind of accident would produce that much blood?

"You awake?" she said, turning towards me, smiling, still half naked and unself-conscious, pulling on olive-coloured combat trousers over black knickers. I saw the tattoo of a butterfly on the base of her back. I imagined your fingers following the outlines of that butterfly, and then I looked away when I couldn't say for sure whose fingers were where. The room was suddenly thick with your lovers and mine: Sarah, Antoine, Lily, Will, and then Cameron and Lydia somewhere—which edge, which fingers, whose tongue was that, whose curve of hip?

Under the pillow where I had left it, my mobile phone buzzed. You had texted me these words: "A kiss for your morning from the night of America." I typed out a reply: "I need you to come home. I've been hurt. I don't know what to do." Then I erased each of those letters, backwards, one by one, till there was nothing left on the white screen. No, no drama. Ill-advised. I needed time, not flurries of questions and anxiety. I wrote to you as I would have done if it was just an ordinary 6th of November morning and I was playing the usual game of cat and mouse, predator and preyed upon, seducer and seduced, that game we played in which we got to change places as often as there were texts.

"I will not kiss you today," I wrote. "Not today. You will have to find other lips to kiss." *Mine are cut and bleeding.* Like releasing a white dove into the sky to seek you out in Florida. *Message sent.* It's all just the same here. I am fine. Nothing to worry about.

"You won't want to look at yourself for a bit," Will said. "It's not pretty. You might want to stay away from mirrors. Who was the text from?"

"Kit," I said. "I've texted back that I'm full of cold and I'll call later."

I tried to feel the size of my face with my fingers, running my finger-tips round the lids of my eyes. Those first tears hurt, so I bit the end of my tongue, hard. I could taste blood in my mouth, see it in the darkness of my sight. I could smell blood in the air.

The phone buzzed again. You were keying in words to send to me across the sea from your hotel room.

"I have just written you a fine long letter," you replied. "So I will kiss you as often as I like. Try to stop me."

"Will?" It was her voice I needed to stop the tears.

"Yes?"

"I can't see very well. Do you think I should call a doctor?"

"No, not unless you want the police here. It's just swelling. It'll go down in a day or so. You'll need to lie low for a bit. You have broken ribs, I think, but I've strapped them up as well as I can. A doctor wouldn't do any more than that. There's nothing else broken but your nose as far as I can tell. That will heal by itself. It'll be OK. I'll stay with you, I promise, as long as I can. You still sure you don't want me to call the police?"

"No. I don't think so. I mean, I don't know. I don't know what to do. I want to get whoever did this, but I don't want the police involved. If they come here there will be questions about me being here and the book, and Cameron will have to get involved. And he's in deep enough already."

"You can say that again."

"What does that mean?"

"Nothing. Listen. I've been sitting here thinking about it since six o'clock. I reckon you have to know now. It can't make things any worse for you because you're kind of at the eye of the storm. Trouble is, the storm's moving all the time."

"Know what?" Behind Will's head a fine rain had begun to sweep across the garden.

"There are things you don't know about Cameron Brown."

So that's how Lily Ridler began. Not by telling me that you had been her lover. In the scale of things *that* fact scarcely mattered. Lily's Cameron Brown fitted into your skin but was not the man I knew. Beware the man who is hairy on the inside, someone said once. The rat man. The wolf man. What does a wolf skin look like from the inside?

You were right. She is—was—an animal activist. In 1998 she'd been chosen to set up a splinter group of an international animal-rights organization. Their aim was to sabotage the activities of Histon BioSciences because it had doubled its use of laboratory animals that year. She was passionate and driven. As I watched her talk, I could see how she might have made a powerful infiltrator, might have been persuaded to wrench secrets from you, allow her body to become a tool with which to blackmail you.

Lily's entanglement began in the spring of 2001. Back then venture capital sponsors, defeated by the spiralling cost of security against animal-activist campaigns, had withdrawn money allocated to build a new, internationally coordinated pharmaceutical laboratory in Cambridge. The animal liberationists hadn't dared to celebrate, she said, knowing that there had to be a major backlash, knowing that a war had started with that victory.

"Did you celebrate last night?" I asked bitterly. "Was I another triumph?"

"Lydia. Christ, listen to you. Are you so fucking brainwashed that you can't see what everyone ought to be able to see? What happened to you last night, and to Emmanuel Scorsa last week, has *nothing* to do with the animal-activist campaigns. NABED has nothing to do with us. Look, use your head. What is the most important thing that animal-liberation groups have preached since the seventies?"

"Nonviolence?"

"Exactly. So why have a group of activists suddenly started to kill animals and attack scientists in the Cambridge area? Why not anywhere else? And why the change of policy, the abandonment of a policy of nonviolence to life which has defined everything we've done since the campaigns began? Why would we jeopardise all that now?"

"So who *is* driving it?"

"In the spring of 2001, after the plans for the Cambridge pharmaceutical lab were scrapped, a group of seven men—directors of some of the multinational pharmaceuticals and others—were summoned to a meeting in a hotel somewhere in North London. They formed an alliance, calling themselves the Coalition for Research Defence. We call them the Syndicate."

"Why Syndicate?" Outside in the garden, the apple trees strained against a wintry wind, lashed with rain.

"Because they're like the Mafia. Inside everything. Wired up to everything. They talk about strategies and wars on terror and—I've read some of the e-mail correspondence—smoking us out. To them we're vermin burrowing under their ground, terrorists standing in the way not just of scientific advancement but democracy and even the safety of the West. The bastards are fundamentalists at heart, not cynics. That makes them more dangerous."

"What do they want?"

"To wipe out animal activism once and for all, at any price. They've pretty much destroyed us in eighteen months. One member of the Syndicate, John Petherbridge, is a senior officer of the Special Branch group established by Scotland Yard to infiltrate terrorist groups. So they've got access to mobile phone numbers, e-mail addresses, CCTV recordings, all the information they need to bring us down. They have major financial backing from the drug companies and, we think but can't prove, even government—or at least MI5—support."

"This is all about drugs?"

"Christ, no. The pharmaceutical companies make big money from the drugs trade. But two of the seven men who run the Syndicate are arms dealers. One of them, Robert Marlow, is particularly dangerous. He's funding gunrunners in Afghanistan."

"I don't get it. What's the connection?"

"Between the arms dealers, Scotland Yard, and the pharmaceuticals? Biological weapons. A consortium of pharmaceutical companies is close to a big breakthrough with a chemical that paralyses the human nervous system. An immobiliser. Works just like those wasps that paralyse their victims. They're on the last stages of the tests now."

"How do you know? And should you be telling me all of this? Mightn't the house be bugged or something?" Lily couldn't hear my mockery.

"This is one of the safest places of all, because of Elizabeth. Why do you think I found my way here? Keep your friends close and your enemies even closer."

"Elizabeth? Was she a member of the Syndicate?"

"Oh, Christ no. Elizabeth never knew anything about that. She was completely lost in her world—optics, glass, light, the seventeenth century. She wouldn't have been interested in what I do, what *we* do. She had her own villains to hunt down."

"Villains?"

"You've not finished reading it yet—Elizabeth's book?"

"Yes, OK. I know who Elizabeth was hunting down. Or at least I think I do. Where does Dilys fit in?"

"Dilys Kite? Oh, she's OK. Just a friend of Elizabeth's. She was round several times a week—she drove me mad. I fell out with Elizabeth when we argued about Dilys."

"Did Elizabeth know about what you were doing?"

"Of course not. They were like a pair of old witches with their crystal balls. All caught up in the past and with the dead. They couldn't see the dying around them, the slaughter. That wasn't for them."

"So what is NABED?"

"NABED is an animal-liberation terrorist organisation. They were set up in the spring of last year. They attack employees of the labs and their families. They are extremely violent. They work in cells."

"They were established at the same time that the Syndicate launched their campaign? Spring of 2001?"

"You're getting the picture."

"Shit—no," I said. "That's completely implausible. Are you telling me that NABED is the terrorist wing of the Syndicate?"

Lily didn't answer.

I went on unravelling, in disbelief: "That they attack their own people, just to discredit . . . ?"

"I said—at any price."

"But Emmanuel was nearly murdered . . ."

"It went wrong. We think something went wrong."

"And you've been working from The Studio, all this time? Lying to me?"

"Yes, I can send e-mails from here that won't be traced."

"But Elizabeth doesn't have an Internet connection."

"My laptop has a wireless connection. There's a transmitter on a house next door that I use. They don't know that I use it. My e-mails piggyback on their line."

"But why should The Studio be safer than anywhere else? How did you know that it wouldn't be bugged?"

"You don't get it, do you? It's simple. Because Cameron Brown runs the Syndicate. Because Cameron Brown developed Morazapine—the chemical that paralyses the nervous system. Because Cameron summoned those men to the London hotel, because Cameron set up NABED, because Cameron *is* the Syndicate."

We'd fallen off the edge of something solid. Neither of us spoke until Lily said, "Do you know where he is now?"

"In Florida."

"Is that what he told you?"

What *had* you told me? You told me you'd been working with Elizabeth on cracking the code in Newton's notebook—the alchemical purification spell. The cluster of letters that began with NABED. Not a coincidence then, just a private joke, a name for the terrorist wing of the Syndicate. Morazapine—I remembered you talking about Morazapine. You'd called it an antipsychotic drug, hadn't you? Hadn't you described how it worked by burst-firing some part of the brain; hadn't you said that it kept madness at bay, that it would be a major breakthrough in the treatment of schizophrenia? Morazapine—I remembered the camels and the incense and myrrh the name had conjured, the white owl flying across the path of our car as you talked, trees branching out like arteries against the night sky. I remembered love. I remembered you. Somewhere in the hot pain inside my head, I remembered you, watching you sleep, your body against my sheets, still, watching you breathing.

After I left you, I'd listen to that song by Counting Crows, the one about trying to forget . . . about thinking for a time that you had. Thinking you were free. The song about how the remembering comes crashing back, like a blow to the stomach, in a spectrum of colours—"Give me your blue rain, Give me your black sky, Give me your green eyes . . . give me your white skin . . . give me your white skin . . . give me your white skin . . ." Yes, I had given myself up again. As if I had no choice. In fact, I had never taken myself back.

With what are you embroiled, Lydia Brooke?

"Morazapine is an antipsychotic drug," I said slowly. "He told me about it."

"Yes, it was to start with. But Cameron also discovered its paralysing effects, which he tested and strengthened in his lab."

"He would never have set out to—"

"Make a formula that would be used in a chemical weapon? No, of course not. But once he put in a fund-raising bid to a company he knew had links to arms dealers, once he'd taken the huge research grant they gave him and the new lab, research assistants, and lab equipment, and the nomination for that international award in neuroscience, he'd given away any control he might have had about the future uses of that formula—"

"He was weak," I said and then, hearing myself defend you like that, I snapped, fragmenting into a thousand pieces. "Get away from me," I said suddenly, into the darkness of the room, as tears began to sting my face. "Get out. I can't hear any more."

"I'll be back in an hour," Will said, quietly. "I'll be down in the garden by the river if you need me."

"Don't come back," I said. "Don't come back."

"I'm taking your mobile and the landline handset with me," she said. "So you don't try to call anyone. I'll be back in an hour. I'm taking your keys; mine don't work in the lock anymore."

Twenty-eight

I wasn't afraid of what she might still tell me; I had to stand and face it. Despite my injuries, I could have walked away that morning, taken the side door and the path through the garden to the gate in the wall, without Will seeing me. I could have called you on your mobile from the pay phone in Landing Lane, reached you in Florida, or wherever you were; I could have left you a message. Or simpler still, I could have phoned the police and told them where to find Lily Ridler.

So why didn't I? Because I was curious, and it wasn't a benign kind of curiosity, it was something dark and ravenous—ravens scavenging over a corpse, dark, urgent, and visceral. For years I'd ignored my endless small suspicions about your words and explanations; I hadn't wanted suspicions enmeshed with love. Yes, I knew you had lied, to me and to Sarah, serially and compulsively, all the time we'd been lovers. Lied, not only as a way of keeping the affair going, not only as a means of controlling a life that had become fractured into multiple secrets, but also because you had forgotten the difference between truth and lies, and recently you had come to lie when you didn't need to, badly. You'd left the Volvo at Trinity and walked to The Studio, you said. I drove to the Trinity car park an hour later. It wasn't there. You were visiting a friend in Nottingham for the weekend, you said. I found the receipt for the hotel in Munich in your wallet. You were driving back to the lab, you said. I watched a dark un-marked car pick you up from Landing Lane.

So I didn't leave The Studio. I walked up and down in the undulating, shoaling light, talking to you. When Will came back an hour later, I said, "You've made a mistake. He could never be caught up in all of this."

"He is."

"I've known him for so long . . ."

"I know. And you've been lovers for years. Don't tell me. He's too kind to be involved in anything so violent. He has children. Pets. He reads Rilke, makes love to you. Look, people are complicated. Your Cameron runs NABED; he orders animals to be mutilated and people attacked to discredit us, all in the name of the freedom to experiment on animals. He thinks he is doing the right thing, of course. He wouldn't do it if he didn't. I've heard tapes of one of the Syndicate meetings. He thinks he's doing what's necessary to defend what he calls civilisation and civilised values. Some civilisation, eh?"

"Do you know how long we've been lovers?"

"Yes. That sort of information is easy to come by. It's that kind of war. You have to know where your enemy's weak spots are."

"So that's why I was attacked last night."

"I told you. We are a nonviolent organisation. What happened to you last night has nothing to do with any animal-liberation group."

"But everything to do with NABED?"

"Yes."

"But if NABED is the terrorist wing of the Syndicate and Cameron Brown is one of them, he would have known I'd be attacked last night. He would have sanctioned it." *Did you? Could you have done that?*

"No, not necessarily. There are things happening in the group—alle-giances are breaking down. Petherbridge is especially dangerous. I would always have said that you'd be the safest of all. Cameron—they—wouldn't go that far. And you being attacked would expose him too—expose you as his lover. Think what the press would do if they got hold of that story. That's a hell of a price to pay, to lose you and his wife at once." Yes, I could see that.

"So it doesn't make sense."

"It only makes sense if there's some kind of internal battle going on.

Cameron is having to fight for his corner. I'm sure the attack on you last night was meant as a warning to him. And that's not good, because he's been acting as a brake in the last few months, questioning some of their decisions, opposing others. Now that the testing stage is almost complete, he's being kept out of certain decisions. He no longer knows everything. But he's still the only one who knows how the formula works or how to develop it. They wouldn't have it without him. He's the linchpin for everything, but not for much longer. With the tests almost complete, he's making himself dispensable."

"What's to be done?"

"There's nothing for you to do. You don't even have to believe anything I've said. You can put it all down to paranoia. We have to sit it out. If I'm right, they've used you to send their message to him."

"What if the message doesn't get through?"

"How do you mean?"

"Well, if I don't tell the police and if I put off seeing Cameron when he gets back from America—until my face has healed, that is—then there's no need for him to ever know. Then the message won't reach him."

"But you have no idea what that will do."

"It'll throw a spanner into the works. Might stop whatever's happening, or slow it down?" I was clutching at straws.

"Best thing you can do is to finish the book and then move back to Brighton. Get out of the cross fire. It won't go on forever. But it is going to get worse before it gets better. Especially now."

I didn't see Will again after she left The Studio that day. I didn't see her again until the court case. I tried to speak to her during the time they held her at the Parkside Police Station, but they wouldn't let me. I wanted to ask about you and her, but I never did because there was never the time, nor could I have found the words.

That last morning, as she left The Studio, heading north again, she gave me a brown envelope.

"You won't like me for this," she said. I had to squint to see the writing, but I recognised the shape of Elizabeth's handwriting before I could read the letters. The envelope was addressed to Will Burroughs at an address in Chesterton.

"She posted me this the day before she died," Will said. "See—the postmark is the sixth of September. There's a note. It simply says, 'Dear Will, sorry to be oblique but I wonder if you might keep this in a safe place for a few weeks. It's a draft of something. A precious piece. I'll let you know when I need it back. It's the only copy, so keep it carefully.' "

"Have you opened it?"

"Yes."

"And?"

"It's a chapter of *The Alchemist*. It's called 'The Crimson Room.' "

"It can't be called 'The Crimson Room.' That's not possible. My chapter's called 'The Crimson Room.' Have you read it?"

"Yes."

"Has anyone else read it?"

"Only Emmanuel Scorsa."

"Emmanuel Scorsa. The neuroscientist in the hospital? How the hell?"

"He's one of us, works undercover like me. He's been working at the Histon lab for a year or so. When he first came to Cambridge, I had to brief him about the layout in the lab. I'm the only one who knows—I worked inside that unit for six months before Cameron took the job there. Emmanuel came to The Studio sometimes at night after Elizabeth died because we thought it was safe. Then you arrived."

"But why did you show him? Were you lovers?"

"No, we weren't lovers. There are rules about that, for Christ's sake. I showed him the chapter because after Elizabeth died I didn't know what to do. Everything and anything was possible—I started imagining even more conspiracies." She paused, uncertain how much to say. "I knew Cameron very well once, as part of my work. When Elizabeth died, some of my people were saying that Cameron was behind it . . . but that made no sense because he and his mother were so close. He talked about her all the time. I couldn't believe . . ."

So Lily's relationship with you had become emotionally "complicated," despite everything you stood for.

"No, you were right," I said. "That's unthinkable."

"They pulled me out for a bit when I got sick. I started to see things here at The Studio—strange lights. My vision got weird. I think I must have had a bit of a breakdown."

"And what did Scorsa say?"

"Not much. He told me to bring the chapter here and leave it somewhere safe. We both knew it was pretty incendiary stuff, though those ideas and theories Elizabeth had about alchemy and murder were also weirdly plausible. I couldn't see the point of all that energy, really. Elizabeth's obsession. You know: a whole ten years given over to uncovering a network of alchemists and then ending up with a theory about a grubby little set of murders in Cambridge. Pathetic, really. Think what that energy and intelligence might have done for us. Do you know how many animals we kill to eat in this country alone every year?" she said, opening her eyes wide.

"I couldn't even begin to guess," I said.

"Eight hundred million animals, every year. Doesn't that just do your head in?"

"So it's been here all the time."

"What? The chapter? Yes, I stuck it behind some of the books in the big bookcase. I didn't want Sarah finding it when she was clearing out the house. It's yours now. Better late than never, I suppose. I just thought it might make your job a bit easier if I gave it to you. Make it easier for you to leave Cambridge."

"But why didn't you give it to me before?"

"I didn't think that Elizabeth wanted you or anyone else to have it. She didn't tell me anything. I was trying to do what she wanted, but it doesn't seem to matter now. Look, if it gets you out of Cambridge quicker, it will have been of some use."

Twenty-nine

In the silence that followed Lily's leaving, I knew that despite the pain in my eyes, I could not postpone reading that final chapter, a chapter I had already sketched in my head from Elizabeth's original notes and inferences. Those facts had begun to speak for themselves. Outside in the garden, nothing moved; the wind had dropped. The lights reassembled on the walls, like a spectral gathering, solemn and still, as if restlessness had ceased, for the moment. I was sure that I knew now what she had discovered, that terrible truth, about a great man's climb to power, about the price Newton was prepared to pay for the red robe, the Lucasian chair of mathematics. Yes, I was sure that Elizabeth had tracked Newton the alchemist to his lair, that she had found him out. This was her chapter:

The Crimson Room

The fact that Newton was appointed to a prestigious fellowship at Trinity College in 1667 is remarkable. He was certainly in the running—his scholarship made him eligible—but he had not distinguished himself academically, and he had given a poor performance in his examination for the scholarship.

Few Newton scholars have anything to say about the unusual circumstances by which the Trinity fellowships had become vacant by 1667. An American academic, Louis Trenchard More, who published a detailed biography of Newton in 1934, is an exception. He presents the vacancies as being the result of good fortune: "On October first [Newton] was elected a Minor Fellow. There were nine fellowships vacant that year, as no elections had been held in 1665 and 1666. One of them was made by the death of the poet, Cowley; two of the other vacancies were caused by Fellows falling down staircases—whether the result of defects in the stairs or of excessive conviviality may be left to the imagination . . . One of the Senior Fellows . . . Barton, had been ejected from the college in the preceding June on the grounds of insanity."[1]

Even Michael White, whose more recent biography of Newton claims that Newton was, as an alchemist, "the last sorcerer," ascribes the vacancies to luck, and seems not to know that the falls of Valentine and Greswold resulted in deaths: "By chance, that year the number of vacancies had been inflated by several retirements and a death occasioned by events which vividly convey the atmosphere of Restoration Trinity. A senior fellow had been recently removed on the grounds of 'mental aberration' of some unknown variety, and two other fellows had been forced to retire through injuries sustained after falling down the staircase leading to their rooms while in a drunken stupor. A fourth, the poet Abraham Cowley, had died after catching a fever brought on by a night spent sleeping in a field after a bout of heavy drinking. Luckily for Newton, this created a lengthy enough list to give him an opening."[2] *Luckily for Newton.*

Richard Westfall fails to mention the deaths of the Trinity fellows at all, regarding them perhaps as less relevant than the vote rigging and corruption in the elections, which he describes as common practice in Trinity at the time. However, he does describe Newton's unusual behaviour in the months from his return to Cambridge in March 1667 to his appointment to fellow status in October 1667. Westfall implies that the young man ought to have been nervous: "As with the scholarship three years earlier, Newton's whole future hung in the balance of this election. It would determine whether he would stay on at Cambridge and be free to pursue his studies or whether he would return to Lincolnshire, probably to the village vicarage that his family connections could have supplied, where he might well have withered and decayed in the absence

[1] Louis Trenchard More (1934), *Isaac Newton*, p. 45.
[2] Michael White (1997), *Isaac Newton: The Last Sorcerer*, p. 95.

of books and the distraction of petty obligations. On the face of it, his chances were slim. There had been no elections in Trinity for three years, and as it turned out there were only nine places to fill . . . How could an erstwhile sub-sizar of whatever capacity hope to prevail against such odds?"[3]

Strangely, as Westfall points out, Newton's financial accounts for 1667 (laid out after his list of sins) show that the young man was acting in a way that revealed absolutely no anxiety about his future: "Neither in Newton's papers nor in the surviving anecdotes does a hint of tension over the outcome [of the examinations] appear. His accounts present a picture of relaxation which almost belies our other evidence of unremitting, introverted study. Soon after his return, he spent 17s 6d [£92 in current rates] to celebrate his Bachelor's Act and on subsequent occasions tossed away another of the £10 [£1,000] he had pried loose from Hannah Smith and then some with 'acquaintances' at taverns. He cheerfully confessed to a loss of 15s [£81] at cards, compensated perhaps by a purchase of oranges for his sister. The accounts radiate confidence as well. He invested £1 10s [£163] in tools, real tools, including a lathe, such as he must have longed for in Grantham—not the purchase of a man seriously expecting to move on a year hence."[4]

In 1667 Newton clearly did not think his stay in Cambridge was going to be temporary. He was already celebrating his future. Could he have known the outcome of the elections in advance? And how would that have been possible unless Barrow, Babington, and others had told him? Where did all this confidence come from? What had he been promised, and by whom?

On being elected a fellow in 1667, Newton turned his rooms into a crimson chamber. Instead of taking the new rooms allocated to him as a fellow, he continued to use those he shared with Wickins, between the Great Gate and the chapel, the rooms that adjoined the laboratory and physic garden. After being elected, he paid for these rooms to be redecorated and bought new crimson furniture and hangings, as well as new carpets and pictures and a whole wardrobe full of expensive clothes.

Newton had shown an obsession with the colour red since he had copied out those earliest recipes for mixing colours in the Grantham notebook; that obsession would persist into his old age. In a list of possessions drawn up by

---

[3] Westfall, *Never at Rest*, pp. 176–77.
[4] Ibid., pp. 177–78.

Catherine Conduitt after her uncle's death, she records "a crimson mohair bed complete with case curtains of crimson Harrateen" and in the dining room "a crimson settee."[5] Other items included crimson drapes and valances in the bedroom, a crimson easy chair, and six crimson cushions in the back parlour.

Red was the colour of power in Cambridge—Barrow, as the Lucasian Professor of mathematics, was the only fellow of the college to wear a scarlet gown. Scarlet robes marked out a special kind of status in the city too, for the aldermen exchanged their ordinary gowns for scarlet gowns on ceremonial occasions, for churchgoing, and for the pomp required for the opening of the Stourbridge Fair.[6]

There was talk in the college now, whisperings that connected Newton to the deaths of Greswold, Valentine, and Cowley, that embroiled Newton in talk of conspiracies and poisonings and murder. Those were suspicious deaths, at least collectively. He and the other newly elected fellows had gained from them. But Newton was the only one who had access to the physic garden and the poisonous plants that were said to grow there. What was the truth behind these rumours?

One figure has been overlooked by Newton's historians. Ezekiel Foxcroft, some ten years Newton's senior, a fellow of King's College and lecturer in mathematics, had been travelling between London, Cambridge, and Ragley Hall in Warwickshire, carrying messages and manuscripts for his mentor, the philosopher Henry More, since the early 1660s. At Ragley Hall, he had presided over scores of complex alchemical experiments in the company of important alchemists, including his own mother and her companion Anne Finch. In his rooms at Cambridge or at Ragley Hall, he was working on the translation of the powerful Dutch alchemical text *Chymical Wedding,* a book divided into seven chapters, seven days of revelation. It was a book cross-hatched with sevens. He had been preparing to take on the mantle of power that had been promised him for a decade or more. The Lucasian Chair of Mathematics, they said, was his.[7]

Then, in 1661, a boy called Isaac Newton came to Trinity College. Hearing from Barrow about the dexterity of the young man's mathematical skills and from Henry More about the young man's alchemical skills, Ezekiel went to call on the young subsizar in 1662.[8] That first meeting was undoubtedly awk-

[5] See Richard de Villamil (1931), *Newton: The Man,* p. 14. London: Gordon Knox.
[6] See Samuel Newton (1890), *The Diary of Samuel Newton, Alderman of Cambridge,* edited by J. E. Foster, p. 72.
[7] Vogelsang Papers, p. 56.
[8] Vogelsang Papers, p. 57.

ward, for Newton, both competitive and territorial, would have instinctively bridled to meet More's brilliant Cambridge protégé, Foxcroft. In time Foxcroft forged a friendship with Newton, over late-night discussions of Euclid and of Descartes and of geometry and algebra. It would not have taken Ezekiel long to divine the heat and steel of Newton's mind, the way he turned numbers into spirits, made them do magic. He saw Newton's fury in the sequences of calculations spread out over the floor of his rooms. God, Ezekiel understood, had chosen this charmless and driven young man, and was now dragging him through night and day to truths never before glimpsed, even by Euclid or Descartes.

In 1664, Newton began a new notebook, entitled "Quaestiones Quaedam Philosophiae."

Struggling against his own envy, for he had been raised by his mother and by her friend Henry More to believe himself to be the greatest of the next generation of alchemists, Ezekiel Foxcroft saw himself dethroned. He came to understand that it was his part to play lieutenant to this general, John the Baptist to this Messiah. He would do so willingly, he told the older men, More and Barrow and Babington; he would show Newton where to acquire the tools he needed, he would bring him alchemical manuscripts from London or from More's library in Ragley. He would accelerate the pace of Newton's discoveries. He was true to his word, at least at first, for this was a new kind of power.

Foxcroft flattered Newton. He told him that he had been chosen, that he was invincible, that he was a kind of god. He pushed him further and further, bringing him manuscripts at night, when Wickins slept and when he and Newton could be invisible. Ezekiel insisted that Newton keep their friendship flawlessly secret. No one must know that the two men met or that they assembled alchemical formulas together in Trinity College rooms. He set Newton initiatory tasks to test his mettle and to strengthen his alchemical powers. Under Ezekiel's influence, Newton came to believe that he could do anything, that everything he did was sanctioned by divine authority, that nothing could stop the flood of knowledge passing through him—secrets about light, colour, gravity, numbers. As the conduit of divine knowledge he was untouchable. Ezekiel had said so.

In 1665–66, Newton scratched out the fundamentals of what would come to be called the calculus.

Foxcroft listened to Newton. When Newton complained that he had no power, that soon he would be forced to leave Trinity and go back to farming, Foxcroft undertook to clear Newton's path to a fellowship. It was a grave decision and one that he made alone. For Newton to be assured of the fellowship, there had to be a high number of vacancies among the existing fellows. Ezekiel realised quickly that there was only one way to achieve this. It would not be easy and the risks were high, but with careful planning and care, murders might be made to look like accidents.

In 1665, in his rooms in Trinity, Newton proved that white light was made up of colours and took to his bed, temporarily blinded.

Foxcroft drew in a draper's delivery boy, Richard Herring, who had friends who worked in the Trinity kitchens. Knowing of the boy's fascination with alchemy, he sought him out in the Red Hart in Petticury, promising to teach him the secret of the philosopher's stone. Instead, telling the boy about initiation rituals, he taught him how to gather and process the leaves of the belladonna plants growing in Newton's physic garden at Trinity. He showed him how belladonna skillfully administered produced an effect that looked like drunkenness: hallucinations, dilated pupils, respiratory distress, and disorientation. Under the right conditions, it could produce a fatal fall. In time and with more promises and some threats, the boy agreed to slip small amounts of poison surreptitiously into the food of two Trinity fellows. In the shadows of a Trinity staircase Foxcroft moved the plot to its completion. Greswold died from a fall in 1665, Valentine in 1666; the plague outbreak gave Foxcroft an additional cloak behind which to work.

In 1666, working by candlelight late into the night, Newton devised a method of calculating the exact gradient of a curve, a method which would come to be known as differentiation.

Not everything went according to plan. In May 1665, Abraham Cowley's fall down a staircase did not result in his death. The poet, suspecting a plot, fled Cambridge to his house in Surrey. It took two years for Herring and Foxcroft to reach him, and to succeed where they had earlier failed. The effects of belladonna also proved to be unpredictable. In 1666, when Herring tried to poison Francis Barton, another fellow at Trinity, Barton fell into a deranged and insane state; he was so sick that it was impossible to entice him onto the staircase outside his rooms. The master of Trinity, convinced that Barton was a danger to himself, sent him away to his family home in the countryside. It was a plague year. No one asked any questions. Foxcroft let Herring believe that the plot had worked, that the boy had succeeded in his final act of initiation, that this was the last death.

Sometime in 1665 or 1666, somewhere between a garden in Woolsthorpe and a garden in Trinity, Newton carved out the rules of gravitation.

What Foxcroft had started seemed to have no end. When Newton complained that the great alchemical secrets were being spread abroad and that they would soon become diluted and impure, Foxcroft undertook to silence all those who had betrayed such secrets, moving in disguise through London streets, calling on alchemists, clearing the way, purifying—in Newton's name.[9]

The blood on Foxcroft's hands nullified all his alchemical experiments; he watched them spoil, he told his mother, Elizabeth, keeping from her the terrible reasons for their spoiling, knowing how much she would berate him for his sacrifice. Now, defeated, weakened, he determined to do all that was left to him and in which he might be useful—the translation of alchemical texts. For a few years the translation of *Chymical Wedding* occupied his mind and compensated in minor ways for his lost powers.

Then, when he thought he might forget, a tide turned horribly against him. Francis Barton returned to Trinity in 1668. Richard Herring, grown especially superstitious since the Great Plague and burdened with guilt, terrified by the sight of Barton strolling across Trinity Great Court, told Foxcroft that he was going to confess his sins to the fellow who had come back from the dead. Foxcroft, convinced that the whole sequence of deaths would become visible once the boy-poisoner started to talk, slipped belladonna into Herring's ale as he played dice in the Red Hart in Petticury on the evening of 10 November 1668, then followed him as he wandered, disoriented, along the riverbank towards his death in the river at dawn. There seemed to be no end.

In 1668–69, Newton, with the help of his friend Wickins, installed an elaborate experimental apparatus in his rooms and constructed the very first functioning reflecting telescope.

Foxcroft's embroilments changed him. He received no thanks from the immortal Newton, no preferments. The blood that stained him in Newton's name went unacknowledged. From the moment Newton had received the Trinity fellowship, he had shunned his old friend, though he had not refused

---

[9] Vogelsang Papers, p. 60.

to drink with others and had even played bowls. Foxcroft could see the look of cold contempt the younger man had for him now. He watched Newton rise, saw him appointed to the Lucasian chair, the chair that Foxcroft had been promised; saw More's and Barrow's adoration; watched the Royal Society lionise the reclusive, ungracious, arrogant young man.

In 1669 Isaac Newton was appointed Lucasian Professor of Mathematics.

Once Newton had assumed the red robes of the Lucasian professor, Foxcroft changed his direction. He determined that his acts would no longer be in Newton's name. Now he had only one desire left: to soil the younger man's reputation and restore his own. He had accounts to settle.

In 1669, Newton wrote up "De Analysi," another milestone in the road towards the calculus.

But still there was no end. After returning to Cambridge in 1668, Francis Barton lived an apparently quiet life in Trinity, but after a strange encounter with a young man on a staircase who confessed that he had poisoned Barton with belladonna, a young man who was found drowned in the river a few days later, Barton began to make enquiries into who had keys to the Trinity physic garden and access to the poisonous plants that grew there.

In 1671, dressed in his red robes, Newton unveiled his telescope to the men of the Royal Society in London. It caused a sensation.

By 1674, Barton's enquiries about poison had brought him closer and closer to a mathematician at King's. Then, according to Alderman Newton's diary, Francis Barton died a violent death from falling:

25th April, 1674: **Saturday morning.** St Markes Day. Mr Francis Barton, one of the senior Fellowes of Trinity Colledge in Cambridge was found dead at the bottome of his Stayres in the house in St Edward's Parish where he dwelt, it being conceived that he fell downe, and had soe laine dead a day or two before it was found out.

Barton, the fifth Trinity man, died by falling down a staircase, only a few months before Ezekiel himself died in suspicious circumstances in a brawl in a London tavern. That series of seventeenth-century deaths in Cambridge, deaths in which Trinity fellows—apparently drunk, but almost certainly drugged—fell down staircases, came to an end only with the death of Ezekiel Foxcroft.

Foxcroft was the brilliant usurped son cheated of his birthright, the Lu-casian professorship, by an ex-subsizar boy for whom he had repeatedly killed. Those deaths in Trinity, perhaps always unknown to Newton, though they had provided the bridge to his glittering future, embroiled Foxcroft for the rest of his life, to the day of his death. Constantly threatening to become visible, they dragged the poisoner further and further into blood, more deaths, greater damnation. With so much blood on his hands the alchemical formulas would no longer work for Ezekiel Foxcroft, and sooner or later Henry More lost interest in his once promising protégé. Meanwhile, Newton took the Lucasian professorship and drew the scarlet folds of the gown and his glory around him.

Here, with all the ambiguities stripped away, was a different truth from the one I had expected. Reading Elizabeth's terrible assured revelations on paper, in an empty house, I had come to recognise my ghostwalker—here in the folds of "The Crimson Room." I sat absolutely still for a long time, wondering about mistaken identities and masks, and the man who had followed me down Garret Hostel Lane and over the bridge, who had passed in and out of mirrors, in red. I remembered that Dilys had said something once about how she saw Mr. F. in red—a dark, wine-red gown.

"But that doesn't make sense," I'd protested. "Foxcroft was a fellow at King's. King's gowns are black." Perhaps her eyes were playing tricks on her.

"I'm just telling you what I see, my dear. You're the historian."

"Why does Foxcroft wear red?" I framed the question now for the first time directly to Elizabeth. Not Newton but Foxcroft in red, *in the red Lu-casian gown.*

"Perhaps he wants to be taken for someone else," Elizabeth answered.

"Yes," I said, "Foxcroft wants to be taken for Newton."

I felt for Ezekiel; I could step into his hatred then as if it were my own. I could follow him beyond Elizabeth's ending. I had come to know him *in red,* my angry masquerading ghostwalker. I sat at Elizabeth's desk in the late-afternoon light, thinking through with Elizabeth, talking directly to her about the stages of Ezekiel's brilliant plan, the plan that had gone wrong, following him beyond the end of Elizabeth's chapter, into Elizabeth's life and then into my own.

Angry and vengeful, Foxcroft's spirit had walked through and beyond his own shadowy death. For three centuries, habituated to guarding the few records that remained, he'd watched the myth of Newton's superhuman genius grow in the hands of scholars and historians. Hidden in the historical records, he, Ezekiel Foxcroft, had survived only as an occasional footnote in Isaac Newton's numerous and extensive biographies, footnotes used to explain briefly only the identity of the man referred to as "Mr. F." in Newton's notebooks, or the man who'd translated a famous Rosicrucian text, *Chymical Wedding*. Yet Ezekiel knew that without the blood on his hands, without all those deaths undertaken in his name, Isaac Newton would almost certainly have returned to Woolsthorpe and obscurity.

Then, while he was stalking Elizabeth Vogelsang, Foxcroft had come to see what might now become possible: revenge. After centuries of invisibility, and years of keeping scholars away from the few records of the Trinity deaths, Foxcroft realised with a strange sense of relief that, despite the obstacles he had put in her way, Elizabeth had already mapped Newton's contacts with the alchemists in Grantham, and that it would be only a matter of time before she would see how the deaths might be connected to Newton's fellowship. He saw that by *reversing the habits of centuries,* by guiding your mother not away from the records of the Cambridge deaths but towards them, he could and would frame Newton. He would make Newton carry the burden and the responsibility for those deaths. He would use Elizabeth to do his work, and then, once Elizabeth's book was published, he could let go. So he began to put papers in places where she would find them; leave books open at key passages, then make them disappear; tantalise her, lay a trail she had no choice but to follow. Red herrings. Scents dragged through the undergrowth to distract the hounds from the fox's path. He put on the red gown so that his identity would be beyond question, so that his ghostly presence would be taken to be Newton's, the spectre of the Lucasian professor.

But he underestimated Elizabeth. Shortly before her death she found the reference to Francis Barton in Alderman Newton's diary and saw it all, sniffed out the fox's trail, noted how the sequence ended with Foxcroft's death, and, brilliantly, guessed the rest. Then she started to pursue the man in red with her relentless curiosity. She had no fear. In Dilys's house she challenged Mr. F. directly, accused him of the murders, tracked him to his den. Foxcroft must have confessed. Perhaps the old alchemist surfaced in him then; perhaps he thought Elizabeth might expiate his sins, take off his burden. Whatever happened at Dilys's house, Elizabeth alone came away with what she wanted, for Dilys was still in the dark about Foxcroft. Then Elizabeth set about rewriting the final chapters of her book. She declared Foxcroft to be the man who had murdered in Newton's name.

Checkmate. The most dangerous game of chess Elizabeth had ever played and a game of truth-telling that led inexorably to her death.

Newton *was* lucky. Very lucky. Not just because he benefited from the deaths of the Trinity fellows but because their murders might, in another time and space, have been attributed to him. They had, after all, been carried out in his name.

Thirty

When Dilys Kite rang on the morning of the 7th of November to say, "Lydia, my dear, you are in very deep," I replied, with a degree of brittleness, "Mrs. Kite, I know. I've never been deeper."

"Are you being looked after?"

"Do you *know*?" I turned the mirror in the alcove near the door so that it faced the wall.

"Of course we know."

"How?" Had my face turned up in one of her crystal balls, its swellings and bruises further distorted by the curves of the glass? Did she think she had summoned a monster? Or did she just "know"?

"There's no time. I am being . . . hounded. And frankly, my dear, I am getting quite tired of it all. I have had to cancel all my engagements this week. I've never had to deal with anything like this before. It's bedlam. This is Elizabeth's unfinished business. And she can't finish it, so *you* have to." Dilys had a way sometimes of talking about the spirits she worked with as if they were a bunch of unruly schoolboys making anonymous calls from a village phone box.

"What's bedlam?"

"My house. Bedlam. He's broken all manner of things. The light switches keep fusing. Pictures fall off the walls."

"Mrs. Kite," I said, "do you have time to come to The Studio? And would you pick up some biscuits on the way? I'm out of biscuits. And I can't get to the shops."

"Of course, my dear, biscuits it will be. And some aloe vera for your face."

"You look just like a woman in my village who's had a face-lift," she said, making the tea. "That's what people will think. That's what you'll have to tell them. Now . . . we need to talk about Mr. F." She had taken the chair next to the fire, which she had stoked up. She had brought a whole host of remedies and pills in a black plastic bag, most of which I'd politely refused.

"Mr. F.? He's in your house?" I repeated, casually.

She passed me a custard cream from the packet. "Yes, Mr. F. That's what he calls himself." Ezekiel Foxcroft. Elizabeth's hit man. But I wasn't going to tell Dilys that. First I wanted to see how much she knew.

"What do *you* know about him?"

"Well, we've heard from him before, of course. But not for some time. I checked my files."

"You keep records of the spirits who contact you?"

"Of course. How else would we know who's been where and when? I keep them in a card file over there . . ."

"Were there transcripts of the visits?"

"Yes. Elizabeth kept them in a file she called—"

"The Vogelsang Papers?"

"Yes, that was her little joke. It used to make her laugh that the Vogelsang Papers was a collection of transcripts from a series of spirit visitations from the seventeenth century. A new form of historiography, she said. Yes, it used to make her laugh."

So the footnotes in *The Alchemist,* her evidence, were to transcripts of interviews with spirits called up at Prickwillow: Cowley, Foxcroft, Herring, Greswold, and the rest. She must have made a transcript of Foxcroft's confession, too. That would have been in the Vogelsang Papers.

"What happened to them?"

"The Vogelsang Papers? They should be here, . . ." Dilys looked alarmed. "Missing?"

"Afraid so. I think they may have ended up on the bonfire. Someone decided they were nonsense. Did you ever raise Newton?"

"We tried once. I told Elizabeth I'd never do it again."

"And Elizabeth had to steal the prism from the Whipple Library to do that?"

"The prism didn't work. I told her it wouldn't. Glass objects hardly ever work. They are too opaque for spirit transfer. It just burned a mark high up on the wall."

"So what did you use instead?"

"A lock of Newton's hair. Elizabeth took it from the display cabinet in the Wren Library. The librarians knew Elizabeth, so when they gave her the locket for examination and left her alone with it, she managed to open the spring mechanism and replace it with a lock of her own hair. It was almost exactly the same colour. A good match."

"Christ. Is it still there?"

"Yes—not much we can do about it now. I can't get in there to switch them around again. But the tourists won't mind. No one will ever know."

"Did the lock of hair work?"

"No. It was a great disappointment to both of us. Oh, to have had one of Elizabeth's index cards for the great man . . . what a triumph that would have been. No. Mr. F. turned up instead, talking nonsense."

And how exactly, Mrs. Kite, do you distinguish between shades of nonsense?

"I'm getting confused here," I said. "You called me this morning because—"

"Because Mr. F. won't leave my house; he's breaking things and he's monopolising the letterboard. He has a message for 'L.B.,' he says. I don't know anyone else with those initials, except you. I do wish they would use full names and not initials. It would be so much easier."

"And the message?" *A message for me from Ezekiel Foxcroft, who died over three hundred years ago?*

"I wrote it down on the back of an index card."

I took the card and turned it over. The message said simply: *No testimony.*

"He was," Dilys added, "very insistent on that phrase: 'No testimony.' He was so insistent, he left deep scratches on my inlay. I'll never get those out."

"I think I understand," I said. "There must be no record. It must end here."

"It makes sense to you?" she said.

"I have one or two things to check," I said, "but yes, I know what he wants from me." I needed time to think.

She didn't ask me any further questions. I always wondered why. A code of hers, I suspect. Something about leaving her clients to work things out for themselves.

Thirty-one

Will Burroughs did not visit Emmanuel or say good-bye to her friend. She was in hiding. You didn't visit him again either; you were out of the country—somewhere overseas. Emmanuel Scorsa was attacked on the night of November 2nd and died on November 9th in the intensive care unit of Addenbrooke's Hospital. Like James Valentine, 336 years earlier, it had taken him exactly seven days to die. Unlike James Valentine, he died under bright halogen lights in a hospital room when his parents, Maria and Marco Scorsa, advised by solicitous doctors, asked for his life-support system to be switched off. He had been murdered, they said, with rat poison—his organs had failed. James Valentine, the professor of Greek, died in his rooms in Trinity, alone in the dark.

Somewhere in the Parkside Police Station an office had already been set aside for a murder enquiry. Forensic scientists had taken samples from underneath Emmanuel's nails and collected evidence and blood samples from his coat and trousers and around his wounds. When the forensic officers had finished working on the murder scene in St. Edward's Passage, police officers took down the white sheeting and the red tape. Bicycles—only a few to start with—began to make their way down the passage and down King's Parade; students making their way to the library, books piled up in their bike baskets; tourists, admiring the crisp morning light and the frost on the grass, stopping to take photographs. Underneath the bridge the punt chauffeurs cleaned and polished the sides of their boats, ready for winter storage.

Everything changed almost overnight, as if a switch had been thrown. A gearshift manoeuvred into place and a foot pressed down aggressively upon an accelerator. The police launched a murder enquiry. Somebody rang you in the States; you changed your ticket and took a plane from wherever you were back across the sea. "Emmanuel died this morning," you texted me. "I'm on my way back." Members of the Scotland Yard Special Unit investigating animal-liberation groups reserved rooms in Cambridge hotels. Files were pulled from filing cabinets, computer databases searched, suspects identified and prioritised. Their names were written down on a whiteboard: Samuel Phelps, Roma Smith, Sarah Drabble, Peter McEwen, Lily Ridler.

The police, the papers said, were looking for members of an animal-liberation group called NABED. For weeks everyone with an opinion seemed to be talking about animal rights and animal ethics. The *Sun* began calling all animal activists "monsters." Radio 4's *Moral Maze* instantly reran an old recording of a discussion programme in which leading animal-rights theorists argued and cross-questioned each other. Cambridge was full of reporters and photographers, and everywhere Emmanuel Scorsa was portrayed, in different ways, as a martyr for scientific truth. No one had yet discovered his membership in the Animal Liberation Army. No one would, not even during Lily's trial.

When you came back from America (or wherever you had been), it was impossible for us to see each other. Plenty of time for my face to heal. Plenty of time for the message my face was supposed to carry to you not to be passed on. I saw you photographed at Emmanuel's funeral, his mother, dressed in black, leaning blank-faced on your arm. I heard your speeches and interviews. I heard you on the morning radio. I saw you once on the national evening news. You were passionate, reasonable, and fair-minded. You spoke about Emmanuel's brilliance, about his sense of humour and his kindness. You made a direct appeal to anyone who knew anything about the murder, asking them to come forward. You announced a reward. And from committee rooms and enquiry rooms and police stations and recording studios, you continued to send me text messages—tender and beguiling—and I continued to answer. "Lydia, when this has all calmed down, I want us to go away." "Lydia, I have some questions I want you to answer." "Lydia, I can't live like this anymore. We have to face some things."

"I know," I texted back. "I know." All through November I answered your texts and your e-mails, uneasily, trying not to give away anything of what I now knew, not in my tone or in my silences. I was trying in the midst of all this fragility to keep an open mind. I resolved to wait to see what would unravel. You were in London for most of November; you e-mailed me from your hotel room or from Internet cafés. Sometimes there would be silence for several days. I was afraid for you, of what might be happening in those silences and in those invisible corridors of power you walked down, or in the dark alleyways around your hotel. I imagined you in those labyrinths like Foxcroft, or those alchemists hunted down in alleyways in London or Antwerp or Pisa, carrying all that dangerous knowledge, the wolves closing in. And while I waited, trusting my future and yours to whatever puppet masters held our strings, I rewrote *The Alchemist*. I neutralised it.

No testimony, said Mr. Foxcroft. And I understood. You see, Cameron, I made a deal with Mr. Ezekiel Foxcroft, robed in red, my ghostwalker, that I would exchange Elizabeth's chapter, "The Crimson Room," the record of his guilt, I would exchange that chapter for the laying of ghosts, for the end of the deus ex machina. It had to stop. He, I thought, agreed.

On the 11th of November, I watched the local evening news. There was still a good deal of coverage of Emmanuel's death. But there were no new deaths. Not a single death reported. It had to mean something. Foxcroft's pledge would hold.

In the hope and expectation of that disentanglement, I also burned all the written evidence—Elizabeth's copy of "The Crimson Room," her notes, Dilys's notes, the file she had left for me. On Elizabeth's bonfire I watched the edges of all that paper curl and twist and char in flames that burned blue, green, and orange. I began a new final chapter for *The Alchemist* and rewrote several earlier chapters, so that there would be absolutely no ambiguity or inference, no trace of Elizabeth's accusation. No innuendo about Newton having benefited from those unexplained deaths, no reference to Foxcroft or the poisonings—just the usual kind of end chapter to a biography of the great man: Newton, the genius. I finished it in a couple of weeks. It was a short final chapter and easy to write.

The Alchemist, as I ghostwrote it, was a good book, but it was not Elizabeth's book. It *is* a good book. Reviewers applauded Elizabeth Vogelsang for her scholarship, for her knowledge of the complex European networks and Newton's connections to them, but also for her understanding of how little, in the end, Newton depended on alchemy for his science—how once and for all the idea of Newton the sorcerer had been laid to rest. A few months ago the book was nominated for the Whitbread Biography prize. It didn't win, though the publishers used the nomination for dust-jacket publicity just the same. I didn't know all of that in November 2002. In November I was just closing things down. I had no choice.

Thirty-two

And then in December you sent me the text I had dreaded. "I'm in Cambridge," it said. "Meet me. I have to see you."

"I'm in Norfolk. By the sea," I texted back, once I'd examined my face and decided it wasn't safe yet. You'd see the scars. I couldn't cover them up.

Another text from you followed mine: "You're at the sea? I don't believe you. Show me. Send me a picture of the sea on your mobile."

There was a picture of an old boathouse on some Norfolk beach on Elizabeth's noticeboard. I photographed the picture of the boathouse framed against the sea and sent it to you. A few minutes later I heard your voice speaking into the answering machine: "I know where that is," you said, laughing. "That's the place my mother used to go to at Heacham. They knocked it down last summer to build a hotel. Nice try. Meet me to-morrow? Lydia—pick up. I know you're there."

I picked up the phone. "I'm afraid," I said.

"It's safe for the moment," you answered, tenderly. "You just have to trust me. Everything's gone quiet. I've seen to it."

"I've forgotten what your voice sounds like," I said. "It's been five weeks."

"They wouldn't let me phone you. I told you. It's been killing me, Lydia, not to be able to see you. I'm so tired. I've never needed you like this before. Meet me. Just for an hour. Please." *And why will they let you see me now? What does that mean?*

"The Green Dragon," I said, taking a deep breath. "Meet me tomorrow night at the Green Dragon in Chesterton. I'll buy you a pint. There's a mummified cat—"

"A mummified what?"

"Cat—a mummified cat—bricked into the fireplace there. To keep off evil spirits."

"It's going to take more than a mummified cat . . ."

"What?"

"Oh, nothing. Just a joke. Green Dragon at eight? I can't wait to see you. It's been weeks, far too long."

You'd taken the leather sofa near the log fire by the time I arrived. I had counted on the light in there being too dim for you to notice the last visible scar, a raised red gash, on my cheekbone. But you did. It was the first thing you saw. You drew close as I sat down, unwinding my scarf and unbuttoning my coat. You ran your fingertips over the wound. Slowly. As if I were a hurt child.

"Cold hands," I said.

"What happened?"

"What do you mean?"

"Your face—looks like you've been in a fight."

"Yes," I said. "A street brawl. You know me. Can't keep out of trouble. No. Just a bad gash from a branch of one of the trees in The Studio garden. I was walking down to the river after dark and slammed straight into it. It's not as bad as it looks. What an idiot, eh?"

"No, you're no idiot."

What did that comment betray? I watched you closely, your face near mine, watched your eyes narrow, reading me. Did you know? Had someone in the Syndicate told you? Sent you a photograph, perhaps? You looked away.

"Adnams?" you asked.

"I thought I was buying this round," I said lightly. "Christ, you said you were tired. You look a hundred years old. And you've lost weight. What have you been doing?" This elaborate game of innocence and ignorance, I thought. How long can we sustain it?

"Thanks. Just working. The usual. Wish I could pack it all in now. But there's too much at stake."

I watched you walk to the bar, surveyed you: the tall, familiar shape, the blue shirt over the worn red T-shirt, the cream trousers, the brown shoes that needed polishing. You were at the end of a very long telescope. I saw that I no longer knew anything. Anything was possible. If someone had told me that you had issued an order for me to be attacked to frighten me into leaving Cambridge so that I would no longer be your Achilles' heel, if they had said that you wanted me out of the way at any price, I might have believed them. And then if someone had said that you would protect me above all else, sacrifice everything for me, that you loved me above all else, yes, I would have believed that too.

We were both embroiled in your network, its surveillance, its cameras and phone-tracking devices, its satellites and computer systems. There was no separating from it or cutting ourselves out from what we knew, no escape to some safe future. There would be consequences to the knowing, casualties. A price to be paid. One of us *has* to find a way out, I thought. *There must be a way out.*

Morazapine, the formula you had made and that only you could develop, whatever you had wanted it to be, had, under your dark husbandry, bloomed into a paralysing drug, a chemical weapon. Yes, whatever you had meant it to be, it now had the strength to paralyse armies, prepare them for slaughter. It could take out whole cities: Tehran, Basra, Baghdad. It would. There *was* a great deal at stake. They couldn't let you go. You were their Daedalus—you carried the secrets to the labyrinth in your head. They couldn't let you just walk away.

"Have you seen the plaque on the wall?" you said, putting two pints down on the table. "To the man who disappeared? Over there, under the shelf in the corner. It's famous."

"I can't read it from here," I said. "My eyes are not so good."

"Some bloke who was a ferryman here. On the shelf just there over the plaque there's a single boot, a hat, and a wicker basket with a tea can and a drinking bottle. Underneath it says, '1896—All that is left in memory of Alfie Basset, who mysteriously disappeared after leaving the Green Dragon and crossing the river in his own boat.' "

"Poor Alfie," I said. "And they never found his body. How was America?" *Tell me.*

"Dull. I wasn't there for very long. I had to come back to deal with the press after Emmanuel died. There's been a lot of political fallout. Meetings and negotiations and deals. It's not good." *You'll never tell me. These evasions between us. Great rifts in the landscape.*

"I saw you on the television."

"And the book? How's *The Alchemist*?"

"It's finished. I've finished it."

"Are you ready to pull out the stopper?"

"What's that?"

"The hand grenade. You said *The Alchemist* was going to be controversial. You said you'd be pulling out the stopper."

I smiled. "Hand grenades don't have stoppers; they have pins. I was wrong. It's a good book, an important book in terms of the history of alchemy, but there's nothing very controversial about it. No grenades."

"Shame. It would have been good to see some ruffled feathers among the historians of science. Lydia, how brave are you?"

"Not very. I was. I'm not so brave now. Why?"

"I want to sit by an open window with a view over water. A room with you in it and silence. A marble bath. Away from here. Right away from here. And then there are things I want to tell you. Will you come? Just for a few days? I want you to know some things. And I can make it safe. I have a few favours left to call in."

"Yes," I said slowly, finishing my pint. "I will. But now I have to go. Really. I'm sorry. I'm not feeling very well." *And I have things to tell you. About the end of your mother's story and a man in red. And I'm not sure I care about safety anymore, not mine at least. Yes, I will come and we will tell each other some things. It's time.*

"You'll come?" you said. "Venice? Will you come to Venice?"

"Yes," I said. Just that. Just yes.

.   .   .

I addressed the envelope to you—Dr. Cameron Brown, Trinity College, Cambridge—and slid a copy of Elizabeth's "The Crimson Room" inside. I had made the photocopy the night before I'd burned Elizabeth's original copy of the chapter and all the related papers. The stamps on the envelope were Christmas stamps, a seventeenth-century Madonna and child, in bright, oil-paint colours, the child holding a red pomegranate. I mailed it that night, slipping it into a postbox on the corner of Union Lane. A gift. Your mother's lost words, returned to you. This was what she had been looking for. This was what she had found. Elizabeth Vogelsang's goddamned seventeenth century—the dark history buried beneath the myth of a great man. A history that would now have to be reburied. But first you had to see it—the end of your mother's story. Another of the blackbird's circles.

Thirty-three

"Cameron's late," Kit said as I helped her and Maria carry the plates into the kitchen on New Year's Eve. The conservatory, where Kit had jewelled her long dining table with ivy, gold, cinnamon-scented candles, pink ginger lilies, and bowls of oranges and figs, looked like a scene from a Caravaggio painting. Opulence and sacrifice. A New Year about to turn. A dinner party.

"I don't think he's going to make it," I said. "He would have been here by now." I checked my phone. There was a text. I felt the pleasure again as a chemical rush through my veins. It said, "Got as far as the Plough and Fleece but Leo is with me. The gods are not with us tonight. Will text later." I turned my phone off.

When I came back to the table I said, "Cameron sends his apologies."

"He's not got this virus that's going round?" Tom said.

"No, he's at another party and thought he could get away, but it turns out he can't."

"Run out of alibis? Not Cameron, surely," Anthony said wryly.

"There's money in alibis," Kasia said.

"Can we change the subject?" Anthony looked in my direction when I spoke, waiting to see how far I might be pushed.

"Oh no, you misunderstand," Kasia answered quickly. "I'm not sitting in judgement. I just find it interesting, that's all. I have several friends who are in your . . ." She trailed off, suddenly aware that everyone around the table was listening.

"Situation?" I said.

"Yes."

"What situation is that?" Tom leaned forward curiously.

"Women having affairs with married men." Anthony knew he was wounding me, but he was too drunk to care. Now Kit was watching me, too. Anthony continued, just as Kit turned up the volume on the CD player so that Madeleine Peyroux's mournful voice broke across our words singing a Leonard Cohen ballad. "Kasia was just saying that she has several friends who are having affairs with married men . . . like Lydia."

Dance me to the end of love . . .

"Cameron's married?" Tom said. "I didn't know that."

"Yes, it's something Cameron forgets too, sometimes," Anthony said.

Dance me to your beauty with a burning violin . . .

"How many affairs do we have between us around this table, I wonder?" I said.

"Lydia . . ." Kit was wary, Maria watching closely.

"Well, if everyone's going to be sanctimonious about it . . ." I said, tracing the patterns of down on the purple skin of an abandoned fig on my plate.

Dance me through the panic till I'm gathered safely in . . .

This wasn't about affairs, wives, and mistresses. None of that mattered. A paralysing drug, an arms industry, espionage, networks that stretched everywhere, infiltrated everything. I peered for a moment into the mechanisms that kept everything going around you, the oiled levers and coils and wheels. And you at the middle of it all, throwing the switches, alone in the labyrinth, working machines you could no longer control.

Dance me to the end of love . . .

"Lydia, cigarette?" Anthony's eyes gave nothing away. "Yes, take me outside," I wanted to say, but didn't. We stepped out into the night. There was a bonfire in a brazier on the patio, which made me remember another fire I had stood next to once.

"I thought you needed rescuing," he said, passing me a cigarette. "Don't stand too close to the fire. Your coat'll catch on the sparks."

"I thought he was your friend," I whispered, cigarette and wood smoke stinging my eyes.

"He is my friend. I've known him for a long time. I adore him. He's extraordinary. He's . . ."

"Clever?"

"Yes, he's very clever. The cleverest man I've ever met. And the most elusive."

"How long have you known about us?"

"Since the beginning." He sounded apologetic.

"Ha. The *beginning*. When was that? You know I can't remember a beginning anymore . . . Did he *tell* you?"

"He had to tell someone. He was in a bad way. I've had to rescue him several times since. He'll have a breakdown eventually, you know, splitting himself like he does between you and Sarah. Leaving you, coming back to you." *And the rest. And all the rest.*

"He didn't leave. I did."

"Whatever . . . It doesn't matter in the end, does it? You always come back. So does he. He was outside, Lydia, a few minutes ago, in the car. He texted me. I was to tell you that he was waiting for you. I didn't get it in time to tell you."

"Why didn't he text me?"

"Because you switched your phone off."

"What did he say?"

"He wanted me to tell you that he loves you. That he only had ten minutes and that he had to go. He's put an envelope through Kit's door, apparently."

"It's too late," I said. "It's much too late."

"You're just tired, Lydia. It'll all—"

"I know. Don't tell me. It'll all look different in the morning."

Everything seemed on fire outside on Kit's patio. The flames from the brazier made everything look like it was blazing—the shrubs, the wall, the trellis, trees. An immense conflagration.

Anthony was piling more logs and branches into the brazier.

"Everything's burning now," I said. "Everything."

"Yes," Anthony said. "We'll burn our way into the New Year. It's going to be a good year. You'll see. All will be well."

Thirty-four

I still have the letter you put through Kit's door on New Year's Eve. Handwritten in black ink on thick, cream-coloured paper, it has two folds, beautifully symmetrical. The tickets were bought from Bennett's Travel Agency on King Street at five P.M. on the 29th of December. I put them in the box you bought me with the heron embossed on the lid, with all the things you gave me that autumn and winter: the silk scarf, the bronze statue of Venus, the oyster shells, the copy of Ovid's *Metamorphoses* and of Walter Pater's *The Renaissance* with the autumn crocus leaves pressed inside. You wrote:

> Dear Lydia, here's an air ticket to Venice. I know it's a crazy idea but it's been so dark of late. I just had this feeling that we should find some winter light for ourselves. Grasp it before it gets taken away. I'll meet you at five o'clock at Cambridge Station on the morning of the 5th. Can't get away before then—things to sort out with Sarah. Bring a warm coat. Venice can be cold in winter. Text me if for any reason you can't make it. C.B.

There's the finest of strands catching the sun at my window, a single spider's thread. The window here has been scratched, and where the sun catches it, in the cut, the colours bleed like stained glass.

There was thick fog that morning. It was four forty-five when I reached the taxi rank next to the pub on the High Street in Chesterton, so I was surprised to see another man waiting there.

"You going to the station?" I asked. "Shall we share the ride?" He nodded in answer and took a step back into the shadows. A few minutes later the two of us occupied the back seat of a taxi threading through Cambridge streets, which were empty except for the red lights of occasional cars ahead of us, streaked and starry. The streetlamps above us across Elizabeth Way Bridge made veils of lit fog. The taxi driver slid the glass panel across between him and us—it was too early to talk.

In the silence I thought of you on the station platform, how I would reach out to touch your arm, imagined how we would talk, at first, of inconsequential things, as the train pulled south through the dawn towards Stansted Airport. I wouldn't ask how you had managed to find five days away from work in early January to travel to Venice or how your lab would allow you to do so at this precise moment without additional security measures. Nor would I ask about your Christmas or ask after Sarah and the boys. That was understood. Best not to ask. I always told myself that you would do the same if our situations were reversed. There are some things best not said, at least not yet, not until that room with a view over water, not until Venice. And then, what then? You would have a plan. You would have worked out what to do—some new machinery for flight. We'd find a way out. Everything was possible now.

I switched on my phone. There was a text from you, marked by a tiny green envelope, sent earlier that morning: dated the 5th of January, three A.M. "I'm at Trinity," it said. "Just finishing off some paperwork in the office. Loose ends." "The Crimson Room." You were reading "The Crimson Room." Or had been. I saw the desk lamp and the pool of light it made and you in it, reading the white sheets of a photocopied manuscript. Cameron Brown reading in a pool of light.

"Shame about the fog," I said to the man sitting next to me. "Apparently there's a meteor shower up there somewhere, or so the papers said yesterday. We'd be one of only a handful of Cambridge people awake to see it. If it was visible, that is."

"Yes, I know," the man in the black coat answered, looking out his window and peering up towards the sky. "They are spectacular. Never the same." He'd seen several? How could that be—was he lucky?

"What would we see?" I asked, studying the texture of his skin, the curve of his profile in the half-light, struggling to remember something. "What would we see if we were standing out there looking up at the sky and there was no fog?"

"Sharp points of light all radiating out from one still centre, in jagged lines. A little like an abstract scientific drawing." His voice had a richness of timbre that reminded me of stringed instruments, sad and slow like a cello.

"Like fireworks?"

"No, not like fireworks—much more chaotic and delicate. Not like a shower at all. More like a storm or thousands of dandelion seeds lifted by the wind at once and pulled in different directions." Still he did not turn towards me.

"An entanglement," I said, a nameless sense of dread rising. "Do I know you from somewhere?"

He turned to look at me then, so that I saw his face fully for the first time. "No, I don't think so," he said, his face stiff and unsmiling. I struggled for a moment, searching his face, half remembering.

"What have I forgotten?" I said in that first moment of recognition, feeling my pulse race, inhaling the thick, smoky aroma of sulphur and balsam as he met my gaze, matching my question with his own, asking, in a voice that was barely audible now, only:

"Did you forget?"

As he turned away, I remembered letters that had appeared on a mirror once and heard the biblical verses they marked: "I will prepare thee unto blood, and blood shall pursue thee," letters that filled the air with the taste of poison.

"Can you stop? Please let me out here," I said to the taxi driver, my voice high-pitched, banging my hand on the glass panel to make him hear, barely controlling an urge to open the door and take my chances jumping from the moving car.

"We're here, love," he said. "Cambridge Station. You all right?"

The fog had given way to soft rain. The man in the black coat headed off down Station Road while the taxi driver lifted my bags from the car.

"Off somewhere nice?" he asked as I passed him the fare.

"What?" I said, bewildered, watching the dark figure diminish to a vanishing point, occasionally illuminated as he passed under the street-lights.

"Never mind. You have a good trip, eh?"

"Thank you," I said.

Floating not into darkness but into a darker obscure.

Checking my watch, I gathered myself back into the morning. A man in a taxi who for a moment in the dark I had thought I recognised. A trick of the brain. Déjà vu. Nothing more. Nearly time. You were ex-pected at five A.M. I bought two single tickets to Stansted, checked on the next train, and stood in the lit-up entrance of the station to watch for your car. I might have been standing at the bottom of the sea and raising my eyes to some faint green twilight.

I ran over the few words I had exchanged with the stranger, struggling to understand.

What have I forgotten?

Did you forget?

Did I forget? Did I?

"No. I've stuck to the bargain," I said aloud.

A few minutes before, I had seen you reading your mother's chapter in a pool of light in your rooms in Trinity College; now I couldn't see you at all. You were nowhere. You were gone. In that hole that had been ripped in the night, ripped through past, present, and future, in that hole I could do nothing but remonstrate with Ezekiel, my voice loud and high and desperate, echoing in the empty station entrance.

"There *is* no record. I've changed the story. You know that. There's nothing left." But I was lying now even to ghosts, phantasms, tricks of the fog. Ezekiel knew that as well as I did. I had *not* erased the last written record, as I had promised. I had sent you a photocopy of "The Crimson Room" with a note that read:

Cameron. Read this. Your mother's last chapter. It went missing but I found it again. She worked it out. She worked it all out. When you've read it, shred it. That's important.

There were no chapel bells to strike the fifth hour as it came and went.

I had wanted you to see Elizabeth's version of "The Crimson Room," wanted you to know where your mother's story had led, her last brilliant discovery. You would shred it. There would be no record, once you had done that.

"There'll be no record," I said again. "He'll shred it . . . Ezekiel? Are you listening to me?" I ran my finger across the scar on my cheek, pinching the skin there to stop my knees from buckling under me. A boy, running for a train with his mother, turned to look at me, a woman talking to the air.

Hand grenades have pins, not stoppers. And sometimes they take longer than you think to go off.

At five-fifteen I texted you: "Held up?" I wrote and waited, holding my breath for one of your usual text replies: "Five minutes" or "En route." When none came, I knew.

Taxis gathered to wait for the next train in from Stansted. I watched the few early-morning travellers spill out from the station, tanned families returning from Christmas holidays at ski resorts, academics travelling alone, a few lone businessmen in suits, carrying briefcases. I watched them queue for taxis and watched the taxis disappear. It was cold.

It was five-twenty when I phoned. I left a voice message: "Cameron. I don't know what to do. Call me. There's no way we can catch that plane now. Did I perhaps miss you? Did you mean for me to meet you somewhere else?"

By seven A.M. Sergeant Cuff, standing beside your body at the bottom of Staircase E in Trinity College, behind the cord of striped red plastic marking off the edges of the "incident," had recorded my words on your phone in his notebook, next to a note that recorded the seven cuts to your face. "Voice message from 'L.B.': 5:20 A.M., 5 January." The words were written out, my words, with that dying fall: "Did you mean for me to meet you somewhere else?"

Thirty-five

They put up a plaque to you today, Cameron Brown, on the 19th of November, 2004, in the chapel at Trinity, nearly two years after your death. That's a kind of triumph, don't you think? You would have liked that. Another of Trinity's famous men. Not a bench in a park, or a statue like they gave Newton, but a bronze plaque in the chapel. Just a plaque, but very simple and in good taste: "To the memory of Cameron Brown, neuroscientist, 1954–2003." Sarah was there and your boys, so I didn't stay. She looks better than the last time I saw her; it hit her hard—the court case and all those stories that had to come out about you and me. There were speeches when they unveiled the plaque. I slipped away.

I have Lily's funeral to go to. She hanged herself in Holloway on the 11th of November, just a week ago, when the wardens turned away for long enough. She said she would, so we knew it was just a question of time. Couldn't go on, she said. She was of no use, she said, in prison. There was nothing we could do about that. Once she had read that last chapter of Elizabeth's book, it was just a matter of time, as it is for me. A question of time. "We are only like dead walls, or vaulted graves/That, ruin'd, yield no echo."

Dilys will come with me to Lily's funeral. But none of Lily's people will be there. They can't, you see. Your people have smashed theirs. It worked in the end. The laws have been changed, the networks scattered. Their time is over. The police investigation failed, of course, to uncover the link between the Syndicate and NABED and instead established that Lily Ridler had conspired in the deaths of Elizabeth Vogelsang, Emmanuel Scorsa, and Cameron Brown, and in the attack on Lydia Brooke, as part of a campaign of violence orchestrated by a terrorist organisation called NABED. She continued to protest her innocence and refused to reveal the names of any of the other members of the group. None have been found.

Who was standing behind you on that Trinity staircase at dawn? An embittered alchemist in a red gown trying to erase the last traces of a historical record or a man in a black balaclava, a member of the Syndicate working to protect the secrecy of a chemical formula that paralyses its victims and will, sooner or later, escalate the war on terror? Two particles moving together across time and space, shadowing each other. One turns one way; the other follows.

Coincidences. How many times does a piece of paper have to fly away in a windless garden for it to stop being a coincidence? I never worked that out.

I dreamed last night that I was running through an ancient city at night, between canals and old walls, cobbled and stained with lichen and mould. It was a rat run. A maze. I couldn't get out. There was no one to be seen. Sometimes it was like a film—a Buñuel—where everyone is forever trying to get somewhere in beautiful clothes, high heels, and silk shawls, but they've forgotten where they're going and they're hungry and disoriented. I ran first my fingertips and then my knuckles along the wall. It felt familiar, but I couldn't remember where I had seen it before. There were alleyways and arches and doorways and sometimes there was water, like little quays alongside the path. Rats swam up against the edge; one scrambled out of the water and onto stone, its great tail slithering like a wet snake behind it. Then it was gone. I had forgotten something important. Something I was supposed to do. I was following something in red— a child who seemed to be weeping, then a cat that was bleeding. Don't worry, I said. I'm coming. I'm coming. Then it was me ahead in the red coat, bleeding, wounded, crying. And I was you, following me. It made no sense.

I woke, falling through moon shadows, sweating; I woke feeling you watching me, lying close.

Is the light, freighted with water, still shoaling across the walls of The Studio? Can the surface of the present still rub away and let the past through? What else might come to be possible? You might know, Cameron. You who have passed to the other side, you who watch me, you whom I see always out of the corner of my eye, whom I catch still on the edges of my vision. You who are always there. Time past and time future, what might have been and what has been, point to one end, which is always present. And you, Cameron Brown, man of fractures and disguises, lie close still, under, between, inside, for we became once, and still are, entangled together, imprisoned, like time, in a skein of silk.

For a Further
Understanding of Newton

AUTHOR'S NOTE

A word about fact and fiction.

All the seventeenth-century characters in this novel—students, fellows, alchemists, aldermen, chemists, and apothecaries—are real people who left records of themselves, some more substantial than others. I have been faithful to those records.

The deaths of Greswold, Valentine, Herring, Barton, and Cowley are as they are reported in Alderman Newton's diary. The alderman clearly thought there was something troublesome about each of those deaths.

Isaac Newton left copious information about himself but there are still some areas of his life which are not well illuminated and will never be; his years spent in the apothecary's house in Grantham are frustratingly indistinct. I have been faithful to what is known, but I have also, like Elizabeth, speculated about what might have happened there.

Ezekiel Foxcroft, mathematician, alchemist, fellow of King's College, left the most shadowy of records of his life. He is known only as a Mr. F., referred to in Newton's notebooks; as the translator of an important Rosicrucian text, *Chymical Wedding*; is named in Venn's list of Cambridge alumni, *Alumni Cantabrigienses*; and is mentioned in a letter or two that passed between Henry More and Elizabeth Foxcroft.

In *Ghostwalk*, I have woven together the closely researched Trinity deaths, Newton's alchemy, and Ezekiel Foxcroft to create a narrative about patronage and murder. That narrative is speculative. Whether that speculation is also factual will never be known.

TIME LINE

1629   Ezekiel Foxcroft is born in Stoke, Shropshire; his mother, Elizabeth Foxcroft, and his uncle Benjamin Whichcote are both philosophers interested in alchemy.

1642   Newton is born on Christmas Day (January 4, 1643, New Style) in Woolsthorpe, Lincolnshire, England.

1649   Ezekiel Foxcroft enters King's College, Cambridge, where his uncle is provost.

1650s   Newton is sent to the King's School in Grantham. Boards at the apothecary's house.

1652   Foxcroft is appointed fellow at King's College.

1660   Restoration of the monarchy after the civil war. Charles II is crowned.

1661   Newton arrives in Cambridge.

1661   Beginning of the restoration of the English glassmaking industry, monopolised by George Villiers, Second Duke of Buckingham, past student of Trinity College, patron of Abraham Cowley. Venetian glass has dominance over world trade until English law restricts the importation of foreign glass in 1664. Buckingham starts to recruit Italian glassmakers for his glasshouses.

1662   Chemist and member of the Royal Society Christopher Merrett publishes his translation of Antonio Neri's *The Art of Glass* (1612), making Italian techniques available to English glassmakers.

1662   Newton teaches himself short-writing, or code; writes a list of his sins.

1662   Samuel Hartlib, alchemist, intelligencer, and centre of an alchemical network, dies in London.

1662   On 30 November: the altar in Trinity Chapel is destroyed by fire.

1664   Newton is elected to a Trinity scholarship; competition and Newton's low
performance in the examination indicate powerful patronage.

1664   In April or May, Newton begins experiments with light.

1664   On 17 December, a comet moves across the skies; Newton watches it. It is
still moving on 23 December.

1665   On 5 January, Richard Greswold, Trinity fellow, falls down the stairs, apparently drunk, and dies.

1665   On 3 April, a second comet passes; plague deaths begin in London.

1665   In May, Abraham Cowley, eminent poet, fellow at Trinity, and cofounder
of the Royal Society, sickens and then suffers from a fall in his house in
Chertsey, Surrey, in which he is badly injured. Draws up his will two
months later.

1665   Sir Kenelm Digby, alchemist, dies at the age of sixty-two.

1665   George Starkey (Eirenaeus Philalethes), alchemist, dies at the age of
thirty-seven.

1665   In his rooms in Trinity, Newton proves that white light is made up of
colours and takes to his bed, temporarily blinded.

1665   In August: Newton buys a prism at Stourbridge Fair; he then leaves Cambridge to return to Woolsthorpe.

1665   After Michaelmas, there's a fire in Trinity Old Library.

1666   In March, Newton returns to Cambridge; plague outbreaks in Cambridge
rise as the spring temperatures increase. Sometime in 1665–66 Newton
carves out the rules of gravitation and the fundamentals of what would
come to be called the calculus.

1666   Working by candlelight late into the night, Newton devises a method of
calculating the exact gradient of a curve, a method which would come to
be known as differentiation.

1666   In June, Francis Barton, Trinity fellow, loses his sanity and is expelled
from the college.

1666   On 22 June, Newton leaves Cambridge for Woolsthorpe; plague has returned.

1666   On 2–5 September, the Fire of London rages. One-sixth of the inhabi-
tants of London are made homeless.

1666   Thomas Vaughan (Eugenius Philalethes), alchemist, dies at the age of
forty-four.

1666 On 9 November, James Valentine, Trinity fellow, falls down stairs apparently drunk. Dies seven days later.

1667 On 25 March, Newton returns to Cambridge and buys equipment that suggests that he is about to undertake a series of alchemical experiments. He performs successful experiments on colour and light.

1667 On 28 July, Abraham Cowley, Trinity fellow, poet, and cofounder of the Royal Society, having fallen ill after being found asleep and apparently drunk in a field near his home in Chertsey, Surrey, dies.

1666–67 Ezekiel Foxcroft begins his translation of *Chymical Wedding* by Christian Rosenkreutz, the third manifesto of the Rosicrucian movement. Published posthumously in 1690.

1667 In October, Newton is elected a fellow of Trinity. He is lucky: three Trinity fellows have died since he came to Cambridge—Greswold, Valentine, and Cowley—and a further fellow, Francis Barton, has been expelled for insanity.

1667 After his election, Newton paints his rooms red and buys more equipment to set up or further equip an alchemical laboratory; his roommate, John Wickins, leaves the college for a short period.

1668 Francis Barton returns to Trinity.

1668 On 11 November, a young man called Richard Herring drowns himself in the river next to Trinity.

1669 Newton writes up "De Analysi," another milestone in the road towards the calculus.

1669 Nicolas Le Fevre, alchemist, dies at the age of fifty-four.

1669 Newton is appointed the Lucasian Professor of Mathematics.

1674 In April, Francis Barton, Trinity fellow, dies after falling down a staircase in Cambridge.

1674 Ezekiel Foxcroft dies.

NEWTON'S SINS

This list, written by Newton in code in 1662 in the so-called Fitzwilliam Notebook, was decoded only in 1963, by Newton's biographer Richard Westfall. *Newton Project.*

Before Whitsunday 1662.
1. Vsing the word (God) openly
2. Eating an apple at Thy house
3. Making a feather while on Thy day
4. Denying that I made it.
5. Making a mousetrap on Thy day
6. Contriving of the chimes on Thy day
7. Squirting water on Thy day
8. Making pies on Sunday night
9. Swimming in a kimnel on Thy day
10. Putting a pin in Iohn Keys hat on Thy day to pick him.
11. Carelessly hearing and committing many sermons
12. Refusing to go to the close at my mothers command
13. Threatning my father and mother Smith to burne them and the house over them
14. Wishing death and hoping it to some
15. Striking many
16. Having uncleane thoughts words and actions and dreamese.

17. Stealing cherry cobs from Eduard Storer

18. Denying that I did so

19. Denying a crossbow to my mother and grandmother though I knew of it

20. Setting my heart on money learning pleasure more than Thee

21. A relapse

22. A relapse

23. A breaking again of my covenant renued in the Lords Supper.

24. Punching my sister

25. Robbing my mothers box of plums and sugar

26. Calling Derothy Rose a jade

27. Glutiny in my sickness.

28. Peevishness with my mother.

29. With my sister.

30. Falling out with the servants

31. Divers commissions of alle my duties

32. Idle discourse on Thy day and at other times

33. Not turning nearer to Thee for my affections

34. Not living according to my belief

35. Not loving Thee for Thy self.

36. Not loving Thee for Thy goodness to us

37. Not desiring Thy ordinances

38. Not long [longing] for Thee in [illegible]

39. Fearing man above Thee

40. Vsing unlawful means to bring us out of distresses

41. Caring for worldly things more than God

42. Not craving a blessing from God on our honest endeavors.

43. Missing chapel.

44. Beating Arthur Storer.

45. Twisting a cord on Sunday morning

46. Striving to cheat with a brass halfe crowne.

47. Peevishness at Master Clarks for a piece of bread and butter.

48. Reading the history of the Christian champions on Sunday

Since Whitsunday 1662

1. Glutony

2. Glutony

3. Vsing Wilfords towel to spare my own.

4. Negligence at the chapel.

5. Sermons at Saint Marys (4)

6. Lying about a louse.

7. Denying my chamberfellow of the knowledge of him that took him for a sot.

8. Neglecting to pray (3)

9. Helping Pettit to make his water watch at 12 of the clock on Saturday night

EXTRACTS FROM NOTEBOOK CONTAINING "QUAESTIONES QUAEDAM PHILOSOPHIAE" (CERTAIN PHILOSOPHICAL QUESTIONS)

These extracts from a notebook written by Newton in the early to mid-1660s, in Greek, Latin, and English, reveal the extent and relentlessness of Newton's experiments with natural phenomena and, particularly, his interest in colour. Notebook location: Cambridge University Library, Cambridge. *Newton Project.*

Of colours

17   Substances belonging to the vegetable or Animall Kingdome when lightly burned are black, when througly burned are white. As Ivory being skilfully burnt affords painters one of the deepest blacks they have &c. But mineralls are to bee excepted from this rule, For Allablaster if never so much burnt will turne no darker then yellow. Leade being calcined with a strong fire turnes into minium which is red, & this minium by burning turnes darker but never to a white colour. Blew, but unsophisticated Vitriol when tis burnt a little by a slow heate to friability, is white being further burnt turnes Grey, Yellow, red, & when perustum it turnes to a purple.

19   Gold & silver melted into a lumpe & dissolved by Aqua fortis the pouder of gold falling to the bottome appeares not yellow but black though neither the gold silver nor Aquafortis be so, & silver rubbed on other bodys colours them black.

20   Most bodys precipitated from the liquor into which they were dissolved are white, but not all.

21   The scrapeings of black horne lookes white.

22   Sulphur adust is not the cause of blacknesse as Chimists hold, for common sulphur be either melted or sublimed turnes onely red or yellow. And the plant Camphire though very inflamable & consequently sulphureous by burning turnes to noe colour but white &c. But then wt causeth blackness in sulphur adust.

23   A Candle looked on through blew glasse appeares greene.

24   Pouder of blew bise mixed with a greater quality of yellow orpiment makes a greene but the particles by a microscope are discovered to retaine theire blewness & yellownesse.

26   A feather or black ribband put twixt my eye & the setting sunne makes glorious colours.

28   Yet either a Lixivious liquor, or urinous salt being poured on a solution of blew vitrioll in faire water makes it yellow & the precipitated corpuscles retained the yellow colour when they were falne to the bottome.

29   A just quantity of Oyle of Tartar poured into a strong solution of french verdigrease turnes it from greene to blew; a Lixivium of pot ashes turnes it to a lighter blew, & spirit of Vrin, or Harts-horne make other blews.

30   {One graine} of Cochineel dissolved in spirits of urin & then by degrees in faire water, imparted a discernable colour to 125000 graines of faire water.

31   Most of the Tinctures which chimists draw which abound with minerall or Vegetable Sulphur turne red; & both Acid & Alcalizate salts in most sulphureous or oyly bodys produce a red. & blew is more commonly turned to red then red to blew

33   White bodys are commonly sulphureous.

35   Tinge water with red rose leaves into which drop a little Minium disolved in spirit of vinegar & it will be of a muddy greene, but drop in a little Oyle of Vitrioll which though an acid Menstruum yet it will præcipitate the leade in the forme of a white pouder to the bottome leaving the rest of the liquor above of a good red almost like a Rubie

36   Oyle or spirit of Turpentine will not mix with water & it & water shaken together apeare white.

NEWTON'S RECIPES FOR COLOUR
AND REMEDIES FOR SICKNESS

These extracts are taken from a personal notebook that Newton kept from 1659 to the early 1660s, now referred to as the Pierpont Morgan Notebook, and are held at the Pierpont Morgan Library, New York. Newton left many drawings and paintings on the walls of his garret room in the lodging house in Grantham—he was clearly using some of these recipes for colour at that point. He also had a tendency towards hypochondria, though his health was generally good. *Newton Project.*

Of Shaddowing.
To shaddow sweetly & rowndly withall is a far greater cunning then to shaddow hard & darke; for it best to shaddow as if it were not shaddowed.

How to prepare your colours.
Such colours as have need of grinding you must grind them with faire water, then put them on a smoth chalk stone, & let them dry. then grind them againe with Gum water & reserve them in muscle shels for your use.

A sea colour.
Take privet berries when the sun entreth into Libra, about the 13th of September, dry them in the sunn; then bruise them & steepe them in Allum water, & straine them into an earthen poringer that is glazed.

A yellow colour.

Take yellow berrys, & bruse them & steepe them a quarter of an hower in allum water then strain them if you will or let them stand in liquour.

A Haire colour.

Take umber or spanish browne grind it & temper it with gum water.

A russet colour.

Take the fattest sut you can get & put it into a pot of cleare water so that it be covered two or 3 fingers & let it seeth well which don straine it through a cloth set it on the fire againe to thiken (but take heed you set it not on too hot a fire for feare of burning it) & so let it boyle gently till it bee as thick as you would have it.

A colour for faces.

Lay on thecheekes little spotts of lake or red lead then come all over it with white, & a little lake, shaddow it with Lamblack or umber, & white lead.

Colours for naked pictures

Take white leade & a little Vermilion temper them & lay them on, shaddow it with bolearmonick in the middle & adde a little sut to the utmost double hatches.

A colour for dead corpes.

Change white leade with the water of yellow berrys & wash the picture all ouer then chang it with blew Indie & shaddow it in the single hatches, & leanest places then take sut, yellow berrys & white lead & with that shadow the darkest places.

A blood red colour.

Sinaper, lake, & vermillion make a good red.

Another.

Take some of the clearest blood of a sheepe & put it into a bladder & with a needle prick holes in the bottom of it then hang it up to dry in the sunne; & disolve it in allum water according as you have need.

A red colour.

Boyle brasill as you did the log-wood. but if you would have it a sad red mingle it with pot ash water, if a light red temper it with white lead.

A Crimson.

Cynaper tops: Cynaper-lake: or vermilion.

Clowd colours.

The lightest is whitelead & Inde blew a like quantaty of each, the next a deale of Inde & a little white, then purple & white with a little brasill, then whit lead & yellow berrys.

How to write a gold colour.

Take a new laid egg, make a hole at one end & let out the substance then take the yolk without the white, & four times soe much quicksilver in quantitie as of the former grind them well together & put them into the shell stop the hole thereof with chalk & the white of an egg then lay it under a hen that sitt with 6 more for the space of 3 wekes, then break it up & write with it.

fflesh colour.

Take white lead grind it with oyle, lake, & vermilion so you may make it pale or high coloured at your pleasur.

A White colour.

White lead ground with nut oyle.

Charecole black & seacole black.

Grind charcole very small with water, let it dry then grind it with oyle. thus make seacole black.

A good cement for broken glasses.

Take raw silke & beat it with glasse & mix them together with whites of eggs.

A bait to catch fish.

Take Cocculus Indiæ unciæ ss. henbane seeds, & wheaten flower of each a quarter of an ounce, hive honey as much as will make them into past. Where you see the most fish cast in bits like barly cornes, & they will swim on the top of the water, so that you may take them up with your hands or a nett. If it rane after the bate is cast into the water or if you put them in other faire water they will come to themselves. You may in the dead of winter in the morning when the sun shines catch fish with your angle bated onely with past wad of wheat flower.

To make birds drunk.

Take such meat as they love as wheat, barley &c. steepe it in lees of wine or in the juice of Hemlock, & sprincle it wher birds use to haunt. Sodden Garlick sprinkled amongst corne sowne.

To catch crows, or ravens.

Take the liver of a beast & cut it into divers peeces, put some nux Vomica into each peece. & lay them where crows haunt.

To catch crows or pigeons.

Tak whit pease & steepe them 8 or 9 days in the gall of an ox. & lay them where they haunt.

To make pigeons, partriges dicks & other birds drunk.

Set black wine for ym to drink where they come.

Another.

Take tormentill, byle it in good wine put barley into it. Lay it where the birds com. this should be don in winter when snow is.

Another way to catch birds.

Make past of barley meale onion blads, & hen-bane seeds, & set it on severall little boards or tiles, or such like for the birds.

A secret for travellers.

Let travelers take a peece of Roch allum, & hold it now & then for a small time in their mouths for when they are hot it will coole them & refresh them & quench their thirst more then beer will. There is also a stone (which the Mounte bancks call a Celestiall or miraculus stone & the Apothecarys lapis prunella) which dos mot much differ from this it is onely better.

A Salve for all sores.

Take a pound of sheeps tallow a pound of turpentine & a pound of Virgin wax, a pint of sallet oyle, a quarter of a pound of Rosin: take also of Bugle, Smalsach, & plantaine halfe the quantity of the other or so much as will make a pinte boyle all these together on a soft fire of coles, always stir it till a 3d part be consumed, then tak it from the fire & straine it through a new canvas cloth, into an earthen pot.

How to write on black paper.

Take the yolk of a new layd egg & grind it on a marble with faire water so as you may write with it. then write what you will with it & when it is dry black all the paper over with ink & when it is dry, you may scrape all the letters that you wrot of with a knife.

A speciall remedy of his, for the tooth-ach, which never failed to give ease to hollow tooth, or other, for a time.

Take Pellitory of Spaine, long paper, Ginger, & Cloves, of each one dram; Ginny-pepper halfe a dram beate all these into a very fine powder; then with Chimicall oyle of cloves, oyle of thyme, & spirit of salt of each a like quantity, make it up into a past & out of that past make little pellets, or cakes, & dry them in the sun; & so use them.

Helpes for the eye sight.

Things hurtfull for the eyes.

Garlick Onions & Leeks. over much Lettice. Goeing too suddaine after meat. Hot wines. Cold ayre. Dunknes. Gluttony. Milke. Chese. White & red coulors. Much sleepe after Meate. Much blood-letting. Cold worts. dust. ffire. much weeping. & watching.

Things good for the sight.

Measurable sleepe. red roses. ffennell. Selandine Vervaine rootes X Pinpernell. Oculus Christi. To wash your eyes in faire running water, & your hands & feet often. To looke on any greene or pleasant colours, or in a faire glasse.

A Water to cleane the sight.

Take greene Wallnuts husks & all as they come from the trees & a few of X the leaves & distill them. Then drop the water thereof into your eyes morning & night for 6 or 7 days together.

Drop 3 or 4 drops of thewater of rotten apples at a time into your eyes.

Wash your eyes with the water of Dasies, both roots & leaves being cleane washed, then stamped & strained.

The juice of the hearbe Euphasia, or the water.

Certaine tricks To turne waters into wine.

1 Into Claret. X
Take as much lockwood as you can hold in your mouth without discovery tye it up in a cloth, & put it in your mouth, then sup up some wather & champe the lock-wood 3 or 4 times & doe it out into a glass.

2 ffor White wine.
Chew the Ball once or twice lightly. &c as you did for claret.

ffor Sack.
Take a drop of Wine or beare vinegar & put it in the Glasse shakeing it about the sides of the Glasse. &c: as you did for claret.

ffor Strong Waters.
Have a cup of Strong Water by you like the other of water which drinke up as if it was the water & doe it out againe into one of the Glasses.

To Cut a Glasse.
Take a plaine Glasse, hold it up side downeward over a candle till it bee pretty hott then take a match of rope, & blowing it all the while run it ouer the Glasse as you would have it cut.

Against the Plague.
Take Alloes, Hepatick, [illegible] cinamon Myrrh of each 3 drams. Cloves, Mace, Wood of Alloës or Lignum Alloës, Mastick, Bole armoniack, of each halfe an ounce. Make a fine powder thereof, which take early in the Morning with white Wine mixt with a little Water.

An Excellent water for Vlcers.
Heate faire water in a vessell never before used: yn power it into quick lime in an-other new vessell. Let it stand till the lime sink to the bottome & you have taken all the spume from the top. then pour the cleare water from the Lime into a cleane Glasse & stop it well up. Wash the Vlcer with it: & lay a cloth diped in it, on the sore. & it cleanses it.

FURTHER READING

On Newton

Fara, Patricia. *Newton: The Making of Genius.* London: Macmillan, 2002.

Gleick, James. *Isaac Newton.* New York: HarperPerennial, 2004.

Iliffe, Robert. *Newton: A Very Short Introduction.* Oxford: Oxford University Press, 2007.

More, Louis Trenchard. *Isaac Newton.* New York: Scribner, 1934.

Westfall, Richard. *Never at Rest: Isaac Newton.* Cambridge: Cambridge University Press, 1983.

White, Michael. *Isaac Newton: The Last Sorcerer.* London: Fourth Estate, 1997.

For the finest resource on Newton, his life and works, and access to published and unpublished writings, as well as links to other Newton sites, see the Newton Project: http://www.newtonproject.ic.ac.uk, edited by Rob Iliffe and Scott Mandelbrote.

On Glass and Prisms

Douglas, R. W., and Susan Frank. *A History of Glassmaking.* Henley-on-Thames: Foulis, 1972.

Godfrey, Eleanor S. *The Development of English Glassmaking, 1560–1640.* Oxford: Clarendon Press, 1975.

Klein, Dan, and Ward Lloyd. *The History of Glass.* London: Orbis, 1984.

McCray, W. Patrick. *Glassmaking in Renaissance Venice: The Fragile Craft.* Aldershot: Ashgate, 1999.

Neri, Antonio. *L'Arte Vetraria,* 1612; translated into English as *The Art of Glass* by Christopher Merrett in 1662. New edition by Michael Cable published in 2001 by the Society of Glass Technology, Sheffield.

Polak, Ada. *Glass: Its Makers and Its Public.* London: Weidenfeld & Nicolson, 1975.

Schaffer, Simon. "Glassworks: Newton's Prisms and the Uses of Experiment." In *The Uses of Experiment: Studies in the Natural Sciences,* edited by Simon Schaffer et al. Cambridge: Cambridge University Press, 1989.

On Alchemy

Dobbs, Betty Jo Teeter. *The Foundations of Newton's Alchemy, or "The Hunting of the Greene Lyon."* Cambridge: Cambridge University Press, 1976.

————. *The Janus Face of Genius: The Role of Alchemy in Newton's Thought.* Cambridge: Cambridge University Press, 1991; new edition, 2002.

Eliade, Mircea. *The Forge and the Crucible: The Origins and Structure of Alchemy.* Chicago: University of Chicago Press, 1979.

For biographies of sixteenth- and seventeenth-century scientists and alchemists, see Richard Westfall's "A Catalogue of the Scientific Community in the Sixteenth and Seventeenth Centuries" in The Galileo Project: http://galileo.rice.edu/lib/catalog.html.

On Plague

Bell, Walter George. *The Great Plague of London in 1665.* 1924; rpt., London: Bodley Head Books, 1951.

Defoe, Daniel. *A Journal of the Plague Year.* 1722.

Porter, Stephen. *The Great Plague.* Stroud: Sutton, 1999.

Williamson, R. "The Plague in Cambridge." *Medical History* 1.1 (January 1957): pp. 51–64.

On Seventeenth-Century Cambridge

Defoe, Daniel. *A Tour Through the Whole Island of Great Britain.* 1724.

McIntosh, Tania. *Decline of Stourbridge Fair, 1770–1934.* Leicester: University of Leiccster, 1998.

Newton, Samuel. *The Diary of S. Newton, Alderman of Cambridge.* Edited by J. E. Foster. Cambridge: Cambridge Antiquarian Society, 1890.

Prynne, Abraham de la. *The Diary of Abraham de la Prynne.* Edited by Charles Jackson. Durham, 1870.

Ward, Edward. *A Step to Stirbitch Fair.* 1700.

Wilmer, Clive, and Charles Moseley. *Cambridge Observed: An Anthology.* Cambridge: Colt Books, 1998.

On Entanglement Theory

Aczel, Amir. *Entanglement: The Greatest Mystery in Physics.* New York: Plume, 2003.

ACKNOWLEDGMENTS

My thanks go first to my father, Roger Stott, who gave so much to the book and to me; my agent Faith Evans, who understood it on first reading; my astute editor Helen Garnons-Williams at Weidenfeld & Nicolson; Cindy Spiegel at Spiegel & Grau; Emma Sweeney, my U.S. agent; Kelly Falconer and Alan Samson at Weidenfeld; and all the readers of drafts: Judith Boddy, Rob Iliffe, Sal Cline, Lucie Sutherland, Stephanie Le Vaillant, Jonathon Burt, Charlie Ritchie, and my son Jacob Morrish. For ideas and inspiration my daughters, Hannah Morrish and Kezia Morrish. For stories of the river, its punt chauffeurs and for descriptions of the way the light rises over the river at dawn, Jacob Morrish, accomplished part-time punt chauffeur and young hedonist. For beauty and entanglement, Jonathon Burt.

For help with research, the librarians of Cambridge University Library, the Wren and the Whipple libraries; Patricia Fara and Simon Schaffer; my colleagues at Anglia Ruskin University; and the staff and students of the History and Philosophy of Science Department at Cambridge. My thanks go too to Diane and Eric Pranklin for stories about a fenland abattoir in winter and to Melanie Piper for help with the illustrations.

I thank the Hawthornden Trust for granting me a month-long writing fellowship in Hawthornden Castle in 2004, where this book was completed, and for the companionship of Daniel Farrell, Susanna Moore, Heather Dyer, and Sarah Stonich.

ILLUSTRATION AND TEXT
SOURCES AND CREDITS